RELENTLESS

P. J. O'DWYER

Black Siren Books

New York

[Handwritten inscription:] September 4, 2012 Dear Amy, Thank you for your interest in Relentless. Enjoy the read! Warm wishes, PJ O'Dwyer

Novels written by P. J. O'Dwyer

The Fallon Sisters Trilogy

Relentless

Defiant

Forsaken

Copyright © 2012 by P. J. O'Dwyer Enterprises, Ltd.

Black Siren Books

331 West 57th Street
Suite 510
New York, NY 10019
www.blacksirenbooks.com
inquiries@blacksirenbooks.com

This book contains an excerpt from the forthcoming book *Defiant*, the second book in the Fallon Sisters Trilogy by P. J. O'Dwyer. This excerpt has been set for this edition only and may not reflect the final content of the forthcoming edition.

Printed in the United States of America

Library of Congress Control Number: 2012933447

ISBN 978-0-9848997-0-8 (hardcover)

ISBN 978-0-9848997-1-5 (ebook)

Cover design by Duncan Long, www.duncanlong.com

Interior Layout & Design by Ronda Taylor, www.taylorbydesign.com

EARLY PRAISE FOR *RELENTLESS* . . .

"*RELENTLESS will take readers on a rollercoaster ride and keep you guessing on several fronts. Highly recommended and a fantastic read!*"

—Monica Solomon
The Romance Readers Connection, 4½ Stars

"*This is a fast-moving story of right against might, with engaging characters that quickly pull the reader into an exciting rollercoaster ride of twists and turns guaranteed to leave you breathless and guessing right up to the very end.*"

—Cheryl Caldwell, Co-Publisher
Honest Horses Magazine

"*Lovers of horses, mystery, and romance rolled into one intriguing package will want to place RELENTLESS at the top of their must-read list for 2012! O'Dwyer's vivid writing hooks the reader in for the ride, but beyond that illuminates the urgent issues surrounding wild horses, slaughter, and horse rescue. This book is a many-sided gem you won't want to miss!*"

—Carol Upton, Co-Founder
Sunshine Coast School of Writing

"*RELENTLESS is a truly well-crafted, well-written story. I look forward to seeing it in print one day in the near future. P. J. O'Dwyer is a gifted author.*"

—Joanna Waggoner
Washington Romance Writers 2011 Marlene Awards

"*RELENTLESS vibrates with emotion and conflict and intensity. I couldn't get enough! P. J. O'Dwyer's got talent, in spades.*"

—Frieda Knizek
Washington Romance Writers 2011 Marlene Awards

"O'Dwyer is a master at putting emotion to paper and making it convincing. RELENTLESS is high intensity at its best. It gives the heart a workout in every possible way—suspense that has it pounding nonstop, romance that has it thumping, and frustration, anger, and deep sorrow that holds it clenched in a vise. I could not put it down!"

—Cindy Taylor
All Book Reviews

"RELENTLESS is an enthralling read, with twists and turns that keep you in suspense. O'Dwyer has crafted a wonderful story that takes you from the countryside of Maryland to the drug wars of Mexico, all because of the love of the horse. Her research for her subject matter is exceptional in this wonderful tale."

—Alex Brown
Author of Greatness and Goodness: Barbaro and His Legacy

"P. J. O'Dwyer's RELENTLESS is a perfect mix of romance and mystery. It was fast paced enough that I didn't want to put it down! Her knowledge of horses, horse rescues, and the horse slaughterhouse controversy was impressive and eye opening. The images she imparts of the slaughterhouse in Mexico will stay with me a very long time. It was a wonderful read, I will recommend it highly!"

—Monika Orendorf, President and Founder
Dusty Trails Horse Rescue
State of Alabama

"An absorbing tale of murder, romance, and horses . . . O'Dwyer creatively expresses the redemptive powers of love and one woman's devotion to saving ill-fated horses. This gripping novel unfolds in surprising ways, and its twists and turns will have readers on the edge of their seats until the very end. This entertaining story provides satisfaction for mystery devotees, romance readers, and horse lovers all in one well-written book."

—Mimi Peabody, Secretary
Alaska Equine Rescue
State of Alaska

"RELENTLESS is an absolutely spellbinding novel that is a must-read for all who know and love horses, and who enjoy a captivating mystery. This novel gives an inside look at the struggles of Bren Ryan, who has lived her life with equines and has an intimate knowledge of sale barns and auctions. Adding business rivalry, murder, and a stranger in town, and you have an enticing read with a true education about the inhumanity of slaughter and the heartlessness of those who make money from sending horses to a horrendous demise."

—Susan N. Thompson, Founder and CEO
Dreamchaser Horse Rescue and Rehabilitation, Inc.
State of Arizona

"Finally, a novel that accurately depicts the rescue world and their struggles to protect the horse from ignorance and greed—RELENTLESS kept me reading into the night."

—Joey Ogburn, Director
Reigning Grace Ranch
State of Arizona

"P. J. O'Dwyer brings to life that perfect combination of horses and romance while eloquently addressing important issues facing the equestrian community. Anyone who loves horses will be able to relate to the protagonist, Bren, who dedicates her life, and her heart, to rescue work. Add in the intrigue of a mysterious murder and this book will keep you turning the pages."

—Melanie Sue Bowles, Founder of Proud Spirit Horse Sanctuary,
and author of three nonfiction books, including:
Hoof Prints: Stories from Proud Spirit
State of Arkansas

"Captivating! Mysterious and visceral, RELENTLESS is a colorful literary fiction that chronicles the vivid life challenges of a dedicated mother and horse rescuer in a world that measures the value of life by the weight on the end of a meat hook."

—Katia Louise, President and Founder
Wild for Life Foundation, Lifetime Equine Refuge
State of California
Director, Producer of SAVING AMERICA'S HORSES – A NATION BETRAYED

"*Thanks to Ms. O'Dwyer for having a horse rescue advocate as her heroine in RELENTLESS. In 2007 the Unwanted Horse Coalition estimated that there were approximately 170,000 unwanted horses in the United States. Building awareness of this issue is so important for those of us working for the horses. Thanks so much for making it an enjoyable read as well!*"

—Judy B. Smetana, Ph.D., Executive Director
Colorado Horse Rescue
State of Colorado

"*RELENTLESS is a fast-paced murder mystery, romance, with realistic, and sometimes brutal, horse rescue thrown in. The who-done-it will keep you guessing 'til the end.*"

—Patty Wahlers, President
H.O.R.S.E. of CT, Inc.
State of Connecticut

"*RELENTLESS—a true page-turner that you didn't want to end.*"

—Robin Weinkam, Treasurer
Changing Fates Equine Rescue of Delaware, Inc.
State of Delaware

"*I've read so many horse books and novels. But once I received a copy of RELENTLESS, I was taken by the breathtaking action of romance and mystery. What a good depiction of the inhumanity of horse slaughter. This great horse novel has a little bit of everything, and is a must read! Thank you for sharing this with me.*"

—Betina Parker, President and Founder
Equine 808 Horse Rescue
State of Hawaii

"*Your success with RELENTLESS is imminent. It was a wonderful tale about the struggles one encounters when defending right and decency against what always seems to be the powerful forces of the antithesis of all that is good. I was enthralled, and I look forward to future novels that will no doubt evolve from your creative mind. Thank you for the opportunity to preview this moving novel.*"

—Tony Mangan, President
Panhandle Equine Rescue, Inc.
State of Idaho

"RELENTLESS is a page burner of a murder mystery with an unlikely heroine, staged in a quiet little piece of animal welfare that is very near and dear to my heart. Bren is a strong-willed, feisty redhead whose #1 life passion is saving, rescuing, and rehoming horses in need, until the day her husband is murdered.

"Even with her heart, her mind, and her time largely consumed with finding Tom's murderer, Bren continues with their life's work of Grace Equine Sanctuary . . . and that mixture of unending dedication leads to a 'never saw that coming' finish you won't want to miss.

"While clearly a fictional tale, O'Dwyer's depiction of certain elements of the underbelly of the equine world is accurate and eye opening to those horse lovers who may have little or no idea of the dark realities."

—AnnMarie Cross, Founder
Crosswinds Equine Rescue, Inc.
State of Illinois

"Absolutely riveting! P. J. O'Dwyer has written a suspenseful masterpiece that draws you into the plot, making you feel as if you are there, feeling the love, hate, and pain along with the characters. A very satisfying indulgence indeed!"

—Stephanie M. Bowser
Friends of Ferdinand, Inc.–Indiana
State of Indiana

"Bren has the heart of momma bear. Nothing will keep her from protecting the rescued horses and the people she loves. Hang on . . . it's a wild ride."

—Karen Everhart, Founder
Rainbow Meadows Equine Rescue and Retirement, Inc.
State of Kansas

"RELENTLESS is a wonderful depiction of the emotional, high-energy life of a woman named Bren and her commitment to saving horses. O'Dwyer shows the human side and communicates the very fast-paced, hectic nature of what we do, which is horse rescue."

—Sunny Francois, Executive Director
Louisiana Horse Rescue Association
State of Louisiana

"A well-written story with all the elements to keep you deeply involved—murder, mystery, romance, and an all-too-real glance into the greed and horror of the horse [slaughter] world."

—Mona Jerome, President and Founder
Ever After Mustang Rescue
State of Maine

"I commend you for finding an entertaining way to bring this ever important issue to the masses in a way that will teach those who would otherwise have no interest or knowledge."

—Christine Hajek, President and Founder
Gentle Giants Draft Horse Rescue
State of Maryland

"I haven't read a novel for 30 years. But after a few chapters, I was forgetting it wasn't real! Even I wanted to do some serious damage to this kill buyer. You won't want to put RELENTLESS down!

"P. J. O'Dwyer has done something by writing this book that I couldn't do in a million years. She has alerted a whole new audience to the horrors of horse slaughter."

—Lorraine Truitt, Founder
Horse Lovers United
State of Maryland

"I loved Bren and Rafe and their story. Bren reminds me of many of my hardworking, hardheaded, horse-loving friends. I really couldn't walk away from the story for long, it was that engaging. Well done, Ms. O'Dwyer, this was a fantastic read. I look forward to the other books in your series about the Fallon girls."

—Charish Campbell
Owner/FEI Rider/Trainer/Holistic Equine Therapist
Chesapeake Sporthorse Hundred Acre Wood
Maryland's Eastern Shore

"Your book RELENTLESS was excellent. Between the horse rescue, romance, and suspense it was very thrilling, and I couldn't get enough. I know that this book will be enjoyed by a wide audience."

—Sarah Transeau, President and Founder
Tranquility Farm Equestrian Education and Renewal Center
State of Maryland

"RELENTLESS, an enjoyable ride of a novel. From the depth of the characters to the reality of small-town life, this novel is one to be reckoned with. O'Dwyer nails the seriousness of the horse slaughter issue through mystery, intrigue, suspense, and romance."

—Lori Stottlemyer, President and Founder
Windy Rock Equine Rescue
State of Maryland

"RELENTLESS is a thrilling romantic murder mystery novel that has creatively woven through its storyline the struggles of running a horse rescue, a timely reminder of the cruelty that horses are still facing today. With 100+ abused and neglected horses coming through our gates on an annual basis, we could not be more pleased that this book spotlights the continuing hardships that equines and the equine community grapple with."

—Caroline R. Robertson, Development Director
Days End Farm Horse Rescue
State of Maryland

"RELENTLESS perfectly describes the heroine in this novel. Bren's passion, determination, and dedication are qualities anyone involved in horse rescue can relate to. The imagery surrounding the conditions and processes of a slaughter house, coupled with the suffering of both the horses and Bren, are powerful and riveting themes the author perfectly intertwines. This book had my full attention from the first to the last page. Real life issues close to my heart, along with romance, mystery, and common, everyday struggles left me wanting more and more! This is a must-read book for all avid horse lovers and the champions who work tirelessly to improve conditions for all horses!"

—Sandra Bertovick, Board Member
Horses' Haven
State of Michigan

"So . . . finally I have met a horsewoman with more excitement in her life than mine, LOL! Just finished reading . . . quite the twisting story. God bless you for speaking for so many lost souls.

"Totally amazed that you were able to put that all together. Horses, kids, dogs, love, money, greed . . . story has it all! I wish I had a drop of your skill, sigh."

—Mary Jones, President and Founder
RIDE-Minnesota, a horse rescue
State of Minnesota

"RELENTLESS has a little bit of everything: a mystery, family, love, and loss. Although a book of fiction, the story depicts the real heartbreak and rewards of today's horse rescue. And is an accurate account of what these beautiful creatures have to endure from the dark side of humanity.

"You can't help but want the best for the main character, Bren, and her family. I loved the book and could see RELENTLESS as a movie."

—Rhonda L. Stephens, Founder and President
The Shannon Foundation
State of Missouri

"P. J. O'Dwyer has taken the longtime, emotional issue involving the love for horses and slaughter while portraying a journey into the life of a widowed mom and rescuer, jam-packed with passion, family, murder, mystery, and love! What a journey it is!"

—Deborah Derr, D.C.
Founder of United In Light, Inc. Draft Horse Sanctuary
State of Montana

"RELENTLESS—the title of the book is the best description of its heroine. Every chapter, every page, is packed with the determination and energy of a woman who could lose everything by pursuing her quest for justice. The twists and surprises are 'relentless'! Couldn't wait to get to the end to find some relief from the excitement! Thank you, P. J. O'Dwyer!"

—Virginia Hudson, Board Member
Western Montana Equine Rescue and Rehabilitation
State of Montana

"The book RELENTLESS made every attempt to portray our countries dirty little secret of horse slaughter in a very precise way. The story line kept you interested and, yet, provided details and information on a topic few really know about. The authors rendering of horrors of horse slaughter were right on. The story and the facts were interwoven together providing substance and depth. Kudos to P. J. O'Dwyer for not only providing a fine novel, but doing the her upmost to present the facts of equine slaughter as they really are."

—Valerie Hinderlider, President (ret.)
Break Heart Ranch
State of Nebraska

"P. J. O'Dwyer's *RELENTLESS* hits on every daily issue that we as human beings and as a rescue are touched by. It reaches out and touches the soul to its inner core. I highly recommend *RELENTLESS* and believe it will be insightful to many."

—S. Pierce, President and Founder
Miracle Horse Rescue & Sanctuary
State of Nevada

"I thoroughly enjoyed *RELENTLESS*. The story stayed with me when I put the book down. There were several elements that made *RELENTLESS* a fabulous read. First, it's a love story focused on the horse world. As a horse lover, any novel involving horses catches my attention. As a horse rescue operator, having Bren, the heroine, involved with rescue and fighting the dirty secret—horse slaughter—well, that's an important subject too often swept under the rug.

"P. J. O'Dwyer tackles the horror and heartache of slaughter, hopefully bringing attention to a cruelty that needs to be stopped. Finally, as an avid reader, I found *RELENTLESS* to be well-written with surprising twists and turns. The action kept me riveted and surprised. I'm truly looking forward to the rest of the Fallon Sisters Trilogy."

—Lisa M. Post, President and Co-Founder
Helping Hearts Equine Rescue
State of New Jersey

"*RELENTLESS* is a must-read for every horse lover. The plot is full of twists and turns while illuminating the dark side of the horse industry—slaughter. It is my hope that this book moves people to support a change in the way America treats its horses!"

—Debbie Colburn, President
Four Corners Equine Rescue
State of New Mexico

"Any book that reminds us of those people involved with horse rescuing is helpful and valuable. Thank you, P. J. O'Dwyer, for writing a book which does that in such a captivating way. This book is a real thriller—mystery fans and horse lovers will enjoy it greatly."

—Erin Pfister, Rescue Coordinator
Akindale Thoroughbred Rescue
State of New York

"RELENTLESS . . . a suspenseful novel that tangles romance with the very contro-versial and emotionally charged subject of horse slaughter. A truly accurate depiction of where America's horses can end up. Two thumbs up for showing the dedication of those who spend their lives rescuing one of the oldest American icons . . . the horse."

—Monica Coville, Founder and President
Equine Rescue League of Cooperstown
State of New York

"I was enthralled by RELENTLESS, waiting with hungry anticipation with the turning of each page. RELENTLESS is appealing for every audience from romance, mystery, and drama to animal and horse enthusiasts. RELENTLESS is a must-read novel!"

—Alison Smith, Director/Founder
Triple H Miniature Horse Rescue
State of North Dakota

"As the title suggests, Bren Ryan is much like that one stubborn friend we all have. She can be frustrating and challenging but her intentions are good. Once I connected with her passion for horses, I wanted her to succeed, in spite of herself.

"If you're looking for an escape from your day-to-day routine and have a heart for horses, then RELENTLESS just might be the trail you want to head down."

—Jeannette "Jet" Parrett
NW Horse Forum
Seattle Times

"I love to read, and RELENTLESS is everything and more that I enjoy in a book. I lost my husband tragically and suddenly three years ago, I have a farm, children, and a horse rescue. I could relate to Bren and that made your story that much more interesting and exciting to me. It is impressive how you focused upon, so decisively, the important, everyday issues that all horse rescues experience . . . hard work, financial worries, heartache, and the most hated of all, horse slaughter and their needless pain and suffering. And then to blend this so successfully in an exhilarating romance and jaw-dropping mystery. Wow!

"I found your book to be one of the best I have ever read."

—Mary Jones, President and Founder
W.H.I.N.N.Y. Horse Rescue
State of Ohio

"What an interesting book. I found it hard to put RELENTLESS down. Thanks for putting the issues out there in a new way for those who want to learn as well as wrap themselves in a good read!"

—Cheri White Owl, ES, CRSS and President and Founder
Horse Feathers Equine Rescue, Inc.
State of Oklahoma

"Thank you to P. J. O'Dwyer for her realistic and compassionate portrayal of the underbelly of the horse trade. Speaking for all relentless horse advocates, Bren's tireless efforts on behalf of equines is a realistic depiction of the challenges faced in caring for these magnificent and sensitive creatures. Romance, mystery, and horses make this a compelling, informative, and completely enjoyable read . . . I truly loved this book!"

—Joan Steelhammer, President/Founder
Equine Outreach Inc.
State of Oregon

"The author of RELENTLESS captures the struggles and sheer determination of Bren, a woman and single mother running a Maryland horse rescue who is also tormented by the unethical antics and behavior of a horse dealer. This book tells the story of loss, grief, pain, romance, and the iron will of woman who will not give up even though the odds are against her. Bren, true to her children, horses, and beliefs, will stop at nothing to protect them and to find the truth. You will be compelled to keep reading as Bren's journey takes many twists and turns along the way and has an ending you will not expect

"A good read for horse lovers and non-horse lovers alike."

—Marlene Murray, President
—Patricia Bewley, Vice President
R.A.C.E. Fund, Inc.
Retirement Assistance and Care for Equines

"P. J. O'Dwyer weaves a riveting tale that kept this real-life horse rescuer reading till way past midnight. I highly recommend RELENTLESS for anyone with even the slightest interest in horses or suspense novels. Ms. O'Dwyer has successfully blended the two into one fantastic read!"

—Jo Deibel, Founder and President
Angel Acres Horse Haven Rescue, Inc.
State of Pennsylvania

"RELENTLESS is a skillful mix of romance and suspense. O'Dwyer spins a believable tale where no one is what they seem."

—Elizabeth Wood, Board of Director (ret.)
South Carolina Awareness and Rescue for Equines
State of South Carolina

"This saga of the plight of the modern-day horse, combined with the twists and turns of exciting characters, keeps the reader's interest for an all-night read.

"The reality of the horror of horse slaughter and insurance fraud in the racing world is brought out in the story, making the book a thrilling page-turner.

"RELENTLESS is a modern-day romance, showing the hardships of horse rescues and the personal tragedy of the loss of a loved one, making this a must-read by all horse lovers.

Sign us up for the first copies!"

—Susan Watt, Program Director
—Elaine Everheart, Volunteer
Black Horse Wild Sanctuary
State of South Dakota

"I love this book! It shows the true meaning of rescue and the trials and tribulations with rescuing horses. It's so much like real life, and her writings are so intriguing you can't put the book down. As a fellow horse rescue, myself, I can understand what she is going through. Kudos to a book well written!"

—Kathy Grant, President/CEO
Mustang Alley Horse Rescue, Inc
Mustang Alley Riding Stables
State of Tennessee

"RELENTLESS—I was so drawn in by O'Dwyer's book I couldn't put it down. I felt every emotion along with the characters—anger, sadness, love, happiness, and revenge. It's a MUST read.

What an eye-opener to the reality and horror of horse slaughter and the ups and downs of horse rescue!"

—Krissi Roberts, Executive Director
Madaresgold Horse Rescue
State of Utah

"Once I started reading this book, I couldn't stop! P. J. O'Dwyer has brought a serious animal welfare issue into the spotlight while keeping readers on the edge of their seat wondering what will happen next. As a horse lover, the founder and director of an equine rescue, a mother and a woman, I connected with this book on many levels. Get the chores done, grab a cup of tea, and cuddle up on the couch with RELENTLESS, you won't regret it!"

—Gina Brown, Executive Director
Spring Hill Horse Rescue
State of Vermont

"Kudos for writing RELENTLESS—a story about America's horses and the reality of what happens to them when they go to slaughter. So many are sent there every day to die a horrible death. It is wonderful to see a book come out that touches on this issue."

—Brenna Wright, Board Member
Spring Hill Horse Rescue
State of Vermont

"I couldn't put it down! RELENTLESS was one of those books that kept me on the edge of my chair through the entire book. It is a realistic look into the plight of thousands of horses, the auctions, the kill buyers, and running a horse rescue woven into a suspenseful romance that will keep you turning the pages into the night and an ending that will shock you."

—Cindy Smith, President
Central Virginia Horse Rescue
State of Virginia

"A sexy cowboy, murder and mayhem, and the power of love make RELENTLESS a galloping good read. Bren Ryan's near-manic devotion to saving horses is no exaggeration. Neither are the cloak-and-dagger mysteries that seem to follow her everywhere she goes. This entertaining and believable story of the underbelly of horse rescue will keep you breathless right to the end."

—Jenny Edwards, Founder and Director
Hope for Horses
State of Washington

"RELENTLESS is a stirring and intriguing story that intertwines the important issues facing our horses. It made me laugh, cry, and left me hanging on the edge of my seat more times than I can count. It has everything a book should have and more: intrigue, love, deception, mystery, unexpected twists, and an underlying truth of the horrors faced by horses."

—Shelley Sawhook, President
American Horse Defense Fund
Washington, D. C.

"P. J. O'Dwyer has successfully disguised an educational message about horse slaughter as a brilliant romantic thriller!"

—Jeanne Beales, Founder
Horse Haven Hollow
State of West Virginia

"Part love story, part suspenseful thriller, set in the backdrop of the life of a woman dedicated to the rescue and welfare of horses, O'Dwyer has not only given us an entertaining story as well as insight into the plight of unwanted horses, but she has also created an American hero with her main character, Bren Ryan."

—Scott Bayerl, Co-Founder and Director
Midwest Horse Welfare Foundation, Inc.
State of Wisconsin

"RELENTLESS will captivate you from beginning to end. The absolute plight of horse rescue, splendidly infused with romance and mystery, will keep you in utter suspense. A truly amazing read!"

—Jenny Cramer, Director
Reaching Hands Ranch
State of Wyoming

"Fans of romantic suspense and horse lovers alike will be captivated by RELENTLESS. Sizzling with passion and taut with intrigue, this novel is a rollercoaster ride that propels the reader from a horse rescue farm in Clear Spring, Maryland, where a murder has occurred and danger continues to lurk, to a Mexican slaughterhouse and an encounter with a deadly drug cartel. Author P. J. O'Dwyer expertly captures the flavor of rural America as well as the ruthlessness of a Mexican border town, even as she exposes the cruel and predatory nature of the horse slaughter industry.

"Headstrong, fearless, beautiful—and widowed—Bren Ryan does not feel ready to accept the advances of a handsome, alluring stranger who has moved in next door. She has poured heart and soul into raising her two fatherless sons and into managing her horse rescue farm. But, in the midst of attempting to discover the truth behind her husband's sudden and mysterious death, she is plunged into a shadowy maze of events that give rise to real concerns about her own and her family's safety.

"RELENTLESS is a must-read for those looking for an edge-of-the-seat thrill ride that pulses with romance. The novel also provides an inside view of the dark world of kill buyers and trafficking horses for profit."

—Sinikka Crosland, Executive Director
Canadian Horse Defence Coalition

"Anyone working in the equine welfare field will tell you that their business is never concluded, that it's 24/7 and indeed—relentless. P. J. O'Dwyer's novel of the same name personifies the passion and dedication demanded of equine welfare workers in the character of Bren Ryan, a tough and true advocate for the horse who, like many of us, allows her work to close off other avenues of her life. Through Bren, we see the best and the worst of ourselves and our business while journeying into the heart of adventure and romance.

"The novel is a true page-turner and engages the reader with its honesty and realism; from family meals to the mean streets of Mexico, the book reflects and amplifies the lives of ordinary people in extraordinary circumstances. Bren Ryan and those around her are not so different from the rest of us who love and serve horses, have complicated relationships with families and friends, and strive to balance our lives to the best of our abilities—Bren just gets to have a few more adventures and a great romance with a hot cowboy.

"Put away the daily routine and pick up Bren and RELENTLESS—you deserve a little romance and adventure!"

—Marcy Emery, President
New Stride Thoroughbred Adoption Society
British Columbia, Canada

"P. J. O'Dwyer 'had me' in the first couple of pages. RELENTLESS depicts the horrid truth of the slaughterhouses of our time, bringing shocking awareness to those who have no concept of their existence.

"I was left mesmerized by Bren's audacity and incredible strength of will, cheering her on and holding my breath as she encounters and overcomes immeasurable challenges, knowing there is more 'real life' depicted within these pages than fiction.

"Thank you, P. J. O'Dwyer, for creating a 'face' for the courageous women and men working to create needed change."

—Marilyn Chapman, President
Earth Spirit Horse Rescue
New Brunswick, Canada

"It should have been written years ago . . . After the first few pages, I was hooked! RELENTLESS draws you in and keeps you guessing. O'Dwyer will totally blindside you with its surprising twists and turns until the very end. I felt as though I was there. Taking every step with Bren, cheering her on, and holding my breath. I couldn't put it down!"

—Judy McGrath, Founder
Maritime Horse Protection Society
Nova Scotia, Canada

"Thank you, P. J. O'Dwyer, for writing this book. You have truly captured the essence of those of us who have cried many times for those we couldn't save. Make my job obsolete. Read RELENTLESS—feel the pain, experience the joy, and eliminate horse slaughter."

—Raven W. Jackson, Farm Manager
Earth ARC Horse Rescue Unit
Nova Scotia, Canada

"RELENTLESS is spellbinding cover to cover. It has everything—horses, dogs, and a suspense filled story that keeps you wanting to get to the next page. I couldn't put it down."

—Rose Gergely, President
Refuge RR for Horses
Ontario, Canada

"A celebration of the human spirit and the tenacity of one woman to stand up, against all odds, to defend those who cannot defend themselves, Bren Ryan serves as testimony to the thousands of animal rescuers who dedicate their lives to creating a better world for our four-legged friends."

—Jana Hemphill, Director
Sadie's Place Horse Rescue
Prince Edward Island, Canada

"RELENTLESS—an enjoyable read that combines horse welfare, a little romance, and suspense that keeps you turning the pages until the very end."

—Bunnie Harasym, President and Founder
Paradise Stable Horse Rescue
Saskatchewan, Canada

"P.J. O'Dwyer's decision to give a percentage of her book sale profits to fund horse rescue is a very kind act. Without generosity like this some horses in need would go without. Thank you for your support and kindness."

—Redwings Horse Sanctuary
the UK's largest horse sanctuary

"This brilliant book brings us to the truth about horse slaughter. I cried quite spontaneously from a deep place within me that the writing touched. Allow yourself to be touched, too. Excellent."

—Jayne Boyles, Founder
Folleyfoot Horse and Pony Sanctuary
Staffordshire, United Kingdom

"Every horse sanctuary needs a Bren Ryan—a woman with a big heart who fights for what she believes in and will stop at nothing to ensure justice. RELENTLESS is a romantic thriller with a twist—not only in the plot, but in the way it bravely addresses controversial animal welfare issues that would otherwise remain unknown to those outside of the horse rescue world."

—Shelley Irving, MA Writing and Trustee
Shy Lowen Horse and Pony Sanctuary
Liverpool, United Kingdom

"P. J. O'Dwyer skillfully weaves the reader into Bren Ryan's tempestuous life, her family, friends, and deadly, often surprising enemies, in a fast-moving must-read for all lovers of romantic adventure."

—Sue Paling
Sathya Sai Sanctuary
Castlebaldwin, County Sligo, Ireland

"RELENTLESS is a thrilling and often gut-wrenching rollercoaster ride that whisks readers into the dark side of the horse world. The sometimes racy read encompasses several genres—from equestrian novel to thriller, to mystery to romance—along the way venturing into territory rarely tackled in modern fiction. RELENTLESS is a true page-turner with many surprising twists. P. J. O'Dwyer keeps the reader guessing to the very end."

—Robin Marshall, Editor
Horsetalk.co.nz/Equestrian News and Information
New Zealand

"Loved it! Just the right balance of suspense to romance with the true reality of horse slaughter as it is today. I could relate well to Bren and her passionate mission of rescuing equines destined for an awful, undignified end. Loved Bren's strong and somewhat tempestuous personality, which is why I guess I could relate so well. The dark, handsome cowboy was a bonus and the deepening plot had a great twist that was totally unexpected. It was the first novel I have read in a while and once I started reading, it was hard to stop.

"Looking forward to seeing RELENTLESS on the shelves so other romantic horse lovers can also share the literary experience. Will definitely be recommending RELENTLESS to those wanting a great read! Great work!"

—Nicki Cherrington, President and Founder
Last Chance Equine
Rotorua, New Zealand

"RELENTLESS provides a realistic view of equine rescue and the slaughter industry in both America and Australia. The story was gripping, intriguing, and had me on the edge of my seat. It pulled at my heartstrings, especially knowing issues that the book was based around are real life issues—an excellent read for not only horse lovers but for anyone who enjoys a story filled with action, suspense, and mystery."

—Amanda Vella, President and Founder
Save a Horse Australia Horse Rescue and Sanctuary
Queensland, Australia

"RELENTLESS is an enthralling romantic thriller—one can't help but be swept along with Bren's passion, in particular the equine welfare issues close to our hearts.

"Woven expertly into the story, P.J. O'Dwyer conveys the shocking reality of the fallout from the very darkest side of the U.S. horse slaughter trade, with a moving narrative that expertly intertwines love, family, and one woman's unshakeable belief in justice. A great read!"

—Jane DiGuiseppe
Quest Equine Welfare, Inc.
Victoria, Australia

In loving memory of my mother, Jean, who shared her love of books and opened up a world of unimaginable possibilities through just the turning of a page. Without you, I would never have had the vision to write.

And to my brother Andy, who taught me that anything is possible no matter the obstacles you face in life—you need only the desire to succeed.

I love you and miss you both.

DEDICATION

I've always believed writers have a responsibility to educate as well as to entertain. It is a precious opportunity when a writer is able to write a story that is both relevant to our time and that can affect positive change through awareness.

That chance event became a reality with the novel *Relentless*. Its title is a tribute to those who struggle each day advocating for the protection and humane treatment of horses and other equines that suffer from abuse, neglect, overbreeding, and the deep pockets of special-interest groups, including the drug industry.

Relentless is dedicated to the women and men of horse rescue. But specifically to the rescuers featured in this book who took the time to talk to a stranger, listen, and agree with enthusiasm to read Bren's story. Your insight and knowledge have made this book a more accurate account of the hard work, long hours, and never-ending commitment which is horse rescue.

Will there ever be a day when horse slaughter is only a past transgression of an earlier era of ignorance and greed? I know it is possible because of your strength and willingness to continue to fight and bring awareness to the ugly truth that is horse slaughter.

I find myself richer in friendships and dedicated to a cause I didn't know was mine until having met each one of you. Thank you for the opportunity to share your story.

ACKNOWLEDGMENTS

Amy Harke-Moore, it has been a true blessing having you in my life. You have made becoming a writer a reality for me. Thank you for your knowledge of the English language and your patience. You are not only a very gifted editor but also a dear friend.

Ally Peltier, your experience in the publishing world has been invaluable in making this book all it can be. Your eye for detail in the finer points of plot, conflict, and tension has given this story the edge it needs to compete among the many romantic suspense novels that line the bookstore shelves.

Carolyn Haley, thank you for being the perfect set of eyes. Your sense of organization, character/location, and time lines has given this project the final touches it needed to ensure consistency throughout. The book absolutely shines thanks to you.

Duncan Long, your ability to create a cover I could only dream about leaves me in awe. You are a rare find and a joy to work with. Thank you for bringing my characters to life.

Ronda Taylor, you've managed to take the impossible and make it a reality. Your sense of style and design have made this book a work of art. Thank you for indulging me in the many changes that have gotten us to this point. The interior of this book is everything I'd hoped it would be.

To all my horse rescue reviewers. Thank you for your expertise and knowledge with regard to horses, rescue, and the slaughter industry. As always, any and all mistakes are my own.

To the Martha Dailey Lookout Club, it takes a village to raise a writer. Or is it a critique-driven writers' group? The friendships and good humor I've shared with you have been one of the highlights of my writing career. I thank you all for your abundance of praise, and, yes, criticism. You've given me what a writer needs in her toolbox—self-confidence.

To the "Fabulous Four"—my father Turk Divver, his wife Pat Moran, my brother Joe Divver, and my favorite cousin Danny Divver. Thank you for believing in me and making this book a reality. I love you guys.

Dawn Rachuba and Lisa Powers, thank you for taking time out of your busy lives to indulge me and read my many drafts. The two of you are what real freindship is all about. You're the best.

And, finally, to my husband Mark of twenty-two years and my beautiful daughter Katie. Without your love, support, and understanding, Relentless would not be a reality for me. I love you both.

FOREWORD

When author P. J. O'Dwyer asked me to contribute a foreword for her new book which revolves around the hidden underworld of equine rescue, my interest was piqued. The field of equine welfare and cruelty had become one of my personal and professional specialties.

In O'Dwyer's *Relentless*, she creatively brings to light an issue that for over ten years I had been researching and investigating. P. J. O'Dwyer's story in *Relentless* thus struck a responsive chord in me. If I could help by lending my voice to the work, I told P. J., I would gladly do so.

It was through the discovery that America's majestic wild horses had been and continue to be brutally eliminated under the guise of humane protection that I first learned that our nation's domestic horses are also being violently killed/slaughtered. During the making of my film, *Saving America's Horses: A Nation Betrayed,* I encountered a steady stream of beautiful thoroughbreds flowing into the slaughter pipeline and wondered how such magnificent, sensitive, and intelligent beings could be derailed from such a life of glamour and plenty into a nightmare of betrayal absent of all humane protections. I was astonished at how many American horses of every breed and discipline disappear every week to face this barbaric fate.

In the process of unraveling the layer after layer of the incomprehensible corruption, I realized the vast majority of our country's population is in the dark about the violent and criminal nature of this seedy trade. I found that the only way to deal with the underbelly of this issue is through transparency—to establish what's happening, document it, and get it into the open where it can be dealt with.

In 2006 Congress put language in an Agriculture Appropriations Bill that cut off funding for horse meat inspections as a short term fix, until a federal ban could be passed. This effectively shut down horse slaughter in the U.S., but the industry opened new slaughter plants in Canada and Mexico where our American horses have continuously been exported for slaughter to this day. Proponents have since continued to push for the reopening of horse slaughter plants back in the states.

Relentless is valuable because it will help to raise awareness about this issue. O'Dwyer's fictional portrait of a horse rescuer's struggle to survive brings heart and soul, emotion and character to those braving the criminal elements within the horse slaughter trade. An unexpected romance adds to the chaotic daily life of Bren Ryan, whose love for horses spurs choices that place her in life threatening situations. It's a story of stolen horses and stolen hearts juggled with equal amounts epic stubbornness and hope. The extremes explored both rivet us and reach deeply into the breathless moments that engage a visceral reflection on the meaning of life.

Having firsthand experience in the underworld of equine rescue and as a lifelong horseperson, I applaud O'Dwyer for capturing the rich sense of fulfillment, commitment, and hard work associated with the daily care of equines. *Relentless* brings to surface the powerful bond we've shared with these loyal partners and companions and calls to humanity for the need to protect them.

—Katia Louise
Filmmaker, Speaker, Credentialed Educator, Horsewoman

CHAPTER ONE

BREN RYAN CLIMBED INTO BED WITH HER SEVEN-YEAR-OLD SON Finn, pulling the covers up nice and tight. She wrapped her arms around him. Outside his window, the spotlight she'd made a point of leaving on at night caught snowflakes fluttering down from a dark December sky, and she trembled.

"Mom?" Finn's voice shook.

She angled him away from her, slipping her fingers through his blond hair, her palm resting on his cool forehead. "You feeling okay?"

He glanced up, a smattering of freckles dusting his pert little nose, presently twisted with worry. "Did it hurt?"

"Hurt?"

"Dad. Did it hurt when he died?" Finn raised his eyebrows, an endearing gesture they teased him about when his glasses slipped down his nose.

She held him tight. It had been almost a year since Tom's death. Finn never asked much about the particulars. Maybe that was because there was enough speculation in their small town of Clear Spring, Maryland, to fill his ears and feed his curiosity.

But she'd done the exact opposite, gaining a reputation for being overwrought, some would say unstable, and relentless in chasing a theory she couldn't prove. Unfortunately, her recent decision and method to remind everyone they still had an unsolved murder and a killer running free would have its drawbacks. "It was quick, Finn. You know how you feel when you're hanging upside down on the monkey bars?"

He nodded.

"He just felt pressure, and then he fell asleep."

Bren clenched her teeth. She would sugarcoat it for Finn but not for her friend, Kevin Bendix, the sheriff of Washington County. She'd been avoiding his calls today and the confrontation that would put them at odds.

Finn settled in against her chest and remained quiet. Bren rested her chin on top of his head. Except for their breathing, it was silent, the slow beat of Finn's heart against her forearm soothing.

Bren took a deep breath and shut her eyes, trying to imagine Tom's footfalls climbing the stairs after he'd locked up for the night. She half expected to find him smiling at her in the doorway of Finn's bedroom, waiting to trade places.

A light tug on her hair brought her eyes open. Finn's small fingers were intertwined in a long, dark red strand of her hair. "Some kids on the bus today were teasing me and Aiden again." He glanced up. "They keep saying Dad's dead because you stole that old fart's horses."

She stiffened. "That's ridiculous."

Bren slipped out from under the covers and stood. "It's getting late, baby." She removed Finn's glasses, placing them on the nightstand, and reached for the light. "Good night, sweetheart."

"Mom?" His eyes, the size of two brown copper pennies, peered up from beneath thick lashes. "Did you?"

Her heart skipped a beat. She grabbed his hand and squeezed it. "No. People talk is all."

He nodded, and Bren relaxed.

"I'll go check on your brother." She kissed Finn's cheek. "If you need me, I'm right down the hall."

"Good night. Love you, Mom."

"Love you, too."

Bren turned off the light and moved into the hall, catching her teenage son coming from the hall bathroom.

"Aiden," she whispered.

He scowled at her and headed for his bedroom, disappearing inside.

She followed, coming to an abrupt stop when he closed the door. Bren reached for the knob, and it clicked. She jiggled it. "Aiden, open the door."

"I hate you."

"I didn't steal those horses, Aiden."

"Dad thought you did."

"Dad was wrong. Now open the door." The lock popped, and the knob turned in her hand.

"What?" Angry brown eyes pierced her through the crack of the door.

"It was the only way to wake this town up."

"Whatever."

That word, in particular, accompanied by Aiden's sarcastic tone, could set her teeth on edge. But tonight she ignored it. "I love you, A—"

He pushed the door shut, and Bren's grip tightened on the knob. She counted to ten.

Let him go. He's hurting.

Tears pinched her eyes. She hurt, too. How could she help her sons when she couldn't help herself? Trembling, she was not the constant her boys depended on or the competent thirty-five-year-old director of a horse rescue farm. She'd fought injustices all her life, protected those who couldn't protect themselves. Yet, all five foot six, one hundred and twenty-five well-toned pounds of her wanted to slither to the floor in defeat. Where was the fierce, wrongly widowed farm girl now? She released the doorknob and escaped down the steps to the kitchen.

The house hummed with the warmth from the furnace, but the chill wouldn't leave Bren. She scrubbed her arms, then reached up into the cabinet above the dishwasher and snagged the pretty-shaped bottle of Crown Royal they kept on hand for holidays and dropped it inside the large pocket of her robe.

She climbed the stairs of the old farmhouse she'd shared with Tom. Tears leaked down her face. She didn't want to continue doing this alone. The horse rescue farm they called Grace . . . the boys . . . life.

She wiped her face with the furry pink sleeve of her robe and entered her room. Her bed . . . hers and Tom's bed sat quiet and made with the comforter her mother had sewn sixteen years ago for their wedding. She hadn't slept there since Tom's death. No way could she disturb it—not tonight. Maybe not ever.

Rather than head down the hall to the guest bedroom, Bren settled down in the wooden rocker Tom had bought when Aiden was born. She couldn't escape his memory. It reached out everywhere, like tiny pinpricks, reminding her she was alive and Tom wasn't.

The cap of the bottle twisted off easily; she took her first swig. She winced when the Canadian whisky burned her throat.

She managed several more swigs and began to relax. Raising the bottle, she toasted herself. "Way to go, Bren. Nice job screwing with your boys' heads." The tears that had dried down her cheeks reemerged, wet and flowing. She took another swig and rocked and held the bottle up again. "To Wes Connelly, you miserable bastard. Whatever it takes, I'll torment your murdering ass until you're broken and behind bars."

Tom's handsome face flashed before her. He'd warned her. His remark the last night he was alive: "Stop antagonizing Wes. I've got too much to do around this farm to protect you from yourself." Headstrong and deliberate were her responses to everything, and Tom, amazingly, had been the guiding hand that had kept her from self-destructing. But Tom had been wrong about one thing.

He was the one who needed protection.

She lifted the bottle again, her hands sliding on the glass. "I'm sorry, baby." She let the bottle sink into her lap and closed her eyes. She continued to rock until she nodded off.

The shrill peal of a cell phone, her cell phone, made her stand up. The bottle of Crown Royal dropped and poured out onto the hardwood floor. "Shit!" She bent over and righted it and lurched for the nightstand. Tom's name glowed on the screen of her phone. The room spun and Bren dropped onto the bed. Gripping the phone tight, she fumbled to flip it open, but the ringing stopped. Tom's name disappeared.

"What the hell?" She scrolled through the contacts and verified the number. It was Tom's.

She hit the number two key and scrolled down her list of contacts until she came to Bendix.

"Bren?" Kevin yawned into the phone. "It's three in the morning. What's wrong?"

"Tom's phone. Where is it?"

He yawned again, and something, maybe his bed covers, rustled into the receiver before he grunted. "Bren, we've been over this a million times. You know we never found his phone."

An hour later, Kevin turned off the lights on his cruiser and stepped out into the chilled, predawn air. "You ever think to run this by me before you take out a full-page ad?" He reached into his cruiser.

Bren didn't need to guess for what.

A copy of Clear Spring's weekly newspaper crinkled in Kevin's fingers. He held up page three. "It looks like a damn wanted poster from the Wild West."

That had been her intention. A decorative scroll at the top and bottom, and the word "Wanted" in bold capital letters.

She lit it up with her flashlight.

Local kill buyer, frequents Jameson Livestock Sale Barn, mid-sixties, wanted for the murder of Thomas Patrick Ryan. Reward for any information leading to his arrest and conviction. Call Bren Ryan or the Washington County Sheriff's Office.

If it wasn't for the desperation behind the act, she'd almost laugh. "Only thing missing is his photo."

"Real funny." Kevin scratched his head, his tight blond crew cut bristling against his fingers. "You'll be damn lucky Wes doesn't smack you with a defamation suit."

"I didn't mention his name."

He smirked. "Nice try, Bren. You knew damn well he and everyone else in this town would get your meaning." Less formidable minus his uniform, he leaned against his cruiser and yawned. "I'm tired, Bren." Snow batted his face, and he grabbed a knit cap from his pocket. Pulling it on his head, he huddled inside his jacket. "And cold. If you have something new, let's have it. If not, I'm going the hell back to bed." He grabbed the door handle.

"Tom called me tonight."

His head whipped back. "That supposed to be funny?"

"It's true." She handed him her phone. "Check recent calls." Bren wrapped her arms around her waist, pressing her barn coat against her. She was freezing. Still in her flannel pajamas, she'd slipped her work boots on bare feet when she left out the back door to meet Kevin.

He flipped open her phone, the screen a blue glow reflecting off his wrinkled brow.

She sidled up next to him. "For Tom's name to appear on my phone, the call had to be made from his phone."

He gave her a sideways glance. "I know how it works," he snapped.

She stiffened and placed her hands on her hips. "Then do something. I shouldn't have to resort to ads in the paper. You're the sheriff. Obviously, I got his attention. Not that I was expecting a phone call."

Kevin scrubbed his face and pushed off his cruiser, handing back her phone. "Since when do you not get Wes's attention?" His brow rose and she got his meaning.

She'd done a lot of things in recent months to screw with Wes. All could have gotten her fined or thrown in jail. Good thing her best bud came in the form of the county sheriff.

"You never canceled Tom's cell?"

Kevin's voice brought her around. "It's stupid." She shrugged. "I needed to hear his voice." Her own voice cracked then. Tom's voicemail was the only recording she had of him. Being able to call his phone, hear his voice made it seem as though he was still with her.

Damn it! The bastard must have enjoyed her desperate attempt to keep from going quietly insane. She winced. "He knows I've been calling Tom's phone."

Kevin's expression softened. "You tell anyone else about the call or the phone?"

"No. But why would he keep it?" She pulled on her bottom lip. "There must have been something on Tom's phone he didn't want us to know."

"We already checked his phone records. None of the numbers would raise an eyebrow. It was just the usual you would expect for a man who is a blacksmith and runs a rescue."

Okay, so it wasn't the caller that stood out. "But what about messages? Did you check those?"

"Bren, technology has come a long way. But there's nothing that would allow us to hear or read a message. We'd have to have the phone."

"That's it. We need to find the phone."

"That's the logical step. But let's keep this between you and me."

"But—"

"I mean it. If he had anything to do with Tom's death—and that's a big if—you'll tip him off, and we'll never find the phone."

"*Okay.*"

He hesitated. "Can you think of anything else Tom might have been involved in before he died?"

Huh? Maybe she'd missed something. She just assumed it was Wes's way of paying *her* back. But perhaps Tom had known something she didn't. "Remember that horse of Rex Boland's? The show horse, Cloud Dancer? They found him dead in his stall over at Wes's place."

Kevin gave her a blank look.

"Yes, you do. A few days before Tom died, the county got back the lab results. They said it was colic. Tom thought the cause of death was too convenient. Plus, Wes's stable is for looks. He never kept any horses in it until Cloud Dancer." She zeroed in on Kevin. "Think about it. Rex Boland and Wes are friends. Wasn't that horse heavily insured?"

Kevin slumped against his cruiser, his hands in his pockets. He frowned. "I think the county knows more about toxicology reports than a blacksmith and his wife, even if they do run a horse rescue."

"Come on. It's not the first horse death. There's been a string of them. Maybe not here in Maryland, but now I think it's the only thing that makes sense. With his job, he got around. If anyone might have overheard something, it would have been Tom."

Kevin took a breath. "I think that's a huge leap. Let's stick to facts, Bren. The phone exists, I'll give you that. So let's revisit the night in question, and you tell me everything you remember."

She paced, the snow swirling around her. "I told you. Tom went out around eleven thirty to get his truck ready for the next day. When I woke up close to two thirty, he wasn't in bed. He wasn't in the house." Her voice rose.

Kevin pushed off his cruiser toward her. "Calm down."

"Don't tell me to calm down." She stopped and narrowed in on him. "Tom's dead, damn it! And for almost a year you've wanted to believe it was an accident." Her fingers tensed on the flashlight. She took a deep breath and continued. "I checked the barn—the hayloft. I came around to here." She stepped toward the barn and centered herself under the pulley outside the hayloft door. "And that's when I heard it. A faint creak, like a floorboard squeaking. Then I felt it. A shadow above me." Her eyes glistened, and she blinked back tears. "All I could think about was Tom. Saving him. I should have done better." Bren sagged. "If I could have gotten him down faster . . . heard his cries for help . . . he'd be . . ."

Kevin put his arm around her shoulder. "Bren, no one's blaming you. You couldn't have saved Tom."

She pulled away and shined the flashlight up toward the pulley system. Only quiet snowflakes danced in the night sky. "You didn't find his phone?" she said, thinking out loud.

"We combed every inch of the barn, the hayloft, and here, where you found him."

"What about the hospital? Did you check his belongings?"

"Yes." Kevin cocked his head. "You sure he had his phone?"

"Positive." Bren flashed the light onto the ground. "When he left the house that night, I saw him snap it into his belt holder." She turned off the flashlight. "I heard it click. It wouldn't have fallen out, even if he was hanging upside down." She tapped her finger against her lips. "Unless it was taken off."

"And you think Wes is your guy, obviously." He shook his head. "I think you're reaching."

"You were there."

Wes had been pissed that day. Waking up to find six good-sized, profitable horses missing instead of headed for the slaughterhouse in Mexico made for a contentious neighbor. Wes assumed she and Tom had something to do with it. They—Grace Equine Sanctuary—had bid against him at auction the night before and lost. He'd raised holy hell with the sheriff's office the next morning after the horses went missing. Kevin barely had his feet firmly on Grace's gravel drive before Wes flew up and intercepted him. Not liking the odds—Kevin, Tom, and Bren had been friends since childhood—Wes threatened his own kind of justice. He never elaborated on his method.

The next night, Bren found Tom tangled in their pulley system, the ropes a jumble around his body and his neck. He'd been strangled, and it sure as hell didn't look like suicide or an accident. She knew Tom. He wasn't careless. And she didn't believe in coincidences, either.

"Yeah, well, it doesn't mean he's guilty," Kevin said. "Wes is a blowhard. Always has been. Besides, he had an alibi. He and Lyle—"

"Lyle and he are buddies. They'd both lie to save the other's ass."

"Maybe, but it wasn't just the two of them. They were playing their weekly game of Texas Hold 'Em."

She could tell by the way his voice faded he wanted to take back those last three words.

Some lawman he is.

She took a step closer, ready to rip into him.

"Don't start. If I had to break up every card game that had cash riding on it—" He waved a dismissive hand. "The point is, he had five eyewitnesses. So he didn't do it." He scratched his head again. "We need to face facts. Like I said before, looks like Tom got tangled in the rope and lost his footing and somehow fell out the barn door."

"If that were true—" She bore into him with quiet irritation, because as much as she wanted to scream it at him, she didn't want to wake the boys.

"—he was very conscientious to close the barn door before he flew out the loft." Oh, yeah. She'd had plenty of time to speculate, and Wes, the dumb-ass, had been just a little too neat with his crime scene.

Kevin took a labored breath. "I'll look into the phone."

"I'm coming." She moved toward his cruiser.

"Now hold up." He grabbed her arm. "I know you're hurting. Trust me, if there's something going on here, I'll find it. But there are procedures that need to be followed. I need probable cause to get a search warrant." He shook his head. "I don't have it."

"That's bullshit." She pulled her arm free. "He's a kill buyer."

"That doesn't make him a murderer."

"Might as well be," she muttered before facing him. "Buying horses out from under Grace that were healthy and could go to a good home is criminal."

"Buying horses for slaughter isn't against the law. Besides, not all of them were healthy."

"We're a rescue. There are more humane ways than sending them off to slaughter."

Kevin regarded her with something that looked very much like amusement. "Since you're so adept at investigation, use your feminine wiles on his son. Maybe Robert Connelly knows something." Kevin's gaze landed on her work boots—untied, with her thin, pasty-white ankles shoved inside.

"Go to hell."

"Just a thought. I heard he paid you a visit. Also heard he's back for good as Wes's accountant."

Bren shrugged. "He's not his father. He's been very supportive since Tom's death, which is more than I can say for you lately."

"Whatever." He placed his hands on his hips. "The point is, I can't have you going off half-cocked. I'm warning you. Let me handle it. Stay away from Wes."

That was impossible. The town of Clear Spring was no bigger than Mayberry. He was asking a lot because if she found herself within breathing space of Wes, she'd kill him.

She spun around and headed back toward the house.

"Hey, where you going?"

"To bed. You find Tom's phone, you'll find his killer."

And if he didn't, she would.

Chapter Two

"Who picked out your sweater?" Bren asked, holding open the door for longtime friends Jeremy Breakstone and his wife Jo, also members on the board of directors of Grace.

Jeremy looked down his nose, crossing his eyes. "I did." His chin rose and he grinned. "You don't like it?"

He must have been an easy mark as a kid. Short-cropped, strawberry-blond hair, a hint of youthful freckles—he could pass for a teenager when he grinned, except he was highly educated, tall, and strong enough to compete with the size and power of the horses as the local equine vet.

Bren reached out with her finger and rang the tiny brass bell sewn onto an embroidered appliqué of a reindeer. "It's festive."

"I thought so." He handed her a cookie tin with last week's copy of Clear Spring's newspaper strategically opened to page three. His eyes practically danced with amusement. "Only thing missing is his photo."

"Shh." Bren tried not to laugh hearing her words coming out of Jeremy's mouth as she tossed her head back. No one was in the hallway. She took the tin and handed him back the paper. "We're not talking about it around the boys."

A pink flush rose in Jo's bronzed cheeks. "We shouldn't be talking about it at all." She shot her husband a censorious look. Leaning on her cane, she frowned at Bren. "How you holding up?" Jo's deep blue eyes held hers.

Bren had struggled all morning to keep from crying. Call it Jo's best-friend-sixth-sense. No amount of smiling or humor directed toward Jeremy's sweater could hide Bren's pain from Jo.

"I miss him." Bren's eyes watered.

Jo motioned Jeremy through the door.

His arm went around Jo's waist. "I'm already gone." Pulling her tight, he kissed the top of her dark head, her hair slipping from its tight bun, loose wisps now framing her face. "I don't do tears." Jeremy crossed over the threshold and squeezed Bren's shoulder. "Hang in there." He started down the hall.

"Not so fast." Jo grabbed the paper out from under his arm. Without breaking stride, Jeremy disappeared through the kitchen.

Jo shook her head. "He's like a big kid." She maneuvered with her cane and stepped inside, folding Bren into her arms. "Holidays make it hard, sweetie."

Bren hugged her back. "I just miss him so much." She wiped a tear from her cheek and sniffed before pulling away. "I've made a mess of things with the boys, especially Aiden. He said he hates me."

"He didn't mean it. He loves you." Jo took Bren's hand, giving it a good shake. "You need to let it go. Trust me. I was in law enforcement once. Wes's alibi is solid."

It was on the edge of her tongue to tell Jo about the phone call from Tom's cell phone. Her expertise as a retired DEA agent had come in handy as Bren had tried to make sense of Tom's death. But she'd promised Kevin.

"Come on." She tucked Jo's hand inside her arm and led her toward the dining room. "Dad's waiting on us. He's cooked the biggest bird you've ever seen."

Since Bren's mother had passed away a few years earlier, her father had learned to cook for himself, offering his culinary skills every Wednesday at her house and insisting he do the major holidays as well. Damn good thing. Today her heart struggled to beat, her limbs moved mechanically but by no means were capable of preparing a sumptuous feast. She'd more than likely burn dinner, her mind preoccupied with who was missing.

Bren was quiet at the table. She filled her plate, passing the food on, but toyed with her fork, unable to take a bite. She watched as the gold flecks running through the ivory tablecloth caught the light of the country chandelier above. The merriment of her family's and friends' voices and Sugarland's newest Christmas CD in the background grated on her nerves. She wanted to clamp her hands over her ears.

Tom was everywhere—in her children's eyes, her father-in-law Paddy's expressions. Bren wanted so desperately to scream, pull her hair out. Have a tantrum. She missed him, his laughter, even his anger when she'd pushed him past the point of reason.

The only thing she'd managed to do was wake the dead. The late night calls from Tom's phone hadn't stopped. The article had gotten Wes's attention. One point for her. But she needed more, and the phone—Tom's phone—was her objective. If Kevin didn't come up with his probable cause, she'd find a way to track down Tom's phone, and she wasn't above breaking and entering to get it.

Daniel Fallon, Bren's father, directed his gaze across the table toward Jeremy. "What do you think about Sweet Prince?" His voice, every bit Irish—he'd never lost his accent since coming to America—was edged with dismay.

Founder of Grace, he lived a brisk walk down the gravel road he shared with Bren and her family in a farmhouse where she and her sister Kate grew up. He'd never quite retired. Since Tom's death, it had been necessary for him to take a more active role. Sweet Prince had become a barb in his side that wouldn't shake lose. Not that he or the rescue had any claim to the horse. Sweet Prince's death, just like the other horse deaths over the last year or so, seemed too convenient.

Kevin popped into Bren's mind. Mr. Know-It-All. Now here she had just pointed out there was something up with the number of colic cases and, boom, another drops to his death.

Of course now Kevin was considering she might be on to something.

Jeremy handed the potatoes to Jo. "Damn shame. I nursed him back from colic once."

"Colic?" Bren's father's usual glittering blue eyes hardened through his bifocals. "You don't find that odd, then? Nine deaths now, all from one cause?"

In his early seventies with a portly frame, and thin, downy-white hair, he could pass for a sweet old man, and he usually was, except she knew her father well. The color in his cheeks wasn't from the warm kitchen where he'd prepared their bountiful Christmas dinner. "I guess law enforcement knows better, perhaps?"

Jeremy set down his fork. "I've wondered, myself. The only other horse death I attended was White Lace, a white Arabian. That was over two years ago in Frederick County. Same thing. Nothing showed up on the toxicology report."

"Was the horse insured?" Paddy asked. He sat at the end of the table. Tom's only surviving parent. Pam had died giving birth to their firstborn—Tom.

Having Paddy around worked to both soothe and upset Bren. It was like looking at her husband thirty years fast-forward. Other than the crew cut and the silver hair, Paddy's compressed lips and furrowed brow reminded her of Tom. Tom when he was mad. Or when he'd questioned her about her involvement in Wes's missing horses the same night she found him dead.

"To the hilt," Jeremy said around a mouth of turkey. His voice, a hard jerk, brought Bren back to the conversation.

Jeremy would have prepared documentation for the insurance claim. He must have gotten a glance at the payout. Bren and Tom had theorized over the deaths that stretched as far down as North Carolina and up to New York. Now that she looked back, to before Tom's death, he'd been a little preoccupied about the whole subject.

"Honey, you all right?" Her dad cocked his head, his gray brows furrowing into one.

"Fine." Bren gave a quick smile before her lips thinned. She took a sip of her water.

"Paddy." Finn pulled on his grandfather's arm. "Show me how to do the coin trick."

"You liked that?" Tall and still carrying a lean, muscular frame for sixty-nine, Paddy wrapped his arm around Finn and grinned.

Nowhere could she register Paddy's loss for his son. Even with the holidays and the one-year anniversary approaching, he seemed content and accepting sitting there, his expressive brown eyes smiling through his reading glasses at Finn.

"He'll never get it," Aiden complained across the table.

"Will so," Finn challenged.

"Give him a chance, Aiden," Jeremy said.

"Are you watching, Mom?" Finn piped over the table.

Bren nodded, her temples throbbing.

Sleight-of-hand not being one of Finn's strong points, the coin slid from his sleeve and out onto the table where it spun like a globe before coming to rest flat on the tablecloth.

"Fail!" Aiden yelled as he reached across the table for the coin.

"The wine, me boy!" yelled her father.

Out of the corner of Bren's eye, the glass of wine at her elbow fell over with such force the glass broke, and red wine, dark as blood, splashed her white turtleneck, the excess flooding the tablecloth before it spilled over the edge and sloshed onto Bren's lap. She sucked in air and slid her chair back, her hands pushing the broken glass away from the edge. A sharp sliver caught the meaty part of her palm. She whimpered.

"Bren, you all right?" asked Jo, struggling to her feet.

"You're bleeding." Jeremy stood, too.

Blood from her palm dripped onto the hardwood floor.

"Mom?"

"Stop whining, Finn," Bren said, his voice tonight just a little too high pitched.

Finn's eyes widened and he clamped his mouth shut.

"Bren, he only—"

"Enough, Dad." All eyes remained on her. "Everyone stop staring at me! Stop telling me what to do. How to feel. I've had it up to here!" She raised her trembling hand, still dripping blood, to her neck and cut a slice through the air. Bren grabbed a napkin to stanch the blood and pushed back against the chair hard, toppling it over. Everything seemed to circle—the chair, broken glass, blood-red wine—Tom's blood!

Oh God.

Bren turned toward the hallway, tripping in a pair of high-heeled clogs. Unable to steady herself, she kicked them off and ran to the steps, the tears blinding her as she climbed the stairs and headed in the direction of her bedroom.

He isn't coming back.

Bren hit the light switch inside the doorway and ran to Tom's highboy chest. She still hadn't cleaned out his things. She grabbed for the top drawer and began scooping his undershirts, socks, and boxers, the blood from her hand smearing the clothes. Bren dumped them on the floor. Going for the next drawer, she did the same, a pile growing.

She ran to the walk-in closet, her socks slipping on the hardwood floor. His clothes hung on the left. She took a tentative step—a mix of jeans, flannel shirts, a few dress shirts, and slacks rested silently on hangers. She moaned. Wiping her wet face with the back of her arm, she slumped forward. The smell of Tom filled that side of the closet, a combination of the barn, their land, and Irish Spring.

As long as she could smell him, he was with her. But while time passed, the scent of him haunted her. He'd be alive if it weren't for her—Bren, always needing to prove a point, always pushing to get what *she* wanted.

Except this time it had backfired—big time.

Bren leaned into Tom's clothes. She gathered them into her arms and took a long breath. Her tears flowed anew as she clung to his flannel shirts.

Then her anger took over, and she yanked them off the pole and threw them to the floor. She reached up and pulled down his hunting gear from the shelf, letting it fall with a thud to the ground. On the floor, she pulled out his shoes and pitched them behind her, grunting and stopping to wipe her face several times.

"Bren." Jeremy stopped her mid-throw.

Bren stood still, holding Tom's Nike tennis shoe in her hand.

"You okay?"

She turned toward him and bit down on her lip, shaking her head.

Jeremy moved forward. He frowned and took the shoe from her hand, then wrapped his arms around her. "I know you're hurting."

She nodded against Jeremy's shoulder. The tears ran down her cheeks, soaking his ridiculous red-and-green reindeer sweater.

"I can't—" Racked by sobs, Bren couldn't finish. She only buried her face deeper into his shoulder. She'd cried on his shoulder so many times over the last year, it wouldn't have surprised her if he was waterlogged by now. She'd woken him from a dead sleep the night she found Tom. He had lowered Tom down while she guided his body to the ground. Jeremy and Jo had both rallied around her when Kevin couldn't put Wes anywhere near their farm the night Tom died and wasn't changing his "findings" to suit a friend who, in his words, needed to get a grip.

Well, he needed to get a grip, too—a grip on Tom's phone. Because it existed.

She pulled away and wiped her face. The cut on her hand still thumped, but the blood had stopped. "I'm a mess." She glanced at her wine-stained sweater and jeans.

Jeremy gently pulled her from the closet and sat her down on the edge of the bed. He glanced beside the bed at the pile of clothes. "The clinic is closed tomorrow. How about Jo and I help you pack up Tom's things?"

"I can—"

He put up his hand. "I know you can, Bren. But let us help. Six hands are faster than two." He sat down beside her and squeezed her knee.

Bren gave him a half smile. "Thanks."

"I know this is none of my business, but how are you doing financially?"

Bren shrugged. "It's tight. With the economy, donations are down for the rescue so I've had to dig into what little savings Tom and I had. But we're managing."

"Didn't you have life insurance for Tom?"

Her shoulders slumped. "We're living off it. What's left anyway. And Dad's social security."

Jeremy rolled his lips and made one of those "I'm thinking" faces. "I'm looking for an assistant. In fact, Monday I was going to put an ad in the *Hagerstown Herald*. The position starts at twenty-seven K."

Bren gave him a questioning look. "What are you saying?"

He pulled back and grinned. "The hours are flexible. Part-time for someone who needs to be home before the bus lets off her kids."

"You can't be serious! I don't—"

"Have experience? You run a horse rescue, have lived on a farm your whole life. Don't sell yourself short."

"When would—"

"The first of the year. Tomorrow I'll drop off a key."

"But I didn't—"

"Say yes, Bren."

Bren pulled away and licked her lips, the taste salty. The money, although generous, wouldn't go a long way considering the expense to run a household, but it would ease some of the burden.

She gave Jeremy one of her most serious faces. "How about vacation and holidays?"

His eyes widened.

She smiled and nudged his shoulder. "I'll take it."

CHAPTER THREE

J AMESON LIVESTOCK SALE BARN, ON THE FIRST AND THIRD FRIDAY of each month, took every ounce of energy from Bren whenever they came to auction. This place, redolent of fear, horseflesh, and piss, sickened her, the laughter and jovial chatter maddening.

Folks milled about the barn like it was a Saturday night social. Some sat in the bleachers lining the chute where the livestock came through as if in anticipation of a sporting event.

"You want the night off?" Jeremy dipped his head to see her face, frowning when he saw her expression.

Even though she wasn't here to bid on Grace's behalf, an equine vet was required to be on standby. As Jeremy's assistant, she couldn't shirk her duties, sour stomach or not. "I'm good." She held onto Finn's hand. "You seen Aiden?" she asked her son.

Finn shook his head.

She'd told Aiden to meet them at the rails, adding with finality eight o'clock sharp, hoping she had drilled that last point into his obstinate teenage brain.

"Mom," Finn whined.

"What?" She glanced down. He was grimacing.

"My hand. You're squeezing it too tight."

"Sorry." She lightened up on his little hand and searched for the time. A big round clock hung above the auctioneer's box. "It's—"

Running feet, slipping on straw, caught Bren's attention. Aiden fell in next to Jeremy and swung the unnerving swath of brown hair away from his eyes. "Here," he announced and nodded toward the clock. "With two seconds to go."

He was cruising toward restriction big time. But he had her—he was on time. Giving him a razor-sharp stare, she pinched together her thumb and forefinger, leaving scant space between them. "You're that close."

Aiden's lips thinned and his cheeks flushed in embarrassment. Bren could sympathize with him a little. No one liked being the center of bad attention, and they had belabored the issue.

They moved toward the bleachers. This time Bren made sure her eldest sat next to her. She leaned into him. "I'm sorry. Friends?"

He nudged her back playfully. "Think you can handle it?"

"For you, I'll try."

Aiden shot a covert look around, no doubt checking to see if there were witnesses, and placed his hand on top of hers. He gave it a quick squeeze before pulling away. That was progress, Aiden-style, and the friction between the two lifted.

The auction started ten minutes late. Several horses were paraded through the chute. The cacophony of Lyle's calls echoed against the corrugated metal walls and ceiling. Horses were prodded and poked through the chute, their eyes wide with fright and ears pricked up in watchful attentiveness. That was what bothered Bren most about this particular sale barn—Lyle Jameson was just plain mean.

Finn huddled next to Bren, his hands pushed deep in his pockets.

"You cold?" she asked him.

"A little."

She motioned to Jeremy. "We're going to get some hot chocolate. You want some?"

"No thanks."

Bren nudged Aiden. "You staying or coming?"

He stood up. "Coming."

They cleared the bleachers and stepped outside. Bren could see her breath every time she exhaled. The stars twinkled like diamonds against a soft, black velvet sky. The moon, only a sliver, sat high in the west. With no cloud cover, the air was brisk, and she shivered against the collar of her barn coat as she stood at the concession stand.

She glanced around. Finn and Aiden had taken off toward a pen of mismatched farm animals waiting to be auctioned.

"Can I help you?"

"Three hot chocolates."

The stomping of feet came toward her, and Finn ran up, his coat flapping. "Mom! We saw the funniest goat."

"Finn. It's freezing." She bent down and zipped his coat. "Remember what I said when we left the barn? Mittens." She reached for his hands and found he was wearing his mittens and tugged the matching cap from his pocket and pulled it on his head. "And hat must be on."

"Mom, Aiden's not wearing his."

Bren peered up. Aiden quickly zipped his coat, and then his eyes followed something in the distance. Bren followed his line of sight. Jenny Smithson, a cute blonde, headed into the sale barn with several other teenagers.

"The hat's lame." Aiden folded his arms, his face unsmiling.

Bren knew when to pick her battles, and this wasn't one of them. She pulled Finn around by his coat. "Don't worry about your brother."

She paid for the hot chocolate and handed each of them a warm Styrofoam cup before grabbing hers. "Let's go. I'm working tonight. Remember?"

She didn't want to give Jeremy a reason to regret offering her a job. Plus the job and all her other duties managing the horse rescue left little time to mope. Now, for vengeance—she'd make time. Only she'd promised to stay clear of Wes. But if he found her, he'd pay her back. She needed to get to him first.

Bren's two-way went off, and she jostled her hot chocolate, spilling it on her gloves. "Shit." She steadied the cup on the top of a barrel nearby and pulled off the hot, wet glove. She grabbed for her two-way phone inside her coat pocket.

"Yeah."

"I've got a horse down. You need to get in here." Jeremy's voice breathed deep in her ear.

"On my way," she said. "Aiden. Watch your brother."

Aiden lifted his head. "What?"

"Your brother." She pointed toward Finn who was kicking stones. "Watch him."

Bren jogged the fifty feet to the barn. When she entered, she noticed a group forming around the rail. The crowd and her adrenaline made her break out in a sweat. She pulled off her coat and tossed it at the foot of the bleachers. She pushed aside the gawkers, squeezed through the rail, and took a deep breath.

At the bottom of the chute lay a black colt on its side. Bren's heart stopped. "What happened?"

Jeremy remained crouched next to the colt. "Spooked the mother. She trampled him."

"Damn it!" Bren came around to the colt's head.

Jeremy checked his pupils while Bren felt for broken bones.

"Knocked him cold." Bren lifted her chin toward the mare.

Jeremy nodded.

This was the typical crap Bren complained about the most. These horses were frightened, the lights blinding. Lyle paraded them too close together, making injuries like this inevitable.

Within minutes, the colt came to. He didn't appear to have any sustained injuries. Jeremy brought him to his feet and began walking him around the twenty-foot squared-off area of the chute. He then motioned to one of Lyle's men. "Lead him in the back into one of the stalls."

"Breakstone, I'm bidding on that pair," Wes yelled over the rail.

Bren clenched her hands and turned around. "Go to hell, Connelly."

Wes stood like a peacock in his plumage, dressed in a three-piece suit and red power tie. His head and face, ruddy and pocked and shades darker against the thick, silver nest of hair, always reminded her of a cork getting ready to pop.

"Lyle?" The word, slippery with intent, fell from Wes's lips. His buddy, his alibi and co-conspirator, surely caught his meaning, even if she and everyone else didn't. The only thing she knew was it didn't bode well for her. Wes's cold, steely eyes continued to hold her gaze. Bren shook with anger and fear. Kill buyers didn't normally bid on colts—small with little meat, they'd cost more to house and fatten up. He was paying her back for the newspaper ad.

"What's your bid?" Lyle tapped the gavel in his hand.

"Jeremy, can't you—"

"Five twenty-five for the pair."

Jeremy's expression hardened. "Come on, Jameson. Bren's right—auction them next Friday. This one," he said, motioning to the colt he held by the halter, "needs to be checked out." He nodded to the broodmare presently tied off toward the end of the chute, snorting and pulling against the rope, her eyes wild with unpredictability. "That one is about to go berserk."

"Time is money, Lyle," Wes added.

Lyle shrugged. "Sorry, Doc. He's got a point."

Bren's head ached. Watching Tweedledee and Tweedledum, she wanted to smack their heads together.

The colt's eyes were wide and awake as he danced on his hooves nervously under the fluorescent lights. He gave a snort and whinny. Jeremy handed him off to her. "He's all yours."

No. The colt and the mare were a pair now, thanks to Wes—a more expensive pair.

Lyle grabbed his gavel. "You bidding, Bren?"

Bren's heart quickened. She and Finn had seen this colt earlier. Finn had fallen in love with him at first sight. She'd been thinking of bidding. She'd promised Finn a colt. If she didn't bid, they'd be Wes's. He'd ship the frightened pair off to Mexico for twenty-eight cents a pound in deplorable conditions, take a hit on the colt, and call it even, knowing he'd gotten his revenge.

Cost be damned. "Five thirty-five."

"Seven hundred." A wicked grin curled the ends of Wes's lips.

Bren took a step, tempted to charge the son of a bitch and knock him on his sanctimonious ass.

Finn leaned over the rail. "Mom?" His voice quivered with uncertainty.

She nodded in his direction. "It's okay, baby."

Straightening, Bren set her eyes on Wes, who grabbed an old lawn chair sitting askew on the dirt floor of the sale barn. He loosened his tie and popped the top button of his white dress shirt, then slipped out of his navy suit jacket, folding it neatly in half and placing it over the rail. Searching his pants pockets, he pulled out a thin cheroot, ignoring the straw strewn about on the dirt floor and bales stacked in the corners and against every available wall space.

Bren tightened her grip on the rope as Wes lit up. The colt's eyes flashed, exposing the whites in the corner as he attempted to rear. She held tight, keeping him grounded, and spoke to him soothingly. The colt let out another snort and a whinny and settled down. Wes sat back into the lawn chair and crossed his legs, taking several drags off his cheroot.

"You know you're stealing this colt from a seven-year-old boy," she said.

"You're bidding, not the boy."

Finn's head turned from her to Wes. He stood alone on the dirt floor, clenching his small little hands by his side. David and Goliath. That was their only shot to save this colt, and she was taking it. Bren patted the colt and moved toward the rail. Spying a wooden crate in the corner, she motioned toward Aiden. "Grab the crate for Finn."

Aiden pulled it over by the rail.

"Hop up, sweetheart." It was a large step, but he managed with the help of his brother.

Bren pulled out a wad of bills—her first week's pay from Jeremy since starting as his assistant and a thousand-dollar donation she'd picked up on the way to the sale barn and planned to use for feed and supplies—and handed it to Finn through the rails. "He's your horse, baby, and you're going to have to fight for him."

He nodded and took the money.

Bren gave him a peck on the top of his head and then lifted her chin toward Wes. "Just so we're straight. This is my son Finn. He's seven and far more mature than you'll ever be. He loves this colt, and he's willing to go toe-to-toe with you to get him."

Wes pursed his lips, his silver eyes twinkling with anticipation under his brows.

It wasn't the money now, it was the principle. She'd eat cold cereal for breakfast, lunch, and dinner to prove *this* point.

Wes settled into the lawn chair and placed his hands behind his head. "Okay, little man, let's get to it."

Lyle began his auctioneer rhetoric. "Seven twenty-five, seven twenty-five, do I hear—?"

"Seven seventy-five," called Wes.

Finn gave Bren a look of uncertainty and she nodded to him. "You're good. Bid in twenty-fives."

Finn nodded and looked at the colt standing idly by. He offered his first bid. "Eight hundred."

Wes countered, and Finn bumped him by twenty-five each time. Lyle's voice continued in auctioneer mode. Bren smiled inwardly. She was so proud of Finn. She'd put him in an awkward situation and he'd rallied, his voice growing stronger with every counter. The crowd cheered each time Finn upped the ante and moaned when Wes topped it. The bid was up to nine seventy-five after Wes's counter, and Finn looked to Bren for guidance, his sweet face flushed.

"Mom?" He raised his eyebrows and squinched his nose to adjust his glasses.

She wanted to hug him. She nodded assurance, and he continued.

The bid had risen to a thousand fifty, and it was Wes's turn. He leaned forward in his chair and took a long drag off his cheroot, then dropped it to the floor, flattening it with his expensive black leather dress shoe. He took a breath and eyed Lyle conspiratorially. Something passed between the two; Bren wasn't sure what that meant for Finn, and she clenched her hands to her side.

Wes let out a chuckle and pushed back in his chair. "I'd say you made a fair enough profit, Lyle, wouldn't you?"

And then it hit Bren like a hoof to the head. This was never about wanting the colt and his mother for slaughter; Wes wanted to make a point. He controlled the sale barn, both he and Lyle. And together they controlled her, since a fair amount of her rescues came from auction.

Kill buying was only pocket change for Wes. He only did it for recreation, which irritated Bren more than if he were doing it to eke out a living. His moneymaker was the Clear Spring Horsemen's Club, where the affluent came to play. Since Bren and anyone she knew were working class, Wes's world was a distant planet and inaccessible.

The gavel came down and the words "gone" reverberated up to the peak of the barn. Finn pumped his little arm in celebration, his cheering section whooped and hollered, and Bren's blood boiled in her veins.

"Why, you jackass," she seethed and started in Wes's direction.

Wes stood and moved toward the rail. His ruddy complexion deepened, and his cheeks puffed with indignation. "You pull another stunt like last month, and I'll see your ass in jail, girl." He pointed his thick, blunt finger her way.

Bren, still in the chute, moved to the left where Wes stood, her body pressed up against the rail, their faces inches apart. "Screw you."

Wes reached out to grab Bren, and she jumped back. The broodmare to her left reared hard, the rope snapping from the rail.

To her right, a dark form came at Bren, jumping the rail and knocking her to the ground. She rolled with it. The air popped from her lungs and she struggled to breathe.

Strong arms held her in place. "Don't move," the stranger ordered in a deep male voice she didn't recognize.

Bren looked up. The broodmare snorted and kicked after being cornered by one of Lyle's men. Another pulled on its rope, leading the mare out of the chute. A third man snagged the colt's lead, walking him around behind the mare.

Wes still clenched the rail. "Damn fool."

Bren tried to wrestle free to get to Wes, but the arms around her tightened, and her captor whispered against her ear, "Relax, honey."

Bren didn't miss the drawl in his voice.

She squirmed. "I'm not your—"

"You don't need to thank me, darlin'."

He was mocking her, which made her blood run hot. His arms remained wrapped around her waist, his muscular biceps pillowing her breast. Strong, jean-clad legs held her legs between his, and she was on the verge of hyperventilating.

"Get off me!" She pulled hard against his hold.

He opened his hands wide, and she tumbled out of his grasp, her face scant inches from the mix of dirt, straw, and manure on the barn floor.

"Jerk," she mumbled before grabbing the first pair of hands, only to find Robert Connelly hoisting her up. Tall and blond and wearing a well-tailored navy suit, there was no denying the successful accountant he'd become. Too bad for him he'd returned to Clear Spring, leaving the Baltimore firm to run his father's books.

"Hey, Bren." Robert's eyes, a light shade of sympathetic blue, met hers through a pair of gold wire-framed glasses.

Slightly embarrassed by her show of bravado earlier, and the fact it was directed at his father, her cheeks warmed. "Thanks, but I'm the enemy, remember?"

"Don't remind me." He turned her around and dusted her back. "You hurt anywhere?"

She tossed her head back. "No. He took all the shock."

Robert nodded to the stranger.

Him, she did not recognize. Although something about him, his eyes maybe, looked familiar. Dark, lean, dressed in jeans and a white button-down, shirttails out, he sat on the barn floor, a Stetson lying next to him. His unshaven face and short, dark hair gave him an ill-tempered appearance as he scowled at her through a pair of hooded eyes.

No one had asked for his help. She had everything under control. So if he was expecting her to shower him with gratitude, he could suck wind because it wasn't going to happen.

Robert glared at his father and released her. "What's going on here?" He glanced at Finn. "You bid against a boy for his colt? What the hell is wrong with you?" Robert placed his hands on his hips, pushing the tails of his suit jacket behind his back.

"Lighten up, Robert. I was just having a little fun. The boy has his horse." Wes's usual commanding voice quavered. The only time he ever squirmed was under the penetrating gaze of his son.

The role reversal was one Bren enjoyed.

Having been dictated to as a child, including his choice of friends and those Wes ordered he stay away from, Robert hadn't had much contact with Bren through the years. She'd seen him infrequently over the past several months, to his father's ire. But judging by the interaction of father and son tonight, it was the son's ire Wes should have feared. He stood to lose more than an accountant.

Robert lifted his fine-planed face to Lyle. "What was the final?"

"Thousand fifty."

Robert whistled through his teeth and gave his dad a look of disgust. He turned to Lyle. "What are they worth?" Then he added, "Don't snow me."

Lyle shrugged. "Three."

Robert reached for his back pocket and pulled out his wallet. He opened it and counted three crisp hundred-dollar bills and gave his dad another look. "You're an ass." He handed Finn the cash.

Finn hesitated.

"It's okay, son," Robert said. "Go ahead and pay the auctioneer."

Robert looked back toward a petite blonde, very pretty, dressed in a light-charcoal designer suit and black heels. Clear Spring was a small town, and news traveled fast. Bren bet this was his fiancée, Susan Hewitt.

"Ready, sweetheart?" he asked. Susan nodded. Robert looked down his nose at his father. "It's late."

Understanding Robert's meaning, Wes straightened off the rail, but he waited until Robert was out of earshot before he leaned over toward Bren. "Keep it up, girl, and you'll end up—" He locked onto something to the right and gave Bren a tight smile. "Don't start trouble for me with my son." The edge to his voice menacing, he turned his back and walked away.

The crowd parted, and Bren cringed when Kevin, dressed in street clothes, pressed forward.

Now she was in trouble.

He eyed her. "I don't need your take. I saw it from the stands."

"But he threatened me."

Wes glanced back grinning and kissed the air with mocked sincerity.

Bren pointed at him. "He—"

"Give it a rest." He nodded to the stranger, still in a sitting position with his legs drawn up, hands resting on his kneecaps. "Nice save." Kevin reached out and pulled him to his feet.

"Not with her." The stranger nodded in Bren's direction and dusted off his jeans.

"Bren." Kevin waved a negligent hand her way and frowned. "Don't get me started."

The man bent down and picked up a black felt cowboy hat, then placed it on his head.

"Nice Stetson. Where you from?" Kevin asked.

"Texas."

"Visiting?"

"No. Looking for land."

"Not enough in Texas?"

"Branching out." The stranger cocked his head. "Third degree?"

Kevin laughed. "No." He reached out and extended his hand. "The name's Kevin Bendix. I'm the sheriff. I guess it's my nature to ask questions."

The stranger shook his hand. "Rafe Langston—rancher."

Bren gave them her back and checked the bleachers, looking for Aiden and Finn. Finding them with Jeremy, she took a step in that direction.

"Hey." Kevin grabbed her arm. "Hold on. I need to talk to you."

Bren's shoulders slumped, and she glanced over at him. "Kind of busy here, Kev. Unless it's about Sweet Prince, you're going to have to wait." He'd had two weeks since Christmas to dig into the most recent horse death.

"Bren," he warned.

"Okay. How about later?" She nodded toward Aiden and Finn in the crowd. "I need to get them home."

"Fine." He motioned with his hand. "I'll be by tomorrow morning."

Wonderful. He would read her the riot act. Except he forgot one thing—Wes had instigated this one.

Bren took a step in the direction of the bleachers but hesitated. To the right of her the cowboy remained. Leaning against the rail, a slow smile tugged at the corners of his mouth, and he followed her with his eyes.

Her cheeks warmed.

Jerk.

CHAPTER FOUR

B REN SHIVERED AGAINST THE PATCHWORK QUILT AND PULLED HER
legs up tight to her chest. Why was it so cold? She couldn't afford
to come down with the flu. There was too much work that needed to be
done and money to be raised.

The nightstand rumbled, and Bren glanced at the clock: three seventeen
in the morning. *Screw him.* She'd taken in three abuse cases yesterday, mucked
out stables, and taken a ride on her horse Smiley toward the back forty to
mend a hole in the fence. She was tired and in no mood to play his game
tonight. Bren ignored her cell phone and pulled the quilt over her head. *Get the
message, asshole. I'm not picking up.* She smiled when silence greeted her back.

The nightstand rumbled a second time. Bren popped her head out for
air, and shot her hand out. The phone glowed a serene blue with Tom's name
bold and dark against the bright screen. The bastard knew what he was doing.
She was beginning to associate anger and fear with Tom. And that pissed
her off. She flipped open the phone and hung up on him, refusing to listen
to his insidious breathing on the other end.

This had been the fifth call since the sale barn incident almost a week
ago. For all the notifications she'd given Kevin, he still couldn't locate the
phone or the caller through what he called triangulation. Seemed the phone
needed to be on longer for that to happen.

Keeping the phone in her hand, Bren grabbed the quilt and wrapped it
around her. Her bare feet hit the hardwood floor, the quilt dragging behind
her like a cape. She checked the windows in the spare bedroom where she'd
taken up residence. They were locked. Then why did she wake up on the tip
of Antarctica? Whatever the reason, it would have to wait because she had
to pee.

Bren entered the hall. She hit the light switch and stepped onto the cold tiles of the hall bathroom and almost wet her pants when she found herself still standing in darkness.

"What the hell?"

Did the light blow? Bren gathered up the quilt and fumbled in the dark until she hit the light switch in the hall—nothing.

Son of a bitch!

Seriously? One of the coldest nights in January. Standing in front of the thermostat, she tried to read the temperature. Frustrated, she lit the box with the blue glow of her cell phone, fifty-seven degrees. Bren's head fell, and she struck the wall with her palm.

My life sucks. Sucks, sucks, sucks!

Gripping her cell phone, she flew downstairs to the kitchen, headed for the drawer next to the dishwasher where she kept the utility bills. Moonlight spilled in over the shutters above the sink, filling the kitchen with a dim, eerie glow. Rifling through the drawer, she snagged a bill, still sealed, and started to rip it open. The side porch creaked and Bren's hand stilled. She held her breath.

Relax. It's only the wind.

She slipped her finger under the envelope flap, peeked, and frowned. The porch creaked louder. Her heart held tight in her chest, and she slid her eyes from the window above the sink to the side door. The haze of a flashlight bolted right, then left, like a dizzy firefly. Bren jumped back, hiding around the corner of the broom closet, clenching her phone and the bill in her hand.

Her chest constricted. The boys. She was all they had, and the only defense against whoever was outside the door. She ripped the quilt from her shoulders, casting it to the floor, and rounded the broom closet. Easing the drawer open where she kept her skillets, she snatched the handle of the cast iron and headed toward the door.

Bren focused on the doorknob. Her heart skipped when it shook. He wasn't going to get the jump on her. Surprise would be her leverage. She turned the lock and grabbed for the knob. The door swung open, and she lunged forward, the skillet raised above her head.

"Lord in heaven!" he bellowed. "You gone round the bend, girl?"

Her shoulders relaxed, and she let the pan down to her side. "Shh. You'll wake the boys."

Bren's father stood several paces back, his face wide with surprise against the glow of the moon filtering under the covered porch. He brought the flashlight up and angled it dead center on her face.

She squinted against the bright light and waved an irritated hand toward the flashlight. "Turn that thing off," she hissed.

"You have lights?"

Shit. If she didn't have electricity, her father didn't, either. She laid the pan on the counter and stepped back, shielding her face—from what was it, the intrusive light or her father's questioning eyes?

Another failure.

"No, Dad. We're on the same electric bill."

Daniel lit the floor of the kitchen with the flashlight and stepped in wearing his winter coat and flannel pajamas with his furry slippers. "Is that all you're going to say on the matter, Bren?" She didn't miss the rancor in his voice.

Bren ignored the question, grabbed the teakettle, and filled it. She reached above the stove and felt for the lighter in the cabinet. She turned the burner on. The pungent odor of gas filled her nostrils, and she flicked her Bic, admiring the orange-and-blue flame coming to life.

"Tea?" She glanced over her shoulder.

Daniel slid a chair out from the table and sat. He scratched his head, his body slumping back against the wooden spindles. "Come out with it."

Bren faced him. Leaning against the counter, she sighed. "I'm sorry. I thought I was handling everything." She gave a weak smile. "Until I woke up freezing my ass off."

"Did you forget to mail it?"

She frowned. "The bill?"

"Hell yes, the bill. Did you forget?"

"I wish." She'd gotten a peek at the contents of the envelope before she'd been distracted with her prowler.

"Bren, you're not funny. Stop this nonsense and tell me what's going on."

The teakettle let out a hiss, and she turned the burner off. Bren poured the steaming water into two cups and dropped a tea bag in each one, then set them on the table. "Sugar?" she asked as she grabbed the sugar bowl off the counter.

Her father nodded.

Sitting across the table, she moved the sugar bowl toward him and handed over the turn-off notice. "We're broke."

His eyes widened. "I'm serious."

"So am I, Dad." Her face fell forward into her hands, and she shook her head and moaned, "I'm a loser, Dad. A big fat zero."

Daniel muttered something and tossed the notice on the table. He pulled at her arm. "Nonsense. I didn't raise losers. You're having a tough time of it. That's all."

Bren lifted her head. "Tell that to Bernie."

"Bernie? The bank manager?"

"One in the same." She sat straight up. "It's not just the electric bill. Tom and I struggled every month to make the mortgage. I'm not good with budgets like he was. I owe Bernie, the bank, close to five K by the twenty-fifth of this month."

"Twenty-fifth. That's two weeks away. How much you have saved?"

Bren shook her head. "Half."

"Twenty-five hundred?"

Bren nodded.

"Savings?"

"None."

"Why the devil didn't you tell me?"

"I didn't want to worry you. I thought I could handle it. It's my problem."

"I'll not listen to this talk. It's our problem." Bren's father tossed his glasses down on her kitchen table. "I guess you think you created this recession all by yourself?"

"No. But—"

He put up a hand. "Just tell me what old Bernie suggests we do about it."

She frowned. "You're not going to like it. I don't like it."

"Try me."

"Subdivide."

He fell back against his chair and rubbed his temples. "Lord, heaven, saints preserve us." He sat up. "He's not serious?"

"It was a suggestion. Kind of like a preventive measure. I . . . we can continue to struggle, but eventually the bank will foreclose."

Daniel tapped his finger to his lips. "He's right. How much do we owe total?"

"Close to five-twenty-five."

"That much?"

"We refinanced a few years ago, remember?"

"All I know is I signed some papers."

"I told you what—"

"I know. It just slipped my mind. At the time I was dealing with your mother's illness."

"I don't want to break up our land, Dad."

"I don't want to be homeless."

There was that, too.

Her father's brows met over his nose, and he placed his glasses back on. "You'd get more with the house."

"Your house? The house Kate and I grew up in?" She leaned over the table. "I can't. I won't—"

"You will. It's just a house."

"But Mom . . . her memories."

Her father put a hand over his heart. "They're here, Bren."

Yes they were, but, still, she loved her childhood home. Unfortunately for Bren, her sentiments ran to objects, as well—the house being one of them, her old bedroom part of it. The kitchen where her family had sat down to dinner every night when she was a child.

Mom was dead. Her sister Kate was married—married to an asshole who kept her under lock and key. Tom . . . Tom she couldn't think about. And Bren was left with her father, whom she was disappointing in a major way. He would never say it. That was her dad. He felt it—had to feel it—but would never consider putting it into words. Failure seemed to follow Bren like a dark shadow.

She grabbed her father's hand. "I'm sorry, Dad."

"It's not your fault, sweetheart."

"What about Kate?"

"She should know. Regardless, I don't think she's in a position to offer a solution."

"Will you come with me to talk to Bernie?"

"Of course." He squeezed her hand.

Being tossed off their land wasn't an option. Losing a part of Grace would have to be.

By the next morning Bren and her father had spoken with Bernie. They signed the paperwork and arranged the auction for the first of February. But now, two weeks later, she was angry all over again.

Bren swung her dark blue pickup into the parking lot across from the Washington County courthouse steps. She'd meant to be on time. Not that she could stop the proceedings today. But walking into this thing with her eyes open, she wanted to know who would end up with a cool hundred acres and one farmhouse below market.

Whoever bought the property would be sharing Grace's driveway, their right of ingress and egress a constant reminder Grace's heart had been sliced in two.

Bren stepped off the curb and cut across two lanes of traffic. Even the sun had chosen to hide this morning. Gray clouds crowded the sky, only adding to the bleak future looming several footsteps away.

"Hey." Jeremy jogged the distance between them.

She met up with him on the sidewalk.

His hardened expression, uncommon for Jeremy, and a paler than usual complexion, sent a streak of alarm racing toward her gut.

"Where have you been?" His lips thinned.

Jeremy and indignant didn't go together. Last time she'd checked, she was off the schedule today. Her only commitment was to Grace and the horse rescue. It was touch and go as to whether she'd even show her face at the courthouse steps.

"Short on volunteers. I had to dole out the medications this morning. And all that money I hoped to make on this year's rescue calendar is sitting at the print shop because I'm here dealing with this crap, instead of picking them up." She grabbed his arm, irritation scoring her brow. "Why are you here and what the hell is wrong?"

Whatever he felt compelled to lay on her this morning couldn't come close to losing the land her family—namely her mother and father—had toiled over for the past forty years.

"Bren, don't freak out on me."

If he was trying to console her, he was doing a piss-poor job of it.

"It's Wes."

With the bank dealings, emptying her childhood home, moving her father in, and her return to the master bedroom and all the emotional baggage after her father refused her kind offer to take it—the room, not the baggage—Wes had been only a shadow on the periphery of her subconscious.

The other factor had been the phone calls—they'd stopped.

Bren spotted Bernie over Jeremy's shoulder, standing on the courthouse steps with his glasses perched on his nose. He flipped through papers attached to a clipboard. Grace wasn't the only trustee sale today. The paper listed seven properties.

"I don't care about Wes," she threw back at Jeremy and moved past him.

"Wait." Jeremy grabbed her arm. "Your property's on the auction block now."

Her heart bolted out of her chest, and she shook his hand off her arm. "Thanks for telling me." Bren's legs followed her heart and took off toward the crowd congregated at the bottom of the steps. She wanted to get a look at her prospective neighbor.

Pushing through the crowd of bulky winter coats and endless chatter, she popped out on the other side. Bren grew cold.

Wes.

He stood with a well-shined, black dress shoe up on the brick knee wall to the left of the courthouse steps. Hand tucked beneath his chin, he leaned forward. She'd seen that stance before. He was strategizing for the win. The prize was her land, her childhood home, and her sense of security, along with that troublemaker—her pride.

"Let me through." Jeremy nudged a businessman and his briefcase and came up alongside her. "He's bidding on your— "

"No shit," she snapped. She'd been grieving for a year, struggling to survive both mentally and financially, and now Wes wanted to humiliate her.

Son of a bitch. I'll strangle you.

She dashed up the steps. A hand brushed her arm.

"Shit, Bren, hold up."

She turned, catching his profile. The only thing keeping her from strangling him, too, was the fact he was Robert, not Wes, and even that was a small margin of consolation. "You're his accountant."

"I only write the checks."

Beyond Robert's shoulder the courthouse door opened. She laughed to herself when Kevin strode out. He'd earn his salary today.

"Bren." Robert was next to her. "I told him I didn't approve of him taking advantage of your situation."

Maybe. Or was he stalling her? Robert was a Connelly. The sympathetic expression lining his face wasn't going to sway her.

"Then don't write the check." Bren stepped around him and gauged the distance to Wes.

Robert's cell phone rang. "Wait." He dipped his head, swore, and took the call.

If he wanted to talk, he should have started by telling her his father's intentions before today. Kevin wasn't at his post, but she could feel him closing in. Too bad.

"Connelly!" she yelled.

His head swung, his eyes tracking the crowd. His lips curled when he found her several steps down and heading his way.

Bren balled her hands into fists. She was going to pay Wes back in spades, and she didn't care about the consequences.

She was within striking distance when Bernie's eyes peered over his glasses, and he frowned. "Is that the final bid?" He focused his attention on Wes.

She rammed her fist toward Wes's chin and tripped over the last step and missed. She swayed and tried to gain her balance.

Wes straightened and grabbed Bren's hair. He yanked her to within a breath of his mulish face and then gave one hard tug without letting go. Her eyes teared up, and she clenched her teeth.

"I ought to backhand you," Wes said, his voice low and savage.

Bren caught sight of Kevin coming down the courthouse steps. With the crowd below, it would be awhile before he got to her. Locking a pair of belligerent eyes on Wes, she stared him down. "Go for it," she said through gritted teeth.

Wes raised his hand. Bren squinched her eyes closed and prepared for the blow. When it didn't come, her eyes sprang open to find a black suede arm and strong male hand gripping Wes's wrist.

"Let her go. Or I'll break it."

Bren recognized the slow drawl.

Wes's eyes widened. "Who the hell?"

Langston's grip tightened, and Wes's face crumpled in pain.

"Your choice."

Wes released her hair and flung it in her face.

She stepped back and pressed her hair behind her ears. Bren studied the stranger she'd tangled with a month ago. He was solid and lean. His jeans clung to his long, powerful legs. He wore a black suede blazer against broad shoulders. His black cowboy boots were sleek as satin. The pulse in his neck throbbing through the open collar of a denim shirt kept her mesmerized. She willed her eyes upward. His face was shrouded in shadow by his black Stetson, but she didn't miss the gleam of those emerald green eyes boring into Wes.

"Apologize to the lady."

Bren's lips sputtered, and she began to laugh.

Langston shot her a look. "Amused?"

"Extremely."

He smiled, his expression softening. "Good." He brought his attention back to Wes. "I don't make it a habit of repeating myself."

"Apologize?" Wes scoffed and slid Bren a dirty look. "You'll have to break my—"

Langston tightened his grip. Wes yelped like a dog getting its foot stepped on and groaned, "Let go."

Langston raised a brow. Wes stood his ground. Langston applied more pressure. Bren swore Wes's bone popped, and she winced when he withered toward the pavement.

"Sorry," Wes gritted under his breath.

Langston let go.

Wes struggled and regained his balance. Once upright, he straightened his tie, adjusted his dangling Bluetooth, and sent an irate glare at Bernie. "Whitcomb, let's settle up. I've got the required ten percent." He waved an impatient hand toward his checkbook, or rather Robert climbing the steps toward them.

Bernie pressed his glasses back toward the bridge of his nose. "Hold up, Connelly. The bid's still open until I issue the final asking."

"Then do it." Wes's eyes cornered his son. "Where the hell have you been?"

"Susan called. Her grandmother took a fall." Robert took a step back and looked at Bren. "You, okay?" Robert's gaze cut to Wes. He glanced at Bren, then back to Wes. "What happened?"

Wes pointed his stubby finger in Bren's direction. "She happened. Now pay the man."

"Premature, don't you think?" Langston asked.

Wes ignored him. "Whitcomb."

Bernie jumped. "Right. For the third time of asking, the final bid is three hundred seventy-five thousand."

"Five hundred thousand," Langston said.

Bren jerked her head toward Langston. "You're joking!"

"I don't joke about money, darlin'." He reached inside his breast pocket and pulled out a cashier's check.

Wes looked from Langston to Bernie. "Five twenty-five."

Robert stepped forward and whispered in Wes's ear, "Dad. Let it go."

"I will not." He pulled away from Robert. "Pay him."

"Cashier's check or cash," Bernie stipulated.

"Robert?"

Robert leaned in. "We don't have it."

"Bullshit."

Robert shook his head, waved a disgusted hand toward his father, and walked away.

"Robert, don't you turn your back on me!"

"What's it going to be, Wes?" Bernie asked. He nodded toward Langston. "This man's got a cashier's check for five hundred thousand."

Wes's Bluetooth beeped, and he spoke into his mouthpiece. "Take your ass back to Baltimore. I don't need your shit."

Bren caught Bernie mumbling something to Langston. The two walked away toward a makeshift table, she assumed to complete the paperwork for the transfer of land.

Wes yanked his earpiece off and nailed Bren with his eyes. "Go ahead and smirk, girl. Next time you won't be so lucky."

"Are you threatening her?" Kevin came up behind Bren and rested his hand on his service weapon. "Because it sure sounded that way to me."

"You take it any way you want, Bendix." He sneered down at Bren. "Either way you lost, girl."

Bren chewed the inside of her lip. He was close enough she could lift her foot and nail him for his smartass comment before he could counter. But then she'd give Kevin a reason to side with him.

"Go home, Wes. It's over," Kevin said.

Wes glared at Bren. "We're just getting started." He brushed past her, nudging her shoulder, and disappeared into the crowd.

"You're damn lucky you don't have a black eye." Kevin stood, hands on hips, peering down at her.

"I was hoping for one."

"What?"

"Then you could have arrested him."

"No. I'd have to arrest both of you. You swung first."

Bren turned away. Kevin gripped her arm and hauled her back. "Like I told him. It's over, Bren."

"It's only beginning. Maybe Wes doesn't have my land, but because of him a stranger is going to be living in my house."

"That stranger saved your ass."

Bren clenched her hands and bore into Kevin. "Whatever."

Langston sauntered back toward them, his black cowboy boots clicking against the pavement.

Kevin whispered, "Be nice."

"You okay?" The Texan tucked a document inside his breast pocket.

Bren folded her arms. Digging her fingers into her sides, she gave him a cheeky smile. "Kiss off." She turned on her heels, caught sight of Jeremy, and stalked to her pickup truck. She should be grateful, but she was too damn pissed.

"Bren," Kevin called after her. "What's your problem?"

"Figure it out."

"Rafe is it?"

Bren slowed and glanced over her shoulder and caught Kevin shaking Langston's hand. "Sorry about her," Kevin said.

That's right, Kevin, suck up to the enemy.

"Looks like you've got your land," Kevin added.

Yeah, what about that? Vultures came in many forms. This one just happened to be tall, dark, and irritatingly good-looking.

Chapter Five

Bren climbed the steps of her childhood home and ignored the pinch in the back of her eyes. The only place she wanted to be after the courthouse this morning was here. She leaned against the doorjamb of her old bedroom. The horses danced—an Arabian, sleek and white; the paint, a mix of chocolate brown and cream, its mane flowing. They'd been stenciled on the wall by her mother. Unlike her sister Kate, her dreams had never left Grace's pasture. The horses were everything to her. Grace was everything.

She frowned. She could have those dreams again—new dreams, if she could let go of the past and this old house. When the paperwork cleared, the half of Grace she still owned would be close to free and clear. She could devote more time to her boys and less to obsessing over debt. Her job with Jeremy was a windfall. Her hours worked well with the boys' school schedule. She saw no reason to give it up.

Having her dad move in had also been a blessing. It'd been over a week since they cleared out the house and he took up the extra bedroom down the hall. It felt safe having a man in the house again. And the boys were getting to know their grandfather. Plus, he was a great cook and demanded a full house at dinner. They were beginning to resemble a family. Maybe three generations wasn't a typical setup, but it worked.

Bren sighed when she took the first step downstairs. The new owner would probably paint over her horses. But her father was right: Every memory she could hope to bring back to life was locked in her heart. Painted walls and sleek walnut banisters and creaking old steps would someday crumble, but her memories were forever.

She took one more gaze around the wide foyer and reached for the door.

The crunch of gravel outside alerted her to a black four-door pickup and light blue sedan pulling up.

Bren stepped back from the thin glass window running the length of the door. Bernie and Langston. *Damn it!* Her life truly did suck. More like her timing. She didn't need Bernie finding her in the house—his pouty expression saying "poor Bren Ryan."

Bren quickly locked the door and slid into the kitchen, prepared to make her exit through the back door. Grabbing the handle, she yanked and then cursed under her breath. She yanked harder, but the door didn't budge. The key turned in the front door, and it creaked open. *Shit.* Not good. She eyed the pantry—not wide enough. Cabinet under the sink—too many pipes. Broom closet. That would work. She opened the closet and pressed her body inside. At five six she wasn't tiny. The top shelf grazed her head, and she hunkered down. Shutting the door, she tried to control her breathing. She hated small spaces.

Footsteps followed. Bernie called out the rooms. "Four bedrooms, master bath, and hall bath are upstairs."

Perfect. Once they hit the second level she was outa here.

"You go on, Rafe. I'm going to finish the paperwork in the kitchen."

Bren grimaced. She was starting to sweat, and it wouldn't be long before she hyperventilated. Her barn coat was like a straitjacket, tight against her, making the cramped space even smaller with its thickness.

Bernie cleared his throat and flicked his pen. Judging by the sound, he was using the center island. The click of a pair of familiar boots hit the hardwood of the kitchen, and Bren pressed back against the closet.

"What you think of the upstairs?"

"It's adequate."

"Four bedrooms."

"It's just me."

"Then you'll have plenty of space."

Sweat ran down between Bren's shoulder blades. *Come on. Enough small talk.* A drawer shut. Then another. He opened the dishwasher. The suction of the refrigerator door signaled he was getting close. *What the hell? Does he kick tires, too?* Bren held her breath. She could sense him in front of the broom closet. The door pressed forward. *Crap.* His hand was on the handle.

"I just need your John Hancock right here," said Bernie.

The door popped out a fraction when he released it. That was too close.

"Enjoy your new house, Rafe. Welcome to Maryland."

"Thanks."

"A little advice. Keep a safe distance from Bren Ryan. Ever since her husband died last January, she's been unpredictable."

"Unstable?"

"It's possible."

"Thanks for the advice."

Their voices floated away, their footsteps grew faint. Bren cracked the door, the air cool against her cheeks. The front door opened and shut, and she closed the broom closet door.

Come on, Langston.

The quiet unnerved her. His boots were distinct against the hardwood, yet there was nothing. Where did he go? The front porch? She couldn't stay here forever. Eventually she'd have to make her move.

The broom closet door swooshed open, the light blinding.

"You are a peculiar woman, Mrs. Ryan."

Bren popped up and hit her head on the top shelf. "Ouch." She closed her eyes against the pain.

Langston reached in and cradled her head and pulled her forward. "You make it a habit of hiding in broom closets?"

"How'd you know?"

"You're not very covert. It was hanging out of the door." He tugged on her barn coat. "Who's your jeweler?"

Bren couldn't help but smile at the heart-shaped pin with puzzle pieces glued on. "Finn."

"The blond with glasses."

"How do you—"

"I remember him from the sale barn. You have an older boy, too, a teenager."

"Aiden." That was a little disconcerting. He remembered a lot about her family.

Bren stepped away from him, putting the center island between them. "I should be going. Sorry about intruding. I was just . . ."

"You can come by anytime."

Bren's hands fidgeted on the center island. He'd bought her land, her house, and yet offered to still share it with her? She had no choice but to share the driveway. But she wouldn't step foot in this house again. "No. It's your house now. I was making sure I didn't leave anything behind."

He cocked his head and studied her. His dark brown brows knit together over a pair of emerald eyes. "You're the horse freak."

"Pardon?"

"Horses. The room with the painted horses." He motioned toward the ceiling.

"Guess that's why I have a horse farm."

"Right." He took a step closer. "I like the room."

Bren pulled her hands apart and stepped back, eyeing the entrance to the hallway. "Good. You ever have a daughter, she'd love it."

"Family's not something I'm looking for."

Bren bit down on her lower lip. He towered above her. The shape of his Stetson, since removed, still molded against his head and made the black locks curl up at the ends around his ears. His face chiseled and rough with a light black beard gave him a dangerous appearance. He took off his black suede jacket and laid it on the counter.

Bren's every nerve ending tingled, and that voice inside screamed for her to hotfoot it out of there. But there was something about him, a familiarity she couldn't quite place. "I should go." Bren motioned toward the entryway of the kitchen. "Enjoy the house, Mr. Langston."

He leaned in over the counter. "Mr. Langston's my father. My name is Rafe."

"Fine, Rafe."

He came around the counter. Leaning against the edge, he crossed his arms. "Can I call you Bren?"

Bren nodded. "Sure. We're neighbors now. We share a common driveway. You might want to think about purchasing a tractor with a bucket. It's still winter, and February in Washington County is heavy snowfall season."

"Don't see much snow in Texas."

"No?"

"Nope. Too warm."

Definitely too warm. Bren inched back toward the cabinet behind her.

"I'm sorry about your husband."

"Thanks." Not at all what she expected him to say. Nor did she expect the way it made her feel. He seemed to genuinely care that it was upsetting to her. "I heard Bernie's crack. I'm not unpredictable. Bernie forgot to mention my husband was murdered."

"What's the sheriff doing about it?"

"Kevin? Not a damn thing. He believes Tom's death was an accident, just like everyone else in this narrow-minded town."

"How do you know it wasn't?"

The one-year anniversary of Tom's death had come and gone. She'd given up sharing her theory with anyone. She knew the truth. But for the first time in a long while someone actually wanted to talk to her about it.

"This is probably upsetting for you. It was insensitive for me to ask. I'm sorry."

"Are you kidding? I could talk about it until lack of breath. That's the problem. No one takes me seriously. Tom knew his way around a barn. He didn't wrap himself up in the pulley system and say a Hail Mary and jump out the hayloft."

"Hayloft?"

"It's complicated." Bren reached in her pocket and grabbed her hair tie and pulled her hair up into a loose bun. She pointed in the direction of the front door. "I could show you. It's the red barn as you come in. Right before you get to my house."

He remained quiet, the expression for a split second in his eyes hard, almost angry, and then it disappeared.

Jeez, Bren. You sound so needy. Rafe Langston would have no interest in helping her sort out Tom's death.

This guy probably thought she was a total fruitcake. Self-consciously she brought her hand down, nervously scratched the back of her head, and let her hand waft down to her side. "You're not interested. It was silly, anyway. I just thought . . . you seemed . . ."

He pushed off from the counter. "How about I take you home? I didn't see your truck when I pulled up. It's getting dark."

He was just like everyone else. She fisted her hands. And here she'd thought he might be different.

"I'm perfectly capable . . ."

He stepped forward. His green eyes smiled at her while he reached back to grab his jacket. "Are there lights in this barn?"

CHAPTER SIX

BREN HAD THE PRETTIEST ASS RAFE HAD SEEN IN A LONG TIME. HE guessed running a farm kept her in shape. "Why are you stopping?" he asked, coming to a halt on the ladder up to the hayloft.

Bren looked down from above him, her dark red hair softly cascading from her bun.

There was no way he could say "no" to recreating Tom's last hours. The sadness lurking in her brown eyes when she'd asked pained him. But just as quick, her expression changed to one of eagerness at the prospect someone, even a stranger, could take her assertions seriously.

Except he'd been so preoccupied with checking her out. Her slender shoulders swallowed by the rough barn coat left open to reveal the soft curve of her breasts beneath her black turtleneck and tiny waist. He'd hesitated. Then that look about her eyes changed to one of embarrassment, and he'd wanted to kick himself for his stupidity.

"The flashlight," she said. "I need to find the light."

Shit. He was doing it again, totally lost in her big brown eyes. "Oh. Right." Rafe reached behind into his jean pocket and grabbed the flashlight he had taken from his truck. Handing it off to her, she lit up the loft and disappeared over the ladder. He followed, lifting his leg over the edge, and eased himself up to a standing position.

She pulled a long string hanging down from the rafters. A single light-bulb popped on. She turned off the flashlight and frowned at him. "Rafe. I want to apologize for my behavior this morning, and the time before that."

"Before?"

"The sale barn."

"When you almost got knocked on your ass."

"I wasn't—"

He held up a hand. "I know, you had it all under control."

Her mouth snapped shut, and she turned away and walked toward the back wall. "When I found Tom, I was outside below the pulley system. I came up here, hoping to lower him down." Her shoulders dipped. "But he was too heavy for me."

She remained quiet for a moment, her eyes hardened. "Tom is, was, all farm boy, Rafe. This wasn't an accident."

Rafe examined the thick braided rope tied off securely by a winch against the wall. He moved toward the loft doors and opened them. They were at least three stories up. "How'd you find him?"

"There was rope everywhere wrapped around his body. Part of it was around his neck. He strangled to death."

Rafe glanced back and frowned.

"Tom knew his way around a barn." She crossed her arms, her brows knitting together.

Rafe shut the hayloft doors. "I believe you knew your husband."

Bren slumped up against the wall. "Then you believe me."

"I'd say there are questions that need to be answered."

Bren slid down onto a hay bale and pressed her head back against the wall. Her eyes closed, and her slender nose flared as she took a deep breath. "That's all I really wanted. Someone to take me seriously."

Rafe sat down on the floor next to her, his back against the barn wall, and patted her leg. "I'm not a cop. I'm a cowboy. I ride. I rope. And I'll take up a fight for an underdog in a minute. From where I'm sitting, you're the underdog, Bren. If you want, I'll help you sort this out. But I'm going to be a little tied up with moving in and looking into buying some cows."

Bren opened her eyes, looked at him, and laughed. "You really are from Texas."

He grinned. "Yes, ma'am. Born and bred."

"So why Maryland? Don't they have cows in Texas?"

"They do. The Langstons raise only beef cattle—Black Angus as far back as I can remember. Let's just say my daddy's not a fan of milking cows for a living."

Bren leaned forward and placed her elbows on her knees, her chin in her palms. "I understand. My sister Kate . . . she's not into horses. She didn't mind riding them, but she couldn't wait to leave the farm. She's a trial law-yer and lives on the eastern shore." Her eyes dimmed, and she frowned. "I miss her. A lot." Her gaze hardened. "But she married a control freak. One who monitors her every move. Last I heard, we—the farm and all its occu-pants—were off-limits."

Definitely a story there. Rafe cocked his head. "What about your parents?"

"Just my dad, now. My mom died of cancer a few years ago."

"I'm sorry, Bren."

She shrugged. "I'm okay with her passing. When someone you love's in that kind of pain, it's mercy." She pulled at a piece of hay from the bale she sat on. "Not real happy with Tom's passing, though." She hung her head down and twirled the hay between her fingers.

He'd never found the kind of love Bren and Tom obviously had. Hell, he probably wouldn't know love if it bit him in the ass. Now, lust he was all too familiar with. And for all involved it would be best to remember, this one was off-limits. The problem was he had a thing for redheads. And Bren Ryan's hair shimmered against the light in the barn. Silky smooth and the damnedest color red he'd ever seen, almost a dark cherry, a flattering contrast to her alabaster skin and the natural flush of her cheeks. Even the dark, long crescent of her lashes seemed natural.

"So tell me about your boys."

Bren lifted her head. Her expression brightened. "Aiden. He's fifteen, every bit the teenager. He looks like Tom. It's been hard on him. He and his father meshed well together. He and I, not so much."

"And Finn?"

Bren touched the puzzle pin attached to her coat and smiled. "Finn's my baby. Sweet and a lovey. He's seven."

"It's hard for a boy, almost a man like Aiden, to deal with his feelings. I've been there. He's not a boy anymore, but there are times he wants to be, but that would be a sign of weakness. So he walks around with a chip on his shoulder."

"Tell me about it. Only thing is, Mom's the bad guy. It's my fault his dog died in the spring. It's my fault his father died in the winter."

"Did you kill his dog?" Rafe sent her a sideways glance.

"No!" Bren pushed him hard in the shoulder, rocking Rafe's body to the side. "Not on purpose." Her voice softened.

"But you had something to do with the dog's demise?" Rafe raised a brow.

"Okay." She leaned forward conspiratorially. "You might not be a cop, but you're damn good at interrogation. If you must know, he was in the truck with me when I got out to get the mail. I forgot to shut the door."

Rafe laughed. "So you really did kill his dog."

Bren scrunched up her face. "Ha. Ha."

"Maybe Aiden needs a new dog. His dog. His responsibility. Keep him out of trouble."

"I'll take it under advisement. But right now I need to get a handle on my life before I can begin to tackle the puppy stage."

Rafe snatched a piece of hay for himself and began to chew on the end. "So tell me. What's between you and Wes Connelly?"

"The Fallons—my maiden name, and the Ryans—that would be Tom and his dad, have always been enemies with the Connellys. We're like oil and water. But Wes is the greasy bastard. He's a kill buyer."

Rafe put up a hand. "Say no more. They're in Texas, too."

She swept her arm up and looked around them. "As the name suggests, Grace Equine Sanctuary is in direct contrast to Wes's outfit. And don't let the name fool you. Sweet Creek Stables should have been named Bitter Creek."

"He sounds like a real ass."

"Yep. Not just an ass. He killed Tom."

Rafe leaned in. "Come again?"

"Wes killed Tom. I'd stake my life on it. He had motive. We've been enemies since forever."

"So you don't get along. Is that a reason to kill someone?"

She tensed and averted her eyes for a moment—definitely more to the story. He'd asked the question. Now he hoped the answer, if she gave one, was the truth and not a watered-down version.

After all, he couldn't help if he didn't have all the facts.

The taillights of Rafe's black pickup blurred in the distance, the small cloud of dust settling. Another set of headlights snaked up the driveway in the opposite direction, flashing intermittently as they passed the wide, sturdy trunks of oaks leading up to the house. It was time to get into mom mode.

As usual, Bren was more concerned with proving Wes guilty of murder than fixing dinner. Confiding in a stranger about the days prior to Tom's death, the implication—if there was any—of the recent horse deaths, Finn's colt, and the missing stock horses at Sweet Creek took precedence.

The old white pickup came to a stop next to her, and her father popped open his door. "There's my girl."

Aiden hopped out from the passenger side, and Finn slipped out behind him.

"Who was that?" Aiden shot his mother a curious look, his brown eyes unsmiling.

"Our new neighbor."

Her father jerked around. "We heard in town you let your Irish temper get the best of you."

Bren smiled. "He gave me a reason, and I jumped on it."

"More like swung and missed." His blue eyes twinkled against the glow of the porch lights. "Who's this Langston fellow? Are we going to get along?"

Bren nodded. "Time will tell. But he's interested in my theory." She avoided mentioning Tom's name because of her boys.

Her father picked up on her meaning. His eyes turned to flint. "Let it go, girl. No good will come of it." He leaned in against her cheek. "Think of your boys."

Bren pulled back, ready to argue her point. Finn's sad eyes and Aiden's angry words almost a month ago invaded her thoughts. She bit down on her lower lip and swallowed, the comeback moving down her throat.

"I don't suppose you thought of dinner?" His eyebrows rose.

Maybe she needed to rethink living under the same roof as her father.

Finn grabbed Bren's hand. "I'm starving, Mom. I haven't eaten since lunch."

She frowned at her father, and then gave Finn a hopeful smile. "How about blueberry pancakes? It's your favorite."

"Yay! Can you make the smiley faces with the blueberries?"

Aiden moaned. "You're such a baby."

Finn stuck out his tongue at Aiden. "Shut up."

"Make me, squirt."

"That's enough," Daniel said. "You two get inside and set the table. I want to talk to your mother about her day."

Aiden pulled Finn's knit cap off and ran toward the steps, and Finn followed, bellowing after him.

The sturdy hand of her father squeezed her shoulder. "Tell me about this Langston fellow and how he stole one hundred prime acres and my house, then."

Bren laughed. "Looks like the gossip mill didn't give you all the facts. Rafe Langston paid five hundred thousand."

Her father's mouth dropped open. "You can't be serious! Then we're almost paid up?"

"Yep."

He scratched his head under his wool cap. "Why would this Langston fellow pay more than it's worth?"

"I certainly didn't ask." She held up her thumb and pointer finger, leaving just a little space between the two. "We were this close to rubbing fannies with Wes."

"Oh, grand. Wes Connelly on Grace land? I guess I should thank this Langston after all."

Bren laced her arm around her father's. "Let's just take it on faith things are turning around for the better."

She walked with her father to the house, all the while planning her next move where Wes was concerned. Opening up to a stranger had been a huge gamble. But other than Rafe Langston, who else did she have? Even her father was not an avid supporter of her need to know the truth.

But Bren wasn't foolish enough to tell Rafe everything. Tom's phone would remain her secret for now. Maybe she was reaching. But she knew nothing about the self-proclaimed cowboy, except she liked looking at him. The dark, moody expression that lined his face and his striking green eyes did weird things to her insides she hadn't felt in a long while.

Rafe Langston, tall and lean and broad, invaded her mind. There was a story riding beneath that tough-guy sex appeal. But those thoughts made her uncomfortable. She had only lusted after one man, and she'd married him—*till death do us part.*

She'd get close to Rafe—close, as in learn all there was to know about the Texas rancher. Somehow she didn't think the only reason he'd moved to Maryland was because he and his daddy didn't agree on the type of cows they raised.

Bren winced—milk cows on Grace land. If Tom were alive, he'd be giving her holy hell.

CHAPTER SEVEN

"Hey, Miss Bren."

Bren turned. Johnny Grayson smiled that crooked smile of his and sauntered up the aisle of the barn with two chestnut horses in tow. A volunteer at Grace since Bren had been a child, he was moving up in years but refused to give into his age.

"How do their hooves look?" she asked him.

"I'd say they're in need of trimming."

She'd already picked up on the gelding's gait. It was off. But the mare seemed to be sound.

"I'll take a look." Bren bent down, her hand gentle, gliding down the mare's knee. She didn't have to examine the entire front right hoof. It was long in the outside toe.

Bren came to her feet and smiled. "You're right." She patted him on his shoulder. "The farrier's working outside this morning since it's mild."

"We're on our way, Miss Bren." He gave her a wink and clucked his tongue, moving past.

"Johnny."

"Yes, ma'am?"

"If you see Jenny out front, can you have her meet me in the office in ten minutes? I need her help inventorying the vaccinations and dewormer."

"Sure thing, Miss Bren."

The three plodded by, brushed by Jo, several stalls up, who was unpacking medicine she'd brought from the clinic.

Bren went back to measuring out the feed for stalls eight and eleven when something wet and warm nudged her shoulder.

Love for the culprit spread through her, and she laughed at his tactics to gain her attention. She scratched behind the ear of the old Appaloosa she'd named Smiley. He'd stolen her heart at the age of twelve, and she had spoiled him ever since.

"You know I love you, boy, but you're not the only one who needs attention. You're going to have to wait for that apple until I'm done."

Grace teetered at the limit of rescues they could accommodate. At capacity they could house, feed, and rehabilitate fifteen horses. They were already at twelve.

"Jo, did Jeremy give you the antibiotic for Whisper?" Bren hollered down the row of stalls in the barn as she mixed the feed with what she had left of the antibiotic on hand.

Something clattered against a stall, and Bren swung around.

"Jo?"

Bren moved down the aisle, her work boots silent against the compact, sweet-smelling earth of the barn floor. She stopped and picked up Jo's cane in front of Daisy's stall.

The chestnut draft horse, all three thousand pounds of her, was positioned in the back of the stall with Jo pushing up against her, attempting to stay upright while she filled the draft's grain bucket. Of all the breeds Jo could be manhandling, she'd picked one that stood and weighed twice as much as an average horse.

Bren shook her head. "If you fall, she's liable to trample you."

Jo stopped, her shapely black brows creasing with consternation. "Don't treat me like a gimp, Bren." The usual airy voice of Jo Breakstone hardened, and Bren was reminded that Jo, before the shooting that had ended her career with the DEA, could run like a gazelle, scale fences with the agility of a track star, and kick the ass of any drug dealer she brought down.

Bren frowned and took one step inside the stall. "Excuse me, Daisy." She patted the mare's side and reached for Jo. "You need to pick on someone your own size." She pulled Jo out into the aisle and handed back her cane. Then she gave a tug on Jo's dark, single braid of hair resting on her chest. "I'm sorry. You know I don't think of you that way. I just don't want to see you get hurt."

"Sorry, too. I'm just grouchy."

"With me?"

"Jeremy."

Bren leaned back and put her hand on her hip. "What'd he do?"

"He left this morning without saying good-bye."

Right. How could she forget? Jeremy trusted Bren to handle the clinic in his absence while he brushed up on his skills in Leesburg, Virginia. "The beast," Bren teased.

Jo's pout cracked into a smile. "Silly, huh?"

"Kind of. Did you call him on it?" Bren grabbed her cell phone, perpetually linked with the office phones until Jeremy's return, and dangled it in front of Jo. "Literally."

"He didn't want to wake me."

Why was she not surprised? "You've got a good man, Jo. He worships you."

"I know. It's not like I don't have the expertise to catch him if he were cheating."

Bren's face went taut. "That's a joke, right?"

Jo laughed. "You're so gullible."

"Real funny." Bren shook her head in a know-it-all sort of way and scrunched up her face. If there was anyone who loved his wife more than Jeremy, other than Tom, she'd be surprised.

"Stop looking at me like that!" Bren dug her boots into the gravel drive leading away from the barn and shaded her face from the afternoon sun. If anything, she should be giving Kevin the third degree. "What about the dead horse? Or Tom's cell phone? Find that probable cause you need to search Wes's house!"

"When was the last time you received a call?"

"Right before they auctioned half my land. Almost two weeks."

"Then it's not a priority. This is. Are you guilty?" Kevin whipped off his Stetson and slapped it down on the hood of his cruiser. He ran agitated fingers through his short-cropped hair. "Answer the question."

"When would I have time to shoot down to the eastern shore to steal horses?"

"You tell me."

Bren crossed her arms. "Looking to run for sheriff of the whole damn state? What do you care what happens in Dorchester County?"

"I don't. Smartass. I care about you. I care about Wes's big mouth spreading rumors. Eventually, law enforcement with more get-up-and-go than the Washington County Sheriff's Department might think there's more to it."

Bren's face softened. "I didn't do it."

Kevin took a long breath and blew it out. "Okay, Bren. I'm trusting you. You just better hope there's not another 'kill barn' horse stealing. Wes is already bending the state police's ear about the coincidence."

"You can tell Wes—"

The rumble of the school bus brought her around, the high-pitched squeal of the brakes piercing the air. Nancy McAllister, the bus driver, had a soft spot for Aiden and Finn, especially after Tom's death. Usually, the two would make the quarter-mile trek up the driveway, but Nancy had decided, if it was okay with Bren and there was enough radius to turn around, she'd just as soon drop them off at their door.

Bren gave Kevin the evil eye. "Not a word, Mr. Lawman."

The doors folded open, and Finn popped off the last step.

Kevin stepped forward and gave Finn a high-five. "Hey, partner. How's school?"

"Hey, Kev." Finn slapped his hand and squinted up against the sun's glare. "I'm a Patrol. See my badge? It's shaped like yours."

"You want to be a lawman someday?"

"Maybe." He gave Kevin a wide smile and then turned his attention to Bren. "Can I get a snack?"

"Give me just a minute to say hi to Aiden and bye to Kevin."

Finn nodded and went to sit on the front steps of the porch. Aiden wrestled with a few more of his buddies in the back of the bus and then sauntered down the steps.

He gave Kevin a sideways glance, his eyes sobering. "Mom behaving herself?" Aiden was intuitive, she'd give him that.

Kevin smiled at that. "Today? Yes."

"See ya, folks." Nancy waved from her perch in the bus.

"Thanks, Nance." Bren waved back.

The doors closed, and the bus began to beep as it backed up. It slowly pulled away, headed back down the driveway, and then cut over to the side to let the black pickup pass—Rafe's pickup.

Kevin hooked his chin toward the truck and glanced back. "You ever apologize for being an ass the other day?"

Bren ignored his comment and concentrated on the truck, hoping Rafe kept going. Rafe had picked up on Bren's and Kevin's friendship at the court- house. She'd never stipulated that their sleuthing wasn't up for discussion, especially with her friend the sheriff. If Kevin was aware she'd involved the rancher, he might think she opened her mouth about Tom's missing phone. She hadn't. Not to Jo and not Wes. Even though she'd wanted to confront Wes that night in the sale barn, it would only work against her. He'd have lied, and she'd have tipped him off. She'd never find the phone then.

She nodded toward Kevin. "See ya." She hitched her chin behind her at her boys sitting on the step. Finn leaned against the rails, and Aiden slumped against his backpack, texting. "They're starved."

Kevin grabbed hold of the patrol car's door handle and hesitated.

"One more thing. Not that it has anything to do with our earlier conver- sation, but a horse, I think it was an English Thoroughbred owned by some hoity-toity Brit, turned up dead at Charles Town Races yesterday."

"The track in West Virginia."

Kevin nodded. "Came over the wire this morning. FBI's investigating this one along with all the others."

She eyed Kevin. "You know that's no coincidence."

"It's starting to look that way."

"It's happened before. I looked it up on the Internet."

Kevin moaned. "Stick to your day job."

Bren made a face. "I think it's time for you to go."

Kevin grabbed his Stetson off the hood. "I know when you're shooing me away."

"Then shoo." Bren motioned with her hands and turned to head up the steps.

The diesel engine coming up the driveway sent splinters of anxiety to the pit of her stomach. Rafe cut the engine off, and she cursed under her breath.

Finn sat up straight. "Who's that, Mom?"

"Mr. Langston. He bought the other half of Grace. Remember?"

Kevin stopped midway inside his patrol car.

"I thought you were leaving."

"Not a chance." Kevin walked back and whispered, "Someone needs to keep you in line."

The door to the truck opened, and a long, lean, jean-clad leg stepped out, his black boots covered in mud. Rafe Langston, from the few times she'd been acquainted with him, kept his boots shined to a high luster. He stepped down, and four large paws followed, springing from the cab.

"A dog!"

Bren's head swiveled behind her. She'd never seen Aiden move so fast. He was up, tossed his cell phone on top of his backpack, and was racing up on her.

Rafe gave her a sheepish grin, his eyes dancing with mischief.

"Oh no. I told you I wasn't ready for—"

She stopped. Those pitiful eyes and droopy ears pulled at her heart. "A bloodhound," she moaned.

"He was destined for the gallows."

"Yeah, right." She frowned at Rafe.

"You said puppy. He's not. He's close to a year. Potty trained and listens real well." Rafe looked at the gangly bloodhound. "Sit."

The hound yawned and plopped his hindquarters on the gravel, stretched, yawned again, and lay down, licking his chops.

"He's lazy, not a listener," Bren complained.

Finn came up next to her and hugged her waist. "Can we keep him?"

"Yeah, Mom," Aiden piped in as he knelt down beside the dog and patted his head. Aiden studied the dog. "We could name him—"

"Roscoe," Rafe interrupted.

"That's cool," Aiden agreed. Lifting his chin, he smiled at Rafe.

Bren hadn't seen that easy curl of Aiden's lips since Tom died. Rafe bent down and rubbed Roscoe's ears. "Aiden, right?"

Aiden nodded.

"I'm Rafe Langston. I bought your grandfather's house." He glanced up at Bren. "I know that's a sore spot with your family. But I hope we can be friends."

Aiden shot a questioning look at Bren.

Bren smiled. "It's okay. Mr. Langston and I have worked through that issue."

Kevin jabbed her in the ribs, whispering under his breath, "It didn't take you long to warm up to the cowboy."

Bren stepped closer. "Don't you have someplace you *should* be?" she said under her breath.

He rocked back on his heels and smiled. "I'm good."

"So we can keep Roscoe?" Aiden asked.

Bren's shoulders slumped at the prospect, and she pinned Rafe with her eyes. "How about his shots? Is he wormed?"

Rafe grimaced and looked down at his mud-caked boots and then gave her a lopsided grin. "Yes, ma'am. I even bathed him myself."

That explained a lot.

"Can I pet him?" Finn pulled on her coat.

"Sure, sweetie."

Finn dropped to the ground next to Aiden. His small hand stroked Roscoe's nose, and the dog licked him. He giggled and peered back at Bren. "He's soft." Roscoe licked him again. "And wet."

Kevin nudged Bren in the ribs. "Give the man an answer."

How could she say no? He'd gone through a tremendous amount of effort. But it wasn't the energy he'd spent as much as the thought behind it. He'd never met her boys officially. Unofficially, he'd only seen them once, and that was at a distance.

"You're the oldest, Aiden. He'd be your responsibility," Bren said.

Rafe winked at Bren, and it warmed her straight through.

"He's meant for tracking," Rafe said. "I've trained my own. I'd be more than willing to teach yours."

"Awesome. Thanks, Mr.—"

Rafe squeezed his shoulder. "Call me Rafe."

"Thanks, Rafe." He turned back to Bren. "I promise to take care of him, okay?"

All eyes singled her out, and she caved. "Okay."

"Yay!" Finn jumped to his feet and spun around, and Roscoe barked.

Rafe gave Aiden a high-five and made his way toward Bren and Kevin. He reached out a greeting. "Sheriff." He grinned at Bren.

Kevin looked to Bren and then Rafe. "I'm guessing she apologized."

"I'm guessing you've overstayed your welcome," Bren added.

Kevin laughed. "Some things never change." He nodded toward the boys. "Aiden, you take care of that dog. And, Finn, you make sure he does."

"Yes, sir," they said in unison.

The screen door slammed. Her father stood on the porch, a white apron tied around his waist, his hands on hips. "What the devil?" His gaze narrowed in on Roscoe. "You can't be serious."

"Meet the newest member of the family," Bren announced.

"He's the saddest excuse for dog if I've ever seen one. He needs fattening up."

Kevin stepped into his cruiser and lowered his window. "You all, take care."

"Kevin, I've got Salisbury steak and mashed potatoes." Daniel beckoned.

Kevin waved from the car. "Got a date, Daniel."

Bren whistled through her teeth.

Kevin frowned and waved a dismissive hand her way. "I'll see ya later."

Her father came down the steps as he concentrated on Roscoe and then the man standing next to her. "I suppose you would be the one responsible."

Rafe reached over. "Rafe Langston. Nice to meet you, Mr. Fallon."

He shook Rafe's hand and hesitated before he let go. "Ah, you got a look about you. Familiar." He adjusted his glasses. "It must be me old eyes. If I've seen you before, I can't place it."

"Dad, Rafe's from Texas."

"Right. Well, maybe I've seen you in town. At any rate, it's time for supper. I've got plenty to go around, Mr. Langston. How about you join us? Bren's already confided there's no Missus—"

"Dad!" Bren cringed. Tact was not Daniel Fallon's middle name.

Her father grimaced. "Not that she meant anything by it," he said, qualifying his statement.

"We get it." She cleared her throat, hoping he'd zip it before she turned a deeper red.

"Mr. Fallon, I think I'll take you up on that offer." Rafe placed his hand in the middle of Bren's back, and her stomach fluttered.

CHAPTER EIGHT

"**H**E DID NOT." JO BIT DOWN ON HER LIP TO KEEP FROM LAUGHING. "Oh, yeah. Made me out to be some desperate widow." Bren mimicked her father from last night and her confession concerning Rafe Langston's marital status, then made a face in the mirror and pulled on the off-the-shoulder, ruby-lace top, barely a veil against her pale skin. The Wonderbra she'd purchased, plumping her medium-sized breasts over the plunging neckline, made her blush. "Do you think I need to show more cleavage?"

Jo pursed her lips, staring at her and Bren's reflection in the oval mirror of Jo's bedroom. "I think this is a bad idea."

Bren closed her ears to Jo's voice of reason. It was not like she looked forward to slinking around the Bear Claw. But bars were where deals were made. Lips moved more smoothly. Men were easy. Secrets escaped unknowingly in the presence of a provocatively dressed woman. Bren smoothed down the snug black suede skirt that did little to hide a pair of long, slender legs. She turned on her toes, tried to take a step, and wobbled in her new, black, shiny stilettos.

"*Jeez.* You're going to fall on your ass," Jo said.

"They're not work boots, but I can manage." Bren reached for the bobby pins and spun her red hair up and secured it. "Hand me the wig."

"I should never have let you talk me into this."

"Don't get cold feet now. You're my wheels." This plan had been henpecking at her brain for weeks. Jeremy's business trip had worked in her favor. Jo's house to prepare for her undercover sting was perfect.

"Here." Jo passed the long blonde wig she'd spent a fortune on at a local beautician store.

Bren let it fall past her shoulders. "Curling iron." She held out her hand.

Jo handed it off, and Bren began to roll the hair around the curling iron as though it were real. She bent close to the mirror and smoothly attached a set of fake eyelashes. She applied charcoal eye shadow and a gray liner, blush, and a shimmering pink glaze on her lips. She stood back.

"Oh my God."

"What?" Bren clenched her teeth.

"You . . . you don't—"

"Look like me?" She raised two well-shaped, russet eyebrows at Jo in the mirror.

"Not at all. Turn around." Jo motioned with her finger.

Bren turned and didn't teeter. Shaking her blonde hair, she studied herself. Something was missing.

Jo dangled the cubic zirconia earrings in the mirror. "This what you're looking for?"

Bren smiled and took them from Jo. "Thanks." She attached them to her ears. Still, there was something else. She ticked off her disguise: lashes, wig . . . lashes. Contacts! The small black handbag with the thin strap sat on Jo's dressing table. She grabbed it and pulled out a pair of foil wrapped blue contacts.

Jo shook her head. "You thought of everything."

"Had to. A hair change is easy. Eyes are permanent. If anyone questions who I am, they won't be thinking of the dark redhead with brown eyes." Bren opened her right eye, blinked, then cursed. She tried again, and this time the lens went in. The next one followed without too much fuss. Bren turned for final inspection. "I know colored contacts are easy to get, but do you really think this group will think that deeply about it?"

"Not a chance." Jo plopped on the bed. "I don't even recognize you."

A smile curved Bren's lips. "You ready?"

Jo thumped down the stairs, and Bren followed, balancing on her heels as they strode out the door. They slipped into Jo's dark Chevy Tahoe and headed toward Williamsport, and the Bear Claw Tavern, ten miles down Route 68. Bren snuggled inside the borrowed faux-fur jacket of Jo's and shivered.

She'd lied to her father as she slipped out the front door in jeans when Jo pulled up, told him they were going out to dinner and that they were going to see a late movie in Hagerstown.

No way could she tell her father what she was up to. It was bad enough she had enlisted Jo's help. And as far as her newfound friend Rafe Langston went, something told her he might be less than thrilled if he knew the details of her plan.

Jo glanced at Bren. "So tell me about your new neighbor."

Bren pressed her head back into the seat. "He's a cowboy born and raised in Texas."

"Why's he here?"

"He said to be a dairy farmer."

"Most cowboys I've ever heard of draw a hard line between beef and dairy."

Jo only confirmed her own thoughts on the matter. "Not sure I buy it, either."

"Did he say much at dinner about his plans?"

"Not much. The boys couldn't stop talking about Roscoe and asking Rafe questions about his ranch back home."

"They like him."

"What's not to like if you're a boy? He even had me enthralled with the life of a cowboy. The three have become fast friends. Aiden even offered to show him the duck blind he and Tom built."

"What do you think?"

"Seems nice enough. Anyone who can make Aiden smile has my vote."

"I saw him at the sale barn when you and Wes got into it. He's hot." Jo peered over and grinned. "And you know it, Bren Ryan."

Bren groaned. "Not interested."

"Liar."

Those sharp green eyes of Rafe Langston came into focus in Bren's mind, and her belly dipped. Eye candy was one thing, but a relationship with Rafe, or any man, no matter how sexy, wasn't going to happen. "He's my neighbor, Jo. My boys' new best friend." That bothered her. What did she really know about the cowboy from Weatherford, Texas? She, for one, found the whole beef versus dairy thing suspicious. Plus, why move clear across the U.S.? Even if he and his father didn't agree, certainly there were farms in Texas to accommodate his needs.

Jo nudged Bren. "What?"

"How'd you like to do a little investigative work? I'll pay you. Name your price."

"Don't do this."

"This?"

"Bear Claw."

"Jo, I have to. If Wes killed Tom, he may have confided in one of them. If I can get one to talk, I'll get justice."

"You worry me." Jo gave Bren a sideways glance. "Who else needs to be investigated?"

Other than Wes, she had a short list. "Rafe."

"Rafe?" Jo shook her head.

"Just poke around."

"Fine. I'll check him out." Jo reached over and squeezed Bren's knee. "I love you like a sister. I'm sure Rafe has nothing to hide. But there's nothing wrong with knowing for sure."

Bren patted Jo's hand. "Thanks." She leaned forward to see the approaching sign. "We're getting close. Don't drop me off at the door. Park down from the tavern, and I'll walk the rest of the way."

"I don't—"

"I'll be fine."

Jo pulled up into the Exxon gas station next to the Bear Claw Tavern. "Got your cell?"

Bren reached into her black bag. "Right here. But this could take a few hours, Jo. I'll call you when I'm done. Clear Spring is fifteen minutes away. Go home."

"I can—"

"No. You've helped me enough. I only need you to pick me up. I'll give you plenty advance notice."

Bren stepped down from the Tahoe and winked at Jo.

"Hey, Bren, what about your voice?" Jo's concerned eyes locked in on Bren under the glow of the interior light.

Bren smiled back and concentrated on her words and a Southern, genteel accent. "Honey, my name's Belinda Harrington. From Greensboro, originally. Went to one of those New York fashion schools. Hoping to settle in Clear Spring and open up my very own boutique right on Route 40."

Jo shook her head and answered her back with a drawl of her own. "Belinda, sweetie, you just make sure your pretty little ass doesn't get caught.

You hear? 'Cause if you don't call me by one"—she glanced at her watch— "I'm calling the sheriff."

Bear Claw wasn't like the typical bars in Clear Spring. The cars, a mix of Audi, BMW, and Lexus, and, of course, Lyle's black Cadillac Escalade parked in the far corner, spoke of businessmen, not farmers. Wes and Lyle worked hard to create that distinction. They were elitists, and flights, not steps, above those who worked for them.

Bren took one more inventory of cars in the parking lot. Robert's black Mercedes was not among those parked. Running into Robert could throw her off target. Lying to Robert, who'd done his best to protect her from his father, would make her feel guilty. But not seeing Wes with his gleaming new, black four-door pickup with the Sweet Creek Stables decal on the door made her send up a silent prayer it would stay that way.

Bren grabbed hold of the brass bear-claw handle and entered. She checked her phone once more to verify the time—nine fifty-two. It was still early for Saturday night. That gave her almost three hours before Jo's curfew took effect.

Bren's eyes took a second to adjust. Then her insides rolled. Over at the end of the bar, Lyle Jameson sat conversing with several well-dressed businessmen. She didn't know the others. Jo assured her she was unrecognizable. She swallowed hard. Still, she'd stay clear of Lyle and concentrate on the others she didn't know.

From the lively chatter, it appeared they were well on their way to intoxication. And that was good. The questions she needed to ask could send up a warning if the men she talked to were sober. The questions were the problem; more, how to pose them without igniting suspicion. She cleared her head and began to think like the tall blonde she'd become.

Belinda Harrington, sexy . . . She winced at that. *Come on, Bren. Focus.* Belinda Harrington, sexy, new in town, looking for prime office space, preferably a vacant shop window on Route 40—Clear Spring's main street.

That would get her started. She stepped farther into the Bear Claw, thankful for the muted lighting and dark-paneled walls. Several booths were occupied with both men and women. It wasn't like this place only catered to men. Of course, none of these women resembled her in the least. That was the point, wasn't it? Her outfit was meant to entice. She had gone to great pains to be alluring without being trashy. Confident she'd achieved her goal, she headed toward the bar. No ginger ale for her. She needed whisky straight, but she'd settle for a seven and seven—a lady's drink.

Bren ignored the glances from the booths and made a path to the bar, her focus the mounted black bear head above the kaleidoscope of glass shelves and liquor. If she made it that far, she'd grab hold of the bar stool and sink down, relieved she hadn't stumbled in her ridiculous heels.

Several steps from her intended target, a swoosh of strength and muscle rushed by her, bumping her hard to the right. She stumbled and reached for the oak post support against the last row of booths and missed as the dimly lit floor loomed. But strong arms held her fast.

"Excuse me, miss. I didn't mean to knock you over." His hand rested on her hip, the other on her shoulder. He studied her. "You from around here?" He was average height and brawny under his gray suit. With her heels, her face was dead even with his. His thick blond eyebrows matched his unruly curls, and he smiled at her. "You're a knockout."

And he was blunt.

Bren remembered her accent. "From down South."

"Whereabouts? Georgia? South Carolina?"

"North."

"A real Southern belle." He stood back and cocked his head. "You by yourself?"

"For now."

"Well, then, how about some company? I need to take care of some business with that gentleman at the end of the bar." He pointed at Lyle. "And then I'll buy you a drink." His eyes lowered toward her breasts, and Bren wanted to shrink from view.

Pig.

She ignored the urge to slap him and smiled real nice. He knew Lyle, who knew Wes. She didn't know what business he had, but she'd find out. "Sure, honey. I'll just take a seat down at this end of the bar."

He squeezed her arm, his large hand encircling her bicep, and she didn't miss the strength behind it. "Order me Belvedere neat and whatever you're having." He winked at her. "Better yet, start a tab. My treat."

He retreated to the end of the bar, and this time Bren grabbed for the post. *Oh God. Shit. Shit. This is too real.* She willed her frayed nerves to recede. *I can do this.*

She sat down and laid her purse on the slick bar top. She placed her hand inside and grabbed for the mini-recorder. It was too soon to activate it. Her fingers trembled, and she pulled her hands down into her lap.

"What will the lady have?"

Bren smiled up at the bartender. His long brown hair, pulled back neatly in a leather cord, shimmered under the recessed lights. "Seven and Seven and a Belvedere neat for the gentleman at the end of the bar."

Placing a clean glass on the bar, the bartender glanced down, his grip tightened. "Miss, do yourself a favor. Finish your drink, and tell him to go to hell."

Bren's eyes widened. "Is there a problem—"

The bartender stiffened and forced a smile "Hey, Donovan. How's it going?" he said to the creep wanting the Belvedere, who slid onto the stool beside Bren.

"Blake," he said to the bartender. "You meet this beauty …?" He slapped his knee. "Hell, beautiful, we never did get properly introduced." He stuck out his hand. "Donovan Skidmore."

Bren shook his moist hand and gritted her teeth. "Belinda Harrington. Nice to make your acquaintance."

Blake stirred her drink and set it down. He raised a questioning brow toward Donovan. "Your usual?"

He nodded. "Better yet, make it a double." He glanced at Bren and squeezed her bare knee.

Bren took a swig of her drink, the whisky a sedative waiting to take hold.

"So, pretty lady, what brings you to Williamsport?"

"I design women's clothes. Looking for a quaint town to open a boutique."

"Well, honey, Williamsport isn't the place."

Bren took another sip, the warmth of the whisky coursing down her throat. "Actually, I found a vacant storefront in Clear Spring between the barber shop and Mercantile Bank."

He nodded. "Better." He shot a look toward the faux fur she was wearing. "Aren't you hot?"

Sweat ran down her neck, and her clothes clung to her. Hot didn't even come close.

He pushed his stool back and stood. His arms went around her shoulders, and she flinched. The fur moved down her skin, and he tugged until it came free. Draping it over her stool, he sat and pulled his stool closer. "Better?"

Not.

His eyes darkened, and he licked his lips. "You design that lacy red thing?" The bartender slid his drink over to him, the glass disappearing inside Donovan's thick hand.

"Victoria's Secret," she whispered, smiled devilishly, and leaned over conspiratorially. "But don't tell anyone."

He sputtered in his drink with laughter. "You're funny and gorgeous. That's one lethal combination."

Bren smiled wide. As long as he minded his manners, she was relatively safe with him. Blake's obvious distrust of the man, a pinprick of warning, remained sharp.

Donovan nodded to her empty glass. He waved Blake over. "The lady needs a refill."

She didn't refuse. Two drinks would make her less edgy. She took a sip. "Tell me, Donovan, what's your business?"

He laughed and put his arm around her shoulders. "If I told you, I'd have to kill you."

Bren went cold, and her neck tingled. "I see you have a sense of humor, too."

His hand moved down her shoulder and squeezed her hand. "We're a match."

His clammy hand, pressing down on hers, made her bite her lip. "Two peas in a pod, we are, darlin'."

Bren continued to banter back and forth. The third drink Donovan ordered for her, she nursed. She kept a vigilant eye on Lyle and watched the door, hoping Wes wouldn't make an entrance. Donovan knocked back at least six vodkas, his speech beginning to slur. He stood and then swayed. "Belinda, sweetheart, I need to hit the men's room. Don't go nowhere, beautiful."

Bren lifted her glass. "Wouldn't dream of it."

He disappeared around the corner, and Bren sagged against the back of the stool.

"I've seen enough folks to know when they're scamming."

Pushing back in her stool, she gave Blake a questioning look.

"Come on, red. Tell me what's going on."

Bren's face warmed. Red? Her hand flew to the wig. Then it dawned on her, her lacy red barely-there top. She relaxed and smiled easily. "Blake, sweetheart. What'd you mean about Skidmore?"

Blake stepped closer. "He's looking to score, Belinda. Unless you plan on rolling in the sheets with Donovan, I suggest you slip out."

Perish the thought.

There was something in Blake's warm, amber eyes that told Bren he could be trusted. He was a bartender. Bartenders always knew what crept below the surface. "How does he know that man down there?" She pointed toward Lyle Jameson.

"Skidmore works for the Maryland horse racing industry. He has a lucrative side job with Lyle Jameson and Wes Connelly."

Bren tried to remain unaffected by their names. "What kind of business?"

"He's known as the 'meat man.' He sells old race horses for slaughter."

Bren grabbed her throat and took a breath. "I had no idea those beautiful horses were slaughtered."

Blake nodded. "Not many do, unless you know your way around horses." He finished drying a glass, leaned against the back bar, and folded his arms. "You don't want any part of Donovan Skidmore. He's a piece of—"

"Belinda, baby doll." Donovan gave Blake a scowl. "I hope you're not spreading rumors."

Blake lifted his hands, palms out. "And tarnish your reputation? You know me better than that, Donovan."

Donovan grabbed the fur jacket on the back of Bren's chair and clamped onto her arm. "I found an empty booth across the way. It's nice and cozy."

Bren hopped off the stool and smiled. "Thanks, Blake, for everything."

"Take care."

Donovan directed her toward the booth and pushed her legs against the bench none too gently. Bren's senses alerted. He was drunk, a little less mindful of his manners, and the grip digging into her arm was more an order than a suggestion.

Bren tamped down the warning. She was in a public place. No harm could come to her as long as she remained in the bar. It had to be close to eleven. She didn't dare check the clock on her phone. Drawing attention to her purse would only draw attention to its contents.

The horses now took precedence, and Bren focused on her new mission. She took a seat in the booth, squeezing his shoulder. "Sweat Pea, how about another drink for Belinda?"

He frowned. "Don't listen to Blake's nonsense."

"I do my own judging when it comes to the men in my life."

He smiled at that and turned to signal the waitress.

Bren pressed back against the wall. The waitress took the order, and Donovan gave her his full attention. "You're driving me crazy with that lacy top." He growled under his breath.

She needed to change the subject. "Blake told me your secret. You live dangerously . . . Never seen a horse up close. Tell you the truth, they scare me. I had no idea people ate them."

He moved closer and stroked her hair.

Bren stiffened.

"The Japanese and French can't get enough of American horse meat."

Bren reached over and stroked his arm. "So tell me, Secret Agent Man, how does it work?"

Donovan looked around. "Promise not to tell?" He stroked the side of her breast.

Bren held her breath and then willed herself to exhale. "Promise." She batted her fake eyelashes and reached down into her purse resting on Jo's fur, pressed the Record button, and nonchalantly placed her hand in her lap.

"How about a kiss first?" The plump, glistening lips of Donovan puckered.

No way in hell, asshole.

"And then you'll tell?"

"Cross my heart." He made a lazy X across his chest.

And I hope you die because I surely will if I kiss that nasty puss of yours.

She gave him what she hoped was an award-winning smile. "Isn't the fun in the chase? How about we start slow?" She leaned forward and kissed his cheek and cringed at the smell of vodka and cheap aftershave.

His hand tightened around her waist and held her in place. He whispered in her ear. "You like to tease."

Bren rolled her lips in. "Mmm-hmm."

His grip loosened, and she settled back down in the seat. "Your turn."

"Seems Charles Town has several noncontenders they need moved, and I got a buyer."

"How many?"

He tapped his ear. "Lick my ear, doll baby."

Euwh!

The horses with their big frightened eyes invaded her mind.

Do it, Bren.

She leaned over and tentatively touched her tongue to his earlobe. Snapping her mouth shut, she pulled away just as quickly.

"Whoa, not so fast." His hand cupped the back of her neck, and he brought her forward.

Bren smiled sweetly. "One lick, one number."

"Fifteen."

"Why so many?"

He tapped his ear.

Damn her curiosity. Leaning in, she took another sample of his ear and pulled back.

"There are other racetracks."

Right. Pimlico . . . Laurel.

He moved closer and nuzzled her neck. "You're a tease, Belinda." He grabbed her hand and held it against his erection, and she stiffened. "How about we cut to the chase?" He moved her hand back and forth against him, and Bren tried to pull away.

"Shy?"

"I like privacy," Bren demurred.

"How about we continue this at my hotel?"

"Donovan." Two of the men she'd seen Lyle with came toward them. The tall one with the shifty gait pointed his finger at Donovan. "Next Friday. Two A.M. Sweet Creek Stables."

"Sheesh, Driggs, you got a big mouth."

Driggs laughed it off and moved past without a word.

Donovan angled in on Bren. "Now, you didn't hear that, Belinda."

Hell she didn't.

She pulled her hand out from under Donovan's. Wes was as good as gone, the son of a bitch, and she'd be waiting for him when that trailer stacked with horses pulled out of Sweet Creek Stables. He'd go against regulation. She'd bet on it. And she'd have the sheriff and her friends from animal control there to nail his ass.

But first, she needed to get the hell out of here.

"Let me freshen up," she whispered in his ear, "and I'll meet you at the bar while you settle our tab."

He slid out and grabbed her arm, pulling her to her feet. He squeezed her butt. "Hurry up."

If she could have, she'd have smacked him. Instead, she moved to the bathroom to call Jo. Standing in front of the mirror, she washed her hands and smiled at the stranger staring back at her. She bent over and rinsed her mouth and especially her tongue. She couldn't wait to shed this getup for her pajamas.

She reached in her bag for her cell phone and cursed when the words "no signal" glowed back at her. Shit. She pushed open the bathroom door and peeked around the small alcove toward the bar. Donovan was gone. Crap. Maybe he went back to the table? It didn't matter. She was a homing device for Donovan Skidmore. She'd take her chances at the Exxon. If she recalled, there was a large Dumpster. She wasn't above hiding behind it until her ride showed up.

Bren slipped out the door and moved down the hall when she was forced backwards against the wall. "Trying to run out on me, doll face?"

Donovan pressed his bulky frame against her, the heat of his sickening breath hot on her neck while he slobbered kisses against her skin.

She pushed hard. He didn't budge. "You're heavy, Donovan."

"Get used to it. I'm going to be all over you."

Bren's heart sped up, and a shiver shot up her spine. "Get off."

He pressed painfully against her stomach and rubbed his erection into her.

Bren tried to knee him, but he pinned her high and tight against the wall with his massive body. "We had a deal, sweetheart, and I'm collecting."

They were tucked away down from the restrooms, toward a back office. There was no foot traffic, and Bren cursed. She'd isolated herself. The music pumped through the back hall and into the alcove. Her only chance was to scream. Maybe someone would hear her from the bathrooms. She tried to scream, but Donovan Skidmore's lips clamped down on hers. She began to gag when he stuck his tongue in her mouth, and then the pressure of his mouth and tongue disappeared. She coughed and wiped her mouth with the back of her hand.

"The lady said she wasn't interested." A dark suede arm swung, its fist smashing into Donovan Skidmore's face. He slumped to the ground.

Bren didn't have to look directly into his eyes to know who the voice belonged to. She hadn't known Rafe Langston for very long, but she was prepared for his fury at her stupidity.

"You okay, ma'am?"

Ma'am?

Bren straightened. "I can ex—"

He dipped his head. "I'm Rafe Langston. Can I take you home? Or call someone to get you?"

Too funny. He didn't recognize her. Bren raised her chin and looked him in the eyes. She didn't want to wait around for Jo to get there. "What time is it?"

He glanced at his gold watch. "Eleven thirty."

"I'll take that ride. But I need to call my friend and let her know she doesn't need to pick me up."

He nodded. "There's better reception outside." He stepped over Donovan's limp body and directed her around it.

Bren glanced back. "You didn't—"

"Kill the son of a bitch? No. Drunks fall harder. He'll sleep it off and wonder what Mack truck hit him in the morning."

He guided her through the bar and out the door, the air an instant relief to her overheated body. "I'll just be a minute," Bren said.

"Take your time."

Bren moved away from Rafe and dialed Jo's number. "Jo."

"I'm on my way."

"No. You don't need to come. Rafe's here. I'll have him drop me off at your house."

"What happened? You all right?"

"I'll tell you when I see you."

Bren snapped the phone shut. Mindful of her blasted heels, she walked toward Rafe carefully.

"Your friend okay with me taking you home?"

Bren smiled. "Actually, that's where you're dropping me off. But to be safe, I gave her your name and your full description."

"Smart move. I'm the black pickup." Rafe pointed several spaces down from where they stood.

Bren nodded and began to move in that direction. She took a cautious step down from the curb, her ankle rolled, and she stumbled. A silent curse left her lips.

Rafe's strong hand grabbed her arm, holding her in place. "Easy." He glanced down at her shoes, his eyes lingering on her legs before he fastened them on her face. "You walk like a newborn filly."

Bren grimaced. "Breaking them in."

"Or your ankle. Belinda? It's okay if I call you that?"

Tell him the truth.

She wanted to. But she enjoyed listening to his Texas drawl, and the possessive way he held her hand was the exact opposite of Donovan's—and that was a good thing.

"Sure." Oops that came out too Northern. "Sure, honey. I'm Belinda Harrington. I really appreciate you helping me out and all."

"I'm glad I could oblige." He frowned at her. "You think you can make it?"

"With your guiding hand, I'll be just fine."

Rafe nodded, kept his hand in place, and began to walk slowly with her by his side. He unlocked her door and assisted her onto the running board. After shutting her door, he came around to the driver's side and got in. He started the truck and sat back. "Where to, Ms. Belinda Harrington?"

"Just take Route 68 and I'll tell you how to get there."

"Sounds like a plan." He put the truck in Drive and turned on Route 68.

Bren chewed on her lip and stared out the window. *The truth will set you free.* The only problem was she had so many lies stored up inside her, if she opened her mouth the truth might not be the first thing that popped out. If she was going to tell him, she needed to do it soon. She had maybe seven minutes before they got to Jo's.

"Not all men take advantage of a beautiful woman."

"What?" She glanced over at him.

"What I mean is, it's still early." He nodded toward the clock in the dash. "Midnight."

So he liked blondes. And that made her mad. When she was a redhead, he didn't give her a second glance. "What do you have in mind?"

"I have a real nice house in Clear Spring. Been looking to do some enter-taining." He glanced over and smiled. "I noticed you like Seven and Sevens."

Ah, he'd been watching her. "Sure, sweetie. You have a liquor cabinet at your place, I'm there."

He reached over and squeezed her knee, and she tingled inside, and then he took his hand away. *Whoa. Back up. I did not experience a flutter of arousal for Rafe Langston.* Then she sagged. He, on the other hand, was squeezing the knee of the blonde tart, Belinda Harrington, which made her angry the more she thought about it.

Bren grabbed her phone from her bag and texted Jo: *Change of plans. He's taking me home. I'll fill you in tomorrow.* She dropped her phone in her bag and settled back into the seat.

The truck turned left down Grace's driveway, her house disappearing in the distance when Rafe passed it, heading toward her childhood home. That irked her, too. He lived in her house. She glanced over at him, and her stomach fluttered. *Damn it.* She liked looking at him, strong jaw, rough with a couple days' growth of beard. Her gaze dropped to his lean legs in jeans, and she bit down on her lip.

Focus. Focus on what? On Rafe? Not good. She pulled her eyes away from his rugged profile. What exactly was the plan here? He liked blonde Belinda. He said not all men took advantage of a beautiful woman. So she'd test it out.

Chapter Nine

R AFE HELPED HER FROM THE TRUCK. SHE STEADIED HERSELF ON the running board and took a tentative step down and wobbled. He grabbed her arm. "Darlin', it'd be a lot faster if I carried you."

She wrapped her arms around his neck, her wondrous blue eyes staring up at him. He took that as a yes and scooped her up against his chest. The tight black skirt rode even higher, and he gritted his teeth at her shapely, smooth legs dangling from his arm.

Rafe smiled to himself and carried her the rest of the way. He sat her down gingerly, unlocked the door, and stepped back. "Ladies first."

She crossed the threshold and swayed. He curved his arm around her and leaned back to shut the door. "Maybe you should take off those shoes."

She gazed up and didn't take those eyes off him. She stepped out of one shoe, then the other, and sank to just below his chin. "You're tall."

He didn't answer. Instead, he frowned at her. "You really shouldn't be traveling alone." He brushed back a long, gold curl, amazed how soft it felt against his fingers. "What kind of business did you have at the Bear Claw?"

She pursed her shimmering pink lips, and his dick swelled. "None. Just checking out the sights."

He caressed her neck and let his hand brush lazily against the soft swell of her breasts. His balls tightened when she rolled those pouty, kissable lips in and a small whimper escaped through her mouth. What did his mama always say? *Play with fire* ... His eyes lit on her red lacy top, his fingers tingling as he traced the design of the lace that exposed her pale skin, and he forgot about his mama's warning. "You were turning that guy on in there, Belinda."

"Not intentionally," she drawled innocently.

"No?" He cocked his head.

She shook hers.

Rafe reached up and ran his fingers through her golden hair. And marveled again at how soft it felt through his fingers. Gripping it tighter, he yanked real hard and didn't flinch when it came free.

"Ouch!" Her hands flew to her head, tentatively feeling around for the mass of blonde hair that was no longer there.

"What the hell did you think you were doing?" he yelled, and his dick that had stretched to massive proportions began to recede with his anger. Hell, he knew what she was doing, same as he—searching for answers into Tom's death. That made him pause. He and Bren Ryan thought alike, and that was scary as hell.

"You're an asshole." Bren tried to pull away from him.

"Not so fast, doll face."

Her face flushed. "Shut up."

"Isn't that what he called you?"

She closed her eyes, as if not seeing him would make him disappear, and then those bright blue, unnatural eyes opened and blazed back. "You let that pig slobber all over me. You watched and enjoyed yourself."

"Darlin', it looked like you had it all under control." He reached up. "You have something in your eye."

She pulled back, the anger fading to concern. "I do?"

"Yeah. Hold still." Damn, but he was enjoying himself at her expense. He only had one stab at it, and she'd really be pissed if he poked her in the eye by mistake. There was a teaching lesson in there somewhere. But if he was wrong, she'd probably kick him in the balls. He latched onto a fluttering lash and yanked.

"Ouch!" She covered her eye with her hand.

The one brow he could see furrowed, and Rafe quickly pushed her back against the wall, averting a direct hit with her knee into his groin.

"That bastard could have raped you. What's wrong with you, Bren? You have two boys to look after. You had no business in a bar like that." He made a point of eyeing her breast and tried like hell to ignore the tightness inside him returning. "Looking like a hooker. I thought you had more smarts."

"He wasn't even close. You overreacted." Her chin rose, and she shot him a defiant look. "Did you just call me stupid?"

"Take it any way you like, darlin'."

"I can handle myself. Now get off me." She gave one solid push that amounted to a big nothing.

"Settle down, Bren. You could no more handle that jackass then you could me if I wanted to take advantage of you."

"You're wrong. Now get off."

Rafe reached up and pulled at a bobby pin. A long, deep red strand of hair slipped down to rest against her bare shoulder.

Her eyes darted toward it and then back to him. "What—"

He reached up again and carefully pulled at several more bobby pins until her hair spilled down to caress her soft, pale skin. If she didn't say uncle soon, his plan was going to backfire.

Her mouth opened slightly.

Damn. As much as he wanted to touch her, to kiss her, he knew he couldn't let that happen.

Not this redhead. Not this town. Not this lifetime.

He pressed up against her thighs, his chest bumping up against her sweet, pert breasts. *Come on, darlin', say uncle.* She straightened, but didn't push him away. If she shoved back, and he prayed she did, he'd let her go.

But he should have known better than to test Bren Ryan's resolve. She'd been through hell, and she was still fighting. He admired her for that. Tom was a lucky man, the poor bastard.

Rafe cupped the back of her neck and tilted her head up so he could look into those eyes of hers and cursed under his breath when he was met with that ridiculous shade of blue staring back. "Your brown eyes are a lot prettier."

She bit down on her lip and didn't say a word, only stared back at him.

Damn it, Bren! She was tougher than a one-legged Indian in an ass-kicking contest. Rafe brushed her lips with his thumb and stroked her cheek with the back of his hand. Nothing. He reached back and slid his arm down her back and pulled her to him and squeezed a firm, rounded cheek and damned if she didn't move closer. His hand traveled up her rib cage and stroked the side of her breast. He angled his head and pondered the sensual curve of her kissable lips. He groaned and let go. She fell back against the wall.

"You win," Rafe said, stripping out of his jacket and hanging it on the hall tree.

Her eyes widened when he unbuttoned his shirt. He wanted to smile at her avid curiosity. She wouldn't get a full view; he was wearing a T-shirt.

He took off his shirt and pressed it against her chest. "Put it on, and meet me in the kitchen. We need to talk."

"I have a coat."

"If you did, it's still in the bar."

"It wasn't even mine." She took the shirt and let her head fall against the wall. "My life truly sucks."

"If you want to use the bathroom, it's around the—"

"I know where it is." She bore into him.

"When you're done, I'll be in the kitchen." Rafe turned down the hall and tried like hell not to laugh.

Bren stepped into the powder room and hit the light switch. Her body still tingled where Rafe had touched her. The thought of his strong, rough fingers against her cheek made her close her eyes. But Tom's face surfaced, and her eyes sprang open along with the wound that she was alive, and Tom wasn't.

She shivered, slipped into Rafe's shirt, and buttoned it up. Feeling around her hair, she grabbed the last bobby pin and pulled it free. She plucked off the remaining fluttering lash and dropped it in the trash can. Taking one last look at what remained of Belinda Harrington, she popped her blue eyes out and let them wash down the sink.

Bren grabbed her black bag off the floor where she'd dumped it when they came in and moved toward the kitchen.

Rafe sat at a small table in a white T-shirt that hugged his muscular chest. He sipped from a steaming mug; another matching mug, also steaming, sat across from him. "Tea?"

"You drink tea?"

"Since I was a baby."

Still chilled, Bren sat down and added sugar, then wrapped her hands around the warm ceramic mug.

Rafe's expression softened. He popped open a tin and pushed it toward her. "Cookie?"

Bren's mouth watered at the aroma of homemade snickerdoodles. "Cowboys bake?"

"You against men in the kitchen?"

"Nope." She dipped one in her tea. Taking a bite, she savored the taste as it blended with the sweet tea. "Delicious."

Rafe sat back in his chair and crossed his arms. "Promise me you won't go off on any more wild-hair adventures until you consult with me first."

"It wasn't—"

He put up a hand. "No arguing. Just promise me."

The concerned expression in his striking green eyes unnerved her. She wasn't Rafe Langston's charity case, but she wasn't a fool either. Tonight might have turned out differently without his interference.

"Promise."

His shoulders relaxed, and he leaned forward. "Do you want to tell me what you were doing tonight?"

"Gathering intelligence."

"I'm assuming this has something to do with your husband's death."

Bren took another sip of her tea. "I told you Wes killed Tom. I need proof."

"Did that include using your body to get it?" His voice rose, and he gripped his mug with both hands.

His insinuation prickled. What did he know, anyway? She pushed her mug away and stood. "I don't need this. Believe what you want. I'm going home."

His hand reached out and grabbed hers. "Don't. I'm sorry." His dark brows furrowed together. "I wanted to kill him."

Bren's stomach rolled with the harshness in his voice for Donovan Skidmore's behavior toward her. "He didn't hurt me."

His lips thinned. "I should have acted sooner."

Bren sat down. "How'd you know it was me?"

"Your hands." He turned her hand in his. "They're not prissy and painted." His thumb rubbed across her clear, blunt nails.

That's what I forgot—my nails.

He brushed the same thumb against her fingers. "They're small, yet strong."

Damn it! Just his touch and the smooth drawl in his voice made her stomach flutter. Bren pulled her hand away. "It was dark."

"You were busy. And I was close enough."

Bren blushed, remembering what she'd done with Donovan to get information about the drop-off. She reached for her black bag. "It paid off." She pulled out the tape recorder. "He didn't have anything to offer about Tom's death. But he knows Lyle Jameson."

"The sale barn owner?"

Bren nodded. "That's why he was there." She picked up the tape recorder. "It's all right here." She hit the Play button and set the recorder in the middle of the table.

Rafe settled back in his seat to listen.

Bren's faux Southern accent and Donovan's heavy breathing made her cheeks warm with renewed embarrassment. Donovan's raspy voice filled the kitchen, "Lick my ear, doll baby."

Rafe stiffened in his chair and shot an angry hand out to silence the tape recorder. "How about you give me the short version?"

Relieved she didn't have to listen to Donovan's creepy voice, she told Rafe about the horses. He listened intently, polishing off three cookies as he finished his tea.

"I did it for the horses," she said.

He frowned. "I figured." He stood up and stretched. "What's your plan?"

She smiled. "Nail Wes. I know him. There's fifteen that Donovan has. That number could rise. Plus, whatever Wes has on hand. He'll only spring for one trailer. He's cheap."

"Which means he'll go against regulation."

"Then I'll have him."

"It won't prove he killed Tom."

"No. But when Kevin cuffs him and hauls him off to jail, I'll have the satisfaction of him knowing it was because of me."

"They'll only keep him overnight. Then what?"

Bren sat back in her chair. She had a feeling he wasn't going to like her answer.

"If losing six horses was enough to make him kill Tom, then losing fifteen would make me an even bigger target."

Chapter Ten

Rafe pulled up the driveway, shaking his head. He'd finally drilled some sense into Bren's brain last night before dropping her off. She wasn't to make a move on Wes without him. The woman had guts; he'd give her that. But guts could get you—

"What the hell?"

Smoke billowed against a darkening night sky above his house, and he hit the accelerator hard. The orange glow flickering in the distance was most assuredly on his property. Rafe pulled up to the house, jumped out of the truck, and left it running. He'd bought a fire extinguisher when he moved in. Didn't plan on using it, but the insurance of having it was one less thing to worry about when owning a home. Not that he planned on owning a home long—at least not in Maryland.

Rummaging through the hall closet, he scratched his head. Where did he put the damn thing? Broom closet. He headed in the kitchen, and, sure enough, he found what he was looking for.

Once back in his truck, he laid the fire extinguisher on the floor, and reached into the back seat. *Fires don't just set themselves.* He grabbed the rifle and box of shells he'd picked up in town, and placed them on the seat next to him. Rafe drove onto the grass and across the field. Once he got close, he reduced his speed and turned off his lights.

It was a damn fire, all right. A frickin' bonfire. From his estimation, there were at least a dozen people either standing next to the blaze or sitting on logs they'd rolled from the woods. Rafe grabbed his rifle, loading a round of ammunition as he stepped out. He crept toward the group, the rap music filtering through the dry, cold air. *Damn it.* He wouldn't need his gun, which was a damn shame.

Guns he could handle—teenagers not so much.

Hell, it wasn't even his kid. But he'd picked the wrong field. Aiden's stupidity was going to get him an up close and personal ass-chewing, neighbor or not. Rafe continued toward the group, his intended target the boom box sitting on the tailgate of an old, beat-up Ford pickup, white just like Daniel Fallon's.

Two strikes.

The shrieks of laughter and chatter kept Rafe's approach hidden. Standing next to the pickup, he punched the stereo off.

The group's rapid movements slowed, then they froze. "Shit!" one of the boys yelled. Then they all started toward the woods.

Rafe stepped forward. "Nobody move." He put his foot on a large cooler and rocked it with his foot. Somehow he didn't think he'd find grape Nehi inside. A tall, long-haired blond boy crept back into the shadows. "Hold up," Rafe commanded. "Get back where I can see you."

The boy stiffened and stepped back toward the group that had congregated next to the fire.

"Take a seat."

Their bodies were jerky and unsure. They stared at one another.

"On the ground."

Their butts touched the dirt in unison.

Rafe's foot rocked the cooler again. "Give me one good reason not to call your parents."

He didn't need to waste his time opening the cooler. Their shocked faces in the firelight confirmed his suspicions. Rafe took a headcount. There were nine in all—five boys and four girls. He guessed their ages to be fifteen, maybe sixteen .One thing he knew for sure—Aiden wasn't old enough to drive. But this was private property. Most teens who lived on a farm drove as early as ten. He'd been driving the ranch when he was eleven. But Aiden had forgotten one thing—this was his land now. Not that he gave a damn about the boy driving on his land—and he'd tell him that, when he was alone with him.

He liked Aiden. Understood the boy. Losing a father at a point in his life when he needed a steady hand could cause a boy to push back in rebellion. Being publicly embarrassed would be the ultimate punishment, but that wasn't Rafe's intention.

Aiden knew who he was and was most assuredly shitting bricks—that was enough for Rafe. "Who drove the truck?"

Rafe waited, wondering what type of boy Tom Ryan had raised.

"I did." Aiden stood up and shoved his hands in his pockets. His head swung, and for an instant Rafe caught sight of his eyes narrowing in on him.

"Grab two of your buddies, and haul this cooler out of here."

"You gonna let us keep it?" one boy piped up.

"You wanna tell me who bought it?"

His mouth clamped shut.

"Load it up, and dump the beer in the woods. I want the empty containers left in the cooler." Kids were slick. They had heavy coats and deep pockets. If he let them go. And that was a big if, until he did a few sobriety tests of his own. He wanted to make damn sure when he dropped them home they weren't packing a roadie to finish in the back of his truck, and with nine including Aiden, that was the best he could do as a chauffeur. But first the forest fire Aiden and his friend had set needed to be extinguished, along with returning Daniel's truck.

Two hours later, Rafe dropped the last one off—a petite blonde Aiden had been stealing glances at while they rode in the backseat. She hopped out. "Thanks, Mr. Langston." She glanced nervously toward her house. "For not telling my parents."

Rafe nodded. "Go on. We'll wait till you get in."

"Bye, Aiden. See ya Monday."

"Later." Aiden pushed back into the seat and shut the door.

"Up front."

Aiden moaned. "Why?"

"We need to talk."

Aiden came around to the passenger door and got in. He slumped against the door and crossed his arms.

Rafe put the truck in Drive and headed back toward Grace. "Your grandfather know you used his truck?"

"I can drive on the farm."

"How'd the others get there?"

"They got rides."

"And the beer?"

Silence.

"You know it's against the law to drink and drive? Not to mention you're underage."

Aiden only shrugged. "I didn't even get a chance to take a sip."

Rafe pulled off the road and slammed the truck into Park. He reached over and clamped a hand on Aiden's shoulder. "You think it's a game? You think your mom would think it's funny?"

Aiden's head swung, and he met Rafe's gaze with belligerent, glistening eyes. "She's a liar." He dropped back in the seat. "I saw you bring her home last night, not Aunt Jo."

Shit.

"You screwing my mom?"

Rafe's hand fell away, and he clenched the steering wheel. "Don't talk about your mother like that."

"What's it matter?"

"Cut her some slack, Aiden. She's been through—"

"Yeah, right."

Rafe slumped against the window. "I brought your mother home last night. I ran into her in town and gave her a ride."

"How come you were coming from your house?"

Damn it. The kid had X-ray vision.

"I forgot something."

"Your shirt. She was wearing that, too."

"Aiden, your mother was cold."

"That's so lame."

There was no way of salvaging this conversation. He couldn't tell Aiden the truth. "How do you feel about me seeing your mom?"

His eyes drilled into Rafe. "You her *boyfriend* now?"

How in the hell had this gone to shit so fast? "I like your mom. If I wanted to date her, I'd want to know you're okay with it."

Aiden shrugged. "She can do what she wants."

"That's not what I'm asking."

"I thought you said you'd be coming around anyway."

He'd forgotten about Roscoe. Aiden wanted to play the tough guy, but what he really needed he'd lost forever. "I've been busy settling in. But my calendar's free. How about Sunday I come by and teach you and Roscoe how to track?"

Rafe pulled up to the house. Daniel's truck sat strategically parked where Aiden had found it before his joyride, but at close to eight o'clock and well past dinner, Bren's truck was missing. "I'll see you in." Rafe popped his door open.

Aiden nodded and glanced up through the swath of hair hanging across one eye. He grabbed the door handle and hesitated. "I think she likes you, too," he said in a quiet voice before hopping down.

CHAPTER ELEVEN

BREN SAGGED AS SHE TRUDGED UP THE BACK STEPS. IT WAS CLOSE to eight thirty. She was cold and hungry. She'd missed dinner after Jeremy called with an emergency. But the horse would survive, and that made her smile. She stepped into the kitchen. "Dad?"

"We held dinner for you."

"You didn't—"

"I gave Finn a snack, and Aiden and Rafe just came in."

"Together?"

Roscoe padded into the kitchen with his droopy ears and sad face. Bren reached out and gave him a pat. "Hey, boy."

Her father nodded at the dog. "They were out in the barn getting supplies ready for Sunday to teach Roscoe to track."

"Rafe's still here?"

He nodded back toward the family room. "In with Finn. They're playing checkers." He stirred the skillet, and the aroma of homemade chili thickened the air. "Why don't you wash up? Supper will be ready in twenty minutes."

She kissed her father's rosy cheek. "Thanks. I'm starving."

Bren peeked into the family room, and her heart warmed. Rafe was on his side on the floor, his long, muscled legs clad in faded jeans. But it was the boyish grin lining his face that drew her to him as he contemplated his next move. Finn sat poised with his counter. Aiden sat in the recliner, his face aglow with his laptop—Facebook, another creation she could live without.

Finn slapped his cheeks with both hands and then squeezed them, his lips resembling a goldfish as Rafe jumped several of his checkers.

"King me," Rafe said.

"You beat me," Finn whined.

"Remind me next time to teach you my secret." He tousled Finn's fair head, stood up, and stretched. He smiled at her, and she went all gooey inside.

"Hi, Mom." Finn beamed up at her.

"Hi, sweetie." Then to Rafe, "Hey."

He grinned and started toward her. "Okay if I stay for dinner?" He glanced back at Aiden, who watched them over his computer screen, before giving her his full attention. "We need to talk."

He brushed her arm with his long fingers and slid his hand down to hers and held it.

Bren blushed. "What are you—"

"Outside." He pulled her toward the front door.

She tried to pull her hand away. Aiden and Finn were watching them intently. Bren peered over her shoulder at her boys before Rafe tugged her around the corner wall. "You two need to wash up," she called back to them. "Dinner's almost ready."

Rafe opened the door and then held the screen door for her, her hand tightly clamped in his.

"Let—" She snapped her mouth shut when the boys came charging by to use the bathroom. She stepped out onto the porch, yanked her hand away, and wrapped her arms around herself. "What the hell's wrong with you? You're going to give them the wrong impression."

"Too late." Rafe leaned along the railing.

Bren moved toward him and narrowed in. "What are you talking about?"

"Aiden saw me bring you home last night."

"So?"

"You were wearing my shirt."

"Oh." Bren dropped into the rocking chair in front of him. "That's bad."

"Yep."

She leaned over and peered up at him. "What'd you tell him?"

"I sure as hell couldn't tell him the truth." Those green eyes twinkled, and he gave her a wicked smile.

Bren stood up and moved toward him, outrage quickly tempting her tongue. "You didn't?"

Rafe shrugged and grabbed her hand.

She wanted to do as she'd done before, but the warmth of his hand and that damn thumb of his brushing her knuckles made it hard to concentrate.

"Don't be mad, doll face."

Bren ripped her hand from his grasp. "Stop calling me that."

"Makes you mad," he said.

Rafe enjoyed setting her off. In some twisted way, he liked looking for reasons to spar with her.

"Tell me what I need to know."

"I'm officially your boyfriend."

Bren's hand flew to her mouth, and she began to laugh. "Seriously. Rafe Langston couldn't come up with a better lie?"

"He caught me off guard."

"How do you propose we go about dating?"

"Look, just be nice to me. Sit down next to me at dinner."

She could do that. But she wasn't holding his hand. Or . . . She tingled inside again when she thought back to last night when he was getting ready to kiss her. "We're not—"

"Hell no. I like blondes. Remember?"

Bren raised her hand to punch him.

He grabbed her arm and pulled her close. "Be nice, darlin'. This is a good thing. You want to stake out Connelly's place. You're not going without me. Now we have an excuse why we're spending time together."

He had her within inches of him. His arm slipping around her waist, he leaned in against her ear and whispered, "They're watching."

Bren stiffened.

"You need to do a better job fooling your boys, otherwise Aiden's going to question what's really going on with his mother."

Bren cautiously threaded her arms around Rafe's neck and whispered back in his ear, "Get cute, and I'll nail you where it counts."

The roughened stubble along his jaw rubbed up against her cheek. "I'm countin' on it, darlin'."

That Texas drawl had her legs wanting to fold like an unsteady card table. She only hoped their little charade wouldn't topple like a house of cards, because the longer she allowed herself to be tangled up with this cattle rancher who had decided Bren Ryan was his charity case, the more she was beginning to like having him around.

And that couldn't happen.

CHAPTER TWELVE

B REN HAD FRETTED ALL WEEK ABOUT TONIGHT. MOST OF ALL, SHE wanted to nail Wes. But the other part of her—the soft, emotional woman part—regretted the guise of a date to get her out past midnight without raising suspicion.

She didn't like lying to her family. Her boys liked Rafe. Giving them the impression Rafe could become a permanent presence added another layer of difficulty when it came time to reverting back to just neighbors.

Rafe tucked her inside the passenger side of his black pickup. His hand brushing her knee before he shut the door made her catch her breath. But then she inhaled, and the woodsy scent of his aftershave lingering inside the cab had her question what the hell she was doing.

This isn't real.

But the man was, and he'd fallen into his part with ease as he sat down next to her, his arm resting casually along the back of her headrest. "Where to, darlin'?"

He'd trimmed his hair since she'd last seen him and was neatly put together in a brown corduroy blazer, crisp, white button-down shirt, and new jeans. She could almost be tricked into believing he'd done it all for her.

"You don't have to take me to dinner." Bren waved at her father and the boys on the front porch step and placed her leather jacket in the back seat. "They bought it."

"You're my girl." He smiled easily and put his truck in Drive.

The words made her stomach dip. Did he even have a clue how those three words he so casually tossed off his lips affected her? "Stop being cute. Remember where cute will get you."

He winced. "I forgot you have a mean streak." When he stopped at the end of Grace's driveway, their gazes connected. Those damn green eyes lingered on her face. "You look real nice."

"Keep your eyes on the road, cowboy." She nodded toward the windshield, stifling a chuckle. If he only knew how many outfits she'd cast aside before she settled on her brown suede skirt and cream-colored off-the-shoulder sweater! But knowing she'd be dealing with Wes later, she'd given up her heels for tonight and coordinated her outfit with a pair of brown flat-bottom suede boots. He'd probably approve of her sensibility.

"Yes, ma'am." He stopped smiling and concentrated on driving. "I'm serious about dinner. I'm starving."

"So what do cowboys eat?"

He gave her a sideways glance. "You're a smart girl."

"There's a Longhorn Steakhouse in Hagerstown."

"We have time for that?"

Oh yeah. There was no way she'd step foot in the local grill tucked off Main Street toting lover boy. "They're not meeting until two in the morning." She glanced at the dashboard clock. "It's only eight thirty." She cocked her head. "Why did you insist on coming so early?"

"How would it look if I picked you up at midnight?"

She relaxed against the seat, his point taken. "Take 70. It's thirty minutes from here."

Rafe guided her toward their booth, his hand warm and low against her back. He took the seat across from her.

Bren leaned over the table. "No one knows us here. You can stop with the touchy-feely stuff."

Rafe raised his hands. "Whoa, doll face. I'm just playing my part."

"Not funny," she said through clenched teeth.

The manager came by and placed two glasses of ice water on their table. "Your waitress will be with you in a minute." He placed two menus down and walked away.

"Loosen up. I was only kidding."

All fun and games for Mr. Langston. But tonight was way too important for kidding around. "Why don't you just figure out what you want to eat and stop trying to be my date. Okay?"

The humor on his face faded, and he grabbed for the menu and buried his head behind it.

Bren sipped her water. She couldn't think of eating. She had her friends at animal control on red alert for tonight. Law enforcement—her law enforcement—was still in the dark, until she actually needed him. If Kevin knew, she wouldn't have gotten this far.

She toyed with the menu and decided on a house salad and took another sip of water.

A tall blonde waitress approached their table. "Hi, my name's Belinda, and I'll be your server."

Bren choked on her water, and Rafe smiled over his menu. "You ready, honey?"

Rafe slid inside his truck and started the engine.

Bren snuggled into the collar of her leather jacket and dusted the snowflakes still perfectly formed on her skirt.

"You'll be warm in a minute."

She blew into her hands. "I forgot my gloves."

Those small but capable hands he'd acquainted himself with dropped into her lap. He could think of some inventive ways to warm her fingers. Instead, he concentrated on the road. "It's only eleven. What's the plan?"

"Sit and wait. They might show up early."

Sitting in the dark with Bren—now he was sorry he'd bought a used truck with a bench seat. There was nothing to stop him from sliding her pretty little ass next to him, except the temptation to do more than talk. Blocking those thoughts, Rafe headed up 70 and took the exit for Clear Spring.

"How much farther?"

"Right up the road. We can park at the Clear Spring Horsemen's Club. It sits across from the front entrance of Sweet Creek Stables."

"He come up with that name all by himself?"

Bren laughed. "A contradiction. Right. Makes me want to spray paint his work of art."

They came up on Wes's creation—a large sign pinned between two stone pillars, lit by landscape lights. The meandering creek on the image, hand painted in pale blue, sparkled with iridescent splendor. The stream's grassy bank included clumps of cattails. Serene. The urge to ram it with his pickup made Rafe clench the steering wheel. But he smiled to himself. "It's still early yet." He glanced over at Bren. "How good are you at keeping secrets?"

She cocked her head with disbelief. "I'm pretending to be your girlfriend. Remember?"

Her wide-eyed accusation stung. There was no way in hell he could forget a thing like that. The problem was he was finding it hard to pretend. "How could I forget?" He reached over and squeezed her bare leg just above the curve of her knee.

Her hard gaze softened, and she rolled her lips in. "Don't make me feel something for you. Because I can't."

He released her leg. The pain in her soft brown eyes made him hurt. "I was just playing with you. I didn't mean to upset—"

"I've been plenty upset. So don't worry yourself." She pointed toward the windshield. "Make the next right. We can park in the club's parking lot."

Rafe made a sharp right and pulled in.

"Park in front and pull in forward."

He chose an area where the parking lot and grass were level, giving him easy access to Route 68 if he needed to make a quick getaway. To be inconspicuous, he parked in between two cars. "This good?"

"Perfect." She nodded in front of them. "It looks pretty quiet. We'll see the trailer when it pulls in. Then I'll call my people."

Rafe laughed. "You have people?"

She cracked a smile. "A whole underground network."

"Ah." Rafe nodded and turned off the ignition. "So do you and your underground network have secret meetings?"

"Most definitely," she said with mock sincerity. "Seriously, you don't think I run the rescue myself. Grace has volunteers and a board of directors."

She didn't have to elaborate on their names. He'd made a point of checking out this nonprofit—specifically the board of directors—after he'd come to Clear Spring and found out that the man he'd been seeking by the name of Tom Ryan had been dead for nearly a year. Except he suspected, based on the ruse of a date, that Daniel Fallon and Paddy Ryan would not be among her underground network tonight. Now, the vet and his wife, he couldn't discount. They were tight with Bren.

Her teeth chattered, and she lifted her chin toward the heating vent. "We still have at least an hour. We'll freeze without the heat."

Rafe reached behind him into the back seat and grabbed the package he'd yet to open. The two porch rockers he'd planned on painting to match the forest-green swing he'd hung on the porch could wait. "You might want to zip up your coat."

"Turn the truck back on, and I won't have to."

He pulled a can from the package and handed it to her. "So, can you keep a secret or not?"

Bren gripped the can. "You're serious?"

"Whatever Bren Ryan wants, I'm here to see she gets."

"What happens if we get caught?"

"Not planning on getting caught." He nodded to the can of forest-green spray paint she gripped in her hand. "You in or not? Or you all talk?"

Bren grabbed the door handle, and Rafe reached for her arm. "Hold up. Ground rules. We cross the highway. You see any cars, we head for the woods until it's clear. Then we do this thing and head back to the truck. Once we hit the parking lot, we play it cool."

"Good plan."

Rafe released her arm and prepared to open his door. It had been a long time since he'd done anything so juvenile. But he'd be lying if he said he wasn't enjoying himself. He'd been angry for so long after he'd found out his life was a lie. He was angry with his parents—jealous of his brother Trey. But the lie that had brought him to Clear Spring, albeit a year too late, he now embraced, along with a friendship he hadn't expected in Bren.

"Hey," Bren whispered, her fingers squeezing his hand that held the other can of spray paint. "Remember what I said about feeling things for you?"

"Yeah."

"It's too late."

Before he could respond, she was out the door.

CHAPTER THIRTEEN

SHE WAS GIDDY. *DAMN IT.* WORST OF ALL, SHE COULDN'T KEEP HER inside thoughts where they belonged. If he asked her to explain, she didn't think she could. Her feelings for Rafe came at her too fast to define. But the one she could pinpoint with accuracy was friendship, and for that to happen she had to like the man. And she did—too much.

Rafe came around the truck and grabbed her hand. "Let's go."

Relieved he didn't seem interested in exploring her statement, she squeezed his strong hand, possessively covering hers, and darted across the highway. He directed her behind the enormous, brightly lit sign of Sweet Creek Stables.

They were breathing hard, more from adrenaline than anything else, when they crouched down in a thicket of landscaped hollies, the points of the leaves poking her bare skin. "Ouch."

"Shh."

"Sorry. But they're poking me." She eyed his thighs pressed against a pair of dark blue jeans. "You have pants."

"You want them?" He made a move to unbuckle his belt.

"No!"

His hand clamped down on her mouth. "We're going to get caught if you don't keep that beautiful mouth of yours shut."

Bren nodded, and he released his hand.

He leaned into her. "We do this fast. No words."

Bren frowned.

"Save it, darlin'. I'm good at reading you. Your friend the sheriff would be on your doorstep. So refrain. We can't prove Connelly's a murderer—yet."

She swallowed. That was the word she had in mind, and it shook her senses to learn just how in-tune he was to her thoughts. She moved away from him, unwilling to admit it. "Give me some credit."

"Wait here." Rafe came around the sign and picked up two large rocks that fit in the wide palm of his hand. Within seconds, breaking glass shattered the calm of night, and the sign, once illuminated, fell in darkness. He came back around and nodded. "Now."

Bren shook her can and uncapped it. Rounding the landscaped hollies, she pressed the trigger. The paint made wide strokes and crisscrosses. Determined to empty her can before Rafe, she kept her finger trained on the nozzle.

He shook his head at her and smiled as he, too, broadened his strokes. So intent on her mission, she missed the headlights cresting the hill before the turn into the club. A steely grip knocked her off her feet, and she fought to regain her balance as Rafe dragged her back behind the sign.

"That was too close."

"Do you think they saw us?" Bren squeezed the can so hard it hurt. The dark sedan passed. The metallic markings of a red-and-gold shield reflected off the door panel.

"Shit. A state boy."

Rafe held her arm in place, and they waited. But the expected U-turn never came.

"Let's get the hell out of here." He pulled her up with him. "Remember what I said. When we get to the parking lot—walk." Rafe took what remained of the spray paint and shoved it inside the waistband of his jeans.

Bren held on to his hand and flew across the double lane road. Once they reached the grass, they slowed. Their eyes connected, and they began to laugh. Rafe looked back from whence they came. "Guess ol' Wes will have some cleaning up to do."

"You are crazy, Langston." Bren breathed heavily. "But a good crazy." She reconnected with his hand, and they casually walked the rest of the way.

A group erupted from the front door of the club, their voices floating on the crisp air, and Bren stiffened.

Rafe caught her eye. "Relax. We haven't done anything wrong. Right? Just act casual."

Bren dropped her shoulders and kept a steady pace toward the truck. The group huddling under the portico cleared the front of the club where the parking lot light lit them up. She gasped.

"What?"

"It's—it's—" Her tongue stuck to the roof of her mouth. "*Wes.*"

"Where?"

She lifted up their joined hands and motioned to the five individuals moving in their direction. "There." Wes, Robert, and Susan she recognized. The other couple she didn't.

"Shit." Rafe jerked her forward. "Keep quiet." They raced to the truck, and Rafe opened the driver's-side door.

Bren pulled back. "Not the front seat. They might recognize us."

Rafe shut it and opened the back door, throwing the cans on the floor. "Get in." He hoisted her up and scrambled in behind her. His hand cleared the seat of Walmart bags, the contents clanking together as they fell to the floor. "Lie down and make room." He pointed to the back seat. His broad shoulders loomed above her before he came to rest next to her.

Bren opened her mouth, and Rafe covered it with his hand and shook his head.

She nodded and tried to control her breathing.

"They didn't see us. I'm sure." He peeked up above the window, the strong column of his neck stretching to see. "What car do they drive?"

"Either a black Chevy truck or black Mercedes."

He slipped back down. "That's good. We're not parked by one." He gave her a wry smile. "Guess the switch isn't happening tonight."

She pursed her lips.

"Darlin', don't look so disappointed. I don't think he's going to miss our paint job."

Bren perked up and then sank into the seat. "What if he catches us?"

"This truck doesn't stand out. I've seen plenty of black pickups in town."

Their voices sharpened, and Bren grabbed for Rafe. "They're close."

He lifted his head, and Bren pulled him back. "You want to get caught?"

"The windows are tinted. They can't see in."

He lay back down next to her, adjusting his body to the side. Facing Rafe, her chest, still heaving, moved up against the solidness of him. The suede skirt that usually fell above her knee rode high against her thighs, the material of his jeans tantalizingly rough against her skin. Ignoring the tingle she had come to associate with Rafe, she breathed deeply through her nose.

"Where are they?"

"What the—Robert, you pinching pennies again?" Wes's voice, a jovial taunt, had Bren listening hard.

"Dad?" Bren didn't miss the confusion in Robert's voice.

"Susan, you sure you want to marry this penny pincher?" Wes laughed as he said it.

Bren shifted and whispered into Rafe's ear. "Maybe he won't notice."

Rafe wrapped his arm around her and pulled her closer. "Stop talking. And stop squirming."

The sudden contact of Rafe's arm against the small of her back made Bren bite her lip.

"I'm sure Susan's parents appreciate a future son-in-law who pays attention to the bottom line," Robert said.

She didn't know how much more she could take. She'd gleaned enough to know that the older couple was Susan's parents. What she really wanted to know was if her and Rafe's defacing of Wes's personal property was going to get them a one-way pass to jail.

Their footsteps quickened. Or were they closer?

Rafe popped his head up. "Shit. Do any of them drive a Highlander?"

She pulled him back down. "I don't know. Why?" Bren searched his face. The grim expression told her all she needed to know. "They're parked next to us." The words no longer a question as they left her lips.

He nodded. "Don't worry. They'll be out of here in a minute."

That thought came and went in a rush.

"Son of a bitch!"

A gathering of voices gasped.

"Dad!"

The shuffle of feet passed. "Are you blind, Robert? The sign."

"Rafe?" Bren pulled on his sleeve.

He brought his face even with hers. The lights from the parking lot glanced off his face, his green eyes smiling at her.

She narrowed her eyes. "It's not funny."

"You may want to call your dad."

"Shh. They'll hear you."

Rafe glanced up. "You've got a few minutes to make that call. I don't want him to worry. I like your dad. But I have a feeling we're going to be stuck here for a while."

"Great. What are they doing now?"

"I can't be sure. But they crossed the highway. Wes is on the phone. I think he's calling the cops."

Bren pushed him away. "I'm going to murder you, Langston."

He laughed and kissed her hard and fast. "You're growing on me, too, Ryan."

"You are so damn lucky." Bren continued up the steps of what was now Rafe's home. She wagged a finger in his direction.

He hopped up on the step next to her and grabbed her finger and wrapped his hand in hers. "No. We're lucky. Your friend the sheriff did a good job pacifying Wes."

"That's only one side of him—the politician. Trust me. If Kevin had recognized your truck or knew I had anything to do with the sign, you'd have seen a whole new side to him."

They continued up the steps. Rafe's fingers loosened, and she instinctively tightened hers.

"I need to unlock the door." He gave her a curious look.

Bren released his hand quick. "Sorry. The step was loose." The board creaked beneath her feet, and she hoped he bought her excuse. But the reality only cemented what she feared—her self-imposed punishment not to love again bordered on collapse. They were becoming a pair. She smiled—a shameless pair. He had involved himself in her business willingly. Believed her when no one else would. And now she'd begun to depend on his strength, enjoy his humor, hold on to him tight. Or was she letting go—letting go of Tom?

Not ready to go there, she blocked those thoughts and concentrated on the man standing next to her.

When he'd kissed her in the truck, the contact, although brief, still lingered hot and tingly. He never made a move after that to continue to explore her mouth or her body, a true gentleman, considering their positions in the back seat. He'd only spoken to her quietly about her life with Tom and his in

Texas—the ranch he called The Brazos. Problem was, she'd grown closer to him in that hour it took Kevin to take a destruction-of-property report than if he had tried his hand at seduction. Or maybe he was covert. He'd touched her hair that had fallen across her cheek and pressed it behind her ear. He'd yanked her skirt down to keep her warm, his hand skimming against the back of her thigh. But nothing to suggest the tight quarters had heightened his awareness of her as a woman.

Rafe followed in behind her and shut the door. He didn't turn on the foyer light. She shivered, the darkness only adding to her confusion where Rafe was concerned. He tugged her back. This time she did lose her footing and fell into his broad chest.

"What did you mean when you said it's too late?"

She steadied herself and placed her hands against his shoulders. A wall of strength greeted her palms, and she pressed her fingers into his tight, muscled chest, warm beneath his brown corduroy blazer.

He remembered.

"Why did you kiss *me?*" she asked, tossing that hot potato right back in his lap.

"Because I wanted to. Because I needed to." His voice was low and rough.

She touched his lean cheek, scratchy with whiskers. "Rafe. I'm a very selfish woman. God's paying me back in spades. Tom's dead, if for no other reason than my stubbornness. I don't deserve your friendship. I don't deserve to feel, period. I shouldn't have said that to you."

He kissed her palm, his eyes closing. "Then we're a perfect match." He opened them. A hardened glint replaced the softness that had once been there. "I'm selfish, too, darlin'." He yanked her off her feet, the taut, lean muscle of his arm flexing under her bare thighs where her skirt rode up. Cradling her in his arms, he supported her weight easily.

Bren's arms clasped around his neck. "Rafe, put me down."

Holding her tight against him, he said nothing. He cleared the hallway, into the family room. The hardwood floor, shining bright under the moonlight, spilled in from the sliding glass door. He sidestepped a rugged pair of brown leather couches, then knelt down and placed her on white, thick shagged carpet between the couch and fireplace. She sank into its softness. He lay down next to her.

He swept her hair into his hand. "I lied. I'm partial to redheads." He let her hair fall through his fingers. "You're nothing like the women I'm used to."

His fingers tightened, directing her face toward his. Their lips, a breath away, made her heartbeat quicken.

"I'm afraid to ask what you're used to."

"I'm not good at sweet talk."

She shook her head. He didn't need flowery words to convince her. Her hand trembled when she raised it to his face. She stroked his roughened cheek. "I'll only hurt you. Don't make me hurt you, Rafe."

The words died when he touched his lips to hers.

She moaned against his mouth, "Please don't."

He whispered against her lips. "I won't if you don't want me to."

Those firm lips brushing up against hers, the strong yet tender drawl of his voice drove her to distraction. God, she wanted him, too. Her body trembled at the touch of his long, rough fingers. But she'd only ever known Tom's touch. Was she ready for sex with another man? What if she disappointed him?

His lips trailed heat down her neck to her bare shoulder, and she cursed herself for shedding her coat in his truck.

"Tell me what you want, darlin'." He nipped at her shoulder, and she arched her back. Her breast grazing the buttons of his shirt caused her nipples to harden. All conscious thought escaped her but one. He'd said women—lots of experienced women. Beautifully refined southern Texas women is what he meant to say—not a rough western Maryland farm girl who had a penchant for raising hell.

Bren pushed hard on his shoulder. "How many women have you had?"

His eyes widened, and he laughed. "Does it matter?"

"Yes, you stupid cowboy. It matters."

He made a move to touch her cheek, and she slapped his hand away.

"I've had only one man. Tom."

Those damn green eyes searched hers. "Tom was the love of your life. I can't compete with his memory, Bren. I know that." He leaned back on his elbows and snagged a strand of her hair between his fingers. "There have been women in my life. I won't deny it. And I wasn't comparing you to them. There is no comparison. You're going to have to trust me." He let his fingers brush her bare shoulder. "I didn't plan on this, either. I've tried like hell not to feel things for you. But it's not working."

Her honest cowboy, complete with manners, and a heart the size of . . . yes, Texas, warmed her straight through. If she didn't move away from his sexy, long-legged body, she wouldn't be able to deny him.

"I should—"

The distinct ring of her cell phone had her clamping down on her hip, searching for it. She'd had it when she came in. "Rafe, help me find my phone. It must have fallen off."

He sat up, pulling her with him, and skimmed the shag with his hand. "Got it." Sitting her down on his lap, he handed it to her.

Bren struggled to flip it open without verifying the caller. "Yeah." She gave Rafe a nod. "It's Jeremy. He was out on an emergency call and passed Wes's place."

Rafe kept an intense gaze on her.

She nodded affirmation to Rafe as she listened to Jeremy, never taking her eyes off him. "We'll be there. Ten minutes at the most." Bren slammed the phone shut.

Chapter Fourteen

Making an ass of himself hadn't been Rafe's intention. He gripped the steering wheel. Intentions be damned, he'd had a hard-on for the woman since he'd been quartered in the back seat with her. He couldn't remember not taking advantage of a good thing when it was within arm's reach. Hell, he'd had his arms around her and didn't make a move. He'd wanted to. Damn, he'd wanted to, but he couldn't get past Tom Ryan.

But when she held fast to his hand on the steps, he'd made up his mind—meddling ghost of a husband or not—he wanted her if she'd take him up on it. And he was that close, until she questioned his past loves.

He smiled. Her temper only added to all the reasons he was attracted to her. Breaking wild things came naturally. He only hoped he didn't kill her spirit when this was over.

He'd been toting her since dinner. Close to three-thirty in the morning now, and she was still energized and working her phone tree to her underground network. Her peaches-and-cream profile and that damnedest color of red hair, which she'd pulled up in a single ponytail, made her look younger than her age.

Not that she'd shared her age. It never came up. But she was thirty-five, just like him. He'd made a point of getting to know all there was about Bren Ryan once he arrived in Clear Spring. But data and numbers couldn't prepare him for or protect him from her. Lusting after another man's wife, but especially Tom Ryan's widow, was a surefire way to complicate the plan he'd set for himself.

He had no intentions of staying once this unexpected hand played itself out.

He shook his head, still strategizing. She should have been a general the way she'd organized her band of horse-loving warriors, her cell phone still glued to her ear. She shut her phone and settled back in her seat.

"What's the plan?" he asked.

"We meet at Sweet Creek's entrance. Jeremy caught the trailer going in. He's still parked, keeping an eye out."

"What about your friend the sheriff?"

She grimaced. "I'll wait until we get there. No sense spoiling all the fun."

"If your vet is right, Bren, this could get ugly quick." Rafe's lips thinned. "Think about your boys and don't escalate this thing."

She angled her body toward him. "I agreed to let you tag along. I know what I'm doing. If I don't needle the bastard a little, let him know I'm the reason they're shipping his butt off to jail, there's no point."

He cursed under his breath. Wild mustangs had nothing on this unbridled woman. He cocked his head. "Stubbornness an inherited trait?"

She made a face at him. "I warned you, Langston. It's who I am."

And he reminded himself that was why he was falling for her. Rafe parked in front of her vet's Ford pickup and turned his lights off. He reached for her arm. "Sit tight, darlin'. You want to talk to the vet, use your cell."

She stiffened and eyed his hand. "Let go of me, Rafe." She held up her phone. "I can think past my nose."

He released her, and she called the vet with the plan. Two minivans pulled up and what looked to be more than a couple of board members emptied out onto the shoulder. He counted at least twelve of them, a mix of men and women dressed for temperatures dipping below freezing.

"Tell them to get back in their vans," Rafe said.

One of her well-shaped brows arched.

Rafe threw up his hands. "Do what you want."

"Thank you." She smiled smugly.

Rafe blew out a breath and leaned against the door. He wanted to see Wes get what was coming to him. Bren's plan would incite him. He only hoped she didn't do something foolish before the sheriff got there.

He had agreed to her plan because, at the time, it made sense. Drawing out a killer was easier than searching for one. He didn't like it, but he could keep her safe. Right? Wrong—dead wrong. And that was what scared the shit out of him. She was unpredictable, and no amount of corralling her guaranteed she wouldn't dodge Rafe's efforts to keep her safe if provoked by Wes.

A dark pickup pulled up behind the two vans. Bren motioned toward it. "That's my officer friends from Washington County Animal Control."

"They carry guns?"

A thin white-haired man opened the driver's side door of the truck in question. He wore a black wool coat and carried a clipboard. The other was a plump woman who walked with a limp. That answered his question. Rafe scrubbed his face with his hands and pulled Bren around to face him. "They're not armed. No one in their right mind would issue them a gun. How far back you think your friend the sheriff is?"

Bren gasped and covered her mouth, her big brown eyes wide with . . . what?

"I forgot."

"Shit! Call him and stay in the truck." Rafe grabbed for the door, and Bren snagged his arm. "Where are you going?"

"To talk to *your* people." He motioned to the phone in her hand. "Make the call—now."

She let go and punched a number into her speed dial while Rafe searched the side pocket of the truck for his flashlight.

"That bastard!"

Bren's words brought Rafe's head up, only to catch the flash of her red hair as she slipped from the truck, her phone falling to rest on the seat.

The lights of a semi rig hauling a livestock trailer pierced the wide, dark lane leading from the winding driveway of Sweet Creek. Bren crossed in front of his truck. Rafe went for the door but stopped when the gruff voice of Sheriff Bendix sounded on Bren's phone.

Torn, Rafe remained in the truck but kept a steady eye on Bren as he grabbed the phone. "Bendix. It's Rafe Langston. Meet me ASAP at Sweet Creek Stables and bring backup." He disconnected and jumped from the truck.

The semi, moving slowly, lit up the roadway in front. People from the vans scrambled forward. Rafe broke out in a cold sweat when a slim figure with a flowing red ponytail marched out in front of the moving rig.

"Jesus. Bren, stop!"

The hiss of air brakes filled the brisk winter air, and Rafe held his breath. Too far to intercept her, he stood helpless, cursing wildly and praying to

God to protect the fool woman so he could kill her himself, if she survived.

The truck lurched and stopped several feet in front of Bren.

The driver lowered his window. "What the fuck is wrong with you? Get out of the way!" He laid on the horn.

Rafe caught up to her and swung her around. Their chests collided. They were both breathing heavily. The headlights from the truck lit them up. The growl of the semi, its driver's angry shouts, and the swarm of do-gooders converging on the scene seemed to drift away. She was alive, and he'd never been so pissed off in his life.

"That's the most asinine thing I've seen you do yet. What the hell were you thinking?"

"It's—it's a cattle trailer. The cheap bastard couldn't even spring for a horse trailer!" Her eyes locked onto his. The pain in those beautiful brown eyes pierced the tough man he thought he was, and he pulled her toward him.

"I'll see that he pays, darlin'. I promise."

She pushed against him. "I need to get them out. God knows what condition they're in."

Holding her against her will was like trying to bottle the wind. He released her, his hand trailing down her arm. Then he squeezed her hand tight and said, "We do this together."

She nodded, and he let go.

"Holy shit!" The vet ran up. "You gave me a heart attack. You were this close!" The vet squeezed two fingers together.

Bren laughed and pinched his cheek.

"Ouch." He rubbed his face and gave her a less than friendly look. "What was that for?"

"To let you know I'm alive."

"Real funny." The vet reached out to Rafe. "Jeremy Breakstone. You must be Rafe. I remember you from the auction. Glad to see she's not roaming the streets alone."

Rafe shook his hand. "Glad you're here, too." He motioned toward the double-decker cattle trailer. "I'll be surprised if they'll be able to walk out on their own."

The driver was hanging out the window yelling and cursing at them to get out of the way. Rafe clenched his teeth. The more he thought about it, the angrier he got. Cattle trailers matched the height of a horse trailer. Only difference was they had two decks, cutting the height in half. Designed for cattle that were short and stocky, the setup worked real nice, not to mention doubled your numbers. But for horses it was a pine box that didn't allow for headroom. No telling how the handlers had crammed them in. One look and a horse would have been spooked senseless.

Standing in the headlights of the cab wouldn't have been Rafe's first choice for waiting out the sheriff. But it kept the rig accounted for. And with Bren's groupies now surrounding them in the pool of bright lights, their animated chatter creating a hubbub of dissension toward Wes, it seemed a good time to pull the celebrity from their midst. Especially since the loudmouth driver, not liking the odds, had withdrawn into the cab with his companion and raised his window back up.

The plump officer from Animal Control rushed up. "Bren. My God—you almost got run over!" She touched Bren's shoulder like she was seeing a ghost.

"Close call." Bren smiled and motioned to the large pockets of the woman's coat. "Ellie, you bring a camera? I need to document this."

Ellie pulled out a digital camera. "You know what we need, right?"

Bren took the camera. "Oh, yeah." She'd done enough seizures, she could do them sleepwalking. She glanced over Ellie's head, the other officer moving toward them, clipping a badge to his coat. "Rob. You going to give authority to open the trailer?"

"You betcha. But I'd feel a heckuva lot better if we had law enforcement give us some backup."

Rafe stepped forward. "Sheriff's on his way."

The old man's face crinkled in question. Rafe reached out his hand. "Name's Rafe Langston. I'm a friend of Bren's."

Rafe shook the frail, bony hand of the older man. "Nice to meet ya. Rob Peterson, officer with Washington County Animal Control."

Bren slipped away and headed toward the driver's side of the cab. Rafe let go of Rob's hand and dodged Bren, blocking her path. "Hey, what are you doing?"

"You heard Ellie. I'm taking pictures." She glanced above to the driver's window and snapped a picture.

The window went down and a wad of chewing tobacco was spat out, missing them by inches. "Do it again, and I'll smash that fucking camera."

Rob walked up, his pencil neck craning up toward the driver. "Officer Peterson, Washington County Animal Control. I'm ordering you to open the trailer under Maryland's cruel and inhumane transport of horses or animals law."

The driver with a heavy, dark beard and dirty-yellow Steelers cap ignored Rob's order and keyed up a two-way radio. "We have a situation here, boss."

Rafe strained to hear the conversation, but the driver closed the window. It didn't matter. He knew damn well who the boss of this operation was. What he knew of Wes Connelly told him it wouldn't be long before he made his entrance. And when he found out "Red" was behind it . . .

Bren stepped up on the running board of the truck and banged on the window. The window came down halfway. "Get off my truck," the driver yelled down.

"Tell asshole that Bren Ryan's waiting for him." She shivered and crossed her arms, hugging her leather jacket to her.

Shit. Rafe moved past the small group and looped his fingers inside the waistband of her skirt. Stumbling back, he caught her around the middle and hauled her off to the side. "Another stunt like that, Red, and I'm carrying you out of here kicking and screaming."

She beaded in on him and took a huge breath through her nose. "This is my fight, Rafe. No one else's." She pointed her finger toward the brick mansion, once dark in slumber, now awake and brightly lit several hundred yards from where they stood. "That bastard killed Tom, and he's going to—"

The crackle of stones alerted them to the darkened driveway behind the trailer, a halo of soft light heralding Wes's approach. Sirens whooped in the distance, and Rafe pulled her farther away from the driveway. "Behave yourself or your friend the sheriff will have no choice but to lock your pretty little ass up."

Chapter Fifteen

Her childhood friend barreled toward her. Sporting a tough military haircut, dressed in his dark blue, bulky patrol jacket, starched white uniform shirt and dark pants, his badge glinted against the lights of the cattle truck's cab.

Bren didn't like how Kevin Bendix, when he was in sheriff mode, looked at her. Caught between the blinding headlights of Wes's pickup angled behind the trailer and the swirl of the patrol car's emergency lights, flickering eerie shades of red and blue—"fugitive" came to Bren's mind.

When Kevin reached her, there was not a glimmer of friend, only eyes as penetrating as a full-blown X-ray, looking at her like *she* was guilty.

"Nice night," Bren said, hoping levity would lighten his mood.

"Cut the crap, Bren." He frowned at her. "What am I walking into?"

Bren opened her mouth, and Kevin held up his hand.

"Short and sweet."

She put her hands on her hips. "Wes, the piece of—"

The door to Wes's pickup swung open, and Bren smiled with malice. Looked like she could tell the murdering bastard herself what she thought of him.

Wes leaped from the truck, his usual tidy mass of gray hair an unruly nest. "Don't just stand there, Bendix. Arrest her!"

The ridiculousness of his statement made her laugh.

Wes turned on her and sneered. "Go ahead and laugh, girl. But you're on private property."

Barely. And if she was correct, the county owned fifteen feet from the shoulder. He had nothing on her.

"You're an idiot. The only one going to jail tonight is you." Bren held up her camera. "Say cheese, asshole." She snapped off a shot and bit down on her tongue when Wes's hand guarded against another click of her camera, and he stumbled.

Finding his footing, he came at her. "I'm going to kill you, bitch."

Come into my parlor, said the spider to the fly. Bren smiled inwardly.

Kevin grabbed Wes's arm, pinning it behind his back.

Wes hollered, and then scowled at Kevin. "I'll have your badge, Bendix."

Kevin leaned in against Wes. "Settle down, Connelly. Or I'm cuffing you." He peered over Bren's head. "Banniker and Smith." The two sheriff deputies, who had just exited their patrol cars, nodded and plowed through the crowd. Wes continued to struggle, and Kevin twisted his arm higher. "You going to behave?"

Wes grunted in the affirmative.

Kevin let him go and shoved him off toward one of his deputies. "Get his statement."

Kevin grabbed Bren's arm and steered her toward Sweet Creek's darkened sign. "I'm trying like hell not to haul you off to jail." He glanced at the sign now scribbled with dark sweeps of paint and whispered, "I ignored Rafe's truck earlier. Figured you two were holed up in the back seat laughing your asses off while I took that damn report." His grip tightened. "But if you don't give me straight answers. I'm pulling that report out of deep-six and charging you both."

Bren pulled away and rubbed her arm. "Do I need to do your job? Pick a violation." Bren pointed to the trailer. "It's overweight, overloaded. USDOT would have a field day, not to mention the obvious. He's using a cattle trailer."

Kevin turned toward the trailer, his profile hardened. He grabbed his flashlight and motioned toward Bren. "Bring that camera."

Bren fell in step.

Kevin stopped at the driver's door of the cab and called up to the driver. "I want to see your papers." He waited until dirty, callused fingers handed them out the window. Kevin glanced at them before shoving them in his waistband. He continued down the side of the rig, snorts and whinnies growing louder the closer they got to the double-decker trailer. He flashed his light between the metal slats, and Bren's heart sagged when several pairs of big frightened eyes glowed back from the darkness. Kevin shook his head. "Christ."

She tugged on his arm. "I need to get them out."

He nodded, his jaw tense. "Get Peterson up here, I want this documented."

She turned to leave and came up short when Kevin grabbed her arm. "If the papers are accurate, there are twenty-three horses. The way they're sandwiched in there, it's hard to say how many are still alive." He looked around. "You knew, didn't you?" He looked her up one way and down the other, his expression grim. "You can give me details later. For now, it makes sense you handle this case on the abuse side. Get Breakstone up here and as many hands as you have. You're going to need trailers—a lot of them."

Bren shook her head. She'd had trailers on standby. But after what the horses had been through . . . "No way. I can't do that."

"What?"

"They're frightened. And I don't want more injuries."

Kevin took a step back and pushed his Stetson up with his thumb. "How you going to move twenty-three freaking horses without trailers?"

Rafe's long fingers pressed into her lower back. "We can lead them. Grace is only a mile behind Connelly's place. We cut a hole in the fence and feed them through."

Kevin scratched his head and mumbled something derogatory with "cowboy" tacked on the end. He glanced back at the group she'd assembled and frowned. "Wes isn't going to give permission to cross his land."

"I will."

The group turned.

Robert Connelly, backlit from a beam of light from one of the patrol cars, stood with his hands on his hips, looking like an avenging angel.

Rafe couldn't deny that Wes Connelly's predicament amused him. The put-together Connelly fell short of his mark tonight. Red obviously had awakened him. He could pass for the belligerent town drunk with his tall-framed body bent over the hood of the deputy's squad car, legs spread apart, cursing lavishly. It took the three sheriff's men, including Bendix, to cuff him and corral his miserable ass in the back seat.

The smirk on Bren's face after the younger Connelly retired for the night, leaving Wes to the mercy of the county jail, was a definite concern for Rafe. He couldn't argue her strategy. It damn well worked. If she was right and Wes had killed Tom, she would be next. Any woman in the same circumstance . . . He shook his head. Bren wasn't any woman.

He smiled at that and concentrated on the woman who was going to snatch his heart and keep it when he returned to Texas. Now sandwiched in the front of the cattle trailer, Bren, down on all fours, held a mare's head and glanced at Rafe while he tightened his hold on the mare's hindquarters.

When they had unloaded the horses, the animals were slick with nervous sweat, tails thrashing. Most had suffered abrasions but were capable of walking out on their own with assistance, except for one.

They'd found her down in the front, with both front legs broken. The old girl had been trying, without success to right herself. Exhausted, she lay on her side, with her head against the metal wall of the trailer, her nostrils flaring.

Since the horse was too heavy and awkwardly placed, they came to the conclusion it was best to deal with the situation inside the trailer. There was no need to make it an even bigger spectacle in front of Bren's boys and the volunteers who were currently, with the help of Daniel Fallon and Paddy Ryan, tethering the horses together.

Rafe smiled to himself. Tom had raised some great boys with Bren. Straight out of a dead sleep, they had dressed, saddled Grace's horses, and come willingly to help lead the horses now in Grace's care. Damn if they weren't crowding his heart, too.

"Hold her steady." Bren's voice cracked, and she turned her head, wiping her cheek on the sleeve of her leather jacket. "Oh my God—I might have caused this, running in front of the rig!"

Rafe's gut clenched. Her pain, somehow, had become his. No other woman had that kind of effect on him. And damned if this one wasn't burrowing into his heart. And the hell of it was, he wasn't doing much to stop it. Tonight, he'd even encouraged it. Good thing she had a jealous streak, otherwise he'd have taken her on the shag carpet and to hell with being a gentleman.

"You didn't, darlin'." No way was he telling Bren the truth. Wes's men had given him up. The mare had slipped when they'd loaded her in, her legs ending outside the slats of the truck. Wes refused to unload it. He'd ordered them to break her legs and shove them back in.

Jeremy knelt down next to Bren. "You know this is only going to calm her down."

Bren nodded. She caressed the mare's face. "Easy, girl. Relax." She continued to stroke the mare, whose wide, frightened eyes were intent on Bren's face.

Jeremy plunged the needle in. "She'll start to relax in a few minutes." He massaged the puncture spot with his fingers and angled his head toward Bren. "I don't have enough for a full dose. I used it tonight on the last call." He frowned. "I can run back to the clinic and do this the right way. It will take me about forty minutes round-trip."

Bren shook her head. "That's too long."

Jeremy scrubbed his face hard. "Damn it. I'm kicking myself." He pushed up and rubbed his back. "Watch her. I'll find Bendix. She should be fine until I get back."

Rafe clenched his teeth. Had he known the fate of the mare before Wes's hasty departure, he'd have given him a good Bible lesson—an eye for an eye. Seemed only right that son of a bitch Wes should suffer the same consequences.

The mare's muscles relaxed, and Rafe, his long legs uncomfortably bent, stooped inside the trailer. He moved to Bren and touched the slender nape of her neck. "How you doing, champ?"

She lifted her head toward him. The battery-powered work light Jeremy had erected in the corner of the trailer lit up her pretty face, wet from tears. "He's a bastard."

He kneaded her neck. "I know. I've come across some mean sons of bitches. But Connelly's a rare breed."

Bren sniffed. "I want to put a bullet in his head." She frowned. "That's what it's come to, Rafe."

"Think smarter, Bren. We'll get him. You got what you want. Sheriff didn't miss his threat toward you. No one did." He pulled her head up against his and whispered, "The thing of it is, I wasn't thinking too clearly when I agreed to your plan. Hell, half the time, when I'm with you, I'm not thinking clearly."

Bren pulled away, her cheeks flushed with anger. "I didn't ask you to be a part of it. Remember?" She shook her head. "The problem with you, Rafe Langston, is you've stuck your nose in something that doesn't concern you at all." Her expression turned thoughtful before her eyes flashed. "Why are you here?" She sat back on her haunches and stared at him. "I don't understand. Why this town? My farm? My fight? It's not yours, you know, and I don't need your take or your cold feet distracting me. I'm going through with it." She gave him her back.

"Bren—"

She swung back. A set of stubborn brown eyes locked onto his. "In or out. Decide, cowboy."

Whoever said only opposites attract didn't know diddly. "You're a royal pain in the ass, Red." His gaze hardened. "Problem is, we're too much alike. I'm not walking away from this thing. Not with you in the middle." He tugged on a loose strand of her hair. "You have the damnedest color hair. I should have known to keep my distance from you."

The frown lines around her pouty mouth lessened. He was sorely tempted to steal a kiss and see her reaction. The thought made his cock swell, and he cursed this redhead who had him panting after something, or rather someone, he knew damn well wasn't his for the taking.

The door of the trailer swung back, and Jeremy and Bendix crested the top deck.

"How we doing?" Jeremy asked.

"She hasn't moved," Bren said.

"Good." Jeremy slid down the ramp and checked the mare's heartbeat. "She should be good. Let's get this over with."

Bendix followed and unholstered his gun. "Get back." He eyed Bren. "That includes you."

Bren adjusted herself but refused to move away. "You're a marksman. I'm staying put."

Bendix rolled his eyes, and then nodded over her head to Rafe, his point understood. Bendix leveled his gun at the mare's head. The audible click, Rafe's signal, he pulled Bren into his arms and yanked her against him. She clung to him. Her body stiffened when the single bullet exploded. The sound, more like a cannon, reverberated off the metal walls of the trailer.

Rafe held her tight. He was kidding himself if he wasn't deriving his own kind of comfort from this wisp of a woman in his arms. Tough cowboy or not, he recognized that pinch in the back of his eyes.

She was wrong. This was very much his business. She was his business, and it didn't please him in the least. Becoming emotionally attached to her and her boys had never been a consideration. And that weighed heavily, because this family had seen their share of sadness. Adding to it tore him apart. But leaving this one to her own devices could get her killed. He would find a way to walk away from her when this was over. He had to walk away. But death wasn't going to swallow her up. That he damn well couldn't live with.

CHAPTER SIXTEEN

Early morning wisps of fog floated above the cornfields. The sun, a soft, golden glow, emerging in the east above Bear Pond Mountain, reminded Bren she hadn't slept in over twenty-four hours.

Trading her skirt and the thin leather jacket for a pair of jeans and her bulky barn coat her father brought from the house, she was reasonably warm considering the temperature. Snuggling into the quilting of her coat, sitting in the saddle, she relaxed against the gentle sway of her horse Smiley.

She patted his side. This thing with her and Wes had started twenty-three years ago with this horse—her horse. He'd been slated for the same fate as the horses last night. Now in his twilight years, he'd become more than just a horse. He'd been the catalyst for Daniel and Dee Fallon to establish Grace.

Bren leaned forward and nuzzled the side of his head. "I love you, old boy." He pressed his head to hers and blew through his nose, his quiet, contented way of replying.

The volunteers continued to drive the horses across Connelly land. Bren hadn't been sure which way Robert would side. She guessed neither was Wes until Robert's icy departure had left him to wonder where exactly he'd be spending the weekend.

After what she'd been through with the mare, she was half-tempted to steal Kevin's gun and shoot Wes and put herself out of *her* misery. Now, hours later, she struggled to keep her eyes open in what Finn had decided, after conferring with Rafe, was his very first cattle drive. Not that they were driving one single head of cattle. With Aiden and Paddy in the lead, they were a ragtag group of riders and tethered horses, exhausted and beat to the ground as they made their way toward Grace and its pastures.

The creak of the worn saddle and Finn's sweet voice quizzing Rafe about his life in Texas lulled Bren. The two rode next to her, Rafe on Bart, a tall black gelding with Finn sitting in front, his small body slumped against Rafe's chest, his soft, white neck craning up to see Rafe's face when he answered the myriad questions Finn fired up at him.

The fence separating Sweet Creek and Grace emerged from the fog looking better than any Emerald City Bren had ever seen. She ignored the gritty feel to her eyes. With twenty-two new additions to Grace, it would be hours before she could consider a catnap. Wes's arrest was only the beginning. If she wanted him to be prosecuted, she needed to make damn sure they had a solid case. More photos would be needed and a formal assessment of the horses' conditions documented before her team reached out to other rescues in the area that would be able to help. As much as she'd like to keep them all, the burden of having a total of thirty-four horses was too great for their rescue.

Bren glanced over at Rafe, tall and rugged—every bit the cowboy. "Is he asleep?"

Rafe angled his head to the side to see Finn's face. He nodded. "His eyes are closed."

"He's a chatterbox."

Rafe bent down to look at Finn again and smiled. "He's great. So if you're apologizing—don't."

"Nope. I think he's great, too."

"Something bothering you?" His dark brows furrowed over a pair of sharp green eyes.

He was getting too good at figuring her out, and she was lousy at hiding her feelings. They always came out in her expressions. "He likes you, too."

"Is that a bad thing?"

"I don't want him getting too attached."

She had a sinking feeling this cowboy wouldn't remain in Clear Spring forever. And the really funny thing was it didn't matter who bought the other half of Grace if he did leave. She was more concerned about his departure from her boys' life—and hers.

Bren slowed her horse. "Whoa." They came up on the fence, and Aiden and Paddy hopped off their horses. With wire cutters, they began snipping at the wire and pulling it from the ground in places where it dug into the earth.

Rafe pulled up closer, his expression less strained. No doubt relieved she hadn't pushed the issue. He nodded toward her father-in-law. "So what's his story?"

"Paddy?"

"He's Tom's father, right?"

Bren's shoulders slumped. With all that had been going on in her life, she'd had little time to check on him. A pang of guilt surfaced. Again, Bren wrapped up in her own struggles. Yet when she had called him at three in the morning, there had never been any question that he would come.

"He took Tom's death hard. He was his only son."

"No other children?"

Remembering the story of how Tom came into the world, Bren shook her head sadly. "No. Tom was his only child."

"His. You make it sound like the man bore his son himself."

Bren gave him a sideways glance. "Now that is a ridiculous statement."

He laughed. "Just trying to understand all the players is all."

"Is all, huh?" She raised a curious brow. "Patrick and Pamela Ryan had one son. There were no more children because Pamela Ryan died in child-birth. Tom was all he had. He loved him, raised him, and mourned his son's passing. And like me, he'll never get over what happened to Tom."

Rafe's curious green eyes hardened, and for a moment, something . . . anger? The rough planes of his unshaven face tightened before he quickly turned away, burning a gaze into Paddy's back as her father-in-law, with the help of Aiden, cleared a path for them to enter.

The group moved forward, and Bren nudged Smiley, her companion still rooted behind her. She reined Smiley in and turned him about, position-ing herself in front of Rafe. "Hey, cowboy." She lifted her face to him. His expression was more relaxed, his eyes fixed on nothing in particular. She angled Smiley up so that she was next to Bart and squeezed Rafe's arm. "Hey, you okay?"

His nostrils flared when he took a deep breath. He turned and gave her a quick smile. "Just fine, darlin'. Nothing a little sleep won't cure." He nod-ded for her to go on.

Bren cleared the fence, and the tension in her shoulders subsided at the soft thud of hooves coming up behind her. Aiden and Paddy's horses were tied off on either side of the fence. The two stood back, prepared to mend it once Rafe cleared the opening.

By noon every horse had been checked by Jeremy. With limited space, the ones healthy enough were released to roam the pasture. Those under Jeremy's care were placed in stalls. Charts listing their condition and antibiotic schedule were attached to the stall doors, and by the end of the weekend, after half had been placed at nearby rescues, they'd be down to more manageable numbers.

Paddy slid up next to her and gave her a quick kiss on the cheek while she tended to a bay, administering eye drops. "You did good, Missy." She smiled at the name. Only Paddy called her that—had called her that since she was a wild thing, of maybe five or six, running the pastures with Tom. The Fallons and Ryans had become good friends over the years, brought together fighting the same enemy they'd fought tonight—Wes.

Paddy's brown eyes, cloudy from age, brightened. He placed his John Deere baseball cap the boys had given him for Christmas over his silver crew cut. Unlike her father, he'd managed to keep most of his hair. "It's been awhile since I've been useful."

Bren gave him a tight hug. "Not true, old man. You've always been there for me and the boys."

He pulled away, grabbed his hanky from his pocket, and blew his nose, wiping his eyes in the process. "And how are the boys doing?" He nodded through the barn doors.

Rafe stood with Finn riding piggyback while Aiden tried to entice Roscoe to sniff out a stuffed animal they were going to hide for him to track. As far as bloodhounds went, Roscoe had the classic look. Maybe it was those sad, old eyes that got him more treats then he deserved. He certainly didn't deserve a treat at the moment, considering he was rolling on his back and ignoring Aiden's commands. Perhaps there was a reason the dog was a rescue.

Bren snickered. "Rafe's a fine judge of champion bloodhounds."

Paddy laughed. "Where'd you get him?"

"Washington County pound."

He laughed again. "No, the man, not the dog."

"Texas. Wants to raise dairy cows." Bren straightened. "One Holstein is all we need. Don't know how I feel about a herd."

"Daniel filled me in about how he came to own his house."

Bren shrugged. "We're adjusting."

Paddy nodded toward the threesome. "They like him."

Her boys missed their father. Having Rafe around filled the void. "Too much, I'm afraid."

Roscoe grabbed the stuffed animal. Aiden gave chase, hollering to bring it back. Rafe's long, lanky frame shook from laughter while Finn's arms tightened around his neck, hugging him.

"Don't let it worry you." Paddy grabbed her hand, tugging her forward. "Come on. Walk me out." They cleared the barn doors, and Rafe turned. A wide grin split his handsome face and then it faded.

Paddy stopped. "I don't think he likes me much."

"Rafe?"

Paddy scratched his head. "I tried to talk to him earlier. Tell him I appreciate all he's done."

"We're all tired. I wouldn't take it personally."

"Maybe." Paddy pulled on his lower lip. "There's a look about him."

"Funny. Dad said the same thing."

Paddy's eyes narrowed. "You said he's from Texas. Whereabouts?"

"Near Dallas, he said. The town starts with a W." She cocked her head. "Why?"

Paddy shrugged. "No reason, except he *is* spending a lot of time with my grandsons—just curious."

Paddy kissed Bren on her cheek. "I'm taking this sixty-nine-year-old body home and taking a nap." He waved toward the threesome. "See y'all."

Finn slid down Rafe's back and ran toward them, hugging his grandfather. "You leaving, Paddy."

He tousled his blond head. "I'm tuckered out, bud."

Finn smiled up. "When will you be back?"

Paddy frowned at Bren.

Seeing Bren and the boys, she knew, only reminded Paddy what he didn't have—not what he still had. His expression merely confirmed that he, too, wrestled with the past, knowing full well he was letting the present pass by without a fight.

"Tell you what, Finn. How about we all get together next Saturday for dinner at my place? I'll make my homemade French fries you like so much with roast beef and gravy."

Finn pulled away, a smile tugging the corners of his mouth. "And your chocolate cake?"

Paddy glanced at Bren and grinned. "And my chocolate cake."

"Sweet," said Aiden as he ran up to the group, with Rafe's even gait closing in behind him. "Rafe invited, too?"

Bren stiffened. Aiden rarely thought of anyone but himself. Call it the curse of the teenager.

"Sure." Paddy clamped a hand on Aiden's shoulder. "I've got room for six."

Rafe said nothing as they said their good-byes to Paddy, except to pull Bren aside. "When you're done, I need to talk to you in the barn." He glanced at Paddy and the boys, then back to her. "Alone."

She eyed those fingers tightening on her arm, the strength with which he held her to that spot a little too much command and control. "Your manners suck, Mr. Langston," she whispered through clenched teeth and pulled her arm from his grip. "We'll talk, once I get the boys settled."

He strode away scowling and mumbling.

What the hell was his problem? They were all tired. If that was his complaint, he needed to mind his own business and go home.

Bren escorted her sons inside the house. "Head to the kitchen. Granddaddy's got your breakfast." Her stomach growled when they neared the open doorway of the kitchen. Her father, who had taken over the duties as cook, had come in before everyone else to make breakfast. As much as she wanted to sit down with a cup of hot tea and devour the bacon-and-egg sandwich resting on her plate, she pressed into her lower stomach to stop the gurgling. "Save some for me and Rafe."

Her father shot her a look. "You're not eating?"

"I'll be back." She kissed his rosy cheek, more from the warmth of the kitchen than irritation. "Just keep it warm. I have one more thing to take care of."

She pinned a smile on her face and walked out the kitchen and through the front door. Oh, she had one more thing to take care of. More like an attitude adjustment. She entered the barn. "Rafe."

Before her eyes could focus, a firm hand pulled her. Stumbling, she fell back against the wall inside the barn. Long fingers, rough with calluses, brushed her cheek, and her heart, beating a frantic pace, began to slow down. "You scared the shit out of me."

"What took you so long?" His voice matched his demanding green eyes, and she got mad. If it had taken her more than five minutes, she'd be surprised

She pushed against him.

He fell back a step but kept his grip on her arm.

"Why are you such an ass?" she demanded.

"I'm tired, that's all. And I'm not going to get any sleep in the near future."

Bren crossed her arms. "Go to bed. No one's stopping you."

"Is there somewhere we can sit down? Before I fall down." Light from the window high above in the eave of the roof slanted over his face. Fine lines edged the corners of his eyes. Bren realized that they both were tired, too tired to argue.

She motioned toward a door. "There's a small office here." She waved him through and followed.

He took a seat and placed his dusty cowboy boots on the old Formica desk, crossing his feet. Bren perched herself on the top of the desk and braced her hands on the edge. "Let's make this quick. Dad's got breakfast waiting."

"I won't have time to eat. There's been an issue at the ranch that's come up, and I need to tend to it."

"What issue?" Bren leaned in.

"It's nothing."

Bren tightened her grip on the desk and then hopped off. "Have a nice trip." She headed for the door and stopped dead when Rafe pulled her back and onto his lap.

"You're a pain in the ass."

Bren pushed against his chest. Broad and thick with muscle, she gave up trying to free herself. "Let me up."

"Not until you calm down and tell me why you're acting like a spoiled brat."

"You're a jerk."

He laughed at her. "Why is that?"

"We're supposed to be friends."

"We are."

"I've told you all there is to know about me. I know nothing about you, except the bare bones."

He sobered at that. "I'm sorry. I didn't think you'd—"

"You thought wrong." She crossed her arms and pinned him with her eyes. "I want to know."

Rafe's hold relaxed. "My daddy, Sawyer Langston, takes his title of rancher to extremes. My mama, her name is Laura, called while you were with Jeremy. Early this morning, Texas time, he was thrown off a colt he's been breaking."

Bren pushed against Rafe to sit up straight. "Is he all right?"

"Broken leg." Rafe shook his head. "At his age, he should have given up the title 'cowboy' long ago. But he's a hard-ass."

Bren smiled. "Apples don't—"

He shook her playfully. "Don't even say it."

"When do you leave?"

"As soon as I can pack a duffel bag. My flight leaves at five tonight."

Bren made a move to get off his lap, but his arms tightened around her. "I'm not done with you. I don't like the idea of leaving. Not now after you've stirred Wes up. I only plan on making sure he's okay and reassuring my mother. She doesn't handle adversity well."

"Rafe." She cupped his rough cheek with her hand. "They're your family."

He turned his face and pressed his firm, dry lips into her palm and kissed it. That made her tingle inside, and she pulled her hand away and slipped off his lap. Grabbing his hand, she directed him up and gave him a good solid push toward the door. If his hesitancy to make the trip stemmed from concern about her safety, he didn't need to worry.

"I'll be fine until you get back. Besides, I've got my dad and the boys to protect me from Wes."

He pulled her to him, and she braced her hands on his shoulders. His arms wrapped around her, long fingers pressing into her lower back. He bent his head, his eyes closed, and pressed his lips to hers. His kiss was tentative. After last night—no surprise. When she didn't pull away, he deepened the kiss, his tongue sliding over her teeth, caressing the inside of her mouth.

Bren dug her fingers in the back of his scalp, the natural curl of his dark locks wrapped around her fingers. The tingle he'd created deep inside her became more of an ache, and she moaned into his mouth.

He pulled away and gave her a quick kiss. "You're beautiful."

Bren left to gape at his quick retreat, took in the gleam of his green eyes and immediately became leery. She pushed him away. "What are you not telling me?"

"I asked the sheriff to check in on you while I'm gone."

"You told Kevin?" She eyed him provokingly.

"Relax, Red." He leaned casually into the doorjamb. "I only pointed out the threat Wes made earlier."

Bren rolled her eyes. "I'm surprised Kevin agreed. He thinks Wes is all talk—no action."

Rafe shrugged. "Maybe he's humoring me. But with all that's happened, it would be sheer stupidity on his part not to take Wes's threat seriously."

"Then there's no need for you to run out on your family."

He pushed off the doorjamb. "I'm not their only son. My brother Trey is there. He'll run the ranch until Dad recuperates. I've actually been glad for the time apart."

His brooding eyes spoke of something more than needing a little distance. She guessed living on a ranch at his age, with his parents, could be stifling. Of course, her living arrangements matched his. So far, having her father under the same roof was more blessing than curse. Whatever festered between him and his parents, it was a foregone conclusion Mr. Tightlips wasn't going to share it willingly, and, frankly, she was too tired to covertly—although she'd been accused of lacking in that department—drag it out of him.

She grabbed his hand. "Come on. Let's get you fed and packed."

Bren slid the barn door closed. Rafe pulled her to him and kissed the top of her head. "I don't have time to eat. Tell Daniel thanks." He took a step back, his hands resting on her hips. "Just lie low until I get back."

Oh, she would. The timing couldn't have been more precise. Monday was President's Day. Courts were closed, so Wes would be under lock and key until then. She gave Rafe a sweet smile. "When are you coming back?"

"Monday night. That gives me tonight, Sunday, and part of Monday to check on things."

Perfect. When Wes got out, she wanted to make damn sure she kept a high profile. Giving Wes every opportunity to make good on his threat meant being accessible. Clearing her calendar, or, rather, rounding up enough volunteers to cover her duties around the farm for the next week, was crucial, and her job with Jeremy was flexible.

She went up on her tiptoes, wrapped her arms around his neck, and kissed him. Darting her tongue inside his mouth, she teased him before pulling away. She nuzzled the side of his ear and whispered, "I'm going to miss not being your girlfriend."

Before he could hold her in place, she sidestepped his arms that were just catching up to her impetuous kiss. He gave her a lopsided grin. "You're a dick tease, Bren Ryan."

"Shh." She put her finger across her lips and glanced back at the house. "They'll hear you."

CHAPTER SEVENTEEN

RAFE'S TRUCK DISAPPEARED AROUND THE BEND, AND BREN CONTINued toward the house. But the purr of an engine growing louder behind her made her spin around.

She frowned at the blue-and-white patrol car slipping up the driveway. Looked like Kevin had begun his patrol checks.

He parked the car and stepped out.

Bren gave him a wide smile. "What do I owe the pleasure—"

"This isn't a social call." His blue eyes nailed her. "Wes is out on bail."

"What? I thought—"

"His lawyer knows the court commissioner. As a special favor, he agreed to come in on a Saturday."

Bren stepped back. "He's free?" The words fell in an incredulous burst from her mouth.

"As a bird."

I should tell Rafe. The thought popped into her brain of its own volition. No. She was stronger than that. Besides, his responsibility was to his family.

She eyed the only one trained to protect her. "What are you going to do about it?"

Kevin, with legs apart, hands on hips, drilled into her with his eyes. "Nothing. I told you, Wes isn't looking to settle a score with you using violence."

"I sent Wes to jail. I think a payback is in order."

"Sounds to me like you planned it, which reminds me. You owe me details."

Her legs were ready to give out. She'd been tending to the new arrivals since sunup. The noon hour was fast approaching, and she doubted Kevin would give her a reprieve. He needed her side for his report. Bren sidestepped him and hopped onto the hood of his patrol car, thankful to be off her feet.

"Hey, that's county property you just sat your ass on."

Bren laughed. "You're so stuck on yourself. I pay taxes. So it's my property, too."

Kevin's face turned red. "We're not kids anymore. Tell me how you knew about Wes."

Kevin leaned his butt against the hood, and she filled him in on her intelligence-gathering. She left out Belinda Harrington and concentrated on the pertinent facts. When she was done, he frowned and scratched his bristly hair.

"Wes is pissed as shit right now. But Wes is a businessman. You don't think he knew eventually he'd get caught red-handed? Oh, sure, he's angry it was you. But it's all part of doing business. He'll get fined in the end. But he'll be right back doing what he's always done. And you, Bren Ryan, aren't going to change it." He took a breath and studied her. "I promised Rafe I'd keep up patrols, but as far as I'm concerned you don't need it. When he gets back, I'll let him provide bodyguard service for you." He gave her a wry twist of his mouth. "He seems to enjoy being your knight."

"He is not—"

He put up his hand. "Save it." Then he grabbed her arm and slid her down from the hood. "You're done policing Wes. I'm hereby ordering you to get some sleep." He frowned. "You look like hell."

"You're full of compliments."

He laughed. "I try." He opened the car door. "I mean it. Forget Wes. I've got your back." He rolled his eyes.

Fine. She'd humor him. She didn't believe one word of his glorified speech. She could take care of herself. Besides, she wasn't alone. She had her dad and the boys home with her until Rafe got back. "I feel safe already," she said and turned to go in.

Maybe she'd spend the time researching the other issue that law enforcement seemed inept at solving and perhaps find something that would tie them to Tom's death. She stopped and gave him a lift of her brow. "Any word on that toxicology report on Sweet Prince you promised to look into?"

"Last I heard, the FBI's taking a closer look."

"What the hell?" She took a step closer. "You didn't think to mention to them they'd investigated this kind of thing before, almost thirty years ago? Or that maybe Tom's death has something to do with these horses dropping like flies? I can show them the articles."

"The FBI's quite capable of figuring out what's going on with the rash of horse deaths. Last time I looked, you weren't trained in investigations."

Kevin had his way of doing things, and she had hers. But if she didn't get off her feet, she was going to slither to the gravel drive. "We done here?"

"For now."

"Good. I'm going to bed." She turned toward the house.

"Bren?"

What now? She didn't bother facing him.

"Let the FBI do their job and stay the hell out of their way."

She wrinkled her nose and waved him off without so much as a glance and headed up the stairs. "I'll take it under advisement."

Bren headed for the steps. Kevin started his patrol car and pulled out. She cleared the front door and crossed into the kitchen, slumping into her assigned chair at the kitchen table, the egg sandwich she'd been hungry for cold and otherwise unappealing. She'd have liked to think Kevin had it all figured out. If Wes didn't kill Tom, then she was at a loss because no one she could think of had motive.

"Bren?"

She brought her head up as her father entered from the back door of the kitchen. "Hey, Dad."

He frowned. "Where's Rafe?"

"He's—"

Aiden and Finn came charging in carrying coats, hats, heavy winter socks, and two orange vests.

"Hey guys. What's with the clothes? You two need to get some rest."

They stopped and studied her, their brows knitting together.

"We're not tired. Granddaddy's taking us hunting up at the lake this weekend." Finn's eyes were bright with excitement. The camouflage coveralls he dragged behind him looked like a body, its legs sliding along the hardwood floor behind him.

Indecision tugged at the corner of Bren's mouth. They were beat, whether they'd admit it or not. But a road trip up to Deep Creek and the hunting cabin had erased any notion of sleep.

"Come on, Mom. We told you about it. We're off Monday. It's a holiday," Aiden said.

Somewhere along the way, she briefly remembered something to the effect. She really needed to do a better job keeping up on her children's social schedule.

"Guys, I don't think with all that's happened . . ."

Aiden dropped the wad of clothes he carried onto the floor and beaded in on her with disbelief. "We've been planning this. You said we could go."

"But, Aiden, you've been up all night . . ." She looked to her father for support.

He dried his hands on his apron and took a seat at the table. "Boys, I know I promised we'd go. But I don't feel it be wise under the circumstances." He patted Bren's hand. "Honey, I had every intention of canceling. It slipped my feeble mind, 'tis all. I'm not leaving you alone with—" He eyed his grandsons, wanting her to know he would not be sharing Wes's threat as he searched for an excuse. "We've got too much to do with twenty-two new additions in the barn."

"That's so lame." Aiden fell back against the kitchen wall and crossed his arms over his chest, frowning.

Bren laughed and put her head on the table. Grace survived on volunteers, and this weekend there was an abundance due to the hubbub generated by Wes's arrest. But still, the thought of being alone in the house at night made her grow cold.

Stop being a baby and let them go

"He's right." She turned her head toward her father. "I'll be fine. You'll be back on Monday. They deserve some downtime before school starts up."

"Bren, I don't think it be wise under the circumstances," he grumbled under his breath.

"Come on, Granddad, you promised," Aiden said.

Her father gave her a guarded expression and motioned her out the back door. She stood to follow, and Finn came up beside her and tugged her arm. "You gonna let us go?" How could she say no? They were not privy to Wes's threat. To them this was like any other horse seizure.

She tweaked Finn's nose. "I'll work on him." She eyed Aiden. "You have no homework?"

He shook his head. "I finished it."

She patted Finn's back. "And how about you, mister?"

"Mine's done, too."

"Okay. Finish packing." She continued toward the door and angled back to say to Aiden, "What about Roscoe?"

"He's going. We're going to work on tracking."

Even better. A mini-vacation for Mom. "You have his food packed?"

Aiden turned toward the pantry where the dog food was kept. "Getting it now."

Bren smiled. It was amazing how congenial her eldest could be when he wanted something. "I'll talk to Granddad."

She stepped out on the back porch only to be met with a pair of intent blue eyes focused on her. "Really, Bren. Of all the weekends to be alone." He scratched his balding head. "I don't feel at all good about it, you know."

He'd feel even worse if he knew the truth, but she wasn't going to spoil this weekend for them, her father included. "Dad, Wes is in jail, and I have Rafe next door."

"Speaking of which, where the devil is Rafe?" A furry gray brow shot up over his glasses.

Here came the lie. "He went home to bed."

She waited, chewing her bottom lip.

"That's understandable, I suppose."

"He's coming by for dinner later. There will be volunteers coming and going. Jeremy will be by to make his rounds, and, thanks to Rafe, Kevin's making patrol checks. I won't be alone."

His frowning face relaxed. "It does sound like there'll be plenty of people to keep an eye on the place and *you*." He pulled on his bottom lip. "But you'll call and check in with us. I'll have the boys call you before bed. Don't make me worry, then."

"I'll keep my cell on me at all times."

"I guess there's nothing to be done about it now." He hugged her tight and pulled away. "Oh, before I forget." He dug inside his pants pocket and handed her a key.

"What's this?"

"To the back door. The boys must be jiggling the lock, maybe the knob, perhaps. It was missing a screw. I couldn't find a match in my toolbox. I ended up buying a new doorknob. Not that it's a big inconvenience, but your usual house key won't work for this one until I have it rekeyed."

The boys rarely used the back door. Last time she'd checked, it was perfectly secure. A shiver trickled down her spine, and she clasped the key, the brass cold against her palm.

CHAPTER EIGHTEEN

Saturday and most of Sunday went by in a blur. Since neither her father nor Rafe were aware she was alone, she made a point of answering her cell phone without delay. Other than Roscoe taking a dip in the frigid lake by way of falling through the ice, her father was holding his own. Rafe's father, now in a cast, had been released from the hospital and was recuperating, with Rafe and his brother Trey managing the ranch with the hopes of Rafe making his scheduled flight Monday afternoon.

Now at close to midnight and with a full schedule for Monday awaiting her, Bren grabbed her laptop off the kitchen counter and flipped off the overhead light on her way up to bed. She snagged the notepad and pen off her nightstand and crawled under the covers. Clicking into her favorites, she found the website and an article she'd bookmarked last night.

Investigating the recent horse deaths that had troubled Tom was something she'd had on her list to do. She had poked around the last couple of weeks. But now she had the time, since she couldn't relax or fall asleep with Wes out on bail.

Tom's edginess with regard to the horses and then his own demise seemed too coincidental. She didn't know how they were connected or even if they were. But it needed a closer look. Especially since the last colic case in Maryland which had a sizable insurance policy had happened in Wes's stable, several weeks before the night she'd found Tom. Maybe she had it wrong. Maybe Tom's death had to do with keeping Tom quiet.

The old article popped up, and she concentrated on the screen: *An American Heiress Goes Missing.*

She made notes and continued to dig through other old articles. It had happened before—happened a lot. Show horses, jumpers, and racehorses—each insured to the hilt, all paying huge insurance premiums. As it turned out, the owners, without exception, had hired one Tommy "The Sandman" Burns. And it would seem that the heiress, for all her aristocratic breeding and wealth, had somehow gotten tangled up in a most abominable conspiracy that had made her expendable.

But if Bren were looking to pin the recent unexplained horse deaths on Burns, who'd turned government witness over thirty years ago, it would be a tough sell—a copycat killer made more sense.

Scrolling down, she hit on his method of murder—electrocution. There it was in full detail, a handmade device. He'd sliced an extension cord down the middle, leaving two strands of wire, attached a pair of alligator clips to the end of each, and when it came time to cash in, he'd attach the clips to the horse's ear and rectum and plug it into a standard wall socket.

Bren eased off the pen she held in a death grip. It was the most disgusting thing she'd ever heard of. The bastard would just step back and watch the horse drop. It was profoundly ingenious, no singe marks, and nothing to pick up in a toxicology report.

Toward the end of the page was a photo of the device. She sketched it out on the pad of paper and tore it off. Studying it, she tapped the pen to her lips and reached for her phone. She could see Kevin's eyes rolling on the other end and let the phone drop into the covers.

The FBI would know about this. They'd investigated it. Bren Ryan wouldn't be telling them anything they weren't already aware of. Lost in thought, she jumped when her phone rang. The word "Dad" lit the screen, and she took the call.

"Hey, you guys having a good time?"

"They're in brushing their teeth." His voice dropped. "You'll not believe what your youngest one did today. Shot a baby squirrel from its perch. It dropped from the tree and landed next to his feet."

"Did he cry?"

"Like a babe."

"He's his mother's child." She understood the need to hunt. But she didn't have to like it. "You guys didn't give him a hard time?"

"No. Of course not. But I'm not one for waste. We gave it to another hunter for his dinner, and we ended up with Uno's pizza."

Her father's laughter mingled with the boys' voices chattering in the background. "Here they come." His voice faded before he whispered, "It's your mother."

Finn's voice came on the line. "Mom, Granddaddy's taking us hiking tomorrow to see the falls."

"That's great, Finn. So you're having a good time?"

"The best. Here's Aiden. He wants to talk to you."

"Hey. Everything okay at home?" Aiden's voice had an unusual edge of concern.

"Sure. Why wouldn't it be?"

His voice lowered. "I heard you talking to Kevin outside the other day."

Bren grimaced. Aiden would make for a fine CIA operative. He missed nothing where she was concerned. Still, the self-absorbed teenager had hotfooted it out of Dodge, and *now* he was worried?

"I'm fine, Aiden. Enjoy your time at the lake."

"So what have you been up to?" She didn't miss his sarcasm.

"I rode Smiley today, helped the volunteers, and now I'm ready for bed." She snapped the computer shut.

"That's it?" His voice was wary.

Her hands tightened on the paper she'd torn off.

"That's it." She crumpled the paper in her hand and dropped it on the floor.

He remained silent, except for his steady breathing.

"Aiden, listen, sweetheart. If you heard Kevin's and my conversation, then you know he's keeping an eye on me." It appeared he hadn't shared his intelligence-gathering. "Did you tell Granddad?"

"No."

"I'd suggest keeping it that way. Otherwise your time will be cut short."

Again silence.

"Aiden? Are you listening?"

"Yeah."

"So we have a deal? I'll see you tomorrow sometime."

"I guess." His voice took on a sullen tone.

"If I was concerned for my safety, I'd tell Granddad."

"Okay. Deal."

Bren relaxed. "Good. Let me say goodnight to Finn and Granddad."

Her father came on, and she wrapped up the phone conversation and then cleared off the bed to sleep.

She turned off the light and settled under her covers. Staring at the darkened ceiling, she gave one last thought to The Sandman and punched her pillow. Bren's eyes fluttered shut, her body floating toward sleep.

A shrill noise woke her. *My cell phone.* Her heart regained its normal rhythm, and she grabbed her phone from the nightstand.

"Hey, what did you forget to tell me?"

The raspy breath shot cold panic through her veins. She struggled to sit up, pulling the covers with her. She didn't need to guess the name on her phone but glanced at it anyway. Tom's name glowed back at her, and she gripped the phone tighter, placing it back to her ear. "Go to hell."

No reply. Bren started to pull the phone away and hesitated. *Damn him.* "Come get me, asshole." She struggled to free herself from the blankets, her bare feet cold against the hardwood. "What's the matter? I'm giving you an open invitation." She continued toward the closet, searching for the key to Tom's gun locker bolted to the closet wall. "It's just you and me. I'm alone. Isn't that what you wanted?" Her fingers slid along the top shelf until she touched cold metal. She opened the locker. Seizing the Browning double-barreled shotgun and the box of shells, she headed back to the bed. "You're nothing but a coward."

His breathing deepened.

"Did I hurt your feelings?"

He grunted into the phone, and Bren smiled. She grabbed the box of shells and dumped them on the bed. Her fingers fumbled as she dropped them inside the barrel, slamming it shut. "I knew you were nothing but a sissy. You're not going to hurt me. You're too afraid of what I'll do to you."

He growled. Bren closed her eyes and pulled the phone away for a second then brought it back. "If you're a man, then show me what you've got." Something crashed in the background, and the phone went silent.

Shit! Sitting in the dark, the reality of what she'd asked for, and quite possibly would get, made her shiver. Dressed in cotton pajamas, she was grossly unprepared for this visitor, other than the shotgun. Bren hopped off the bed, lugging the shotgun, and headed to the closet. She grabbed jeans and a sweater, and kicked her boots with her feet toward the bed. Dropping the clothes and setting the gun down, she pulled her pajama pants down.

A loud creak made her stand stock still. *Shit!* She pulled her pants back up and grabbed the gun and sat down on the edge of the bed, pointing the gun toward the door.

Pajamas are good. She nodded to herself and slipped her bare feet inside her boots.

Almost ten minutes crept by. With the gun raised, she had a crick in her neck, and her muscles ached. She moved toward the headboard. Now supported, she leaned back and raised her legs, resting the barrel on the top of her knees. She took a deep breath and tried to relax her shoulders.

As plans went, it had been born of impulse. One of those impulsive acts that tended to backfire. Weary and not fully recovered from her all-nighter on Friday, she wanted to close her eyes. Needing support for her elbow, she adjusted her pillows and propped up her arm. She caught herself nodding off and tried to stay awake.

Bren awoke with a start. Her hand flew up to her face, the sensation of an icy finger against her cheek still radiated cold. Then she remembered the gun, no longer tucked under her arm. She scrambled to her knees, frantically searching the covers until she clasped onto the hard barrel.

He hadn't seen the shotgun.

She sat up and leveled the gun, but the darkness made it impossible to see. Her door creaked shut, and she bolted to her feet. He was here—in her house—*in her room.* Cold air drifted past her, and she trembled. Something moved to the left, and she gasped. The window ... She headed toward it. Left open, the screen, slashed and blowing, scraped against the window frame.

Heavy footsteps stomped down the steps, and she tightened her grip on the shotgun. Chasing him through the house in the dark didn't make for good odds. He could be hiding, waiting to spring. She eyed the window. Her bedroom looked over the back porch. She could clear the window and shimmy down the trellis and head him off in the front. Keeping the gun pointed ahead of her, she climbed out the window and fell on her ass with a thud when her boot slipped on a slick coating of frost. She cursed under her breath and tried to scoot forward. The roof chafed her butt until she could push off with one elbow to squat with the gun, drawing a bead on the shadows below.

She could sit here. She could freeze her ass off in the process, too. Or she could suck it up and put her foot over the edge and hope the trellis would bear her weight. She hunkered down and slid her butt across the roof, trying to ignore her skin scraped raw through her pajama bottoms. As she peered over the edge, her stomach pitched, and she pulled back. She'd climbed out her bedroom window plenty of times as a teen. Age certainly had made *her* a sissy.

Maneuvering with the gun, she turned herself around and dangled her foot over, searching for a foothold. She found it. Trying her weight, the trellis gave a little, and she grimaced. She was wasting time. If he hadn't chosen to wait her out in the house, he was making tracks away from Grace.

Ignoring the dip in her stomach, she pressed the gun between the trellis and her body, her feet searching for a firm slat, and continued her descent.

By her calculations, she had maybe a couple feet to go. She gripped the gun, leaped back, and prayed she didn't crumple to the ground. Her boots hit the mulch bed, and she stumbled backward, slamming into something rigid.

"Ugh!"

The sound came from behind her, and Bren tried to gain her footing and her escape.

Strong arms came around her and pulled her backward to the ground.

Oh God!

The fall, a hard punch to her back, sent the air from her lungs. Arms tightened, and she thrashed side to side—nothing. His face, rough and scratchy, pressed up against her cheek, his breathing labored. "What part of lie low do you not understand?"

"Rafe?"

She stopped fighting. He sat up with her, and Bren turned around, her legs straddling him. She wrapped her arms around his neck. "God—I'm so glad to see you!" Her legs and arms shook with sudden relief, and she pulled back with avid curiosity. "Why *are* you here?"

Though it was dark, the moon cast a glimmer of light in the shadows, making it possible to see him. He grinned at her. "In case you haven't figured it out, darlin', I'm crazy about you," he said in that lazy Texas drawl that did weird things to her insides. His strong arms went around her. Those long-fingered hands, callused from working his ranch, pressing so intimately into her bare skin above the waistband of her pajamas, made her go hot and tingly. When he angled his head and brought it close to hers, everything seemed to fade away, except for his lips so very close to hers. He moaned then and cursed under his breath and kissed her hard on her mouth before pulling away, making her body smolder for . . .

"What the hell are you doing climbing on the roof in your . . ." He glanced down. "Those horses on your pajamas?"

Bren's cheeks warmed, and she ignored the laughter in his voice. "Get off me, Rafe. He's in the house."

"Who?"

"Shh. Wes. He came after me," she whispered back.

He stiffened, his hands falling to rest on her knees positioned on either side of him. Bren's fingers pressed into his chest, the corded muscles resilient beneath her fingertips. To the left of him lay her shotgun. She made a move to get off him, her left hand on top of the cold barrel. The ground rose and fell swiftly, the gun sliding from her grasp.

What the hell?

Rafe was next to her, setting her on her feet, the shotgun firm in his hand. Bren reached for the shotgun and Rafe pulled it away. "No way in hell, Bren." He eyed her and then the gun. "Where'd you get it?"

"It's Tom's." She reached for it again, and he removed it from her.

"What the hell is going on? Why's Wes out of jail?"

"I'll explain later." She tried to take off, her target the front of the house, and came up short when Rafe tugged her back.

"Explain now." Rafe craned his head toward the front of the house and frowned. "Where's Daniel and the boys?"

She didn't have time for explanations. Rafe was here, and that was good. Having him close gave her courage. She didn't need the gun. She had him.

She yanked free. "He's going to get away." This time she did escape and ran toward the front porch.

But those damn cowboy boots clomped behind her, narrowing the distance, and his long fingers slid inside the waistband of her pajamas. "I'll rip 'em."

Bren stopped and flung around. "You're a jerk."

"And I bet you have a pretty little ass. So be my guest." A smile lurked around the corners of his mouth.

Nice he could find humor when she couldn't stop shaking with post-traumatic fright and maybe a little anger. "You're a grade-A ass."

"I missed you, too." He tugged her by her pants, rolling her into his arms. "Relax, Red." His eyes lingered on her face. "He's long gone by now if he's not holed up in the house."

"Then we search it."

"*We're* not doing anything." His voice carried an authoritative tone that made her spine stiffen.

She folded her arms and glared up at him. "You're not the boss of me, Rafe Langston. I'm coming." Manly of him to take her only weapon and tell her to step aside while he searched the house, except he'd forgotten one thing. "What if he doubles back, cowboy?"

For being so tough, Bren held fast to Rafe's belt, her bony knuckles digging into his side. Judging by the open front door swinging in the wind, the culprit was long gone. Rafe hit the light switch as they came in. They cleared the hall, checked the powder room and hall closet—both empty. The kitchen turned up the same, and he double checked the back door. It was locked. He moved through the family room, with Bren pressed up against his side. He focused on the steps and crept upstairs with Bren in tow. He flipped on the light to the hall, then the boys' and Daniel's bedrooms. They were orderly with beds made, which answered his earlier question—they weren't there. He checked the hall bathroom and entered the last bedroom . . . Bren's bedroom. Awkward at the prospect of crossing the threshold where Tom had made love to his wife, he hesitated.

Bren bumped into the back of him. "Why did you stop?" she whispered.

He glanced down. "You're sure he was in your room?"

She pointed ahead.

Shafts of silver light filtered through the open window. What was left of the screen scraped against the frame. The overwhelming need to protect her surfaced, both unfamiliar and uncomfortable, and he pushed it away, along with physically unlatching her hold on him. "Stay here." He gripped the shotgun and hit the light switch.

He checked the closet first, then the bathroom. He peered under the bed, but the only thing under it was a crumpled sheet of paper, which he snagged.

"What's this?" He unfolded it, got a glimpse before she took it.

"It's nothing. I had some time, so I researched the horse deaths. It's just a drawing of a device." She folded it and set it on the dresser.

Somehow he doubted it, but he didn't push. Continuing his search, he went to the window. The frost on the porch roof glimmered against the light of the moon. He leaned the gun against the wall, and shut the window, and motioned for Bren to sit on the bed.

She sat, giving him a most angelic expression.

"It's not going to work." He placed his hands on his hips and frowned.

"What?"

"That sweet turned-up nose and your big brown eyes. Where'd you ship your family off to?"

Her brows furrowed. "I didn't. They already had plans to go hunting. I forgot."

"The Daniel Fallon I know wouldn't leave his daughter alone." She remained silent, but the jut of her chin gave her away. "Ah, you didn't tell him I left."

She looked away.

"Damn it, Bren!" He crouched down in front of her. "He could have killed you." He scratched his head and caught sight of her cell phone on the nightstand and grabbed it. "I tried calling—"

She lurched forward, grabbing at it.

He pulled it away. "What are you hiding?" He hit recent calls.

"No." She jumped off the bed and tried to snatch it. He lost his balance and grabbed for her, pulling her down with him. Her hand shot out, and Rafe raised his arm, allowing him to search. The name below his had him pushing her off him.

"How is that possible?" He drilled her with his eyes.

She blinked but made no move to explain.

"Answer me."

That deep red hair of hers fell forward, hanging in shimmering waves around her face. Glittering brown eyes smoldered, and she looked ripe to peel his ass. Maybe she didn't owe him an explanation. Maybe he was acting a bit childish, considering he knew damn well Tom Ryan couldn't make a phone call to his wife. But jealousy, no matter how ridiculous, didn't sit well.

Rafe pulled her to him. "For a minute, I actually thought he might be alive."

She yanked free and moved away, pacing the floor. "He's not." She stopped and glared at him. "Relieved?"

Yep. But he wasn't fool enough to admit he was glad Tom Ryan was dead—and he wasn't, really.

"No, confused. Why would Tom's name appear on your phone?" Then he realized something. "You kept it as a spare? The boys called you. Damn it. I'm a knothead."

She shook her head. "Only Aiden has a phone—since before Tom was killed."

"Then—"

"We never found Tom's phone. But Tom's phone found me." She pointed to Rafe's hand. "He called tonight."

"Who?"

"*Wes.*"

Rafe stiffened. "He threaten you?"

"No. He never says anything."

Rafe came to his feet and tossed the phone like a venomous snake to the bed. "You certain it's Wes?" He moved closer.

She gave him a tired look. "Of course it's Wes. He killed Tom. He took his phone."

He took her arms at the elbows and steered her toward him. "You never canceled it."

She lifted her chin, her eyes swimming with unshed tears. "It was my only link to Tom—his voice."

"How long's this been going on?"

"Only since December."

"Bendix know?"

"I told him." She shrugged and sidestepped him. "He's still checking into it."

Rafe scrubbed his face. "So he let that bastard terrorize you?"

The tears streamed down her face, and Rafe held her tight to him. "It's all right, Bren." He scooped her up and sat her on the edge of the bed. He knelt down in front of her and untied the shoelaces to her boots and slid them off her feet.

Her small fingers sifted through his hair. He lifted his head. The look she gave him was utter surrender. He wanted her, but not like this. The circles under her eyes hinted that sleep had evaded her. Well he'd fix that and quick. He kissed her forehead and tried to stand.

She held him in place, her fingers holding fast to his hair, her eyes searching. "Don't you want me?"

Rafe groaned. "In the worst way, darlin'." He wiped the tears from under her eyes. "But you need a good night's sleep." He cradled her in his arms and laid her down, pulling up the covers. He kissed the delicate curves of her lips. "No one's going to hurt you. I'm not leaving." He caressed her cheek.

Grabbing for the phone resting inside the fold of covers, he held it up. "Kevin needs to know what's going on."

She nodded.

He pressed back a shaft of her hair from her face. The moist crescents of her lashes fluttered shut. Her small hand clung to his, and his jaw clenched.

Screw the circumstances that had brought him into her life. He was so far gone over her, he'd be damned if he was going to have a conscience for wanting Bren Ryan for himself.

And as far as this battle she stubbornly refused to consider anyone's but hers, he was officially taking it over. She'd fight him on it. But he'd welcome her anger. In a woman with that kind of determination and grit he could forgive a little hardheadedness, especially if she'd earned his respect. And Bren Ryan had most assuredly earned his respect, not to mention, she'd stolen his heart.

He only hoped she wouldn't stomp on it once she learned he had deceived her.

CHAPTER NINETEEN

R AFE'S PICKUP HIT THE DIP HARD ON THE DRIVE LEADING TO PADDY'S house, and Bren gripped the handle of the passenger door. Aiden, Finn, and her father, oblivious to the restless solitude upfront and the stone-faced man in the driver's seat, chatted away in the back seat.

For the fifteen minutes it took to reach her father-in-law's, Rafe's fingers continued to dig into the deep navy of his jeans, moving in a back-and-forth motion. For all of the tough-cowboy attitude, she could see straight through to his soul. He was nervous.

That little nugget of truth she'd keep to herself. No sense rocking the John Wayne persona he had built up with her boys, not that her boys even knew who John Wayne was. But they knew Rafe, liked him, in fact. He was from Texas, a rough-and-tumble state, that had ranches instead of farms—cowboys instead of farmers.

She'd allowed herself to lean on Rafe since he'd rescued her almost a week ago. Smart move. Turns out having a liaison in the form of a take-no-crap cowboy was the way to work her buddy Kevin. Without complaint he had opened up an investigation into the break-in. Of course Wes's alibi was solid. No surprise there.

Over that time, Rafe had taught Aiden the finer points of cowboy life. He could rope a sawhorse while riding. Hoop and holler as good as any cowboy out west.

Then there was the sad excuse of a dog Rafe had dropped off, his attempt at giving Aiden some responsibility. Of course the novelty had worn off, leaving Roscoe her new best friend and her all-around responsibility. But in all fairness to the breed, Roscoe in the last week had honed his tracking skills in a most convincing manner and had scouted out every stuffed animal and article of clothing Rafe and Aiden had put to the test, making him a regular celebrity in the house when it came to praise and treats.

"Rafe?" Finn's hand squeezed his shoulder.

"Yeah, partner?"

They had become inseparable. Whatever Rafe was doing, Finn was not far behind. In fact, Finn's favorite place to be was on his back. The extra baggage never seemed to bother Rafe. Didn't matter what he was doing, he'd accommodate Finn's request to ride piggyback.

"After dinner, I'm going to ask Paddy to show you my daddy's room."

Bren caught the slight frown to Rafe's brow. "Looking forward to it," he called back over his shoulder.

"His old room is like a freaking museum," Aiden added.

Rafe's jaw clenched, and Bren's suspicions went on high alert. He was jealous of Tom. She smiled inwardly.

Rafe pulled up to the two-story Cape Cod and parked. The boys scrambled from the back seat, and her father, spry for seventy-two, stepped off the running board with ease. The boys bounded for the front porch, and the door swung open before they could knock.

"Right on time." Paddy stepped out dressed in brown corduroy pants and matching flannel shirt. He tweaked Finn's nose. "Want to dunk the fries?"

"You waited for me?"

"I sure did." Paddy stepped aside. "They're in the kitchen."

Finn ran past, and Paddy called back laughing. "But wait for me." He patted Aiden's shoulder. "I got the latest Mario Brothers for the Wii."

"Sweet." Aiden pushed past and headed for the family room.

Paddy hugged Bren and shook her father's hand. "How you been, old friend?"

"Just grand, Paddy, and yourself?"

"Keeping busy."

Bren's stomach knotted. There was one more introduction. Bren pushed Rafe in the back forward. "Paddy, you remember Rafe?"

His eyes lit on Rafe. He had no choice but to crane his head upward. Something registered in those deep inset eyes of Patrick Ryan before fading away to nothingness—would Paddy see Rafe as an outsider trying to take his son's place?

"I sure do. Good to see you, Rafe." Paddy stuck out his hand.

Rafe gave one shake and released his hand abruptly. "You, too," he mumbled, and Bren jabbed him in the ribs.

Paddy stood back, giving them entrance, and Finn hollered from the kitchen. Paddy waved them in. "Excuse me, the little french-fry chef is beckoning." He disappeared down the hall.

Rafe made a move to enter, and Bren hauled him back. "Be nice," she said through gritted teeth so only he could hear. "You hurt that old man's feelings because you have some bug up your ass about God knows what, and I'm going to hurt you, Langston."

He smiled at that. "Promise."

She threw up her hands and motioned him through. "Just go."

Paddy and Finn kept a vigilant eye on the fries sizzling in the fryer on top of the center island. Her father grabbed the newspaper and settled in the lounger in the corner of the family room, and Rafe sat on the floor next to Aiden. Like a big kid, knees drawn up and back resting against the couch, he was totally immersed in trying to beat her sweet teen at a game Aiden had mastered years ago.

At least Rafe was occupied, which left little room for bad behavior, unless she counted the occasional cursing when his car slid off the roadway of the game and he lost.

After setting the table and getting the go-ahead from Paddy, Bren stepped into the family room. "Dinner's ready."

Her father peered over his paper and smiled. "And it's a good thing, too." He stood and rubbed his belly. "My stomach has been none too quiet."

Aiden jumped up and left Rafe on the floor and headed into the dining room.

Bren placed her hands on her hips and contemplated the rough planes of Rafe's face, wondering what type of boy this cowboy had been while growing up. He obviously had a thing for winning. It was as if he had selective hearing, his gaze intent on the plasma-screen TV, his Mario character yipping with glee as it maneuvered successfully around a curve.

"It's time to eat."

He continued to toggle the remote, and Bren's patience thinned. She reached down and snagged the remote from his hands.

He scowled at her. "Why'd you do that? I was winning."

"Ever heard of winning the battle but losing the war?" She cocked her head to study him. "Bratty doesn't become you."

"Nor bossy, you." He hoisted himself up, stopped, and picked up the brass frame off the end table. He studied the photo without a word, set it down, and gave her his back as he headed toward the dining room.

Bren, left to stare at his back, clenched her fists. This Rafe she did not like—moody and ornery, all because he was uncomfortable around Tom's father.

When Bren entered the dining room, Rafe, minding his manners, sat stoic in his chair. Finn chattered to Paddy without taking so much as a breath, her father and Aiden frowning, the two directing a covert gaze toward Rafe.

Bren shrugged and took the seat next to Rafe.

"Will you do us the honors of saying grace, Daniel?" Paddy asked.

"I will at that."

Her father recited the prayer she knew by heart, and everyone dug in. Rafe filled his plate and ate in silence while the rest of them entertained one another about the recent rumor mill around town, which centered mostly round Wes and the horses Grace had been entrusted to care for.

"So, Rafe, Bren tells me you're from Texas," Paddy said.

Rafe stopped eating. His back went rigid, and his fingers visibly tightened on his fork. He finished chewing and glanced at Bren, no doubt sensing she was watching his reaction. He swallowed and smiled at her and turned toward Paddy. "That's right. I've lived in Weatherford for thirty-five years."

"Finn tells me you're the real thing. A real cowboy."

"I didn't have much choice growing up on a ranch."

She kicked his ankle.

To his credit he didn't yelp in pain, but merely grunted quietly and shot her a gaze that could singe her fiery-red hair right off her aching head, thanks to Rafe's rude behavior.

Paddy chose at that point to let the matter lie. And Aiden, more intuitive than she had believed possible, steered his grandfather toward a conversation of an ATV that Paddy was thinking of purchasing for the boys in the spring.

When dinner was over and Paddy and her father offered to do the dishes, Bren shooed them into the family room with the boys and offered up Rafe to tidy the kitchen instead.

Bren prepared the sink with warm water and soap, and Rafe brought her a stack of dishes. When he turned to gather more, she grabbed his arm. "You need to grow up."

"Last time I checked I was."

"You know what I'm talking about. I didn't need a boyfriend. This was your—" She peeked around the corner to be sure they were still alone. "You need to get comfortable with being around my family—my whole family—including Tom's father, no matter how weird that makes you feel."

He glanced down at her hand, holding him in place. "I don't know what you're talking about." He pulled away and began putting the condiments back in the refrigerator.

Bren scrubbed the dishes, jammed the plates into the dishwasher, and slammed the door.

Rafe came up behind her. "You forgot this." He held the serving fork from the roast beef, and Bren was tempted to grab it and shove it up his ass.

Instead, she gave him a tight smile, snatched it from him, and tossed it in the sink. "Outside." She motioned toward the back door. When he didn't move, she yelled, "Now."

"Mom?" Finn peeked around the corner. "You guys all right?"

"Just fine." She smiled sweetly for Finn.

Finn gave a nervous glance toward Rafe. "Paddy's going to show us my daddy's room. You want to come?"

He pasted a phony grin on his face and turned to answer Finn. "Sure, partner." He made a move to follow and stopped, giving Bren a derisive look. "We done here?"

"Oh, we're done." She wiped her hands on the tea towel and tossed it in the sink.

Bren went in and sat with her father while Aiden, Finn, Rafe, and Paddy visited what had become, in Aiden's words, Tom's museum. She didn't need to see his trophies from Little League, the basketball he'd used to throw the winning shot for the Clear Spring Panthers, their high school alma mater.

She'd lived it.

She didn't need a stroll down memory lane to tell her just how awesome Tom Ryan was as a friend, lover, and father.

Bren leaned against her father's portly frame and wrapped her arm around his belly. "How you doing, Dad?"

He hugged her tight. "I was just about to ask the same of you, sweetheart."

She smiled up at him. "Sometimes I feel like that little girl growing up. I'm just trying to find my way."

He squeezed her. "You will, Bren. You're life has been a true upheaval recently, to be sure."

Try train wreck.

She nodded against him. "It hasn't been easy for you, either. Losing the house."

"It worked out. We got a dog out of the deal. And you and Rafe seem to be getting along." She didn't miss his double meaning, except today she wasn't feeling too friendly toward Rafe.

The familiar click of Rafe's cowboy boots made Bren glance up. He stood in the doorway of the hall leading from Tom's old bedroom, his expression grim. "I can't stay for dessert."

Bren stood and went to him. "You sick?"

"No. I just need some space," he said under his breath.

Bren waved him toward the door. "Take all the space you need, cowboy." The day he'd found her in the broom closet of her father's kitchen, he'd told her his intentions.

Family's not something I'm looking for.

She should have been thankful for his candor. Too bad she'd forgotten Rafe Langston's warning until now.

He touched her arm. "That's not what I meant."

Bren pulled away. "Go." She walked toward the door, her head held high, and opened it for him. "Paddy can take us home. Have a nice life, Mr. Langston."

His expression hardened. "You do the same." He cleared the doorway, and Bren slammed the door. She turned and stopped midstep. Aiden and Finn stood in the hallway with Paddy frowning.

"I take it he had other plans?" Paddy asked.

Bren shrugged. "Who's ready for dessert?"

CHAPTER TWENTY

PADDY TURNED THE SUBURBAN AROUND SLOWLY, TRYING TO AVOID a cloud of dust, and stopped in front of Bren's house. The boys piled out, saying their good-byes over their shoulders.

"Thanks, Paddy." From the back seat, her father rapped Paddy's arm with his hand. "Next time we do dinner here. And I'll not take no for an answer, do you hear?"

Paddy smiled back. "Looking forward to it."

Her father headed toward the house, the boys ahead, their coats unzipped, flapping in the wind as they climbed the front steps.

Bren kissed her father-in-law on the cheek. "Thanks for dinner. It was delicious." She grimaced. "And the ride." She reached for the door handle when Paddy grabbed her arm.

"What do you know about this Rafe Langston?" There was an edge to his voice, ill suited to the Patrick Ryan she knew and loved.

Bren let go of the handle, eyeing him suspiciously.

He shrugged. "He doesn't like me much. Does he?"

Bren's eyes widened. She'd been telling herself it had something to do with Rafe competing with Tom's ghost or realizing he was getting too close to something he had no intentions of ever having—a family. Or maybe what she experienced in the barn with him after the "cattle drive" *was* real. She threw her hands up. "Any ideas?"

He shook his head. "None. I've never met him until the night you called and we rescued those horses."

Bren pulled on her bottom lip. "That's what he said."

Paddy's gaze hardened. "You sound like you don't believe him."

Or you.

But that was insane. How was it possible Rafe could know Patrick Ryan and he not know Rafe?

Drawn in by Paddy's caring brown eyes, she had no reason to question his truthfulness. So that only left Rafe. "I want to. But he's not my favorite person right now, considering how he's behaving toward you."

He patted her leg. "I'm a lot tougher than you think, missy."

Yes. Patrick Ryan had suffered tragic loses in his life, and Bren would do what she could to spare him any more hurt. Meaning this thing between her and Rafe was at a dead stop until he 'fessed up as to his odd behavior. Bren patted his arm. "I'll get to the bottom of it."

He smiled. "I have no doubt."

Bren reached for the door again and stopped. "Paddy? When Rafe was in Tom's room, how did he act?"

He shrugged. "What do you mean?"

"What was he doing?"

"The boys were showing him some photos—mostly when Tom was small. A few of you and Kate, Tom, and Kevin when you were teenagers. Why?"

"Before dinner he picked up the photo of you and Pamela."

"The wedding photo on the end table?"

She nodded.

"And?"

"Nothing. He stared at it and put it back."

"Huh. Not that it's odd."

"No. I know." She'd done the same many times. Photos were like a looking glass into one's past. But what was Rafe looking for in Paddy and Pamela Ryan's past?

Bren shook her head and laughed. "I think I'm letting my imagination have its way." Bren glanced at the clock. "I'm a chatterbox. It's almost nine. I should let you go." She hugged him. "Let's keep this between you and me. Not that there's really anything to tell. I just don't want the boys thinking I don't trust Rafe." She grimaced. "That sounded bad. You know what I mean."

"Oh, sure. My lips are sealed." He patted her knee. "I know you'll figure it out."

Bren hopped out. The Suburban turned around and headed down the driveway. Glad Paddy had such faith in her abilities. Too bad she didn't. Right now she didn't even want to see Rafe, let alone talk to him. Bren took the steps and rounded the porch, taking the door that led into the kitchen.

"Where are the boys?" she asked her father.

"Getting ready for bed. I promised them popcorn, and we're watching *Transformers: Revenge of the* . . . something." He twirled a spoon in his hand and grabbed a steaming cup before sitting down at the table. "I've a need for some hot tea. How about you join me, then?"

Anger always tended to increase her body temperature. "I'll just have water." She grabbed a bottle from the fridge, welcoming the chill of the plastic against her hand. She sat down next to her father.

"He likes you, you know." Her father stirred his tea. "Men, when they're in . . ." He cleared his throat. "Like. They act like jackasses." His blue eyes twinkled, and the smile he tried to hide made her uneasy.

"Well, he can stay a jackass."

Her father laughed. "You're a hard one, Brenna Maeve Fallon Ryan. I know you're angry with him. But I witnessed the whole ugly affair, sweetheart. The man's hurting. If you care about him, then make it your trouble to find out what's ailing him."

"I don't."

He dropped back in his chair. "Now you're telling tales, my girl. I see the way you look at him. You're in . . . like with him, too."

The front doorbell rang, and they both jumped.

He glanced at the clock on the oven. "Almost nine thirty—'tis a bit late for visitors."

Bren stood, and her father grabbed her hand. "Getting back to our conversation, and no, you're not saved by the bell." His blue eyes, usually full of mischief, hardened. "I know what I see, even if you can't. So don't go wasting your breath denying it, then."

The doorbell rang again.

He nodded toward the foyer. "Go on. Get the door."

His warm fingers released her hand, and Bren rushed to get the door, trying to gather her thoughts. If it was Rafe, she'd more than likely slam the door in his face. He'd caused her quite a lot of trouble tonight. She'd just gotten a talking-to from her father. Somehow she'd reverted back to that teenager. Awkward didn't begin to describe how she felt discussing her love life with her father.

Bren grabbed the door handle and opened it, prepared to throw him off her porch. But all that bravado dwindled.

"Hey, what are you guys doing here?"

Jeremy and Jo stood huddled in winter coats. Jeremy gave her a peculiar look. "Who were you expecting?"

Not rehashing it. Not with Jeremy and Jo. "No one."

"Uh-huh." Jeremy craned his head and peeked inside. "Where's Rafe?"

"He has his own house, remember?"

Jeremy peered around the corner.

"I'm not hiding him. He's not here."

Jo stepped forward with her cane and pushed Bren aside as she entered the house. "I'm too cold to play twenty questions."

Jeremy followed, and Bren was left holding the door. Frowning, she shut it. "Dad's in the kitchen. Want some hot tea or coffee?"

Jeremy eyed her. "You're awful testy tonight." He motioned with his hand. "You said Daniel's in the kitchen?" He headed in that direction.

Jo reached for Bren's hand. "You can tell me later."

Bren smiled. "Deal." Then, on second thought, she gently held Jo in place. "How's that investigation going?"

Jo gave her an odd look. "Investi . . . oh." Her expression changed to one of mutual understanding. "You mean Rafe?"

"Shh." Bren glanced around. "Yeah. That one."

Jo frowned. "Don't be mad. I thought with the way things were going you wouldn't want me poking around."

Bren fell back a step. "Going?"

Jo gave her a quizzical look. "You know what I'm talking about."

Bren's cheeks warmed.

Jo leaned in. "Has something happened I should know about?" she whispered.

Their first fight.

Those three words gave her perspective. But he still wasn't forgiven until he explained himself, and she wouldn't be sharing with Jo until she knew herself what was really going on.

"No. He just made me mad."

Jo smiled. "Don't they all."

She remembered not too long ago Jo wasn't feeling too charitable toward Jeremy, either. Bren laced her arm through Jo's. "It was silly. I'm over it." She steered her toward the kitchen. "So what are you two up to?"

"We're going to the Purple Cow and thought—"

"That's a dive."

Jeremy glanced over his shoulder while he prepared a cup of tea. "The last time we went you didn't seem to think so."

The last time had been a lifetime ago. She'd been with Tom.

"Why don't you go with them, honey?"

"Yeah. Call Rafe, and we'll make it a foursome," Jeremy said.

"That be a sore spot," her father added.

"Dad." She gave him the evil eye.

"Oops." Her father stared down into his tea cup.

Jeremy looked from her father to Bren. "What's up with you and Rafe?"

"Tonight he's a jerk. Let's leave it at that." Bren glanced at the ceiling above and the bedrooms beyond. "You'll be all right with the boys?"

"Popcorn and a movie. We'll be fine. Go with Jeremy and Jo and try not to think about, you know."

He made it sound like she had an incurable disease. God save her from herself. She was freaking lovesick over her stupid cowboy. She nodded toward Jeremy. "You buying?"

He laughed. "You coming. I'm buying."

Bren didn't bother changing. Jeans and a sweater and her leather jacket, she was good to go. The three of them climbed into Jo's Tahoe, and they arrived in no time. The Purple Cow on Main Street was sandwiched between the drugstore and barber shop. An obnoxious, brightly lit purple cow, its legs made to look like they were dancing, greeted them high above the entrance.

Jeremy paid the cover charge, and they stepped inside. A Garth Brooks tune filled the bar. Just like the sign outside, the inside decor was purple. Tiny purple lights twinkled in the ceiling. Round tables were stuffed around a dance floor, the band on a small stage in front and a pool table to the left with pinball machines shoved against the wall. She'd called it right: It was a dive, but a friendly one. All the locals hung out here, effectively making it a neighborly kind of place.

Jeremy squeezed through the crowd, greeting those he knew, which, because he was the equine vet in western Maryland horse country, numbered many. He motioned Jo and Bren forward when he found a table.

They took their seats, and Bren relaxed, glad to be sitting in the dark.

A pretty waitress made her way to them. "I'll have whatever's on tap," Jeremy said. "Wine or beer, Jo?"

"White wine."

Jeremy nodded. "Bren?"

"Miller Lite."

Bren took a sip of her beer when the waitress set it down. Jeremy started a tab and scooted his chair in. "What do you think of the band?"

One of the lead singers, a woman dressed in jeans and a sparkly silver top, began to sing Gretchen Wilson's "Redneck Woman." Bren nodded.

"She's good," Jo said.

"Daniel said you guys went to Paddy's for dinner. How's he doing?" Jeremy asked.

So he was going to make her stretch her vocal cords. "Fine."

"Heard Rafe left early."

"Yep." She took a sip of her beer.

Jo patted her knee. "How are the horses doing? Jeremy told me about the one that didn't make it." Jo was her best bud, steering the conversation away from a subject she didn't care to continue.

"They're good." She lifted her beer bottle and tilted it toward Jeremy. "Thanks to your husband."

Jeremy frowned. "I'm just sorry about the mare."

Bren leaned in. "It couldn't be helped." That's why Bren enjoyed her job working with Jeremy. He truly cared about the horses. He had preferred to give that mare a lethal injection—not a bullet to the head. But he wasn't prepared. None of them were.

"You hear anymore about Wes?" Jeremy asked.

She was under strict orders not to discuss Wes. She'd been glad she'd been asleep when Rafe had called Kevin after the break-in.

Bren shook her head.

The band took a break, and the sound system piped in a slow song by Carrie Underwood. Jeremy stood. "Jo, can I have this dance?"

Jo glanced at her cane resting over the back of her chair.

Jeremy knelt in front of her. "You don't need it, sweetheart."

"You be all right while we're gone?" Jo asked Bren.

"Of course. You two go. I'll be fine."

Jeremy scooped Jo up in his arms and whisked her away.

She loved her friends. She should be grateful they invited her to tag along. What was she going to do at home? Sulk. Bren took the last sip of her beer and decided to order another at the bar.

"Bren Ryan. It's been a long time. How have you been, sweetheart?" Elsie Morton, longtime resident of Clear Spring, with her silver-platinum 1950s updo, cleared the bar and gave her a hug. She stood back. "You look good. How are Daniel and the boys?"

Bren tried to connect Elsie with the Purple Cow. "You moonlighting a second job?"

Elsie patted her arm and came back around the bar. "No. Bob let me go. Business is down. When . . . if," she amended, wagging a finger, "business picks up, I'll be back slinging hash. But for now it pays the bills."

A waitress slid in behind the bar. "Sorry, Else, I need one gin and tonic and ice water."

"No problem." Elsie dumped ice in a glass and filled it with the hose from the bar. She glanced up at Bren as she threw a lime in a glass and mixed the drink. "What can I get you, sweetheart?"

"Oh. Ah, Miller Lite."

Elsie grabbed one from below the bar and twisted off the cap and handed it to her. "Put it on Jeremy's tab?"

"Yes."

Elsie turned away to take additional orders at the bar, and Bren drank her beer. Tonight, she sucked as company. The thought of calling a cab to take her home was tempting. She angled her stool. Jeremy and Jo were still dancing. She missed not having that special someone.

"Hey, doll face."

A hand pulled back on Bren's hair. The instant cool air on her neck disappeared when wet lips touched the side of her throat. Bren spun around. "Get your—"

For whatever reason, she expected to be looking into the eyes of Donovan Skidmore. Only she'd missed the mocking drawl when he'd surprised her. "I expected you'd be halfway to Texas by now."

"Nope. This is my home now." Rafe's speech was definitely slurred.

Bren stood up. "I'm with friends. So if you'll excuse me."

Rafe made a wide sweep of his hand, tipping his beer up. "Don't let me hold you up."

Bren ignored him and started to walk away.

"Rafe, buddy. How've you been?" Jeremy gave Rafe a hard shake of his hand. "We're sitting up front. See Jo?" Jeremy turned and waved toward his wife. Jo caught the signal and waved back. "We've got room for one more."

Bren stiffened. No way in hell would she be subjected to sitting next to Rafe and pretending everything was peachy. "He's leaving."

Rafe's lips tipped up into a smile. "Changed my mind." He put a hardy but drunk arm around Jeremy's shoulder. "Lead the way."

Bren decided to follow and retrieve her jacket and purse. She'd spring for the cab.

When they got to the table, Rafe pulled out a chair. "Ladies first." He grinned at her.

She beaded in on him, grabbed her things. "I'm calling it a night."

"Bren?" Jo's voice brought her around.

Bren frowned. "I'm really tired. I'm going to grab a cab."

"We'll take you home," Jeremy said.

"No, you two are having a good time. I don't want to spoil your night."

"She's right. I'll take her home." Rafe's long fingers stroked her hair, and Bren pulled away.

"Don't touch me."

Rafe pulled his hand back as if he'd been stung. "Relax, Red."

"Stop calling me that."

A couple walked by, the man brushing up against Rafe. Rafe stumbled forward. "Hey, partner, watch who you're pushing."

The man made a dirty face and kept moving.

"Did you hear what I said?" Rafe yelled over the music.

Bren reached for him, snagging the collar of his black suede jacket and yanked him down to eye level. "Cowboy, this is Maryland, not Texas. We don't have bar fights."

He blinked at her. "You're cute when you're mad."

She pushed him away. "And you're an ass when you're drunk."

And that was the problem. He was drunk. And he *would* drive home. Maybe wrapping himself around a tree would drill some sense into his obstinate cowboy brain.

Bren stepped forward and dug her hands into the pockets of his black suede blazer.

"Hey, Red."

She took an irritated breath through her nose and ignored him and stuffed her hand into the front pocket of his jeans.

A sly grin creased the rough, dark planes of his cheeks. "You're turning me on."

Bren groaned and shoved her hand in the other front pocket of his jeans. *Damn it, where'd he hide his keys?* Rafe, tall and lean and inebriated, was easy to manhandle. She spun him around with little effort. He teetered, and she grabbed his jacket, her fingers sliding into the back pocket of his jeans. She smiled when her fingers hit the warm metal. Yanking the keys from his pocket, she took him by the arm and directed him toward the door. She called back to Jeremy and Jo. "I've got my ride." She slung her coat over her arm and her purse over her shoulder.

The two laughed and waved her off.

Chapter Twenty-One

THEY CLEARED THE FRONT DOOR, THE COLD AIR A RELIEF FROM the heat of the bar. "Where's your truck?"

He grabbed for his keys, and she pulled her hand away. "In your dreams, cowboy."

Bren searched the parking lot. Finding Rafe's black pickup in the far corner, she pulled him with her. He tripped and then found his footing. Bren rolled her lips in, trying not to smile. "Let's go. The sooner we get out of here, the sooner I can climb into bed."

"Count me in." Rafe picked up his step.

This time Bren did laugh. "Not with *you*. I'm putting your drunken ass to bed. Your bed. Your house. Alone."

He frowned at her. "Party pooper."

She wouldn't waste her breath. Instead, she moved her hand down and clasped his, tugging him like the defiant little boy he was. She leaned him against the truck and unlocked the passenger door. "Get in."

He teetered, grabbed the door frame, and climbed in.

After shutting the door, she went around to the driver's side and got in, dropping her purse and jacket in the back seat. She glared at him. His legs spread wide, his butt on the edge of the seat. "Sit back so I can buckle your seatbelt."

He slid back, and she reached across him.

Big mistake.

His arms came around her, and he flipped her onto his lap and nuzzled the side of her face. "Don't waste your time on me, darlin'."

She pulled her face away from him. "Trust me. I'm not. I need a ride home."

His grip on her waist loosened, and she moved off his lap. She motioned to the seatbelt. "Buckle up. Or you're paying the fine if I get pulled over."

He reached for the seatbelt and snapped it into place and didn't say another word.

Bren started the truck and put it in Drive. Chewing on her bottom lip, she welcomed the silence. Leaving Main Street behind her, the road opened up. Pine trees a blur on either side of her, she pushed the truck to sixty. Grace's sign came into view, and she made the left into the driveway. She passed her house and kept to the gravel road leading to Rafe's. She glanced over at him. He was awake, his dark head leaning against the passenger window while he stared out.

What the hell was his problem? He could have been killed. The pang of loss made her clench the steering wheel. Then she got mad. Tempted to ram his front steps, she turned the truck hard, stirring up dust, and slammed on the brakes.

Rafe sat up. "What the—"

She reached over and slugged him in the arm. "You're an asshole. I've told you everything there is to know about me. Tom's death just about killed me. I hate you for making me feel anything for you." The tears burned her eyes, and she blinked, and they rolled hot down her cheeks. "Damn you!" She wiped at her face. "Now I'm crying over *you*."

Rafe unsnapped his seatbelt and slid across. He put his arm along the seatback, his thumb rubbing away the tears from her wet face. "Don't cry, Red." He moved closer. "I'm an asshole. I admit it." Long, clumsy fingers reached out and stroked her hair. "Tell me, darlin', how I can make it up to you?" He slurred his words.

That drawl, still irresistible and even more pronounced with alcohol, had Bren willing to give him a chance to make it right.

A blubbery mess, she sniffed and wiped her face. "I want the truth. What's going on with you tonight? What the hell happened at Paddy's house?"

His jaw tensed, and his fingers, still twining through her hair, stopped and fell away. Eyes intent on her face, only seconds before, dropped to his hands. He gave a nervous laugh. "There's nothing to tell."

Bren grabbed the door handle. Whatever he could have said—the truth—couldn't have been more hurtful than the lie that slipped from his lips. If he couldn't trust her, if he believed her gullible enough, or was it more of an acceptance on her part that only snippets of his life—the parts he chose to share—were up for discussion, then he was wasting her time. Her eyes flared with warning. "I was ready to give you my heart. *All of it*, you stupid cowboy," she said through gritted teeth. "Bury Tom once and for all. You saved me a lot of heartache. Unlike Tom, you are a liar. Why, I thought you even measured up to him." Her voice cracked.

Rafe visibly winced; his hand resting on her thigh tightened. "You're right, Red." He moved closer, pressing her hard up against the door. His eyes, hard glints in the dark, bore into her. "I'm not Tom, and I'm weary as hell trying to compete." His hand shot up and pulled her face to his. "I'm here, not Tom," he said, his voice rough with anger. "All I've ever wanted, I could never have." His voice became reflective. "How do you choose a favorite? How can you choose one without knowing the other?" He shook his head in disgust. "Tom was the golden boy. He was a keeper, but not me."

Bren frowned. "You're drunk." She pushed him away and opened the door, a cold rush hitting every exposed part of her body, and she shivered. *Damn him.*

"Where are you going?" He grabbed for her.

She jumped from his grasp. "Home."

He laughed. "In those pretty little boots." He mocked her, staring at her feet.

Yeah. In my pretty little boots with my head held high, asshole.

She couldn't do anything about the shoes, but she'd be damned if she'd freeze her ass off. Bren grabbed for the back door of the truck. She snagged her purse, slipped into her coat, and slammed the door. When she turned, Rafe stood behind her, blocking her exit. "Get out of my way, Rafe."

He put his arms out on either side of her and rested his hands on the edge of the pickup's bed, pinning her against him. His thighs pressed her to the truck, his chest a wall of muscle refusing to give an inch. He dipped his head. "We breaking up, doll face?" he drawled.

Tempted to knee him for his smartass comment, she refrained and went for the kill—his heart. "You only said that to hurt me. You're real good at that lately."

His face twisted angrily. "That's right, darlin'. That's all I've wanted to do since I came here." He touched her hair, his hands shaking slightly. "Hurt you," he said, his voice softening. Then the tenderness was gone, and he laughed. "I needed your farmhouse like I needed a dairy farm." He pushed off the truck and waved her through. "Run away, Red. And keep running."

Bren stood frozen. What was he saying? Come to think of it. He'd never bought one single cow.

"Did you hear me?" He bent down, again, his unshaven face dark and scowling inches from hers. He grabbed her arm hard, yanked her past the truck, and pulled her to him. He looked dangerous and capable of hurting her if he wanted.

Bren shuddered. He didn't resemble the man she thought she'd come to know. The gentle, kind man was gone, replaced by an angry, unfeeling bastard.

"Tom's dead, Bren." His voice sliced the air with finality. "He's never coming back, darlin'." For a moment regret flashed in his eyes before it dissolved into an ugly emptiness. "So get used to it."

Bren fisted her hand and brought it up, connecting with his nose. "Go to hell."

His head tipped back, and he cursed. He let go of her arm and grabbed his nose, blood running through his fingers. He eyed her and grinned. "You got a mean right hook, Red."

God, he was exasperating. It was all fun and games now, but wait till the alcohol wore off. Bren gave him her back and started walking. She hated him—hated him for making her fall in love with him. *She was in love with him.* She threw her head back in abject resignation and disgust. She was in love with him, and she couldn't stand to be within a fist's throw of him because he was acting like a spiteful child.

But more than that, he was hiding something from her. Even in his drunken state, he hadn't eased off and confided in her—he was that good at keeping his head about him, and keeping a truth he couldn't confess that ended any future they might have had together.

What did he mean about the house and dairy farm? He acted like it was all a big favor for her. She didn't even know he was still in town until the auction. She didn't even know *him*. And now she was sorry she did.

And that damn heart of hers would cooperate, or she'd disown it.

CHAPTER TWENTY-TWO

B REN REFUSED TO THINK ABOUT LAST NIGHT. OR LET THE DARK clouds and constant mist keep her from her morning chores. She showered, checked on the boys, who slept contentedly, unaware that today would bring another change to their lives. She sighed and took the steps. It wasn't just about her anymore. They had come to love Rafe, too.

The aroma of bacon filled the main floor of the farmhouse. It was Sunday. Which meant her father was busy in the kitchen preparing his sumptuous bounty of eggs, bacon, and fried potatoes before church.

"It smells good in here."

Her father turned from the stove with a spatula in hand. "Good morning, sweetheart." He hooked his chin toward the ceiling. "The boys still asleep, I imagine?"

She nodded and came up beside him and stole a piece of bacon before giving him a quick kiss on the cheek.

"Are you hungry, then?"

Her stomached grumbled. "I am, actually." Golden-brown potatoes and onions bubbled in oil, an open carton of eggs off to the side with a gallon of milk next to it. "How much longer before it's ready?"

"The potatoes still have twenty minutes. I thought I'd call the boys down in half an hour."

She took the last bite of her bacon. "Works for me." She walked over to the fridge and grabbed a baggie with an apple she'd cut up for Smiley. "I'm going to head out to the barn and check on the horses."

Her father smiled back at her. "He's your favorite, he is."

Bren grinned. "Only because you gave him to me."

He lifted his spatula. "You mean fought for him, then."

"Aye, I stand corrected." Her father never did confess to how he had outsmarted Wes, and at twelve she hadn't cared, so long as Smiley was hers.

"Did you have a good time last night? I didn't hear Jo's truck pull up."

She let the memories fade and reconnected with her father. "We had fun." She sighed. "They really have something special, those two."

His penetrating blue eyes met hers. "When you're open to it, mind. It's never too late to love again, sweetheart."

Not wanting to hear the bastard's name, she headed for the back door of the kitchen, stuffed her feet in her boots, and grabbed her coat off the hook. "I'll be back," she called over her shoulder and slipped out the door.

The cold mist floated, dampening her face and hands. Her hair hung in limp, moist waves against her cheeks, and she pulled it into a ponytail. The creak of the barn door, announcing her arrival, sent nickers throughout the barn.

Smiley had a stall in there at night, unlike the other horses they'd rescued. Those roamed the pastures and took shelter in the open barns if they didn't need special care. Smiley was healthy. But at almost thirty-two, the cold was hard on his joints. She loved all her horses, but there was a special connection between her and Smiley. She could see it in his eyes, the way he tracked her in the barn. Or nudged her with his nose if he felt she was ignoring him with her barn work.

Bren reached into her pocket for the baggie. Prepared to open his stall, she stopped, her chest constricting. His stall was empty. Her hand seized the stall door, and she slid it open. Her legs trembled. "Smiley." His name floated from her lips.

Her cold hands pressed against her cheeks, now warm with growing fear. She'd put him in before they went to dinner at Paddy's. Right? Yes, right.

Maybe the boys . . .

Hope dawned, and she ran to the house. Jumping the steps two at a time, she barreled through the front door. "Aiden! Finn!" she yelled upstairs. "You let Smiley out?"

Her father flew through the doorway of the kitchen. "Lord, child." His face dropped, and she could only imagine her frightful image.

"Dad," she cried. "Smiley. Did you take him out after I left?"

"Smiley? No. It was dark, Bren. We never left the house." He moved toward her, his arm coming around her. "What is it? What's wrong?"

Bren slumped, her head dipping, and she wrapped her arms around her waist. She shook her head in disbelief. "I I-he's not there."

"What?"

Bare feet slapped against the wooden steps. Both Aiden and Finn stood frozen, looking down, their faces rosy from sleep, hair ruffled.

"Mom?" Aiden asked warily. "What are you doing?"

Finn only stood wide-eyed, staring.

"I can't find Smiley." She needed to breathe. He was here, probably in the paddock. "Maybe one of the volunteers let him out." A lot of people came and went during the day. She moved to the front door and grabbed the knob. "I'm going to check the pastures."

"Not alone you won't." Her father moved to the bottom of the stairs. "Aiden and Finn, get dressed. Your mother and I will saddle the horses." He frowned at Bren. "He's here, sweetheart. Don't worry."

Bren saddled the bay named Hercules, and, her body quivering, hopped into the saddle. She glanced down at her father. "I'm going ahead." Searching two hundred acres would take time. She needed more riders. The only one close enough was Rafe. Going to ask for his help would take intestinal fortitude. But with no other options, she motioned to her father. "Tether Jocko to Hercules."

He hesitated.

"For Rafe. We'll search his half, and you and the boys can search ours."

He nodded. "Smart girl." He tied the horse on, and Bren cleared the barn.

She kicked Hercules into a gallop and ignored the sharp pricks of cold rain hitting her face. Rafe's truck remained where she'd left it. She hopped off and tied Hercules and Jocko to the rail of the steps.

The hell with knocking.

She grabbed the knob, hoping he was too drunk last night to think about security. It twisted in her hand. Grunting her satisfaction, she flung the door open. "Rafe!"

Nothing.

Damn him!

She bounded up the steps and pushed open the master bedroom door, her hands balling up into fists with indecision. The only sound came from the bed and a heap of blankets, and the man snoring who most decidedly was dead to the world.

Hangover or not, he was getting up.

Bren moved to the window and snapped the shade, letting it roll like a tight spring until it rattled the window and stopped.

"What the hell?" A tousled black head popped up, and he squinted against the morning gloom. "I must be dreaming," he moaned and let his head drop to the pillow.

"Consider me a nightmare." She came around the bed and pulled the covers back.

Her eyes widened.

Naked, except for a pair of white cotton briefs, he shivered. Those long, rough fingers of his shot back, searching.

She yanked the covers back further. "Get up." She clenched the soft comforter. The only naked male body Bren had ever been acquainted with was Tom's.

His face, rough with dark stubble, scowled up at her as he threw a muscled forearm over his face and rolled to his back. "Damn it, woman! Shut the shade."

Bren pulled her eyes away from the wide expanse of his chest, covered in a light sprinkle of dark hair. She found his undershirt and tossed it at him. "Get dressed, Langston. I need you, and I'm not happy about it."

He sat up, a pair of tight thighs, rough with dark hair, swung to the edge of the bed, his feet hitting the floor. His head fell into his palms. "That makes two of us."

She ignored him and grabbed his jeans.

His head shot up, his eyes tired and bloodshot, the tightness in his jaw proof he was less than pleased to be wakened so abruptly.

She hesitated, the denim of his jeans cold between her fingers. "I need another rider, and you're all I've got." Her voice cracked. "Get dressed." She tossed him his jeans.

He caught them. His expression softened.

"Please," she whispered and turned to leave.

He grabbed her hand and frowned up at her. "What's up, Red?"

"I'll make you some coffee. Meet me in the kitchen." She pulled her hand away. "I really need your help, Rafe." The tears spilled onto her cheeks, and she turned away and headed down the steps.

God. Why did she have to blubber so, especially in front of him? She didn't need his pity. She only needed another body to help search. Opening the kitchen cabinets, she came up with a small Folgers red can. Good. He needed all the caffeine he could get. She started the coffee and found a travel mug. When the coffee was ready, she filled the mug and snapped on the lid.

The familiar click of his boots in the foyer were a welcome sound, and she met him in the hallway. His hair was wet and combed, and he finished buttoning his denim shirt when she handed him the mug. "We gotta go." She turned toward the door, and he pulled her toward him.

"What is it?"

Her face crumpled a little. "Smiley's missing."

"*Your* horse?"

She nodded. "Dad and the boys are searching the other half of Grace. We need to search yours."

She pulled away, but he held her in place. "You think Wes is trying to pay you back?"

She nodded, her lips quavering.

He pulled her into his arms and kissed the top of her head. "You bring me a horse?"

"He's out front."

Rafe let her go and grabbed his Stetson and gray raincoat off the hall tree. He frowned at her and grabbed a baseball cap next to it. "Here. It'll keep the rain out of your eyes."

They mounted their horses. Within an hour they had searched almost every inch of Rafe's land. She two-wayed her father, and they, too, had come up empty.

"Bren!" Rafe yelled. He had ridden the back forty that separated Fallon and Connelly land and stopped along the fence. "Think I got something."

There in the mud were faint horseshoe tracks leading under the barbed-wire fence, and directly above were cuts in the fence that had been recently mended. They were not the mends Aiden and Paddy had made during the herd rescue a little over a week ago. That group had come in fifty yards to the left next to the weeping willow tree.

A moan escaped her lips. "He's got Smiley." She slumped in the saddle. "If Wes hurt him, I'm going to kill him." The complete validity of her statement frightened her. She meant it. She'd kill Wes Connelly. Bren brought her horse around and eyed the fence. She had enough running space. If only she could get enough height.

"Bren?" Rafe asked warily. "What are you thinking?"

She ignored him and turned Hercules away from the fence in a sprint. She pulled on the reins, turning him around. She kicked him hard in the sides and hoped he lived up to his name. His feet left the ground, and he flew over the fence, horseflesh and muscle straining to clear the sharp points of the barbed wire. He hit the dirt on the other side. Her tailbone taking the shock, she clenched her teeth and grunted through the pain.

"Damn it, you're a menace!"

Bren couldn't help but smile. "You in or out, cowboy?"

Rafe pulled his mount around and kicked the horse's flanks. He, too, flew over the fence, cursing as he landed several feet from her. The rough planes of his face stiffened. "We do this together, Red. Don't outrun me." He motioned to her pocket. "Call Kevin and have him meet us at Connelly's."

His tone left no room for argument, and she complied. Giving Kevin no leeway, she only told him where he would find her. Against his lingering protest, she slapped the phone shut.

The burnished-red stable with its adorning cupolas rose stark and foreboding against the gray mist. Smiley would be there, and she'd simply retrieve him. For Smiley's sake, she'd avoid confrontation. She only wanted her horse safely back on Grace land. Then she'd slap Wes with theft to go along with the rest of his charges, and her friend the sheriff could do the honors.

Bren slowed, and Rafe did the same as they approached.

He pulled Jocko in front of her, and she yanked back on Hercules's rein. "What the—?"

"We're on private property."

"He's got *my* property." She nudged her horse forward. "We're wasting time."

"I'm not planning to get shot for a damn horse."

"Then go back. I can do this myself."

He shook his head. "You're such a pain in the ass, Ryan."

"Name-calling isn't going to help."

He pushed his Stetson back, his brows twitching together, and pondered their next move. Even-keeled and thoughtful, he surveyed their options.

"Maybe we can do this without raising a fuss." He motioned to a clump of trees several yards from the stable. "I think we're close enough. Let's tie off, search the barn. We find the horse, we grab him and go."

"Smiley."

"What?" He gave her an annoyed lift of his brow.

"His name is Smiley."

He mumbled something under his breath and headed toward the clump of trees. She followed, and they both tied their mounts. He grabbed her hand. "Remember what I said, Red." She couldn't avoid his scrutiny when he pulled her nose to nose with him. "We do this together."

She eyed his hand wrapped around hers. The strength with which he held it and the utter possessiveness made her catch her breath. The anger from last night seemed more a ridiculous temper tantrum. If she was completely honest, there was one more thing she hadn't confessed to him or anyone. The guilt she carried for Tom's death wasn't an unfounded emotion. Standing there in front of Sweet Creek Stables brought that night back in renewed clarity. She had sealed her husband's fate just as surely as if she'd thrown him from the barn doors of the loft. She was a hypocrite in every sense of the word.

"You coming?" He tugged on her hand.

She reconnected with him and let the past fade away. The present dictated her complete attention.

Chapter Twenty-Three

THE KNOB TURNED EASILY IN RAFE'S HAND. HE MOTIONED BREN through a side door of the stable, the sweet smell of hay immediate. Fluorescent lights hummed above. Stalls on either side greeted them. Tack neatly stacked on a huge metal shelf on the opposite end. Crisp leather saddles hung on metal racks in front of each stall, the exact opposite of Grace's horse tack, both in condition and use. Wes hardly rode—he was a showboater to his huntsmen friends. That worked in their favor. If Smiley *was* here, he'd be easy to find.

Rafe motioned to the right. "Take that side. I'll take the left."

She nodded and moved to the first stall, her legs shaking with anxiety for what she hoped to find. But the stall was empty. She moved to the next one, only to find the horse was not hers. She continued checking stalls and glancing back toward Rafe. The same question on her lips, but he shook his head no.

Several male voices came from outside the stable. Bren stiffened and turned to Rafe. He crossed the barn floor and grabbed her. He pointed toward an empty stall and pulled her inside. The two huddled in the corner. On his haunches, he pulled her in between his thighs and held her against his solid frame. She opened her mouth, and he put a long finger against her lips and whispered, "No talking."

She nodded and moved closer.

The metal doors thundered open, and light poured in. Bren bunched Rafe's shirt in her hand and tugged him down to her.

"They're inside," Bren whispered.

Both Bren's and Rafe's breathing seemed to shout at her, making Bren aware they could be discovered. The men, and she couldn't tell who or how many, moved closer. One spoke in Spanish. Her hand tightened. If his words had significance, she couldn't understand them. The others she didn't recognize.

"*¿Donde está mi dinero?*"

Bren pulled on Rafe's shirt again and whispered, "You speak Spanish?"

He nodded.

"What'd he say?"

Rafe brought his head down to her ear. "He wants his money."

What were the chances they'd witness a payoff? And for what? Bren pushed up and was immediately brought down when Rafe grabbed her around the waist.

He narrowed in on her. "You want to get caught?"

Bewildered, she met his angry gaze and whispered back, "But the money—"

His arms pressed tighter around her middle. "Shh."

Bren clamped her lips shut. She needed to focus. Headstrong and deliberate weren't going to get her answers. Patience would pay if she could ignore her impulses and stay rooted and quiet.

Another man shuffled in and moved toward them.

"Where's Connelly?"

"The boss don't involve himself in these kinds of transactions."

Remaining in the corner of the stall was a huge handicap. Seeing was believing. And Bren wanted to see what was going on. Grabbing Rafe by the shirt again, her quiet little way of letting him know she wanted to speak, she pulled him down to her, and he bent his ear toward her lips. "I can't see."

He drew back and frowned. Nodding, he clamped a hand on her arm and directed her toward the front of the stall but to the right where a saddle and blanket hung across the top and front of the wide slats of the stall. Bren peeked through. There were three men. One short Hispanic nervously paced the aisle. Another of medium height dressed in overalls and a baseball cap leaned against a stall with a heavy work boot resting on a watering trough. The other guy, wearing jeans and a leather bomber jacket, pulled a wad from his jacket pocket. Crisp bills, the denomination yet to be disclosed, were counted out. "This is for José over there."

The guy with the overalls handed it to Jose. He then added something in Spanish, and Bren sent a questioning lift of her eyebrows toward Rafe.

"Two hundred," Rafe said.

She nodded.

Bomber Jacket counted several more bills and handed them to the one in overalls. He took the money, dipped his head, and counted it. His head shot up. "It's only half?"

Bomber Jacket laughed. "I don't make the rules. Mr. Connelly said half. Then half when it's delivered and done."

The words sent a warning so sharp that Bren gasped, and she shook with fear. When it's delivered and done . . . She glanced up at Rafe, her eyes wide with horror.

He pulled her to him, the strength of his arms the only comfort against what she feared was Smiley's fate. In a low voice she had to strain to hear, he said, "Do you trust me?"

Considering their behavior toward one another last night, his question was utterly soul-searching. He was with her now, holding her trembling body, refusing to let her either crumble or self-destruct. Either of which would give them up.

With him her emotions could never be harnessed.

He made her laugh and even cry, which angered her. Weakness she detested. He had become her best friend unwittingly. He felt things for her, too. Whether it was love or a kindred spirit kind of thing, she couldn't say.

She pulled him down to her level and searched those eyes she had come to read. "Yes . . . yes, I trust you."

He grinned at her. "That's my girl." He peeked through the slat and came back to her. "Let them hang themselves."

She nodded and concentrated on the men whose voices had become agitated.

"Call his ass down here." The one in overalls loomed above Bomber Jacket, who stepped away and grabbed his phone from his jacket. The chirp of his two-way phone echoed. "Boss, Mason wants to see you."

The phone chirped back, the boom of Wes's voice, her clue that he didn't appreciate the interruption.

Overalls, whom she deduced was Mason, grappled with the phone and yanked it away. "Connelly, you son of a bitch. We had a deal. You renege—" The threat swallowed up when he smashed his lips to the phone and turned away to pace as he leveled his ultimatum in deep whispers.

Mason tossed the phone up in the air. "Catch, Pritchard."

Another name Bren stored away. She pressed her forehead into the rough grain of the wooden slat, her eyes blinking through the crack.

José paced the dirt floor, muttering. Mason plopped on a stool, resigned to his fight, and Pritchard kept his eye on the wide entrance of the stable. The crunch of gravel and the slam of a door brought all three around. Wes arrived and stood, legs apart, hands on hips, an angry dark silhouette backlit against the murk of gray and swirling mist. "You threaten me, Mason?" He took measured steps toward him.

Mason pushed up from the stool. The abrupt movement sent it toppling with a thud onto the dirt floor. "I don't work in draws, Connelly." His grizzly voice gripped the damp air and held, his threat open-ended.

Wes's hand shot up, and he scrubbed the back of his neck with irritation. "You'll get your money. Once I've got delivery confirmation."

"To hell with your confirmation." Thick work boots clumped toward Wes. "All I did was make arrangements."

Wes straightened. Mason had his attention. "I'll see you share the same cell. So keep talking," said Wes.

Terror edged along Bren's spine, the twinge of sudden loss hovering around her. The noose Rafe talked about, agonizingly slow, only gave innuendo. These men were conditioned experts at shadowing the truth. Her fingers, stiff from squeezing the wooden slat, lifted tentatively. The stall door tempted her to make her presence known and demand answers.

But Rafe, sensing her agitation, grabbed for her waist, his warm fingers slipping under her sweater. "Don't."

She bit down on her lip, her throat tight. The ache of tears threatened to expose her fear. "Rafe." Her voice shook. "There's no time." She jerked away from him and grabbed the stall door, but he was on her in seconds. He jerked her back. The baseball cap she wore flew off and her hair fell past her shoulders. Flat on her back with Rafe on top, his weight made it a struggle to breath. "Get—"

His hand came down on her mouth. He pinned her with his eyes, and she flinched with the intensity.

A car door slammed, then another. Their attention swung to the thin strip of space between the dirt floor and the first slat of the stall. His fingers eased and slid to her shoulder. Two black tires and shiny hubcaps winked at them. The thick blue letters "Sheriff" stenciled against a gleaming white paint job announcing the advent of law enforcement made her stomach twist.

There would be no more intelligence-gathering.

José grabbed his head between his hands and bent over muttering. "¡Oh, no. La policía! Ese caballo blanco me persiguen Yo nunca estuvo de acuerdo. El dinero no vale la pena."

The only words she could pick out were *police* and *white*.

Rafe's fingers dug into her shoulder.

"What's wrong?" The hairs along the back of her neck bristled.

He relaxed his grip. "Nothing." His neck craned upward, his eyes trained on the tiny space.

"You know what he said." She yanked his head down even with hers. "Don't lie to me."

"Bren." His brows knit together, and he shook his head.

Her grip tightened on the base of his neck. "Smiley." The name tore from her throat.

He said nothing, only reached to smooth a red shaft of her hair that rested along her cheek and tucked it behind her ear.

Strength born of unbearable loss, she rolled out from underneath him.

With stunned reaction, Rafe reached for her, but she scooted away. Grabbing the stall door, she pulled herself up.

Rafe cursed and came to his knees.

She slid open the stall, the wooden door rumbling in its track alerting the men deep in verbal battle. She struggled to find something—a weapon, because she meant to murder the son of a bitch, who stood frozen, eyes gaping, wondering what the hell Bren Ryan was doing holed up in one of his stalls.

She spotted it. A vicious smile curled her lips, and she grabbed the pitchfork shoved in a bale and strode up to Wes.

José sent up a high-pitched squeal and darted for the doors. He ran smack into Kevin. Kevin, in his lawman guise, imposing Stetson square atop his head and frame like Gibraltar, teetered backward. "What the—Bren—Rafe—" His words caught and held, and Kevin let José slide by him when he locked onto Bren. With a determined step, she closed the gap with pitchfork in hand, her victim clear in the wide-eyed accusatory gaze of her childhood friend.

"Shit!" Kevin moved forward and called back to his deputy. "Grab him!" He pointed to the fleeing José, who had already whizzed by the patrol car, making tracks for the gravel road leading out onto Route 68.

Another patrol car pulled up. Mason and Pritchard made a move.

"Hold up." Kevin put out his hand.

Two deputies entered the stable.

"Detain these two and get their statements," Kevin ordered.

The deputies closed in, and under duress Mason and Pritchard were led out.

Kevin placed himself between Bren and Wes, his arms flung out like a crossing guard daring her to step off the curb. He glanced back at Wes, who was standing off to the side, his eyes warily keeping tabs on Bren and the pitchfork raised in combat. "You want to fill me in, Connelly?"

"She's—" He pointed an accusatory finger toward her. "—fucking crazy," he sputtered and made quick eye contact with Kevin before his gaze swung back to Bren. "Do something, Bendix, before she kills me."

And that was her intent. He'd made arrangements to have her horse stolen. She'd figured that out, even with the little Rafe had shared when it came to José—his way of keeping her contained. Well, she was a freaking powder keg now, and reason and good sense were beyond her. She'd deciphered the conversation between Mason and the thug named Pritchard. *Not until delivery confirmation.* Smiley's fate, spelled out in those four words, would be a reality if she didn't get answers, and quick.

Everything faded away, the swirl of the patrol cars' lights, the red and blue bouncing off the walls of the stable. Rafe, his presence a force she sensed without looking back, and the confused face of a friend/lawman who surely believed she'd gone round the bend, remained on the periphery.

She had only one target, and the bastard had just sprung behind Kevin. A pitchfork in her hands, definitely lethal; Kevin would be smart to move out of the way.

Short of Kevin drawing his gun on her, she kept coming. "You're as good as dead, you son of a bitch!" Her threat aimed at Wes, she never took her eyes off him.

"What the—" Kevin became speechless when she made the first jab to the side of him and missed when Wes dodged to the right. "Damn it, Bren. Enough!" Kevin grabbed the pitchfork handle, his hand slipping by degrees as she yanked it back.

"He stole my horse," she grunted and pulled back and aimed to the right but missed again.

Kevin's face went taut. "Put the goddamn pitchfork down."

Like hell. Trembling with rage and the need for answers, coerced or otherwise, she stayed focused on Wes. "Tell me the shipping company, you bastard."

"Shipping?" Kevin glanced back at Wes. "What the hell's she talking about?"

"How the fuck do I know?" Wes's words came out in a rush, his face turning a deep shade of red.

"Sheriff." Deputy Johnson, the one who had gone in pursuit of José, came back winded. "I couldn't catch him. He's probably over the border by now."

Kevin winced at the comment and motioned for him to take a position to his right. "And for crissake, don't discharge your guns." Kevin placed his hand on his service weapon and glared at Bren. "Don't escalate this."

"This," Bren seethed, "is his doing." She shot a burning gaze into Wes. "He stole my horse, damn it!" Her voice cracked, and the pitchfork slipped in her slick hands. She tightened her grip. "Give me the name of the shipping company and the slaughterhouse." She jabbed the pitchfork to the left.

Wes sucked in air, stumbled back, and reached for something at his waist. The glint of a silver semiautomatic followed, and he drew down on Bren. "Come at me again, you crazy bitch, and I'll kill you."

Bren tightened her grip on the pitchfork and swallowed. He would, too, and he'd be in his right to shoot her. She was on his land, brandishing a weapon, with every intention of jamming it dead center into his miserable person.

"Whoa, whoa, whoa!" Kevin's face turned ashen, and he pulled his service weapon and drew down on Wes. "Drop the gun, Connelly."

"Fuck you, Bendix." Wes's head pivoted, and the two deputies took position on either side of him. "She's as good as dead, she makes another move."

Oh, she wasn't twitching a muscle. Wes looked too comfortable in the way he handled the gun. He'd killed Tom. He'd kill her, too.

Wes pierced her with menacing eyes and took a step forward, his finger heavy on the trigger.

Bren closed her eyes, prepared to take the bullet that would end her life, when a scuffle brought them open. Kevin had reholstered his weapon and come up behind Wes, taking him to the ground in one swift motion, the gun hitting the dirt floor same as Wes.

Strong arms came around her and yanked the pitchfork from her hands. "It's over, darlin'," Rafe whispered into her ear as he clamped her tight to his chest.

Bren slumped against him. The two deputies swooped in and assisted Kevin, yanking Wes's arms behind his back, cuffing him while Kevin grabbed the gun and dropped the pistol's magazine onto the dirt floor. He cleared the chamber with a metallic click and dumped the remaining bullet out onto the ground.

"Does someone want to tell me what the hell is going on here?" he demanded.

Wes lifted his head, his breathing labored with the deputies still on his back. Everyone else turned their attention to the voice coming from the wide opening of the stable.

Bren recognized him immediately—the fair head of reason. The only sane Connelly who seemed to have radar designed to intercede when rational thinking had all been lost between his father and her.

Kevin's head whipped around. "You know anything about Bren's horse?"

"Horse?" Robert took a tentative step inside the stable, dressed casual in a dark running suit and tennis shoes. He frowned in confusion as the deputies hoisted Wes to his feet.

"She claims your father stole him and shipped him off for slaughter," Kevin said.

"I didn't steal her goddamn horse!" Wes sputtered.

"He did it. José said so," Bren shot back.

Rafe slipped his arm around her waist. "Easy, Tiger, you got want you wanted," he spoke quietly against her ear.

She bit the inside of her mouth. Sure, Wes put his best murdering foot forward by brandishing a gun. But it still wouldn't save Smiley unless she got answers.

Kevin tucked Wes's gun inside his waistband. "You better hope to hell you registered it," he snarled at the man. Then to his deputies: "Read him his rights and arrest him."

"Robert." The distress in Wes's voice brought Bren around.

He looked to his son, an expression of uncertainty lining his face.

Robert waved a dismissive hand toward his father. "I'm done with you." His eyes then met Bren's—pained and almost looking through her. "Whatever I can do to help, you let me know," he said and walked away.

The deputies shuffled Wes through the wide opening of the stable, and for once Wes was speechless.

An unexpected twinge of regret surfaced inside Bren, and she realized this thing between Robert and his father was no longer funny. She'd never meant to hurt Robert. He'd done nothing to deserve this.

Kevin stood in the way of the exit, talking into his radio.

She eyed him. If he tried to stop her . . .

He caught sight of them coming toward him. His jaw tensed. "You're not going anywhere until I get a statement so I can charge the son of a bitch."

Bren's back stiffened.

Rafe placed his hand on Bren's lower back. "He's on our side, Red." He grabbed hold of her arm and pulled her forward. "Give the man a statement. Then we're going to see Bean Counter. He's the only one who can help us now."

Chapter Twenty-Four

RAFE PACED THE MARBLE FLOOR OF THE EXPANSIVE ENTRYWAY OF the Connelly home, the click of his boots echoing in the hallowed hall. Wide, opulent staircases, strung on either side, wended their way to the second level like an elegant strand of pearls carved in oak. Bren fidgeted, tapping her work boot against the gleaming marble floor. The contrast between working-class and high-class was stark and uncomfortable the longer she stood in such fine surroundings, waiting for Robert to succeed at his task.

"You sure you trust him?" asked Rafe.

"Shh." Bren strained her neck and peered through the tall double glass doors of Wes's office. Robert sat behind an ornate cherry desk, his glasses perched atop his head, digging through a stack of trucking manifests.

Rafe's fingers locked around her arm and yanked her back. "That's not an answer."

"We're here, aren't we? If he had something to do with Smiley's disappearance, you think he'd be rifling through his father's desk trying to find evidence?" She shook her head. "No, because he'd be signing both his and his father's arrest warrant."

His fingers relaxed, his one brow arching. "No loyalty to family?"

She glanced back at Robert, his head dipped in concentration, thumbing through the stack. "I don't claim to know how his mind works. But from what I've seen, he's a good guy. You can't pick your parents."

Rafe's grip tightened again, his eyes hardened.

"Hey." She stared at that hand, long fingered, wide palm, so male—and squeezing the life from her arm. "That hurts." She tugged her arm.

He let go as if she'd turned to flame. "Sorry. Go on."

How to explain the Connellys? "It's only been Wes and Robert for a long time." She leaned close to Rafe's ear. "Robert's mom left when he was small. She couldn't stomach Wes's side action. Couldn't stomach Wes." She gave a wry smile. "Smart woman, except I can't imagine leaving your son." She shrugged. "Robert, other than the business, is Wes's life. Only Robert chose to distance himself after Wes footed the bill for his higher education."

"So what's Bean Counter doing here?"

"Wes can be persuasive. Who knows? But I wouldn't put it past him to threaten his own son with his inheritance." Through the glass door, Robert's back was toward them, his hands deep in the files of a matching cherry credenza. "In Wes's twisted way, he loves his son. Manipulation is his way of keeping Robert close."

A smile touched her lips. Except the times *she* witnessed their interaction, the two only had cross words between them.

"The point is, he's not his father's whipping boy."

Rafe gave her a look of disbelief.

"He's his son. But he speaks his mind."

Those green eyes didn't soften one iota. Fine, he didn't see what she saw in Robert Connelly. Too bad. She waved an agitated hand at him. "He's doing it because it's the right thing to do. I trust him."

Besides, she'd deal with the devil himself if it got her what she needed— the trucking company and its destination. Without it, they had a fifty-fifty chance of picking the right slaughterhouse, though there were only two slaughterhouses Wes could use. Canada and Mexico were worlds apart. If they were wrong, the distance was too great to make up for lost time.

If they were going to be able to track and catch the tractor trailer in time, they needed to get a move on. No thanks to her and the standoff in the stable, she'd let precious time slip by.

She tugged on Rafe's arm. "Any word from Kevin?"

"Not yet. I don't think your buddy Wes plans on rolling over any time soon."

She closed her eyes, only to see those big brown eyes of Smiley staring back at her. He would be frightened out of his wits. The memory of the rescued horses in the cattle trailer made her shudder.

Positive thoughts, Bren.

Canada or Mexico; twelve hours by truck one way, thirty-six in the other—she wouldn't consider Smiley's emotional state in either case. She needed to function. For the moment, he was alive, and that was what she focused on. She only hoped the authorities detained the truck like they were supposed to. She might just catch up before it crossed the border. There was time to intercept the carrier if they could just find the manifest.

Rafe's fingers pressed into the back of her neck, kneading rhythmically. "Bean Counter still digging?"

She straightened and peered through the glass of the French doors. Rafe's phone went off and she jerked.

"I'll take it outside." The phone pealed again, and he took the call. "Yeah."

Bren raised her brows. "Kevin?"

He shook his head. "No, Trey." He spoke into the phone again. "Hang on." He covered the phone and connected with Bren. Any gleam of hope disappeared. "We're grounded until we have a flight plan." And his brother Trey, a licensed pilot, remained idle until they could confirm their destination.

That stubborn chin, rough and dark with stubble, lifted abruptly toward Wes's office. "Let's hope Junior in there finds it's Ciudad Juarez."

Mexico would be preferable. What little Rafe had told her—Trey had connections there.

Rafe kissed her cheek. "I'll be outside. How about you do your damnedest to move Bean Counter along."

One of the double oak entry doors clicked, and Rafe was gone. Bren hesitated. Maybe it was this house that bothered her.

She reached for the crystal doorknob. This day of murk had become a contradiction. By late afternoon the sun had peeked through, taunting her with its goodwill. By early evening it had given way to a mix of purple and pink hues through a window high above where she currently struggled to open a damn door.

Robert's blond head rose. A tired smile tugged at the corners of his lips. "Hey. I'm sorry this is taking so long. I figured the old man would have shoved it in his normal hiding spots."

"Your father, if nothing else, is predictable."

"Yeah, well, I didn't see this coming."

Bren gripped the edge of the door. *Me neither.*

"Where are my manners?" He motioned to a chair in front of the desk and laughed. "You know, since I was old enough to notice girls, old enough to bring one home to meet . . . *my father* . . ." He frowned at her. "I always wanted it to be you."

The air became difficult to breathe. *Me?* A girl his father despised?

She sank down, the give of the leather chair a relief to standing.

He leaned over, his blue eyes searching hers. "You really had no idea?"

She pointed a determined finger at him and laughed nervously. "You really know how to surprise a girl." She managed to smile. But the truth was, her brain struggled to make sense of his confession. But then again, the children of a feud that had stretched decades learned you don't fraternize with the enemy. "Guess ol' Wes . . ." She cleared her throat. "Your father wouldn't have taken too kindly to you romancing the one he always referred to as 'girl.'"

"Try disowned." He laughed, and the foreboding sense that something was amiss lifted. "Needless to say, I got over you real quick."

Robert's cell phone rumbled next to his elbow on the desk. He glanced at it and gave her an apologetic smile. "Excuse me, Bren. I need to take this."

She nodded, and he took the call.

"Hey, sweetheart, you had me worried." The stress along his jaw lessened. "Next time answer your phone. So I'm not thinking the worst. I'll see you tomorrow morning. Love you, too."

He ended the call. "Sorry about that."

"Everything okay?"

"She drove to Richmond this afternoon to see friends of ours. There was a pileup on Interstate 95." He rubbed the back of his neck. "She had me concerned when I couldn't reach her."

"She's fine, then?"

"Yes. The accident was behind her, but she let her cell phone run down." He grimaced. "We'd planned to drive together until all this happened."

Bren moved her chair in. "Robert, I'm really sorry I've messed up your plans and put you in the middle."

He shook his head. "Bren, I'd do anything for you."

Bren reached over and squeezed his hand. "I hate putting you in the middle."

"It's not your fault." He gave her a quick smile before his expression turned serious. "He created this mess. I'm just sorry for what he's done."

The front door slammed. The click of Rafe's boots echoed in the hall.

Bren swung around. Rafe, tough cowboy, filled the doorway. His jaw set, the dark stubble of beard made him a formidable opponent for anyone willing to piss him off. And Robert, his hand still tucked under hers could be the catalyst to wage such a fight.

"Let's go, Bren." Rafe's voice, possessive and clipped, needled at her. Jealousy, if that was what she witnessed, didn't suit him.

"I'm not done here."

"Mason cracked. I just got off the phone with Kevin. It's Mexico."

Anger faded. Bren smiled at Robert apologetically. "I have to go."

"I hope you succeed."

"Thanks, Robert." Bren squeezed his hand one last time and stood. She didn't have to turn around to know Rafe's eyes sizzled with proprietary intent—a branding she didn't appreciate. He might own cattle, but he didn't own her. She cleared the doorway and snatched Rafe's arm, pulling him into the hall. "You're rude."

"And you're a fool. He was hitting on you."

She wanted to laugh—she'd grabbed *his* hand. "He has a fiancée."

"Ah, then we have nothing to worry about." His tone mocked her, and he rolled his eyes.

She refused to comment. And the "we" he had so easily used to mean "them" was left to explore another day, because Smiley was out there, and she meant to save him.

Chapter Twenty-Five

B REN SHOULD HAVE KNOWN WES WOULD HAVE PAID SOMEONE SO
his load could pass the checkpoint and keep going with Smiley.
Her legs shook as she climbed out of the back seat of Trey's Honda Accord.

Then her whole body trembled. "That's a drainage pipe." Bren backed
up and looked to Rafe, eyes wide with shock. She motioned with her hand.
"What about crossing the border back there?" About a mile back, well-
marked, there was a bridge that permitted both foot traffic and vehicles. A
simple car drive—boom, they were there.

Before Rafe could formulate a response, Trey, his brother from hell—and
from the looks of it, he wanted her to climb into the bowels of hell—popped
his head from the trunk of his Honda Accord and scowled at her. "Because
you don't have a passport, *Bren*."

Mr. Command and Control she did not like.

Their introduction swift, Bren had barely had time to register the differences between Rafe and his brother Trey, except for one—their eyes. Where
Rafe's shimmered green with warmth, Trey's did not. They were a bottomless
gray that glinted with dislike for her.

That was fine. She wasn't here for a popularity contest. Maybe he considered her quest folly. After all, they were risking their lives for a damn
horse. And it was true she didn't have a passport—had no reason to have a
passport. Until some asshole stole her horse from Grace's warm stable with
plans to slaughter him in a country she had no desire to ever step foot in.

Rafe's long fingers wrapped around her arm and pulled her toward him,
and he gave her a hard shake. "Stop antagonizing him."

Her mouth fell open with an irritated breath. "I didn't do anything."

Standing in Rafe's shadow, his bristly, black chin jutting with authority, she quaked with anger. She wasn't playing army. She wasn't taking orders, even if he and Trey treated her like some pimple-faced teen who'd just enlisted. And the damn faded army jacket Rafe wore, its pockets stuffed with rations, flashlights, and anything else he believed vital to their mission, wasn't going to sway her.

She peered around Rafe's wide shoulder at Trey, his blond hair cut ruthlessly short, his head still tucked inside the trunk he tinkered with. She fisted her hands at her side. Didn't he know their enemy was the clock?

With a metallic slide and click, he shoved something into his waistband and slammed the trunk. He hustled toward them, all bulk and muscle, his biceps big as her thigh, straining against a gray T-shirt, a leather jacket in one hand.

"Rafe." The demand in Trey's voice made her jump.

Rafe turned. "Yeah."

He handed him a silver semiautomatic, which Rafe, also, shoved into the waistband of his jeans.

Bren's eyes popped wide. *Shit!* The clock wasn't their only enemy.

Trey slipped into his jacket. "I need to move the car. I'll be back in ten minutes."

"What about the border patrol?" Rafe said.

"We're good. There shouldn't be another for a few hours."

The silver Honda disappeared in a low cloud of dust amidst a terrain that was flat and dry. Strange-shaped vegetation with fronds and sharply pointed cactus grew from the dirt. Behind her a few industrial buildings poked against the blue horizon with only a single winding road, the same one Trey had taken, connecting the white, windowless structures.

They stood several yards from the drainage ditch and the wide metal opening of a corrugated pipe. Above on an incline rose a chain-link fence that stretched forever in either direction. Curled razor wire at the top warned anyone who thought of jumping borders to think again.

Trey seemed to know a lot about border patrols, immigration. She tugged on Rafe's hand. "He's uptight."

"Comes with the job."

The job. "Roping cattle makes you pissed off at the world?" She shook her head. "He doesn't much care for me." She sat down on a large rock and shrugged. "I'm not a cow, Rafe. And if he comes back with an attitude because

I refused to be tossed off as excess baggage to your parents, I'm going to kick him in that tight ass of his."

He didn't laugh, but his eyes glinted in amusement.

"What's so damn funny?"

"Trey's not a cowboy."

"But you said he was running the ranch while your father . . ."

"He is. But the day-to-day operation is a well-oiled machine. We have employees."

"Oh." She cocked her head and brought her hand up against the sun to keep from squinting. She had just assumed. But Trey could fly, could get her from their connecting flight in Dallas to El Paso quicker than any commercial flight, and he had connections in Mexico. "Pilot?"

Rafe shook his head.

"Ooh, so mysterious." She stood with her hands on her hips and set him an irritated gaze. "Then what the hell does he do?"

"He's DEA."

DEA—now the cog turned. Drug enforcement.

The wide, dark hole took on a new frightening meaning. "It's a drug tunnel." If it sounded like an accusation, it damn well was. Would they be the only occupants of said drainage pipe? More to worry about than dark, tight spaces, she whirled on Rafe, her eyes glinting with disbelief. "Is he crazy?"

"No. He's pissed." Rafe came at her, looked over his shoulder to be sure they were still alone, and pinned her with not-so-warm green eyes this time. "Bren, this is his job. If we're caught, he could lose it."

"If we're caught, we could die."

"It's not as dire as that." His expression softened. "It's an abandoned drug tunnel."

So she should relax? *Wrong*.

Bren's shoulders slumped. She'd asked for this. Trey Langston was only giving her what she wanted. And thanks to her need for revenge, she'd driven them to defy borders with the real possibility of rubbing up against the most unsavory of human beings—drug smugglers.

The dark hole loomed, taunting her resolve. Although big enough for her to enter and still stand to her full height, there was no way to tell if it continued that way until they reached the other end.

The other end . . .

Bren wrapped her arms around her waist and trembled into her thick, dark-blue hooded sweatshirt.

Where was the tough farm girl now?

"How far is it?" The question she had meant to ask inside her head left her lips, her voice ripe with apprehension.

"You can always stay behind."

The condescending voice gave her a start. "I thought you were parking the car." She glared at Trey.

"Be nice, darlin'." Rafe pulled her next to him.

"Even better." Trey smiled, a set of dimples softening the severe planes of his chiseled, bronzed face, and for a moment he actually looked friendly. "I found a clump of overgrown tumbleweeds."

Right. They were in Texas after all.

Trey motioned toward her. "Ladies first."

She wouldn't demean herself by asking how far again. She could do this. Grabbing her backpack, she slung it over her shoulder and moved toward the black opening, which emitted a cool dampness like an abandoned cave. She took measured steps along the rocky, thin stream of the drainage ditch, the water lapping at her boots. All thoughts of her life in western Maryland gobbled up into the mouth of a whale. She clamped down on the strap of her backpack and walked inside.

Trey passed her and walked several yards by flashlight until the tunnel changed. Gone was the corrugated floor of the pipe, replaced now with compact soil. Trey hit a switch. Electric wire looped the walls every fifty feet like garland on a Christmas tree. Where a shiny, glass Christmas ball would be, a single lightbulb hung, its glow fanning out into shadows until they came upon the next. The walls and ceiling, shored up with mortised timbers and sheathed in mildewed plywood, closed in like a crypt, and Bren kept walking, the tip of her boots hitting an occasional stone along the carved-out dirt floor as they traveled in silence.

Mr. Command and Control, true to his nature, had taken the lead after realizing his bullying wasn't going to dissuade her. Bren reached back, searching for Rafe. The strength of his rough, long fingers encircled her hand once again, and the anxiety riding high in her chest relaxed a little. They'd walked the better part of twenty minutes when Trey slowed and the tunnel narrowed and ended. Rusty metal rungs embedded into a concrete wall rose about ten feet to a trap door.

Trey turned to them. "This is it." He motioned to the wooden panel above. "It slides back. There's a chest above that I need to move." Trey bent down, the hardened planes of his face even with Bren's face. She wanted to gulp the minute those gray eyes glinted under the amber glow of light. "Life or death, Bren. No in between. Got it? These bastards will slit your throat."

Now she gulped.

The real ball of fire she'd been several thousand yards back cooled to a piece of lead. She couldn't move. Instead, she remained glued to Trey's incisive gaze. Frightened or not, she'd come this far. She glanced up at the door that would lead to a world so unlike the one she'd come from. Her eyes came back to rest on Trey's grim expression. "I'm not leaving Smiley. He's my horse." The last word she could barely get out.

Something in those unfeeling gray eyes of Trey's softened. His broad hand came down on her shoulder, and he squeezed. "Determination. I like that." He smiled at Rafe. "She's exactly as you said."

Whether Trey chose to help because of his loyalty to his brother, his love for horses, or avid curiosity about her, she couldn't say. But something told Bren he found her quite peculiar. Call it intuition or the amused look that passed between brothers. Her face warmed. She didn't particularly like being made fun of. But before she could voice her complaint, Trey handed her the flashlight and started up the ladder.

Bren kept the light to his back, lighting up the area around the trap door.

He reached the top. The wood creaked when he pushed the trap door open. Shafts of light and dust particles filtered down into the tunnel. He struggled with something up above—from the groan and scuffs, she assumed furniture. Gray light poured in, and Trey levered his body up until he sat on the edge.

He lifted his chin toward Rafe. "Bren goes next. Your job's to slide the door back, move the chest into place, and meet us at the jeep outside the back door."

Trey bent down into the hole, his blond hair aglow from the brightness of the flashlight. She turned it off and handed it to Rafe. Trey motioned with his hands in a give-me fashion, and she began to climb. Strong, capable hands reached down, and Bren grabbed hold of Trey. He clasped onto her and pulled her up. Turning her around, he pushed her over the opening, and Bren crawled on her hands and knees and pushed off the cold floor to stand.

The room, no bigger than an oversized closet, was dark except for light spilling underneath a door to her left and cracks of sunshine edging the drawn window shade. Besides the wooden chest Trey had moved, no other furniture existed. Only shelves lined one wall, with cans and jars filled with food, the colorful labels of fruits and vegetables, not the words, hinting it was a cantina's pantry.

Shadows passing underneath the door with the light drew her attention. Beyond it, voices chattered, the words foreign. Glasses and silverware clinked, and her heart sped up. But the other door to the far right, made of metal, loomed, and a cold dread spread through her chest.

Trey gripped her arm. "Let's go."

Bren looked back at the opening in the floor. Rafe's head cleared the opening, his handsome face turning in her direction. He gave her a crooked smile and winked. Her heart gave a hard pinch, and she frowned. She didn't like leaving him behind, even for a few minutes.

Trey tugged more urgently. "Now, Bren. Rafe's right behind us."

Bren nodded and allowed Trey to pull her toward the door. The metal hinges squealed resistance the moment Trey eased back on the doorknob. Bren's eyes darted toward what she deduced was the dining room. The chatter continued without interruption, and she relaxed.

Bright sunlight made her squint. Trey peered around the door. He reached for her arm, never keeping his eyes off the street. "Black jeep parked up and to the right."

He pulled her through the door, the warmth of Mexico's sun immediate against her cheeks and hands. Bren followed Trey's nodding head. Across the narrow street, sandwiched between dilapidated yet colorful seafoam and pink buildings, sat an open-topped jeep. She took a step forward and hesitated. The more she moved into the open, the more she imagined being picked off with a bullet. Trey tugged hard, and she was forced to move. But when a Mexican, dressed in army pants and a white T-shirt, emerged from a doorway across the street and casually leaned against the jeep, sheer terror froze her in place.

Trey glanced down, his scowl deep with aggravation. "Relax. He's one of us."

Really? He didn't look like an American. He looked dark and dangerous and totally Mexican.

Trey's grip on her arm reminded her of a blood pressure cuff, always checking her fight-or-flight pressure. He must have been measuring it now because his grip was squeezing the hell out of her bicep.

Trey dipped his head, and she was surprised to see compassion in those usually impassive, cold eyes. "You with me?"

Bren swallowed, her one hand clenching the strap of her backpack. "Yeah."

The Mexican—the closer they got to him, the more her heart raced. He remained leaning on the jeep's hood. Bronzed skin and short dark hair, his arms bulged with muscle. He turned toward them, and that was when Bren made out the dark gun hanging off his hip.

Oh God, oh God, oh God!

Bren slowed and her shoulders bunched.

"Relax. I told you. He's one of us."

Her shoulders leveled off, and she let go of the breath she held in and picked up the pace until they came within a few feet of the jeep and the scary dude with the gun.

"*Buen día, mi amigo.*" Trey clapped him on the back and shook his hand. He angled his head toward Bren. "Bren, this is my good friend Serg Cruz."

Serg smiled, his teeth gleaming white against his leathery skin. "So this is the chica you were telling me about." He took a step toward her. She'd always thought Mexicans were short. But Serg towered over her, his wide shoulders casting her in his shadow. "So we meet in the flesh, eh?"

Obsidian eyes flashed down at her, and the tiny hairs along her neck spiked. Friend or not, she didn't like the way *Serg* drank her in like some fluted glass of bubbly champagne he didn't expect to be placed at his table. He licked his lips.

Like a second skin, Bren attached herself to Trey, both hands clamping onto his arm—no way was she letting go.

Serg laughed. "Why so afraid, *chica*? I don't bite."

Bren's face warmed.

Trey stepped in front of her, her hands falling away, for once his rudeness welcomed. "Gas tank full?" His voice was clipped. Clearly done with their introduction, he set his attention on the jeep. He bent down to check the undercarriage, stood, and moved toward the front and popped the hood. "Fresh battery?"

"Yes, amigo." Serg nodded. "Extra guns under the back seat if we need it."

Trey shut the hood with a thud and wiped his hands on his jeans.

"Hey."

She froze until a warm hand clasped her shoulder. Bren swung around. "I don't like him."

Rafe's brows rose. "You talking about Serg?"

"You know him?" Her eyes widened.

"Mexican Marine. They, in this case, he, works with Trey on the Mexican side."

Bren hunkered down in the back seat next to Rafe. The gun given to him by Trey no longer rested concealed in the waistband of his jeans but on the seat next to him. Hands rough with ranch work, but yet capable of tenderness, held tight to the grip of the semiautomatic, his finger resting on the trigger.

A knot of uncertainty lodged in her throat. Her selfish need to save her horse might end in one or more of their deaths. Ciudad Juarez was not a vacation destination like the posters she'd seen in the window of the local travel agency in Clear Spring. There were no sugar-sand beaches and gemstone shores like Cancun. The streets were crowded. Cars zoomed past, spewing fumes into the air. The people, their faces set on the task of the day, crossed streets amid armed police dressed in fatigues like Serg.

She wished she'd closed her ears to Serg and Trey, their conversation an extension of their work and the troubles one border town could suffer at the hands of a greedy drug cartel. Murder became murders in staggering numbers, their mutilated corpses left indiscriminately on city streets, the message: Power and profit—king.

Bren focused on the man who had caused her immediate discomfort and relaxed. They wouldn't have gotten this far without him. He spoke the language, knew his way around, including the location of the Rastro Municipal Slaughter Plant, and could recognize trouble, specifically, a member of the Juarez drug cartel. She hoped if they did run into one it stayed in the singular.

The jeep rocked Bren at seventy miles an hour, her hair losing the battle as dark wisps flew in her eyes. Serg had said twenty minutes—no more. They were close, pinned between ragged mountain ranges in front, rising up against desert flatlands of the Chihuahuan Desert, the thin ribbon of asphalt snaking the dust-laden landscape. Arid with only squat grasses, their lackluster narrow fronds, covered in dust, waved with the speed of the jeep when it rushed by.

Bren glanced back, willing the trailer carrying Smiley to miraculously appear. Serg's bronzed arm shot up. He glanced at Trey, his full lips curving with satisfaction. "Up in front."

Trey peered over his shoulder. "This is neutral territory, working class." He hooked his chin at Rafe. "Conceal your gun."

Rafe slipped it back into his waistband. His hand reached out and squeezed hers. "Positive thoughts, darlin'." She took comfort in his engaging drawl.

But she couldn't dispel the emotions already threatening her speech, so she nodded back. The jeep slowed, and they hit a checkpoint. Serg handed over a document, spoke brief Spanish, and the Mexican dressed in jeans and bright yellow shirt opened the gate.

To the right were cordoned-off areas, the fields within them dusty, the earth cracked, giving the horses currently milling about nothing to feed on.

They came up on a trailer, and she jabbed Rafe in the side. "Binoculars."

He gave her a questioning lift of his brow. "For what?"

"The license plate on the trailer."

He dug into the inside pocket of his army jacket and pulled them out. Bren squinted against the eyepieces and focused the lens—her heart dipped when she read "Texas." Bren handed back the binoculars. There were so many horses. Her hands began to shake. How would she find him? There were other trailers up in front. The heads of horses struggled, pinned in between metal piping. The echo of hooves, stomping against the metal floor of the trailer as they tried to get their footing. *God, I beg you. Let him be alive.*

Serg parked the jeep and hopped out, followed by Trey. Bren grabbed the roll bar and followed. As Rafe came out behind her, he pulled her to him. "Don't flip out, Bren. I mean it. You can't help them." The lines of his handsome face grew taut, his words sharp with warning.

She could do this. She took a deep breath and tried like hell to ignore her surroundings. She had eyes for one horse only. She'd find him. Let Serg explain, and she'd simply take him home.

Take him home . . . take him home in what?

Bren shot a look at Rafe. "We don't have a trailer."

He frowned. "Let's make sure we have a horse."

She opened her mouth but snapped it shut. She wouldn't argue his point. She didn't come this far to fail. Of course they'd have a horse. She wasn't leaving without him.

Serg took off his sunglasses and angled his head toward Bren. "Chica, tell me again what your horse looks like."

"He's an Appaloosa."

"App-a-loosa."

Panic rose in her chest. Her spokesman had no idea what the hell an Appaloosa was. She swallowed and wet her lips. "He's white with spots on his rump." Bren searched the pens and the tops of the trailers. Most were black and chestnut, with just a few white blazes poking up amidst steel bars. Frustrated, she took a step forward and grabbed his arm. "I'll show you."

Trey stepped closer. "Not a good idea." He eyed Rafe. "Keep her contained. Serg and I will check on the horse."

And here she'd thought Trey was growing on her. She'd obey. But if they failed to turn up her horse, she'd be in the thick of it. And someone better the hell speak English, and if they didn't, cussing was pretty universal. They'd get her meaning.

CHAPTER TWENTY-SIX

BREN PACED BESIDE THE JEEP. "I SHOULD HAVE GONE WITH THEM." She stopped in front of Rafe, her big brown eyes wide and glistening. "I know my own horse. If he's here, I could find him faster, Rafe." Her voice cracked on a plea.

He had no doubt. But letting Bren lose in a slaughter plant, her eyes unveiled to the ravages of their operation, wasn't going to happen. It sickened *him*, and he raised beef cattle.

"Be patient, Red. Give them a chance." He leaned against the front of the jeep, keeping a steady eye on her. He knew this one. Knew what she was capable of. They didn't need to escalate this visit—easy in, easy out. He'd given Trey a copy of the shipping manifest. Once management cross-referenced the manifest with the horse, they'd figure something out and get her horse back to Maryland.

"Hey, I asked Trey if he knew Jo."

She stopped pacing and gave him a curious look. "Why would he know Jo?"

"Jo worked for the DEA, right?"

She looked around, agitated, like she knew he was making small talk to take her mind somewhere else. "Is this going somewhere?"

"I just thought he might know her, or of her."

"Well, do they?" A well-shaped russet brow arched.

"Nope."

She placed her hands on her hips. "I know what you're doing." She tapped her finger to her lips. "You're trying to distract me. Besides, I think if she did know him, she would have put two and two together after having met you.

She would have asked you about him." She turned back to pacing, her signal that his ploy to engage her in some other way wasn't working.

He settled his back against the jeep and kept her in his sights, checking his watch. The last two days he'd watched her break a little with the burden. Seeing her that way did strange things to his insides, and he didn't like it one bit. He had half a mind to level anyone who had caused her pain, but sitting inside a jail cell would make it difficult to keep an eye on her.

He eyed her now. A bundle of anxious energy wearing a path in the dirt, crossing and uncrossing her arms, her head a constant bead on anything that moved, and that damn pacing . . .

Ah, hell.

Rafe pushed off the jeep. "Red." He grabbed hold of the back of her sweatshirt when she passed him for the hundredth time and hauled her back against him. Wrapping his arms around her narrow waist, he whispered against her ear, "Relax, darlin'." He kissed the back of her head. "It won't be long now."

She turned in his arms and nuzzled into his chest. "I just want it to be over." She peered up, soft black lashes fluttering against the afternoon sun, small creases of worry bracketing her pale yet pretty lips. "I want to go home, Rafe. I hate this place. It's foreign and angry and scary and . . . and I just want my—"

The high-pitched neigh had Bren straightening in his arms. "What the hell—" Her head came up, and she abruptly pulled away, taking careful steps backward. Her arms swung back and forth at her sides in a contemplative gesture, as if weighing her options, her eyes like lasers looking for . . . what?

He groaned and pushed off the jeep.

And she stopped, giving him a curious look, like a spooked filly before it reared. Her hands were hidden inside her sweatshirt sleeves. Only the tips of her fingers visible, they curled with agitation. Her eyes, large and seeking, lit on the pens to the right of them—none of those horses, at the moment, appeared to be in dire distress.

She kept searching.

"Bren?"

She shuffled backward, her head swiveling for sound. Other than the snorts coming from the trailers, the high-pitched cry made no repeat. But she kept moving away from him.

He placed his hands on his hips, his gaze deliberate. "We're staying put."

She frowned. "Come on, Rafe," she whispered. "I just want to check things out."

No way in hell could he let her do that. There were things about this place she didn't need to know. He took steady steps toward her. "Darlin', I'm pulling rank." He reached for her, and she jogged backwards, turning toward the first horse trailer.

"*Shit*, Bren, get your ass back here." Rafe charged after her. He couldn't let her get to the corrugated buildings.

Her hands ran along the metal pipes of the trailer, her head bobbing up and down as she searched the frightened group of horses packed tighter than a can of sardines. She passed the first trailer and jogged several more yards to the second. Rafe was on her now, only a reach away when the same neigh rent the air, freezing them in place.

Bren cocked her head and cupped her ear. "It's coming from over there."

Shit. The buildings.

Rafe edged up on her and grabbed her arm, his breathing no longer suspended.

Keep her contained. *Yeah right.*

He had about as much control over her impulsiveness as he did with his own destiny. And right about now he was seriously wondering what the hell he'd been thinking, bringing little Ms. Horse Rescue to a damn slaughterhouse.

"Bren," he warned.

Her eyes flashed. "Let go, Rafe."

"We're on foreign soil, darlin'. I'm not looking to be thrown into a Mexican jail. Leave it alone. The odds of it being Smiley are slim at best."

Her face paled, and Rafe wanted to kick himself. If she hadn't considered that possibility, she sure as hell was now.

"Bren?" He eyed her straight up, his one brow arced. "Don't make me bodily carry you back to the jeep."

He waited.

The combative stance of hers gentled. "You're probably right." She shook the arm he still held in a death grip. "But can you ease up?"

Damn. But he'd forgotten how small she was and felt like a total jackass for manhandling her. He let go and pulled her toward him and kissed her forehead, his arm sliding to her waist. "I'm sorry, darlin'. You just can't take off—"

The shrill ring brought Rafe around to his phone shoved inside the front pocket of his jacket. Keeping his arm around Bren, he fished it out. Seeing Trey's name, he answered it, his grip on her loosening a fraction.

She slipped from his grasp and charged toward the buildings.

"Shit!" he hissed into the phone. Listening as he went after her, letting Trey know she was moving their way, he slammed his phone shut.

"Bren!" Damn it, but she was trying his patience. He'd tried to spare her. But her own obstinacy was going to get her an eyeful. She ran past several workers, gray aprons looped around their necks and waists. White masks hanging below their chins. They jumped out of her way, speaking in rapid Spanish, the words lost on Rafe.

Bren slipped behind the first in a series of buildings. Another crippling death cry pierced the air, followed by the deep-throated shouts of men. Bren screamed, and Rafe took off in a dead run. The gun Trey had given him dug into his back, and he prayed like hell he wouldn't be forced to use it. He should have known his easy-in-easy-out plan would be blown to hell. Everything the woman was involved in caused a freaking disturbance.

Rafe rounded the same building. Now on pavement, the audible click of his boots made him acutely aware he was headed in the right direction. Railings came up on him, the concrete dipping to the left, which he felt sure was the beginnings of a ramp into the plant, and without a doubt the direction she'd—

More shouts broke out, and the unmistakable female voice he'd come to associate with trouble shook with alarming agitation.

"Let him up, you murdering bastards. Now!"

And the fear she'd do something real stupid struck terror in his veins.

He came up on the railing and stopped.

Stupid didn't even come close.

Armed with a power-washer hose, the amount of pressure yet to be determined—he'd guess painfully high—she took aim. It wouldn't kill, but if she pulled the trigger, it'd sting like a bitch. He shook his head and frowned. Sure as shit she'd pull the trigger. Bren didn't know the meaning of negotiation. Before long, they'd have the whole Mexican police force surrounding them. He didn't even want to think about Trey's reaction.

But the scene at hand had him shoving Trey's concerns aside. Rafe had heard the stories. Never paid it any mind. His business was cattle, and The *Brazos*—the family ranch—slaughtered them, too. But there were humane ways of doing it, and this damn sure wasn't one of them. Rafe's hands fisted, anger hot and pulsing thumped in his chest.

On the concrete, in front of the double doors leading into the plant, lay a black gelding on its side, at least seventeen hands. Its coat rippled with sleek muscle. Handsome came to mind, except for the gashes on its neck, ripped open, exposing raw horseflesh. Its eyes bulged with terror. The white blaze along its nose was saturated in his own blood, the hind legs bound, a steel chain looped and attached to a winch. His guess, they'd been in the process of dragging the gelding into the slaughterhouse when Bren interrupted them.

The workers, and there were two dressed similarly to the ones he'd seen earlier, stood back, their aprons covered in blood, their hands each gripping a glinting puntilla—a sharp, deadly knife. Their barbaric, and Rafe would add criminal, method used to slaughter the most admirable of companions had him sorely tempted to blow a hole straight through them.

But brandishing a weapon—and unlike Bren's, his was deadly—on foreign soil was a frightening prospect.

The gelding's agitation brought him around. It continued to thrash about, attempting to stand, its snorts and high-pitched neighs a torment that ate at his very soul.

And his heart ached and applauded the red-headed hellion positioned on the attack. Only problem was, she had no claim to *this* horse, and her actions would pay her back in spades when it came time to negotiate for Smiley's release.

He didn't know for sure, but these two men, their knives dangling from their hands, dark complexions with mouths agape, looked completely harmless and just as confused and unsure as Red. Not everyone in Mexico was a drug runner. Most were hardworking, trying to get by and feed their families.

But he'd been wrong before. Wrong about a lot of things, actually, and he didn't want to be wrong about this. So he kept watch of their hands as best he could while trying to corral Bren and coax her into surrendering the pressure wand.

He came up behind her.

Small and vulnerable, her slender shoulders trembled. With her hands in a death grip on the wand, she dared the two plant workers to touch her or the horse. She meant business, but her weapon of choice wasn't going to keep them at bay forever, and the longer she continued the standoff, the longer the horse would suffer. He was going to die one way or the other. It wasn't clear if his legs were broken. But as Rafe neared both Bren and the horse, he was certain, by the amount of blood pooling under his belly, he suffered from multiple stab wounds.

"Bren, honey, listen to me. He's suffering. You can't save him."

She glanced at him then, tears streaming down her cheeks. "I want my horse." Her voice cracked, her head tilted to the side, and she wiped her wet face on her sleeve.

Rafe quickened his steps, and she tread backward, trying to keep the two workers and Rafe in view. She stumbled over the hose and quickly regained her footing. She pointed the wand at the heavier of the two Mexicans.

"You're killing him." She sobbed and looked at Rafe, her face flushed and puffy from crying. "They're killing him."

The words fell on a whisper of despair, and Rafe cursed his inability to bring this to a quick end. "I'll take you to your horse, darlin'. I promise. Just drop the wand."

He motioned for her with his hands, but her body twisted in agony as though she were suffering the same painful attack as the horse.

"You found him?" Her voice rose, and she sighed in an effort to control her breathing. She took a tentative step forward, peeking past the gelding into the shadowy entrance of the plant. But she retreated at the heavy work boots clopping, voices growing and moving in their direction.

Rafe glanced to the right and winced. In front, Serg and Trey—Trey his main concern, sporting a scowl of contention—led the group of plant workers. Most wore aprons covered in blood and calf-high rubber boots, wet and glistening under the afternoon sun.

"What the hell, Rafe?" Trey came up short, staring down from the top tier where the railing ran perpendicular to the plant. His hands gripped the railing, and he gave Bren his full ire, leveling a gaze that usually made anyone on the opposite end cringe.

"Bren, these people are not the enemy. It's their job," he said, his voice gentling as he made his way around the railing to stand next to Rafe. He leaned in so only Rafe could hear. "What the hell happened to her?"

Rafe motioned to the gelding, now quiet and resigned to his fate, his chest expanding with ragged breaths. "She's in the business of saving them." Rafe shook his head. "It's part of her."

Trey's hand rested on his shoulder. "Brother, you're too close to this one. Let me take a stab." He winced and waved him off. "I'll handle it."

Coward or not, Bren's emotional state sucked the life out of him. Sweat pooled between his shoulders. His heart, more like rapid fire, beat against his chest—no way in hell could he make direct eye contact with those panicked brown eyes of hers.

Trey moved down the ramp. "Bren, Rafe and I will take you to your horse." He motioned to one of the Mexicans wearing a short-sleeved dress shirt, the buttons tugging against his pendulous belly. Trey spoke in clipped Spanish and motioned for him to come around.

Bren glanced nervously toward Rafe.

"Darlin', listen to Trey."

Her lips quivered and she fastened a wary gaze in Trey's direction. "Y-you found him?"

"Yes, Bren."

She shook her head and looked to Rafe with uncertainty, her fingers tightening on the wand. She let out a soft cry and dropped the wand and reached for him.

Rafe pulled her to him. Never letting go of her hand, he led her up the ramp behind Trey.

Trey hooked his chin toward Rafe. "Around back."

Rafe stopped, put his arm around her, and whispered against her ear. "No more funny stuff, Red. My heart can't take it."

She sniffed and nodded yes.

Trey glanced over her head to Rafe. "We're going around back." He led them to a heavy white door with one small square window, the glass covered with condensation from the inside.

Trey pulled Bren aside and placed his hands on her shoulders. "I misjudged you, Bren. And I'm sorry. I wish I had men as determined as you under my command. The trailer carrying your horse arrived early this morning." Trey's jaw tightened. "He was slaughtered around noon."

A sob bubbled up, and she wrapped her arms around her waist. Her slightly puffy lips, from crying, rolled in and her eyes welled with fresh tears. "Nooo!" She pulled away, doubling over at the waist.

Rafe reached for her and scooped her tight, her body one big spasm. Her warm tears soaked through his sweatshirt to his T. She stiffened and lifted her head, and Rafe's gut clenched at the determination lurking in those eyes of hers. This wasn't over by a long shot, and he knew it.

"I want to see him." Sobs continued to rack her. "I need to know for certain, Rafe."

"Bren, sweetheart, it's not something you want to remember."

She shook her head. "I want to see his hide." The soft underside of her throat bobbed. "Know it's really him."

Strong as iron and he wanted her to bend. Wanted her to accept the truth and walk away from this nightmare. But bendable, he'd learned, wasn't in Bren Ryan's nature.

Rafe nodded to his brother. "Let's make this quick."

Trey knocked on the door. Within seconds, it opened, and Trey spoke Spanish to a stocky plant worker wearing a white smock half-buttoned over a thick winter coat. He nodded and opened the door to admit them.

An immediate chill hit Rafe's face and hands, and he realized it was a huge walk-in refrigeration room. He pulled Bren off to the side. "Damn it, Bren, what are we looking for here? Tell me. I've seen carcasses after slaughter. You haven't. You don't need this memory burned into your subconscious. What is it going to take to prove he's dead, short of you searching?"

Her face crumpled. "I just need to see the mark on his hide. It's a smiley face. Once I see it . . ." Her head dipped, and she sniffed before lifting her chin again. "I'll know for certain." She touched his pocket. "The digital camera. That bastard Wes is going to pay for what he did to Smiley. I need you to take a picture when I find him." She rubbed the side of her face hard and took a heavy breath. "The manifest, too. I'll need it for court. I'm not going to fall apart here. I promise." Her lips thinned. "Smiley deserves better."

Rafe nodded and dug into the deep pocket of his army jacket. He couldn't help but smile. She'd harassed him about this jacket from the start, and all the shit he'd shoved into every available pocket. With the camera in one hand, he grabbed hers with the other, and followed the Mexican worker around a corner, past several metal tables, hoses, and floors with several drains until they were motioned to the left.

Bren's hand tightened in his. Hung by their underbellies by heavy meat hooks were several carcasses. Definitely horses—their tails and manes fluttering under the ventilation system above. Split down the center of their sternums, some of the hide pulled back to reveal the meat of their hindquarters, their hooves and heads severed. Rafe's stomach roiled.

He glanced at Bren, her profile stiff, eyes fastened straight ahead. There were five in this row. Two chestnut, one black, a bay, and one Appaloosa. He assumed the Appaloosa was Smiley. The worker had directed them to this row specifically. Rafe tugged on her hand.

"Is that him?"

She connected with Rafe. "I-I need to check his left hind quarter." She took the one step needed to bring her within reach. Her hand raised tentatively, her index finger lightly touching the hide. She stroked it, a whimper escaping through her trembling lips.

Rafe moved beside her. "Where is it, honey?"

She motioned upward, her hand shaking, silent tears slipping down her cheeks. "There." Her voice was barely a whisper.

Damned if she wasn't kidding. Rafe stepped closer, a perfect smiley face—two eyes, a nose, and a curve for the mouth shaped from the speckles that had given him his name. Rafe quickly took several photos and shoved the camera in his pocket.

He grabbed Bren's hand, her fingers trembling in his grip, and every muscle in his body tensed. He was done allowing Bren to use herself as bait to draw out a killer. If Wes had killed Tom, and that was a big if in his mind. As much as he wanted to pin Tom's murder on him and have done with it, he wasn't completely convinced.

But he was convinced about one thing. Wes Connelly enjoyed causing Bren pain, and that really started to piss him off. Now her hand, usually steady and sure, shook with grief. Her pretty face, wet from tears she should never have had to shed, pierced his soul, and he realized right then and there he'd had it up to his six foot two frame with her being hurt.

Somehow Bren stopped being Tom's widow and started being his girl. Not his intention, but he didn't have time to ruminate on how he'd gotten into such a predicament. He needed to get her the hell out of here—out of Mexico. By the time they got back to town it would be close to nine. Enough time to clear the tunnel and cross back into Texas.

He'd call Kevin tomorrow. Let him know the outcome and hope it was enough to keep Wes in jail for now. If not, Rafe meant to personally kick his ass, put his dick in the dirt, and make him think long and hard about causing her anymore heartache. If Wes needed a new target, he could take aim.

CHAPTER TWENTY-SEVEN

BREN DARTED TOWARD THE HORSE, HIS HINDQUARTERS AND THE thrash of his gray tail so familiar. She found him. After hours of searching the paddocks of Grace, he stood foursquare, his head hidden from view as he grazed. He was a glutton for the spring clover.

She came up on him and grabbed his bridle, swinging him around, and froze with horror. Decapitated, only jagged bone, bloody raw flesh remained. Her stomach dipped, her jaws clenched, and an explosion rocked her awake with such force, she screamed in utter terror.

"Bren!" Strong fingers dug into her shoulders. She blinked, and the dark of night blazed red hot. Screams and shouting scrambled her thoughts, and her mind tripped and fell through nightmarish valleys trying to right itself into the present.

But when her brain caught up to real time, she realized the present was the last place she wanted to be, and she flung herself into Rafe's broad chest, her arms looping around the strong column of his neck. "I don't want to die."

All around her the rat-a-tat-tat of guns peppered her eardrums, and she trembled.

What the freaking hell?

She'd fallen asleep in the jeep against Rafe while Trey and Serg rounded up the necessary paperwork she needed to prove what Wes had done. Maybe she'd been asleep for a little over an hour. It was her way of forgetting the awful memories of today. But waking up to a city in bedlam, vehicles ablaze and vehement shouts in a language she couldn't understand, left her a jumble of nerves.

Rafe's arms encircled her waist, his lips grazing her ear. "Neither do I, darlin'." He held her away from him. The hard planes of his face fluttered against the angry flames engulfing the city. "We're going to make a run for it." His fingers slid down her shoulder and gripped her hand tight.

Damn good plan. She was all for that, and she squeezed his hand back with bone-breaking intensity as he drew her with him from the back seat.

Serg and Trey came around on either side of the jeep and reached under the seat in back. Simultaneously retrieving assault rifles, Bren got her first inkling of just how dire their situation had become.

Trey motioned forward. "We head for the cantina," he shouted to compete with the growing roar.

Bren threw a quick look over her shoulder. Rolling up behind them, convoy-style, were heavy-duty pickups. Men stood in the open truck beds, surrounded by thick roll bars levering massive firepower. They blended into the dark of night, leaving her in doubt as to friend or foe. She sank her grip into the rough material of Rafe's army jacket. "Who the hell *are* they?"

"Military." Trey brushed by her. "We're in the middle of a goddamn turf war." He motioned for them to follow and gave Bren a disconcerting look before his gaze cut to Rafe. "Human trafficking is big business. Watch her."

Trey didn't elaborate, only angled his body with Serg through abandoned vehicles and the rush of people clearing the streets. But the meaning was not lost on her or Rafe. Judging by the added pressure placed upon her fingers, she'd find herself minus a hand if they got separated.

The pop and zing of bullets brought her around, and she yanked hard on Rafe's arm, his tall frame bending to accommodate her. He lent his ear but kept his eyes trained to their immediate surroundings.

"Where's your gun?" She searched his person frantically until she spotted it resting along his lean muscled thigh in his other hand.

"Red, forget the gun." He jerked her hard, his eyes tense and tunneling into her. "Focus on what I'm telling you. This is some serious shit we're in. Stay with me." His fingers flexed almost painfully around her hand. "And don't let go."

Like that was ever going to happen. She pressed closer to him, hoping his strength would transfer to her. Bren's legs shook. Her heart ran a race of its own, its beat pounding against her chest. An explosion to the left and the fireball that ensued had her ducking, her one available arm curved to protect her face. Hell had nothing on this place. Flames danced with fury around them. Gasoline burned her throat, and the real fear the gas tank would explode had her reassessing paralyzed fear for move your ass or lose it.

There was one good thing about scared shitless—it could provide a burst of energy when it was most needed. Those legs that stood frozen in place seconds ago pumped with intense speed, dodging cars and the crush of people. They followed Trey and Serg's lead and hopped the curb. Having their own strike force out front aided their forward progress. In the distance, maybe two blocks up, she recognized the seafoam-green building under the street lights. Edging their way against shop windows, they crossed a side street, and she concentrated on the scalloped frontage of the building trimmed in coral. One more block and they'd be within steps of a door that would lead them out of this hellhole.

But their escort slowed, the hesitation nearly sending her full force into Trey's back. They stood in the lee of shadowing buildings, and Bren hoped it was enough to conceal them. Heeding Trey's earlier warning, she pulled her hood over her head, hoping she blended in with the men in her company, only scrawnier.

Trey spun around, his chest expanding, his breath coming in short pants. "Plan A's off the table." He nodded out in front. The side street, their only access to the back door of the cantina, was blocked by a military jeep manned with two soldiers. "No way we're getting past them." He looked to Serg. "Any ideas?"

"Only one, amigo." His thick dark eyebrows met in the middle of his angular nose, and he nudged his chin in Bren's direction. "We need to get chica off the street. The tunnel for tomorrow when heads are cooler and the cartel runs out of bullets." He wiped sweat from his forehead and angled his rifle down the sidewalk. "We go this way. Holiday Inn's a couple blocks up and back toward the park."

The thought of remaining there overnight sent a panic through her, and she shivered. Rafe released her hand, his arm slipping around her waist. He pulled her snug to him. "Cold?"

She shook her head. "Scared."

"Scared is good." She couldn't be sure, but from the sound of his voice he was smiling.

"Not funny. I want to go home," she whispered back.

And that tunnel is empty and waiting. Or is it?

Not that it mattered—the risk, anyway. Because Trey and Serg moved forward, and Rafe trapped her hand in his and pulled her with him, her fingers curling in response. They stepped off the sidewalk away from the soldiers and covered several more blocks. People darted and scurried across streets trying to find cover. Serg motioned up ahead. "One more block. We go right."

Bren's legs burned. But she refused to give in. Life or death, Trey had said. If she'd thought he had been a bit dramatic, shame on her. Rounding the corner, they headed past a Laundromat, lights on but empty—same with a small market and restaurant. The green fancy H in the word "Holiday" shimmered in the distance, and Bren kept pace with the men. A single shot rang out, and she ducked. Snapping her eyes shut, she held her breath. A wave of panic washed over her, waiting for the jagged pain to explode in her chest. When it didn't, she exhaled and kept running.

Trey motioned them on ahead of him and Serg. "Rafe," he said, winded, trying to catch his breath. "Hotel's up two blocks."

"Come on, Red." Rafe pulled her forward. Her head was still turned toward those trained to battle Juarez's drug trade with significant firepower, and she hesitated. Trey and Serg moved back in the direction they came, now only shadows.

"Bren." The edge to his voice brooked no argument. She moved with Rafe toward the hotel and concentrated on the glint of his semiautomatic, still gripped in his other hand. "You just as good at shooting as you are at roping?" Her words came on uneven breaths.

"Bull's-eye every time, darlin'."

A little cocky. But if they had to fight to survive, she'd go with cocky anytime. "How many bullets?"

"Twenty-one."

Was that even enough? She didn't want to know. Twenty-one bullets stood in between her and—

The thought never had time to truly register. The ground shook beneath her feet, and a dark swath of soldiers came at them. Overtaken, Bren and Rafe battled to stay together. But the warmth of his hand fell away, only the chill of the night air left to brush her palm, and the strength that had kept her from spiraling into the frightening abyss of despair was gone.

"Rafe!" Her desperate cry, lost on the wave of insurgency, ripped from her throat.

He cursed and tried to fight his way back to her, his familiar form disappearing among the soldiers, along with the fading of her name. He was gone.

"Rafe!" Her voice cracked, and cold, stark terror seized her. Surrounded, they thumped and paddled her like a pinball, shooting her from side to side. She struggled to remain on her feet. But the force overwhelmed her, and she fell to her knees. Pebbles dug into her shins, and her arms flew up to protect her head.

Her heart beat so fast she feared it would stop. Huddled into a small ball, her backpack protecting her from the jolts of their legs as they ran past, she prayed. A boot caught her calf, pinching her flesh, and she bit down on her lip to keep from crying out. The trembling ground around her steadied, the boots no longer echoing in her ears, and she lifted her hands from her head and peered through the last of the fatigue-clad legs passing by. They were gone, and she was left alone in a heap in the center of the street.

Shaking, Bren stood, searching for Rafe. No one remained. Alone in full panic mode, she tried to run. Pain shot through her legs; she staggered, her muscles still too tense for a sprint. In front, another street came up. She checked the street in either direction—only swaying palm trees and blinking traffic lights. Across the intersection a wrought-iron fence encircled a playground, and she hoped this was the park Serg had mentioned. She searched for her bearings, but only a tall, concrete building several blocks up, minus the fancy green H, remained—her North Star.

How had she gotten so turned around?

She crossed the street and hugged the fence, her destination the building ahead. She needed to keep moving. The pop of gunfire still pelted the air in the distance. She needed to find Rafe. Her mind raced, and horrible thoughts crept in. She was sick with worry—worried he'd been shot or worse—dead. Tears burned the backs of her eyes.

If she lost him . . .

The screech of tires brought her around. Two dark Suburbans rounded the street behind her, their headlights off. *Shit!* She needed to hide. But where? She searched the deserted streets. A fence, interrupted by the entrance to the park, beckoned along with a set of hedges on either side. Bren tackled the distance quickly and shoved her body into the tangle of shrubs. She took deep breaths to steady her breathing. The earthy scent of boxwoods reminded her of her garden. Before she left, the spring pansies had just begun to peek through.

Her hands clenched. *I'm not dying in this hellhole.*

Angry shouts and the pop of gunfire erupted again, and her oath to deny death forced her to recant in a desperate plea of mercy.

Please, God, don't let me die! She hunkered down, and gripped the iron fence.

Her fingers tightened on the bars. Her leg muscles trembled. She kept her eyes trained on the park. The lights in the park were off, but the glare from the streetlight on the corner picked up on the red roof of the jungle gym.

The colorful swings swaying in the breeze gave way to sweeter, innocent days when death didn't hang in the air like an awful stink trying to suffocate her.

Finn's sweet face invaded her thoughts, and she sobbed. She missed her boys, and her heart smarted with the realization she might never see them again.

Doors slammed shut, along with her future. Heavy soles beat against the sidewalk and entered the park. She pressed back into the thicket to keep hidden. Several more men entered, holding assault rifles. Dressed in black, wearing stocking masks with only holes for their eyes and mouth, they danced and shouted and shot randomly into the air. A scream, high-pitched and savage, came up behind her. Something moved past her through the gate. Gone was the stomp of angry boots and shoes on the sidewalk, replaced with friction and drag and an earsplitting wail, fierce and keening.

Bren froze. Fear clutched her throat. What in *hell* was that? An animal?

It came again, a more urgent shriek. No, it had to be a human sound—frighteningly human. My God, what had she stumbled into?

Bren remained still. The risk of movement too great, she remained rooted to the ground. Her fingers cemented to the bars of the fence, afraid drawing back her hands would alert them to her location. She'd pray the overgrown limbs, thick with leaves, would conceal her pale skin against the black iron.

Bren gasped. Hog tied, a man writhed against the ropes binding his ankles and his wrists. His colorful striped shirt rode up his back. Bare skin scuffed along the pavement. His head thrashed back and forth, his face staring upward.

He cried, the words a jumble of Spanish that meant nothing to Bren. The others paraded around him, taunting him with jeers and kicks to his side and head. A taller black form approached, his arm swinging up from behind his back with malice, and the gleam of a machete took shape, and the blade swung down viciously. A gut-twisting shriek echoed in her ears and was silenced. Blood spurted like a geyser where his head should have been, and Bren shook in horror as they hoisted the ropes binding his ankles over a thick tree limb several steps from where she crouched. It swayed just like before. Just like . . . *God* . . . *Tom's body*. Dark and menacing, its arms dangled and the nightmare she'd lived with for months left her wide awake and petrified.

She so desperately wanted to shut her eyes, but she needed to keep *them* accounted for. Nausea assailed her and she swallowed in desperation. Clenching her teeth against a second wave, she remained entrenched.

Another man slung his rifle behind his back and reached for the head. His fingers grabbed the head by its hair, and he held it high. His comrades laughed and slapped each others' backs while he walked toward the fence and Bren.

Bren whimpered. The irrepressible sound sent jagged spokes of fear racing over her skin. Dark pant legs and boots stood straddled before her. The drip of blood, steady and horrific, plopped on the supple leaves inches from her face. The man stepped back. Another round of bullets sprayed the night sky, and panic rushed her. Boots and heavy shoes filed past the gate into the street. Their voices, filled with mirth, vanished with the abrupt slamming of doors.

They were gone.

Bren chewed on her lips with indecision. Her fingers, still white-knuckled and oddly sticky, remained on the fence. Terror-fed adrenaline spiked, and she shot up to her feet and screamed. The head, jammed on the spike of the fence, stared back, now a hideous death mask, eyes bulging, mouth frozen open.

An iron grip seized her arm, and she could taste her own fear as it spun her around. "Bren!" His voice was so rough, she scarcely recognized it as his.

She shook. Her fingers tight and sticky, she raised her hands.

His eyes hardened, and he pulled her from the entanglement of shrubs. "I got you, darlin'."

Silent tears flowed down her cheeks. She couldn't even wipe her face. The blood—his blood—stained her hands, and it hit her swift and sickening. She now knew the meaning of having someone's blood on her hands, and the truth that could only live in her nightmares awakened. The blood was no longer that of a stranger's in a hellish land.

It was Tom's.

Chapter Twenty-Eight

Bren couldn't keep her teeth from chattering. Warmth eluded her. Had eluded her since Tom's death, and tonight as she witnessed the most barbaric of acts, she realized that the tortured soul she had become would never experience true warmth unless she told someone what she had done.

Rafe slipped the room passkey through the lock. It beeped then buzzed, and he opened the door.

Still frozen and standing rigid in the hotel's corridor, her hands held out, fingers stiff with dried blood that she'd refused to get anywhere near her person, Rafe pulled her inside. He flipped on the light and dropped their backpacks against the wall. A soft glow illuminated the hotel room from around the narrow entryway where she could make out the beginnings of matching comforters draping two beds. Rafe directed her into the bathroom and hit the light. It was small, with only a single shower behind a frosted-glass door, a toilet, and narrow vanity with one sink.

"You have any open cuts?" Their eyes met in the mirror—his tense, hers blank and staring.

She shook her head. "N-no." She clenched her teeth to stop them from chattering.

He frowned. "You're freezing." His hands came up, brusquely rubbing her arms.

She nodded. "A l-little."

He turned on the faucets and began pulling up her sweatshirt sleeves. He tested the water and directed her hands underneath. It was warm. The instant contact of the heat against the cold of her skin burned slightly. The water, turning a rusty pink, swirled down the drain. He hit the pump soap.

Working up a lather, he reached for her hands.

While he scrubbed, his long fingers moving vigorously in between hers, she noticed the differences in their hands. Where hers were small and pale and slightly trembling, his were generous and male, shades darker, and moving in controlled motions. He rinsed her hands and grabbed the hand towel off the bar on the wall and dried them. As he flipped the towel over his shoulder, their eyes met in the mirror again.

Gone was the gentleness he possessed while administering to her blood-caked hands. He scowled at her. "Do yourself a favor and forget about tonight."

Not a chance. She lifted her chin to him in the mirror. "I—"

"We're done, Bren." He spun her around, gripping her shoulders. Her breath caught. "I almost went nuts when I couldn't find you. We let this thing go before it kills us."

They were a pair, the two of them. Both exhausted, dirty, and still smarting from their near escape. But she couldn't agree. Not about this. Unlike Tom's death, she had verifiable proof. Wes *was* guilty. She might never prove he'd killed Tom, but she wasn't walking away from Smiley's murder. Putting him behind bars, even for a week or a month, would at least give her some satisfaction.

"I can't." She wanted to elaborate, but any more than one- or two-word sentences were beyond her. And even if she possessed the ability to lodge a stronger complaint, Rafe's severe expression and the distress in his voice outweighed any harsh reply.

Her teeth chattered anew. God, she wanted to be warm, and his body, which took up an ample portion of the tiny space, gave off the most wonderful heat. She trembled right down to her toes and moved closer. But even his strength and nearness couldn't extinguish the horror of tonight. And it flooded her senses with overwhelming alarm.

"Don't you understand?" She reached for him, tugging on his arm. "It's always there. I can't let it go. *It won't let me go.*" Her voice cracked.

Not going to lose it. Not now.

But every ounce of suck-it-up-and-deal dwindled, leaving her with the awful image of that body. "I-it swung . . ." Her hand flew to her mouth. "*Oh my God, Rafe.* T-they cut off his head!"

His hands slid down her sides, and he hoisted her onto the edge of the vanity and kept a firm hold on her waist. "It wasn't Tom, Bren. He was a nameless face—a drug dealer. He got what he deserved." His eyes narrowed in on her. "Jesus." He took a deep breath, and his fierce gaze softened. "What you saw . . ." He hesitated and reached to caress her face. His voice gentling, his eyes still incisive, determined. "I should have said no to you. No to this savage border town."

But she had seen it, heard it—way before tonight. The awful sound. It played back with frightening intensity, and she clenched her hands to keep them from covering her ears. "The creaking was just like before." Her head fell back, and she closed her eyes.

Rough fingers gently kneaded the back of her neck. "No, honey, it wasn't."

She opened her eyes and shook her head. "I couldn't save him." Toms' lifeless body took shape in her mind. "His face was the most frightful shade of purple," she whispered.

Rafe tilted her chin up. "You've got to let it go."

She swallowed hard. "I've never experienced that kind of panic." Her teeth began to chatter again. "U-until tonight. T-then I thought I'd be n-next."

He raked his fingers through his hair and cursed. "You and me. That's what's important here. I'm not willing to take any more risks. Not with you."

"But I can't—"

"Damn it, Bren!" He gripped her by the shoulders. "Listen to what I'm telling you. We're done. This thing between you and Wes ends tonight." He yanked the towel off his shoulder and balled it in his hands and tossed it on the vanity. "I'm dead serious here." He cupped her chin, his eyes glinting a warning to let him finish. "We've turned up zilch. Even your buddy Kevin couldn't prove Wes killed Tom. I was all for helping you. I don't scare easy, darlin'. But tonight, when I thought I'd lost you, it just about killed me."

"I'm sorry." She slumped against the mirror and turned away from him. For once she had nothing to say. Everything he said was true.

"Hey." He knelt down in front of her. His hands slipping under her bottom, and he nudged her to him.

If she so much as peeked at him, she'd be tempted to give in.

"Look at me." His voice was gruff and demanding, yet when she engaged him, met his eyes, they belied the tough guy she'd come to know as Rafe Langston and hinted at the pain she, too, had felt when they had been separated tonight.

"It's not your fault, darlin'. I should have never let go." He hugged her legs and laid his head on her thighs.

Her heart caught at his expression of tenderness for her, and she reached out, twining shaky fingers through his thick, unruly black locks. Pulling gently, she directed him up. He was handsome and strong and curiously sensitive, and it touched her deeply. "I caused all this, not you. I think God was just giving me a *what for.*"

He shook her lightly. "It doesn't matter." He searched her eyes. "Did you mean what you said the other night . . . about your heart?"

The roughness of his voice made her go all shivery. Yes, she'd meant it—fallen for him when she shouldn't, lost her heart in degrees starting the night in the hayloft of her barn.

Don't make me love you.

"I'll only hurt you, Rafe."

"I'm hurting already." He kissed her mouth. "I knew I should have stayed clear of you." His hands slid under her bottom, and he pulled her still closer. "I told myself you were trouble."

She smiled at that, but she wasn't getting a reprieve. For the most part, her covert activities were benign. Her schemes were only meant to save lives, not end them—except for one. "Tom is dead because of me, Rafe."

"It wasn't your fault."

"Don't be nice to me." Tears stung her eyes, and her throat ached to tell him the truth.

His hands moved under her sweatshirt and pressed lightly against her spine, his eyes softened. "What is it, Red?"

She held his face between her hands, the dark whiskers along his cheeks prickly. She hadn't meant to get close to him. If anything, in the beginning, he was an irritant. Or maybe *she* was just irritated. "You're the only one who believed me—would help me. You're my best friend, Rafe." Those damn tears she tried valiantly to keep from spilling over betrayed her.

His fingers tensed along her back. "Hey, don't cry." He frowned and slipped a hand out from her shirt, brushing away a tear from her cheek. "Want to know a secret?" He cocked a brow up and grinned. The exaggerated gesture lightened her mood and coaxed a half smile from her lips. "You're mine, too."

And there it was. This stranger she'd wanted no part of had broken through her walls, and the awareness that she'd known him all her life—at least bits and pieces of him—was stronger than ever.

She couldn't explain it. Simply, there was no explanation, and she'd given up trying.

Still shivering, she scooted closer, her knees bumping up against his solid chest. She brought her hands down to rest on his shoulders, the resilience of firm muscle tensed, and his reaction left her no doubt he was bracing himself.

"You need to know the truth, Rafe. About me." The words were there. She only needed to say them, and she would be free.

Tell him.

"I lied when I told you that night in the barn I had nothing to do with Tom's death." Her fingers tightened on his shoulders. "I'd still have Tom and Smiley if I hadn't gone after Wes. I should have let those damn horses go." Her throat went dry, and she whispered, "I didn't, Rafe." She held fast to him. "All the stories around town are true. I stole back the horses we lost at auction to Wes—slipped out at night while Tom slept, crossed the fence onto Connelly land, and stole them out from under him. I had help, but it was my idea."

He remained quiet for a moment, only reaching up to press back a strand of her hair. "I already guessed that."

"You did?"

"We think alike. I would have done the same."

She let go of his shoulders, her hands on her hips, and pinned him with her eyes. "And that's exactly *why*, cowboy, we're filthy dirty, pouring out our souls to each other, holed up in some hotel, surrounded by lawlessness."

His lips quirked. "Scary, you and me."

"Very." She shivered again. *Guess confessions are only as good as the confessional box.* She'd hoped for relief from the chill that kept her in its grip.

"You're still cold." He stood and slid her off the vanity and rubbed her arms.

The tiniest of heat moved along her skin. His hand moved to cradle the back of her head, his rough fingertips pressing into her scalp, radiating warmth, and she moved closer.

He tipped her chin up. "You didn't cause Tom's death. Whether you took the horses or not, that's no reason to kill."

"No. But I should have thought it through—weighed the consequences. Tom would be alive."

Something in the depths of his eyes hardened, and he bent his head, his lips grazing hers, and whispered, "He's not."

The quiet rasp of his voice, the mere touch of his lips ignited a desire she hadn't had in a long time, and instead of giving in to it, she stiffened. But the usual feeling of betrayal eluded her, attempts to recall Tom's face—difficult. The only face she saw was Rafe's. The only touch she felt—his. Her heart raced.

Oh God.

The memories of tonight swamped her. He was right. Vengeance didn't spell victory—*try misery.* She'd lost the love of her life. How many more had to suffer? How many more could she afford to lose?

Her hands moved up, putting some space between them. Still keeping her hands on his expansive chest, she concentrated on him. Rough and tumble, dark and dangerously handsome, he made her senses reel. The solid warmth of him was intoxicating. It made her woozy with the kind of need a woman could only have for a man.

And then there was that damn feeling that she had missed connecting a dot somewhere. Was it an expression? Or maybe his eyes, so familiar, sharp and piercing at times, but mostly devastatingly warm and caressing.

Whatever it was about Rafe Langston, the thought of losing him hurt with such intensity she felt as if she would die. Her fingers gripped his army jacket. "You jerk." This time his eyes were alert and questioning. "I thought I'd lost you, too."

His arms went around her, and she snuggled so close, the drum of his heartbeat was one with hers.

"Not gonna happen, darlin'." He kissed her, his mouth experienced, sure, and firm with such undeniable possessiveness she trembled.

She'd never been kissed like that before. Not by Tom. Not by anyone. It was hungry, hard, and explosive. Yet, that nagging sense of knowing him poked her subconscious—the reasoning close enough to grasp but the understanding of it beyond her.

He touched his tongue to hers, and that tingle of unexplored newness, replacing any conscious thought, spread through her like liquid fire, and she sighed into his mouth.

Blessed heat had returned, and it warmed her clear through.

CHAPTER TWENTY-NINE

CONFESSIONS BEING WHAT THEY WERE, IT WOULD HAVE BEHOOVED Rafe—considering their admitted status of best friends and all—to ante up and put his cards where Bren could see them. But the truth of it was, his only concern was getting her naked. He was too far gone over her to think about the days ahead, to pull back and reassess.

Her lips were soft and pliant and moving beneath his in a seductive dance. Suddenly his heart beat faster, and then Tom Ryan's ghost nudged him, a little. He opened his eyes. Hers were closed. Amazing as it was, Ryan didn't seem to be on her mind. Good. He wasn't interested in taking a cold shower.

What he wanted was what could have been his all along—he wanted her.

Rafe slipped his hand under her sweatshirt, its thickness hampering him as he tried to touch more skin. "How about we lose this?" he ground out against her lips and tugged on the edge of her sweatshirt.

She lifted her arms, and he pulled it over her head, the band of her ponytail slipping off with it. He tossed her shirt to the tile floor.

She shook her head. The weight of her hair dusted her shoulders and her back. The contrast, reminding him of alabaster and rose petals, couldn't have been more erotic.

He twined his fingers through the dark-cherry waves cascading over her shoulder. Motionless, their eyes connected, and then they both stared at his other hand caressing the curve of her waist.

When their gazes locked again, her eyes were big and brown and . . .

Shit. Was she frightened?

Her legs trembled against his thighs, and she held fast to the folds of his jacket, tugging. "Take it off." Her soft, impatient demand gave him his answer. At least for now, she was willing.

He shimmied out of it and tossed it to the floor. Going for her jeans, he struggled with the button and zipper until her jeans hung loose around her waist, allowing his hands to cup her bare, curvaceous bottom. He pulled her tight to him. "I wanted to take your clothes off the first night I took you home." It was a guttural growl—an admission of weakness. He'd been angry at her stupidity, using herself as bait with a jackass like Skidmore. But mostly because he'd realized that night he had the hots for Ryan's widow.

It had been his first warning to walk away, and the last reason he would have considered it. He hadn't found a woman yet who could hold his interest, much less put a dent in his heart—she'd scored on both.

They struggled with each other's clothes, tugging, lifting, and touching skin. Down to next to naked, she reached behind her back to unclasp her bra.

"Whoa, darlin'." He pressed her up against the vanity. "You were holding out on me. Let me see." He eyed her approvingly. "And here I thought my farm girl would be wearing cotton briefs."

"Cute." She lifted her chin, blushing. "I like the feel of silk better."

He nodded. "Silky and see-through, Red." He cupped both breasts and brushed a thumb over each nipple and watched with interest as they poked steadily against the white lace of her bra, her areolas shrunk and darkened against its sheerness. His mouth came down and covered her nipple, his tongue barely touching it.

She writhed up against him and sank her fingers into his scalp, holding his head against her. "Don't tease me, Rafe."

He suckled her and lifted his head. "Not true, honey. You're teasing me."

He kissed her, their tongues touching, stroking, and his body responded. "You're making me hard, darlin'." The quiet rasp of his voice surprised him. He'd had his fair share of women. Even rocked their worlds—at least that was his impression. But none had ever rocked his.

He crouched down. His rough hands experimented with the white lace, the russet swath covering her sex a shadow beneath the swirling design. "Pretty panties." He brushed her there with his fingertips, then lower.

She gripped the edge of the vanity. "Oh God, Rafe." The catch in her voice and her sigh would be his undoing. Devastatingly sensual, laced with surrender, it invaded his bloodstream, hot and consuming.

He caressed her, the sudden dampness through her lace panties made him dizzy with desire, and he rose to his feet. Deliberately wedging his thigh between her pale, shapely legs, he marveled at the silky sexiness of her. He lowered his head and kissed her neck, his lips grazing her ear. "Bren, honey, take a shower with me?" He rocked his thigh up higher between her legs. The tiny sound of pleasure she made had him reaching behind him. Rafe slid the shower door and fumbled with the cold metal of the faucet. It squeaked, and the hard pressure of shower spray filled the tight bathroom.

"Rafe?" There was a note somewhere between pleasure and distress in her voice.

He turned around.

She chewed on her bottom lip and moved away. "Maybe it'd be best if you . . ."

His eyes searched hers. "What's up, Red? Do I frighten you?"

Making love to him was a damn huge step for her.

"Come here." Her pretty lips thinned, and he pulled her toward him. She fell into him, her fingers slipping into his crisp, dark chest hairs. His pulse quickened.

She held his gaze. Her hand moving across his stomach, she moved lower, dipping her hand inside his underwear.

He pulled in a jagged breath. "You know what?" He strove for calm, which was increasingly difficult considering she was stroking him from root to tip. "I've got a real thing for girls who don't frighten easy." He kissed her then, his hand slipping behind her back, fingers working the clasp of her bra until it gave, and the straps fell down her shoulders.

She released his dick, and he groaned. She slipped her hands between the two of them, resting them tentatively on his pecs, looping her arms around his neck.

"Truth or dare, darlin'." All he needed to do was step back. But he didn't need to worry about making a move. Dare was on his side. She'd choose to lose the bra before she'd admit she had fallen for a cowboy.

She gave his chest hairs a tight pull.

"Ow." He frowned down at her and rubbed his chest.

"Not funny." Her eyes flared. "A woman who hasn't done it in a long time could get carried away and hurt you."

He gave her a lopsided grin. "I was kind of hoping for that."

"Were you?" A well-shaped brow arced in challenge.

"Yes, ma'am." He slid the bra off her arms. Soft, jiggly breast pressed up against him. He lowered his head and closed his mouth over hers. Her mouth was warm and soft and incredibly sweet. He touched her tongue. Hot sparks rocketed him, and his balls grew unbearably tight.

He stood back. She was lovely—lush smooth skin, toned lithe body. His fingers and mind tingled. He cupped her breasts, pale and full and perfect in his hands. He ran his thumbs over her nipples—extended and pink and vying for his attention. "You're beautiful." He flicked them with his tongue.

She drew in a short breath and placed her hands on his shoulders, her fingertips working their heat through his skin. He moved lower, kissing her stomach above the lacy edge of her panties, his fingers hooking into each side. He pulled them off.

Tight, sexy legs trembled beneath his rough palms, and he couldn't get enough of her ivory skin against the bronze of his working-man's hands. His fingers ran the length of her silky legs, her hips, to rest on her small waist. He came to his feet. His eyes swept her, taking in every contour and curve, his finger tracing the edge of the soft, thin delta of russet curls.

He couldn't move. But his mind reeled. His heart raced.

"Not what you expected." Her face grew flushed, and she turned away from him.

Shit. He wanted to kick himself for giving her the impression she was less than perfect. Not his intention. If anything she took his breath away.

"Hold up." He grabbed her by the waist and turned her toward him. She struggled, and he tightened his grip. "Don't rush me." The crush of their bodies, and the tender breathless way in which her eyes caressed his face, sent a rush of heat surging up his belly that spread through him, scorching his heart. "Cowboys are slow—methodical."

Her gorgeous brown eyes flickered, changed, and fastened on him.

He stroked her cheek, warm and rosy with maybe a combination of embarrassment and anger. "Bren, I'm not pretty with words. All I know is you're better than any birthday or Christmas present combined, and I want to take my time unwrapping you."

"I think you've done that."

"Yes I have." He held her tighter. "Now I'm going to tinker with my gift. Touch her." He ran his hand down her spine. "Tease her." He rolled her nipple between his fingers, and the little gasp she tried to hide made him grin. "And kiss her." He lowered his head and dropped a hard kiss on her mouth. Pulling back, he held her eyes with his.

She rolled her kissable lips in a considering kind of way, but remained silent. No problem. Talking was optional. He opened the shower door and drew her under the water.

She squealed, "Damn it, Rafe!" Her lips sputtered with water, her legs unsteady

He held onto her until she got her bearings. Her skin shimmered under the water. Dark, wet shafts of hair clung to the rise of her breasts, soft and provocative. She was intoxicating, and he wanted his hands on her flesh with an intensity that drove him senseless.

"Hang tight," he said, his voice thick with need, and shed his underwear. He stepped in, the heat of the water prickling his skin like pins and needles.

She had already ripped off the wrapper of the purple puff thing and began soaping it up, giving him her shapely back.

He kissed her neck and wrapped his arms around her. Reaching for her hands, he took the soap and puff from her. "Let me wash you, darlin'." He started at the base of her neck, slow, circular motions over her delicate shoulder blades, past the curve of her waist, and took his time over her soft, round rump. Crouching behind her, he held her hips in place and took a nip of her tender flesh with his teeth.

She moaned and turned, giving him access to swirling russet wet curls. He washed her there, messaging the soapy puff between her thighs. As the warm water rinsed the soap from the soft curls, he kissed her mound. Wet and warm, she smelled of soap and woman, and his body grew hot and heavy.

He stood and let his erection brush her there, and the contact inflamed him. Taking the puff, he continued to explore her sensual curves, letting the soapy iridescent bubbles glide over her skin. When he came to her breasts, he touched them lightly with the puff. Her nipples grew stiff, and he lowered his head and rubbed his scratchy cheek against the pale slope of her breasts. He kissed them, the water streaming over her, sensual rivers slick beneath his lips.

She cupped his head and brought it up. "My turn." Her eyes, huge and dark, rested on his face. She took the puff and made arcs across his chest, the roughness of it snagging his nipples, he stilled her hands with his.

"You're going to make me—"

"Come?" Her eyes rested on him—swollen and erect. "I want you to come." She touched him with the puff, swirling his pubic hair, the soap running down his legs.

He quelled her hands and took it from her. Dragging her head up, he kissed her. Slanting his mouth over her sweet, pliable lips until she opened her mouth to him, he licked his way in. She was warm, her lips tasting of soap. He delved deeper, caressing the inside of her mouth.

She suckled his lips, tugging, and the suction she created drove him insane. Her breasts grazed his chest, and he broke the kiss. Pert pink nipples begged his attention, and he laved them with his tongue.

Her fingers pressed into his head. "Rafe," she moaned. "Oh Rafe, please take me." Her hands moved down his back, stroking him, her fingers pressing hard into his muscles.

The small shower made her request a challenge, but he'd never backed down from one yet. He spun her around. Kissing her neck, then her ear, he grated through clenched teeth, his voice thick. "I'm going to take you from behind." He kneaded her buttocks.

She nodded. "Just don't stop."

He couldn't have anyway. She was all he ever wanted, could ever hope for in a woman. No matter how they'd come to this point, he wouldn't apologize for where they ended up.

She was his. He felt protective, possessive, wildly territorial. And he knew as long as he lived, he'd want her the rest of his days.

He tilted his hips forward and nestled his erection in the cleft of her cheeks. He kissed the nape of her neck, taking love bites as he went. He stroked her breast and teased her nipple taut. His hand slid past her flat stomach and cupped her sex, his finger sliding inside her. He moved them, gently stroking the little nub until she whimpered and pressed the side of her face against the shower wall.

Her profile, smooth as sweet cream, glistened under the shower spray. Her cheeks, flushed and perfectly sculpted, were a masterpiece of beauty against black, dense lashes, wet and fluttering shut.

He pressed a string of kisses along the delicate curve of her jaw, while his finger continued to stroke her, tease her. She was wet, her muscles clenching his finger, and her hips began to move against his palm in rhythmic motions.

She bit down on her lower lip. "I want you inside me, now." Her voice was husky.

"Not yet."

Her hands flattened on the shower enclosure. He removed his finger and wrapped his arm around her waist. Holding tight, he positioned himself. He drove into her slowly, the sensation utterly soul-shattering. "God, Bren, you feel so good." He kissed her cheek.

"Love me, Rafe." She said it in a soft, urgent voice.

"I do, darlin'." He held her hand with his against the wall, and he thrust into her again. "God help me. I do." His words were choppy as he tried to hold on to his slipping control.

He continued to rock them toward a tumultuous orgasm. The curve of her tight bottom undulated against his thrusts in perfect rhythm.

"Oh, Rafe, don't stop. Please don't stop. It feels so . . . right . . . so amazing . . ." She took a deep breath through her nose and bit down on those perfectly shaped lips, so wet and sexy.

He groaned with the need to kiss them hard and senseless. Her body began to tremble, and he held her snug to him, letting the warm shower spray pelt his back.

"Rafe," she moaned. Her body convulsed in his arms. "Oh God, Rafe, Rafe . . ."

He thrust deeper. "Bren." His voice was hoarse, and he buried his mouth into the hollow of her neck. He kissed her and continued to seek his own release. His body shuddered, and he came violently. Breathing in gasps, he spun her around, enveloping her in his arms.

Slick and wet and warm, she rested against him. "Hold me."

His arms tightened around her. "I wasn't planning on letting go, honey."

She lifted her head, her eyes voluminous, lids heavy.

He caressed her cheek and eyed her speculatively. "Love me, Rafe?" It came out half amused, half questioningly. "Is that something you normally say during the height of lovemaking? Or did you really mean it?"

"I don't usually say things I don't mean."

"Is that the best you can do?"

She reached up on tiptoe and kissed him. He kissed her back and shook her playfully. The undeniable curve of her mouth against his told him she was enjoying his pain. His lips moved against hers. "Call me old-fashioned, darlin'. But I want to hear the words."

His one eye opened. Her eyes remained closed, and she was content in kissing him back. Rafe broke off the kiss.

Her eyes sprang open, and she laughed. "You're awfully concerned about this." She pulled him toward her. "Isn't it obvious how I feel about you?" She ran her palms over him until they rested on his shoulders. One small hand slipped to the back of his neck, nudging him forward, pulling him to eye level with her. Her eyes were intent, serious, and all for him. "I love you, Rafe. So much it hurts, baby."

He kicked his conscience to the dirt, closed his ears to honesty, and concentrated on the here and now and kissed her breathless.

The truth could wait. Dealing with a hellion who could do pissed-off in a heartbeat was best handled on American soil. For now he only wanted to take her to bed, cuddle next to her until he fell asleep.

CHAPTER THIRTY

THE TRIP BACK TO MARYLAND HAD BREN REASSESSING HER NEXT
move. She had all but agreed to herself and Rafe in Mexico that
she needed to stop her obsession with trying to prove Wes killed Tom before
her boys lost both their parents.

Being back in her house since returning two days ago with her boys and
her father made her acutely aware how much her family meant to her. God
she'd missed them. After seeing her boys off to bed last night, she promised
herself—no more drama.

Then there was work. Her three-day absence couldn't have come at
a worse time. She'd left Jo to handle the clinic while Jeremy remained in
Kentucky at an annual meeting he looked forward to every year in prepara-
tion for the Kentucky Derby. It was time she concentrated on being reliable,
and it started with relieving Jo.

Rafe pulled his pickup into the equine vet parking lot and parked. The
mundane life at the clinic she would take over jumping borders any day.

"Red." Bren didn't miss the apprehension in Rafe's voice. He reached out
and squeezed her thigh. The pressure of his fingertips, warm and assuring,
radiated right through her jeans.

She lifted her head, not surprised to find a pair of brooding green eyes
leveled with challenge.

"Sleep is the last thing I need."

He tightened incrementally on her thigh. "You're relying on anger to
get you through this."

She stiffened. "I'm not going to forget what Wes did to me."

Before he could object, Bren raised her hand. "I already agreed to let Kevin handle Wes. Except for the horses in Grace's care, documenting their condition and testifying in court, I'm hands-off." As much as it pained her, it was for the best. If she'd learned anything in Mexico, it was what was truly important. She only hoped Wes's attorney didn't finagle his release.

Her stomach twisted. What they'd done to her horse . . . She couldn't bring herself to imagine. Even the digital photos Rafe had taken, she'd refused to look at. She didn't need a photo when the carnage was burned into her memory.

Kevin had the memory card now, along with the manifest connecting her horse to Sweet Creek Stables. Seemed Wes had never calculated getting caught and never thought to have Smiley shipped from another location not connected to him.

She smiled at that. Dumb-ass had sealed his own fate. So she relaxed, knowing his bail had been denied and no amount of friendship or good-old-boy system was going to get him sprung anytime soon.

So now she only needed a distraction to keep her from wishing the time away until Wes could be brought to justice. And work, the clinic in particular, the horses and her rescue operation, fit the prerequisite in keeping her occupied.

Rafe caressed her cheek. "So we're square on the Wes issue?" His brow rose in question.

"Absolutely."

He moved across the seat, his lean, muscled thigh pressed up against her leg. "Good. I'm looking toward the future." He threaded his hand through her hair, the rough pads of his fingertips pressing into her scalp, and he pulled her toward him.

She rolled her lips in and then out, knowing full well his intentions, and heat flooded her insides with longing. Her eyes closed. The warmth of his breath so close to her mouth made her tingle. She loved kissing him. Loved . . . The thought was lost when his firm lips came down on hers. She kissed him back, parting her mouth to allow his tongue to explore and stroke. He tasted of coffee and the Werther's butterscotch he'd popped in his mouth before they left the farm.

The future . . . Did he mean with her or in general? Waking up to his long, lean body, his legs wonderfully male and coarse with hair, intertwined with hers, made her face warm with wanting him. But was what they had shared in Mexico one of those things brought on by grief and fatigue, or was it real?

His arm went around her waist, pulling her snug to him, his long fingers slipping inside the waistband of her jeans, and when he cupped her rounded cheek, she moved closer. He deepened the kiss. Their lips moving against one another caused her to moan inside his mouth. Warmth pooled between her thighs. God, she wanted him. But not like two teens in the front seat of his truck in front of the clinic. Cold reality quashed her growing libido, and she groaned, pulling away her lips. "We can't. Not here."

She didn't miss the draw at the corners of his mouth. She pulled away abruptly. "You jerk. You know exactly what you're doing."

His eyes glinted with guilt, but his smile only increased. "I'm horny, Red. Horny for you." He made a move to continue the kiss, and Bren grabbed for the door handle.

The rumble of his phone distracted him. His fingers slid out of her pants, the sensation still a hot brand along her skin.

Rafe snapped the phone open, his eyes never leaving her. "Yeah." He smiled. "As we speak."

Bren's eyebrows rose.

"Trey," he whispered. He motioned to her. "Business. I'll meet you inside."

She nodded and got out of the truck, shutting the door.

At seven thirty in the morning, the clinic parking lot stood empty as she made her way to the entrance. Purple crocuses had begun to peek out from the mulch bed in front of the bay window of the clinic, and Bren smiled. Only a few more weeks until spring.

The doorknob moved smoothly in her hand, and she stepped in and closed it behind her. The old paneling that had since been painted a lemon yellow greeted her, photographs of horses hung strategically around the walls. The desk to the right sat empty. Bren continued down the hall. "Jo."

Originally a country veterinarian practice, it had two examining rooms on either side equipped with stainless steel tables. She peered inside each room. No Jo. Bren made her way back to the front. With her hands on her hips, she decided to make quick work of finding her and grabbed the phone, prepared to hit the intercom button, when the tab of a folder sitting underneath several others caught her attention.

Typed on a neat white label, the name intrigued her: "Rafe Austin Langston." She didn't even know his middle name—Austin as in Texas. Bren's fingers touched the tab. She loved him. She had put Tom's memory to rest in Mexico.

She was alive, and as much as she'd change places with Tom, she couldn't. She had to continue with life, and as she'd found out in Mexico, a ghost—no matter how much she missed the man Tom had been—was incapable of touching her physically. And she very much enjoyed being touched by Rafe. Her cheeks warmed, and her hand automatically flew to her face.

God, I'm embarrassing myself. What an innocent she really was. Tom was the only man she'd ever . . . until . . .

The heat to her cheeks intensified, and she shook her head to clear her brain and concentrated on her find.

Jo must have felt bad after their conversation on Saturday night.

It didn't matter what Jo had come up with, not now. But her hand dug beneath the stack anyway, until she slipped the folder with Rafe's name out. Born in Texas, he was a cowboy who, from Trey's account, was a damn good cattleman. Who had a damn good head on his shoulders for business and knew damn well that dairy farming had tanked years ago.

Yet he'd bought half her farm to build a dynasty on a cow that resembled a domino and could very well fall like one if tipped, sending his hard-earned money down with it.

She knew Rafe was no dairy farmer. Had been pretty sure all along, though she'd been too preoccupied with her own agenda to give the ruse much thought.

Bren glanced through the window. He remained in the truck, leaning against the door, his cell phone pressed to his ear—occupied. Good. She flipped open the file. She scanned the first document, a credit report. She wasn't a banker. The columns with numbers meant nothing to her. But the last column, titled "Balance," she could understand, and the zeroes confirmed what she already knew—he was financially secure.

There were several pages of handwritten notes she recognized as Jo's. The bulleted items: Washington County Hospital; Baldwin and Chase Esq., an attorney firm located in Hagerstown that hadn't been in business for over two decades; and Vital Statistics Administration located in Baltimore.

She set the lined yellow page aside and flipped through the remaining sheets of paper. Her hand stopped. The name, typed in capital letters, she knew better than her own—"Thomas Patrick Ryan"—followed by his birth date and time of birth. Understanding bloomed, and Bren's fingers tightened at the centered, bold type and decorative scrolls highlighting "Certificate of Live Birth."

Why would Tom's birth certificate be in Rafe's file?

"Bren."

Bren's head shot up. Jo stood in the doorway leading from the hall, her black hair tied back in a high ponytail. She leaned on her cane.

"I—I was looking for—" Bren glanced back through the window. Rafe remained in the truck. "Jo?"

Jo frowned and moved toward her, the thump of her cane growing louder and more ominous. "Bren." Jo stood at the corner of the desk. "We need to talk."

Bren held up the copy in her hand. "This is Tom's birth certificate. I don't understand why—"

Jo touched her arm and squeezed it gently. "It's the last thing I expected."

What was she saying? Bren's hand flew to her mouth, and her head swung to the window. He wasn't in the truck. Bren grabbed Jo's arm. "Rafe's with me." Her fingers pressed into Jo's bicep. "Tell me what this means before he comes through that door." Her eyes flew to the door, and she released Jo.

What was taking him so long? The walk from the truck to the front door of the clinic took less than thirty seconds.

The birth certificate slipped from her fingers when Jo pulled it from her and placed it flat on the desk. Jo pointed next to a block that read, "Plurality."

Plurality?

What the hell kind of word was that? The word next to it made her head spin—"Twin." Bren gripped the edge of the desk and reached for the chair. Her butt hit the soft seat with a thud.

"But I've seen Tom's birth certificate. We needed it for our wedding license years ago—for the boys' baptism certificates." She motioned toward the birth certificate. "I've never seen this one."

"It was the original filed by Washington County Hospital. You may have never seen it. The one you're talking about . . ." Jo flipped open the file and grabbed another piece of paper. "Is this the one you have?"

"Y-yes."

"It's issued through the Division of Vital Records. It doesn't require them to list multiple births."

"Tom had a twin." The words fell off her lips in a whisper. "Why didn't he tell me?"

"Bren, I don't think Tom knew."

Jo grabbed the chair in front of the desk and scooted it around and sat.

Those striking blue eyes of hers held Bren's. "There's more." Jo moved papers around in the file and snagged another from the back. "It's not my place to confront Paddy, sweetheart." She squeezed her hand. "But he owes you an explanation."

"Jo." Bren pressed back on her hand. "Tell me why this is in Rafe's file."

She spun the paper around. The words "Adoption" surfaced first, the names "Sawyer and Laura Langston" next. Cold shot through her chest, and then heat warmed her face, and she moaned. "*My God.*" Her hands shook and came to her face. "He's—"

The doorknob rattled, and Jo and Bren's eyes widened and locked on each other.

"Tell me." Bren stood and begged, pulling on her arm. "Now before—"

The door swung open. "Ladies." A lazy smile tugged at the corners of Rafe's mouth. "Jo, you having trouble with varmints? Raccoons, maybe? Your trash cans were knocked over. Made a big mess—bags ripped, trash . . ." He stopped and frowned. "I grow horns?"

Oh yeah, and a long pointy tail to go with it.

Bren grabbed the birth certificate off the desk. She walked with measured steps toward him. "You son of a bitch." She raised her hand and connected with his cheek.

"Ow!" Rafe's hand flew to his face. Green eyes simmering with anger turned confused. "What the hell?"

Fingers stinging, Bren grabbed the keys from Rafe's hand. Shock, on his part, made the retrieval easy. She pushed past him and slammed the door. *This could not be happening.* Bren couldn't even say the words. She swung open the truck door, the copy of the birth certificate now crumpled in her hand, and tossed it on the seat. She hopped in and slammed the door.

Mr. Patrick Michael Ryan would receive her, and he had better not lie to her this time—like he didn't recognize his own son scowling at him across the dinner table that night. No wonder Rafe had been intrigued by the photo of Patrick and Pam Ryan—they were his parents. God, now she knew why Rafe had felt familiar to her. Then she remembered what they'd shared—had been sharing since his timely arrival into her life—and she felt sick.

The click of cowboy boots alerted Bren that Rafe had regrouped. She struggled with the keys in the ignition and reached up frantically to lock the doors. She cursed when she pulled instead of pushed the door lock. The passenger door flung open, and Rafe jumped in as she reached for the shifter.

"Damn it, Bren. Talk to me. Where are you going?" Still rubbing his cheek, he gave her a confused look. "Why are you so damn angry?"

She put the truck in gear and tossed the paper between them on his lap. "You figure it out, cowboy."

He didn't bother looking at it—his attention all for her. "You didn't answer me. Where are you going?"

The truck lurched, the paper sliding between them as she took the turn and headed toward Paddy's.

His face twisted with anger. "Darlin', you're starting to piss me off."

She glanced over at him, her fingers a stranglehold on the steering wheel. "Go to hell, Rafe Langston." She smiled viciously. "But before you do, *darlin'*, why don't you explain to me how it feels to screw your brother's wife."

She hit a bump, and Tom's birth certificate, that she'd flung at him earlier, began to slide off the seat. He grabbed it and took a momentary glance before his fingers gripped the paper that had effectively reduced him to what he truly was—a liar.

"Shit," he said and looked at her, a flush growing beneath his bristly cheeks. "Bren." He reached out and stroked her arm. "I can—"

She shrugged his arm off. "Don't touch me. You disgust me."

Her eyes burned, and hot tears ran down her cheeks. "You're a damn liar. Just like your old man." She wiped her face on her sleeve, and the truck swerved.

Rafe sucked in air. "Jesus." His hand came down hard on the steering wheel, and he steered her out of the curve. "You're going to kill us both."

She gave him a menacing lift of her chin, the tears refusing to stop. "I hate you."

"Fine, hate me. But stay the hell on the road." His expression hardened. "You think this is all about you? Not everything is about Bren Ryan." His eyes glinted with anger. "I was the one given away. Why did he choose Tom over me? What did he have that I didn't? I lost my life, Bren, when Patrick Ryan chose to throw me away. I lost my brother long before you lost a husband."

She took her eyes off the road. It was impossible not to. How dare he take this out on her.

His stubborn jaw remained level, his green eyes pinning her with accusation. Deep lines bracketed his mouth, his lips a tight line. Did she even know this man? She trembled. Had his anger for the slight done to him over thirty years ago been enough for him to exact *his* revenge—starting with Tom?

Her stomach lurched. "You sick bastard. *You* killed, Tom." Her hands clenched the steering wheel. Oh, how she wanted to slap his face again. But reality reduced that fireball burning in her stomach to an ember smoldering with what he would do to her next, now that she knew.

Paddy's property came up quickly, and she pulled down the winding gravel road. She wouldn't think about it. All she had to do was get to the house, slam the truck into Park, and run like Godzilla himself was breathing fire at her heels. Regardless of what Paddy had done or knew, he'd offer her refuge from Rafe.

His farmhouse came up, the front porch and door her target. She slammed on the brakes, prepared for the hard stop, and jammed it into Park, reaching for the door the second the vehicle lurched to a halt.

Rafe's arm clamped around her waist, and he pulled her roughly against his chest. He was breathing hard, as was she. He yanked her hand off the door handle and forced it down to her side. "Damn it! Don't make me restrain you." The edge to his voice frightened her. Every tendon in his neck flexed, a single vein bulged along the side of his forehead.

Bren stilled. Twice her size, his fingers long enough to encircle her neck with ease, he could squeeze, and there would be no way she could call for help or sustain a fight long enough to tire or weaken him. Everything she had believed about him, about Tom, swam menacingly toward her like a shark's fin, and she could only thrash about waiting for the attack that would end her life.

Chapter Thirty-One

Damn it—she was afraid of him! That was the last thing Rafe would have ever expected from Bren. And it ate at him to know he was the cause. He wanted to tell her. He should have told her the moment he'd sent her to the ground in the sale barn. But he never intended to actually meet his brother's wife.

Hell, he didn't even know he had a biological brother until recently. He'd been adopted. His parents had never hid that from him. For the longest time he never gave his biological parents a thought. He just assumed they had a really good reason for giving him up.

Maybe his recent curiosity had come with age. He was ready to settle down, have children, and had no idea the genetics he'd inherited, except for what he could see in himself.

So he'd approached his father. And Rafe almost shit bricks when he pulled out a file. Said he didn't like surprises in business or family.

That was Sawyer Langston—cover your ass, which included the adoption of a male infant from Maryland.

Rafe had let that folder sit on his desk for over a year without so much as lifting the flap. But when he did, he couldn't breathe. The more he thought of it, the angrier he got. He believed he was the only one. *That* he could handle. He just assumed his biological parents were dead. Well, maybe part of that was true.

The son of a bitch. His real father had thrown him away. But not his brother Tom. Why? At the time he was content to remain in Texas and stew over the lot he'd been handed. It was pure selfishness at its best. He had a wonderful set of parents and a brother. He needed to get over it. But the knowledge that Patrick Ryan existed tore at his insides. He would have left it alone if not for Tom Ryan. Rafe was curious about him. So he hopped a flight to Baltimore, took up residence in the Holiday Inn in Hagerstown, and went to find his brother. Except the last thing he expected was to find the man had been dead for almost a year—thanks to the "Wanted" poster his widow had posted in the local paper he'd bought at the diner the next morning.

It ate at him for days. Had he not been so stubborn and opened the file sooner, maybe he could have prevented his brother's death. But just like Tom's widow, he wanted answers. It didn't take long to figure out who the kill buyer was. And he knew where to find him—the sale barn.

Only he hadn't counted on one red-headed, undisciplined hellion stealing his heart. And she had. Now if he didn't explain himself and take his comeuppance, she was going to eliminate him from her life.

He met her blistering gaze and shook her. "I didn't kill Tom. I only found out about him recently. I didn't know he was dead until I got here."

Bren twisted her hand between them. Pulling it up, she flattened it on his chest. Her body relaxed a fraction and her expression began to soften with understanding. "You're still a liar." She pushed harder against him. "I'm asking you to kindly move your ass to your seat. I apologize for jumping to conclusions. But all this could have been avoided had you just told me up front who the hell you were from the beginning."

He tilted her chin up. "I never meant to get close to you. I tried like hell to stay away. The thing is, Bren, your fight has always been my fight. I never planned to cross paths with you that day in the sale barn. But I didn't see any way around it."

Her soft, pink cheeks stiffened. "I could have handled the horse."

He shrugged. "Just like your finances."

"I didn't ask you to buy half my farm. I didn't need you to meddle in my life." She struggled to free herself, and Rafe tamped down the smile threatening the corners of his mouth. She was a damn fighter, and he loved her. He wouldn't be forced into letting go for nothing. And this thing—choosing to not tell her about his true identity—he'd done to protect her. Well, he wasn't the bad guy here. Patrick Ryan was, and Rafe didn't much care for him. But Bren did. She loved him equally as her own father. He couldn't bear ruining all she believed to be true and upstanding about Patrick Ryan.

Rafe pulled her against him. "I'm in love with you, Red. You make me do things I never do drunk. I've never had to explain myself to a woman, either. And damned if I know why I'm doing it now. Except I meant what I said. You're not like any woman I've ever known, and that scares the hell out of me."

She stopped fighting, her breathing still heavily, her soft breasts pressed against his chest. She stared up at him, pain evident in her brown eyes. God, if looks could wound, he'd be bleeding buckets.

He reached up and hesitated when her eyes veered toward his hand. Startled and looking at him like he was the last man she should trust, he caressed her cheek. "Truce." He nodded toward the old man's house and couldn't help but grit his teeth. "He owes us both an explanation."

She nodded and kept her eyes trained on him. "I can't forgive you."

Damn it, he knew she meant every word, and he'd accept it for now. But, eventually, when the bits and pieces of his life fell into order, his only mission would be to collect this ready-made family for himself. Technicality or not, they belonged to him now.

Rafe reached over her and grabbed for the door handle and then angled back to Bren. "You're not going to kick me in the balls once I let you go?"

"I guess you'll have to trust me." She wrinkled her face at him.

"Now, that's mature." He opened the door and motioned for her to step out, then placed his boots on the gravel drive and stood. She walked ahead and Rafe followed. For being such a tough guy, his stomach was tied in knots.

They climbed the steps, and Bren knocked on the door. Footsteps shuffled and the door swung open. Rafe concentrated on the old man's face. He'd already deduced from the photograph he'd studied when he was there for dinner that he'd gotten his looks and eye color from Pamela Ryan.

Perhaps the only thing Patrick Ryan shared with Rafe would be the scowl presently tugging at his lips as he witnessed his and Bren's solemn faces staring back at him. He caught himself and chuckled. "Missy, you surprised me." He turned to Rafe. "You over your snit since last I saw you?"

Son of a bitch. Could he still sense, after all these years, the son he despised lurking beneath the cowboy he'd become? Rafe opened his mouth, prepared to send a zinger his way. Patience he'd long since lost.

"Paddy," Bren said. "We need to talk to you. We'd like to come in."

Paddy stood back, allowing them entrance. "I'm sorry. I just finished taking a catnap. My brain must be half asleep."

They followed him into the family room. "Have a seat." He walked into the kitchen. "Lemonade?" He held up a pitcher. "Freshly squeezed."

"No, thanks," Bren said and picked up the exact photo Rafe had held not even a week ago. Did she see a resemblance as he had? She kept the frame in one hand and motioned with the other. "Paddy, come in. We're not thirsty. We need to ask you a few questions."

Furry white brows rose over his wire-rimmed glasses. "Oh?" He placed the pitcher down and shoved his hands in his pockets and remained glued to the tile floor in the kitchen. Then his shoulders slumped a bit, and he walked steadily toward them. "What's on your mind, Missy?"

Bren held up the photograph. "You must have had some thoughts as to why Rafe left here upset after dinner the other night."

He shook his head. "Nope. I figured he disliked my food or something." He angled his head toward Rafe. "You don't like me much." His brows furrowed, and he shook his head.

Unbelievable. Either he was delaying the inevitable or he actually had no clue who Rafe was. Bren took a tentative step toward Paddy, her hand sliding up his arm, the expression in her eyes one of sympathy for a man who was seconds away from being blindsided. And Rafe could not feel one ounce of remorse.

She motioned Paddy to his recliner. "I think you need to sit down."

"Why?" His eyes narrowed at Bren and then glanced toward Rafe. "I'm not tired. I don't want to sit. Something happen to the boys?" Alarm rose in his voice, and he frantically looked from one to the other. "What is it?"

Bren eased him toward the chair and gently sat him down. She kneeled down next to him and glanced back at Rafe before giving her father-in-law all of her attention. "You don't recognize him."

"No." He squinted at Rafe. "For heaven's sake. He's *your* friend. I recognize that."

For the first time she smiled at Rafe. "Yes, he is. But, Paddy, he's more than just my friend. He's your son."

The old man's face dropped, the loose skin around his throat jiggled, and he swallowed. "My son is dead." His voice became rough. The words marked with finality.

Bren moved closer, her face growing more serious. "Yes. Tom is dead. And I know you miss him. But you had another son, Paddy. I know you did. You don't have to deny it." Bren pulled the birth certificate she'd snagged from the floor of the truck and laid it on his lap. "Tom's birth certificate proves it." She turned toward Rafe. "Rafe is your son. He knows Paddy, and he wants to know why you gave him away."

Paddy shook his head, his hands coming up to shield his face, and he cried out, "He can't be! God forgive me. My son . . . my son was . . ."

Bren squeezed his knee. "Tell us the truth. Rafe deserves to know the truth, Paddy."

His hands came down, and tears ran down his puffy, wrinkled cheeks. "He can't be my son." He motioned with his hands. "My son was crippled." He eyed Rafe through his fogged-up, wet glasses. "You can't be Patrick. They said my Patrick would never walk."

He sobbed and reached for the front pocket of his slacks and pulled out a hankie. He blew his nose hard and wiped his face with vigor. "I was twenty-two, married with a child on the way. One child—until the delivery doctor informed Pam and me she was carrying twins. I couldn't believe it, but our happiness turned quickly when Pam lost consciousness. The babies were breech. Patrick came out first with forceps and Thomas, they were able to right him, followed next." He removed his glasses and wiped them with his hankie. A new sob, heavy with burden, escaped. "God, it happened so fast. Pam's heart rate dropped, and they pushed me out the doors. They worked on her for a long time. But they couldn't bring her back."

His hands fell to his sides, and he hung like a rag doll against the cushion of his recliner. "I'd lost my wife. My world. I had two sons I thought were perfectly healthy until they told me Patrick didn't look right. They wouldn't admit they'd done it to him with their damn forceps. They told me he'd never walk. He'd need constant care."

He looked at Rafe, broken and red-faced, his neck soaked and navy-blue knit shirt stained with his tears. "I could hardly think of raising two sons, let alone one who would never walk. To raise a handicapped child was beyond me." His eyes locked on to Bren's. "I had no choice, Bren. I had to give him up."

Patrick Ryan rocked and sobbed, the springs of his old recliner groaning with age.

Rafe didn't give a damn. He was too old to be delivered from his embitterment. Patrick Ryan had lived with his own demons for years—that was some consolation.

There had never been anything wrong with Rafe. If Patrick Ryan hadn't been so quick to write him off and sign the adoption papers, he'd have found out the doctors were wrong.

Rafe nodded to Bren. "I'll be outside."

Bren handed him the keys.

He couldn't bring himself to give the old man an out. Patrick Ryan had thrown him away like damaged goods. And that he could never forgive. The woman he loved had lived in Clear Spring her whole life. Brother or not, he would have won her fairly. He grimaced. Damn, but if Red knew the male chauvinist thoughts running through his head, she'd clobber him. Rafe shut the door behind him and headed for the truck. After about ten minutes, Bren emerged from the house, her gait the only indication she was ready to peel him a new ass.

With no choice but to assume the passenger seat since Rafe had regained control of his truck, she yanked the door open. "You, Rafe Langston, are an asshole. That old man in there is devastated. Even I can't be angry with him. He did what he thought was right at the time. You can't condemn him for something you know nothing about." She squared her shoulders. "You need to grow up."

"Can't help the way I feel. I didn't ask for this. He chose my life for me." A smile tugged at his mouth. "I guess you should follow your own advice and forgive me."

"And you can hold your breath until you turn blue." She turned in her seat and gave him her profile.

Knowing when he'd been beat, he put the truck in Drive and headed for Grace. The cab of the truck remained uncomfortably quiet until Bren's cell phone went off. She fumbled with it and placed it to her ear. "Hey, baby. I'll be home in a few minutes."

Her shapely auburn brows met in the middle of her forehead. "Sorry, sweetie. Rafe has other plans. You can camp behind our house."

Damn, with all this drama, Rafe had forgotten about his promise to take Finn and Aiden, and that poor excuse of a hound, camping in the field behind his house. Red wasn't getting her way on this one. Maybe she enjoyed making him out to be a no-good, uncaring . . . uncle. He smiled at that. Damn, he was an uncle now, and Uncle Rafe was not going to disappoint his nephews. Rafe snatched the phone from the crook of her neck, her hands busy snapping her seatbelt in place.

She turned a decisive gaze toward him, her brown eyes shooting daggers. "You—"

"Watch it. They can hear you." He placed the phone up to his ear. He had a fifty-fifty chance of getting it right, but judging by the name sweetie, he guessed he was talking to Finn. "Hey, buddy, we're still on." He nodded. "I know." He gave Bren a big smile. "Your mom was confused."

Bren reached out to snatch back her phone and Rafe switched ears, pulling his body toward the door. He eyed her with amusement, and whispered, "Be nice, darlin'." He continued his conversation, telling Finn what to pack and supplies needed for their campout tonight. "Once I drop your mother off, I'll pull out the tent and drive on over to pick the three of you up. We'll pitch it together before dinner."

He snapped the phone shut and handed it back to her. "In case you haven't compartmentalized everything yet, they're my nephews, Bren. I love them just as much as I love you. And I'm claiming what's mine. So you better think about how you're going to explain me to them when we get back tomorrow. I'm not going to be an absentee uncle. And if you'd stop looking at me like I'm some damn criminal, you'd find it in your heart to forgive me for not telling you the truth."

She crossed her arms over her chest and dropped back into the seat. "Don't threaten me, Rafe. You got your way this time." Her eyes, determined and dark, glinted his way, a midnight blue ringing the depths of those gorgeous brown eyes—not that he could see it with the glare of the sun filtering through the windshield, but he knew it existed. Like he knew everything about her. Right down to the freckle on the curve of her pretty little ass cheek.

"Forgive and forget, darlin'. I'm not going anywhere. So you need to get used to my existence." He winked at her.

She growled and turned her face away.

Rafe laughed aloud.

I love you, and you love me back. I can wait. Trust me on that.

CHAPTER THIRTY-TWO

"ARE YOU GOING TO INVITE ME IN?" DRESSED IN SILLY FLANNEL pajamas with penguins turned every which way, wearing her black peacoat overtop and a pair of fuzzy light-blue slippers, Jo leaned heavily with one hand on her cane. Her other hand wrapped around a large plastic bowl, brimming with freshly popped popcorn. Several DVDs were pinned under her arm.

Bren laughed. "You're crazy, Breakstone." The warm, buttery aroma made Bren salivate, and her hands, of their own volition, took the bowl from Jo, losing a few precious pieces when they spilled to the wooded floor of the porch.

"Hey, watch it, Ryan. That's my dinner." Jo grinned at her.

"I forgot. No hubby."

"He called before I left. He wanted me to ask if you'd continue holding down the fort. Another horse, a show jumper, died down in Louisville near Churchill Downs. Jeremy and the other vets were asked to assist in the investigation." Something in Jo's eyes changed. More guarded perhaps . . . or something . . . Maybe Jeremy's business trips were taking a toll on her. If she was still worried about him cheating on her, she hadn't mentioned it recently.

"Huh." Bren gripped the doorframe. "They don't think it was from natural causes?"

Jo thumped her way through the door and struggled with the movies while pulling her arm out of her coat sleeve. "I thought we could watch a couple chick flicks, eat some popcorn, and catch up on girl stuff." She glanced around. "Daniel left yesterday for Ireland?"

So she was ignoring the question. Odd. Bren let go of the doorframe and the crazy notions rolling around in her head. Jo and Jeremy's marriage was none of her business.

"He wanted to cancel because of everything. But I pushed him out the door. He'd planned to go back and visit months ago." Bren helped Jo with her coat. "What did you bring to watch?" Bren cocked her head, trying to get a glimpse of the covers. She frowned when she read Hugh Jackman's name. Of all the leading men in Hollywood, he could be Rafe's twin.

Ugh. Twin. Like I want to be reminded.

"What else did you bring besides *Australia?*"

Jo pursed her lips, and eyed the second movie, and grimaced. "*Someone Like You.*"

"Ah, God, Jo." Bren's hand flew to her face and slid down, taking her cheek with it. "You're killing me here." She grabbed the two movies from Jo and held one up in each hand. "Tell me you don't notice the resemblance."

Jo shrugged. "He's hot. I know that." She gave her a wide smile.

Bren had a sneaking suspicion that the movies had been strategically chosen.

Yeah, too hot to be my brother-in-law. My lover . . .

Her face warmed. *Or Uncle Rafe.* She hadn't even considered how she was going to tell her boys. Nice he chose to drop that hot potato on her lap. Why was this *her* problem?

Jo grabbed the movies and hobbled into the family room. Leaning her cane against the overstuffed plaid couch, she plopped down and glanced back. "Come on, girlfriend." She held up one movie. "Romantic saga?" Then the other. "Or comedy?"

Bren couldn't help but see the irony and wanted to say *both*. Instead, she moved toward the kitchen and called back. "What do you want to drink?"

"You have Diet Coke?"

"Pepsi."

"That's fine."

Clearing the kitchen, Bren set down two tall glasses on the coffee table, the fizz of fresh carbonation spritzing her hands. She plopped down next to Jo, pressing her head into the soft cushion of the couch. "You decide which one." She angled her face toward Jo.

Jo reached over and squeezed her hand. "Everything okay with you and Rafe? It all came together so fast once I started digging. You were in Mexico when I found out."

Bren breathed in and sat up straight. "I knew there was something familiar about him." She'd seen it the night Rafe had caught her in what was now his house. It was the way he lifted his brow. Both Tom and Paddy shared that same gesture. She'd just never thought to connect *her* dark handsome stranger to Tom.

Ugh. Bren grabbed the throw pillow, pulling it to her chest. "*Eewh* incest."

"You dope." Jo grabbed the pillow and beaned her in the head. "He's not related to you. He's your brother-in-law, not your brother."

Bren grimaced. "I know that."

"Good. Now how'd it go with Paddy?"

"Not good. I've forgiven him. But Rafe's being a jerk." Bren shook her head. "Patrick Ryan was young, overwhelmed. He made the wrong decision. And he's had to live with his mistake, which came calling today."

"So what are you going to do with Mr. Tall, Dark, and Handsome?"

"I should kick his ass back to Texas." Bren frowned. "But I love him, Jo."

Jo's arm went around Bren and pulled her next to her. "Honey, he loves you, too."

"He said he never had any intentions of making himself known to me or the boys. I believe that. He only came to find his brother." She frowned. "Then stayed to find his killer." Neither had happened.

Jo snuggled closer. "Ah, the siren and her bewitching red hair were too much for the dashing rogue."

Bren snorted and pulled away. "You actually read that stuff?"

Jo laughed. "All the time."

"Seriously. What am I going to do?"

"Next time you see him, tell him you love him. Figure out a way to break the news to the boys, and live happily ever after."

This wasn't a fairytale—although it did have its villain. Speaking of which . . ."On a different note, what are the odds Wes will serve jail time for Smiley's murder?"

"It's hard to say. He's been slapped on the wrist for cruelty in the past, so there's a history. This is different, though. He stole your horse, paid for transport, and had it slaughtered. It's possible he'll get a few years."

Bren pulled on her lip. "Nothing like a murder charge, though."

Jo nodded. "If you're right and Wes really did kill Tom for revenge, he's covered his tracks well. I don't think any more digging is going to bring that to the surface." Jo sighed. "I think you need to focus on the present and not the past."

Jo was a dear friend. Her words were a gift, and if Bren had enough sense, she'd accept the advice and her life would cease to have so much drama. Then again, drama followed Bren like her own dark shadow. It was part of her. Trying to rid herself of it—impossible.

Bren sobered at the thought and let her body sink deeper into the cushions. She needed to get on with her life. Wes couldn't hurt her anymore, short of hiring a hit. Considering he'd be the prime suspect, that scenario wasn't likely.

"Hey." Bren nudged Jo, a sly smile curving her lips. "Since we're having girl talk, while you were investigating Rafe, did you find out his brother works for the DEA?"

She gave her an odd look. "Yeah, I saw mention of that when I was checking into the Langstons. Trey was their biological son. I think he's a few years older than Rafe."

"You never ran into him when you worked for the DEA?"

"It's a big organization. I never met him."

Something told Bren Jo wasn't being completely honest. Maybe it was the selective words.

I never met him.

But Bren had an inkling that the name Trey Langston made Jo uncomfortable. She might not have made the connection to Rafe before. What were the odds? But it seemed highly probable she knew of him.

One of these days, when the two were old and gray, she'd wheedle it out of her. But for now, Hugh Jackman beckoned. And she really needed the distraction—Rafe's look-alike or not.

Bren grabbed the movie off the coffee table. "I think I could use a laugh. And you're spending the night, so get comfy. You can stay in dad's room. Even has clean sheets."

Chapter Thirty-Three

BREN AWOKE WITH A START. HAD SHE DREAMED IT? SHE REMAINED stock-still, her fingers tightening on the blankets. The sound came again, but it was different this time, like heavy soles crunching pebbles or glass?

Jo?

Bren reached for the light on her nightstand and struggled with the small switch until an audible click broke the silence. The relief that light would accompany it shot disappointment straight to her gut when she remained in darkness.

"Shit," she moaned. "Not again! I paid the damn electric bill."

She threw back the covers, her toes curling the moment they met the cold wooden floor. She tugged down Rafe's shirt, the one she'd shoved in her backpack when they were rushing to get to the tunnel in Mexico. It was unwashed, and, not wanting to remove his scent, she'd traded her horse pajamas for it before she slipped into bed. Admittedly juvenile and purely teenager, it had purpose—she'd fallen asleep.

The heavy pine door of her bedroom creaked when she opened it, and Bren moved down the hall. An eerie blue light from the far window down the hall glanced and shimmered off the walls. Jo's door was open, and Bren peeked inside. Her bed was empty. Bren gripped the doorknob. The glass . . . Maybe she was in the kitchen. Bren continued down the hall, peering into each bedroom and the hall bath, all empty. She took the first step, the carpet runner soft and giving beneath her bare feet. And then she heard it. A click. A footstep.

Jo only had soft slippers.

The gun. Bren made a move. Damn it—she didn't have it. Rafe, thinking she'd shoot herself in the foot or do real damage to someone else, had confiscated it.

Bren listened hard. Maybe she hadn't heard the footstep. She didn't hear anything now.

She wanted to call Jo's name, but her instincts were leaning heavily toward suppressing that need. Although the tingle of fear racing across her skin was unfounded—her only enemy was in jail—she'd go with her gut and hope the ridiculous notion of a hired hit man was wrong, and one didn't jump out and satisfy his contract.

She took her last step off the stairs and hesitated. She was defenseless. Bren peeked around the corner into the dining room, expecting the curtains to flutter, but they remained still. Just like her heart, which wanted to stop beating the moment she caught spindly tree limbs dancing menacingly across the lace.

Breathe.

She let out the air she'd been holding. *Get a grip. There's no one here, damn it.* The country dining room sat untouched. The last time she'd served dinner was Christmas, and that broken woman didn't exist. Whether her intuition was right or she was having a case of the creeps, she snagged the silver candlestick, one of a matching pair she and Tom had received as a wedding gift. It was the closest thing to a weapon she had. She pulled the wax candle from it, laying it on the buffet, and set her sights on the kitchen.

The tingle that something was amiss became stronger. The house was too quiet. Bren gripped the candlestick and moved tentatively toward the doorway to the kitchen, the intermittent gray light from a passing window the only light to guide her. She edged around the wall and peeked into the kitchen. Sharp slivers of cobalt blue, the remains of the only glass left of an original set of eight, glittered on the floor, catching the night-light's glow from the wall outlet.

Her shoulders tensed and then relaxed a fraction at the gallon of milk sitting on the center island. She shook her head. The glass she could clean up. It was an oddball, anyway. The candlestick she'd been holding like Lady Liberty's torch, she let drop to her side. Where the hell was Jo? If she was looking for a broom, it was in the laundry room. Bren angled her head and glanced inside the small room to the left, only to find the washer and dryer and a laundry basket on top.

Coming around the center island, Bren grabbed the cap to the milk, the simple task interrupted when Bren's toe touched something furry that moved.

Every hair on her body stood at attention, and she willed herself to look down. Her adrenaline spiked, and her hand dipped to retrieve Jo's furry blue slipper. Its softness a sense of security, she held it to her chest. But her safe and secure world tilted when she saw Jo's body lying motionless on the floor.

Bren dropped down next to her, the candlestick falling. Her hand trembled above Jo's forehead, the gash jagged and oozing, dark with blood. "Jo! Oh my God."

Her hand flew to her mouth. Oh God, I need a towel—something. Her legs shook, and she struggled to her feet. And then she felt it. The shadow. It darkened the floor in front of her, cutting Jo's pale body in half as it swayed across the soft features of her face.

Bren stiffened. She pushed up from her knees and swung wildly. A solid punch landed at the base of her head, and she fought to remain standing. Her arms gaining mobility, she fisted her hands and swung, but her target dodged her and came around. A movement in solid black, it pinned her arms to her side. Her back moved up against something resilient yet substantially larger than her—a man's chest. His breath, heavy and hot from exertion, brushed her bare neck, and she shivered.

"No!"

She struggled, and he shifted his body. Forcing her over, he pushed her face down on the center island. Her arms flailed, and she managed only to knock the gallon of milk to the floor with a hollow thud, the milk splattering her calves. He pressed her cheek against the granite countertop, cold and hard, her last thought before something soft was shoved into her face, the smell pungent and sweet—everything went dark.

Bren's eyes fluttered open. She couldn't see. Her hands flew to her eyes to make sure they actually were open. They were. But the sudden movement reawakened the angry thump at the base of her head. She pressed her fingers into her scalp and stopped at the knot behind her ear, cringing at the size. But the fluid movement of her hand gave renewed hope. She moved her legs. He hadn't tied her up. Bren ignored the pain and sat up slowly. Her hands reached into the darkness and came up short when she touched a stone wall, cold and damp. She pulled her fingers in.

He's coming back for me.

Her heart sped up. She slid forward, the give of springs beneath her bottom making it clear she was on some sort of bed or cot. She blinked into the darkness, hoping her eyes only needed to adjust. Her sight unchanged, the dark only became a frightening obstacle. She scooted toward the end of the mattress, her toes scraping cold ground. She bent over to touch it and dropped to her knees, recognizing the pungent, moldy earth. Her fingers dug into the floor, dirt slipping under her nails. She must be in some sort of basement.

She wasn't dying in this hellhole.

She stood and held out her hands, afraid of what she might bump into. She couldn't waste anymore time. It didn't matter where she was. She needed to get out. There had to be a door. She only needed to find it. She took tentative steps until her hands ran into another cold, wet wall. She continued groping, trying to find the door. One hand rested on the wall, her fingers coming into contact with something slick and glossy, the other trying to find a way out. Frantic, she shuffled her feet forward and winced when her toe struck something hard. Her hand dropped—it was a table. She moved her hands across it. Slick paper sticking to her sweaty fingers and palm, she pushed it aside until her finger bumped into something smooth and hard. Her hands formed around it. It was wide and round and fluted at the top—a glass sconce. Lantern. God, please let there be a lighter . . . matches.

Her hands trembled, anxiously feeling around for anything resembling a lighter or a matchbox. Everything else she pushed to the floor. Then her fingers ran across something—a small rectangular box. She snatched it, the top of the box moved like a sleeve, and she thought she'd crumple with relief. Her fingers dug inside, touching several pieces of thin wood and rounded tips, and she fumbled the box. It fell. A quiet thud and then the scattering of matches made her cringe.

"Shit!"

Bren dropped on all fours. Her hands shaking and moist, she searched the dirt floor. Her hand bumped into the box first, and her knee landed on several wooden matches, the weight pressing them into her skin. She lifted her knees, afraid she'd snap them. They remained glued to her clammy skin, and she plucked them from underneath her knee and held the box firm in her other hand. There were three matches. She needed to use them sparingly. Standing, she kept the matches in one hand, the matchbox in the other. She moved toward the table and felt around with her fists and arms until her knuckles bumped up against it. Bren transferred the matches to her other hand with the matchbox and lifted the glass off the lantern. If she managed to light it the first try, she wouldn't need the others. She leaned over, struck the match, and held the flame up and touched it to the wick. The match burned lower, the wick refusing to take the flame. Choking back tears of frustration, she drew the match down toward the bottom of the lantern where the kerosene was kept. It was bone dry. The flame burned her finger. She bit down on her lip, dropped the match with a curse, and was plunged back into pitch blackness.

Damn it. She had only two tries left to get it right. The next match she'd find the door and hope there was no lock to wrestle with. If not, the third match would be used to work the lock. She prayed it was something simple she could break through.

Bren shivered. Barefoot, wearing only Rafe's shirt and her panties, she was chilled through her skin by the dampness. But she was alive and wanted to stay that way. She pulled on every fragment of strength. Jo's limp body invaded her mind, and she swayed, not knowing if she were even alive. She needed to get her help. But first she needed to get her wits about her and calm the rattle of fear shaking her insides.

She took the match, pinning it between her fingers and rubbed it along the box until she met with friction. She struck it, her mind racing with what she had to do when the flame came to life. She held it up and began to search the walls.

She gasped, and her pulse beat furiously in her temples. The walls made of stone, the joints twined in moss were covered in photos. There were small snapshots, some larger, but the theme was the same—they were all of her. He'd blown them up, her face life-sized and carefully trimmed in her likeness, her brown eyes staring their warning.

Terror turned her blood to ice. A wave of dizziness came over her, and the room, with its apocalyptic collage, seemed to spin.

The heat of the match brought her around, and she remembered the door. But it was too late. The flame singed her finger, and she dropped it, the orange glow burning the matchstick on the ground. The thin wood curled into a gray ember before darkness descended.

Bren fell to her knees, her hands covering her face.

Tears escaped through her fingers, and she dashed them away. *Think, Bren.* She lifted her head and remained there quiet, except for her sniffing. Then she stopped, and her back went rigid. She remained on her knees and listened. Shuffling—it came again, closer. Scraping. The jiggle of a lock—she held her breath—an audible click.

Heart pounding to the point it would beat out of her chest, she struggled to her feet. Her breathing came in quick, hard pants.

God, don't let me hyperventilate.

Hands out in front, she searched for the bed and the only place to hide until he found her.

And he would find her. She knew with every rising hair along her neck she had miscalculated in a fatal way. There was someone far more evil than Wes Connelly fixated on her. And what he would do to her and for how long caused her terror-numbed brain to freeze up. She couldn't begin to search it for his identity. She would know soon enough.

Her main focus now was to survive him.

Chapter Thirty-Four

WHAT THE HELL WAS HE DOING? RAFE HUDDLED UNDER HIS sleeping bag.

Freezing my ass off, for one.

Uneven ground and twigs poked his back no matter which way he turned, which was increasingly difficult with Roscoe's boulder-sized, jowl-hanging head resting on his shins and Finn pinned against him.

He guessed that Finn's "*I'm not afraid of the dark*" mantra, after Aiden had ridden him before lights out, had fallen short of its mark.

Brothers . . .

Finn shivered, and Rafe touched his soft cheek. Cold. He should have realized a seventy-degree day in mid-March would plummet to near freezing by two in the morning. Rafe concentrated on the mesh window in the tent's roof. Blanketed under heavy clouds, the metallic smell of rain all around him, his heart weighed a miserable ton. What did his mama used to say? She was full of advice—Mrs. Sawyer Langston—and she was his mama, the only woman in his life who could set him straight when he'd find himself in the doldrums for one reason or another.

Nothing weighs heavier than a sack of regret, Rafe Austin Langston, and you best remember that.

So he didn't know Tom Ryan, but he knew his boys. He loved them like his own. Even with all the shit with them, they were his only glimpse into the past and what he and Tom would have shared. It would have to be enough.

A cold raindrop nailed him in the eye, and he blinked.

Wake up, cowboy.

Regret he was done with. He loved her. And whether Bren wanted to believe it or not, she damn well loved him, too. She was just too stubborn to admit it. He had a good mind to gather his nephews and go get her right now. His lips curled with wicked humor—that burned her ass, too. They were his nephews, and he had every right to remain a part of their—

Aiden let out a sneeze and huddled deeper into his sleeping bag. Rafe pulled Finn closer, the boy's small body trembling against him.

He'd never hear the end of it if he got her boys sick. And, selfishly, it gave him a good reason to see Bren. Not that she'd welcome him in the middle of the night. But considering he was returning her boys . . . *Shit.* That didn't make much sense. His house was closer.

Ah hell. I'm doing it anyway.

Never too late . . . He checked his watch and grimaced—two ten in the morning. Or too early to set his world right. He nudged the hound with his knee. A droopy eyelid rose, and the dog licked his chops, his loose-skinned jaw nestling deeper against his leg. "Up, Roscoe," Rafe ordered, his voice a low grunt, so as not to disturb the boys until he'd packed them up.

Rafe forced Roscoe's head up again with his knee. The dog yawned, pulled himself to his feet, and shook his head. The melodious jingle of his tags, a prelude to a harmonious existence with a redhead he was bound and determined to sway into marrying him. He smiled and hoisted himself up.

He took the cutoff from the main driveway to Bren's house.

"Sweet—we're home." Aiden pushed Finn off his shoulder. Finn mewled, transferring his head to Rafe's arm. The three were packed in the front seat with wet-smelling hound and supplies in the back. Rafe couldn't help but smile. Family was growing on him, even the damn dog.

But the spritz of rain, enough to blur his vision, and monotonous grind of the wipers didn't help bolster his courage. He checked the clock in the dash and winced, almost two-thirty. He was half-tempted to turn around and call it a night.

Rafe maneuvered the truck close to the house.

"You can have camping. All I want is my bed." Aiden grabbed for the door handle before Rafe could put the truck in Park.

"Hold up. We can't go in raising a ruckus. Your mother will have my hide."

Aiden gave him a sly grin. "Maybe you should drop us off then. She's already pissed at you."

Rafe smiled. "Better me than you. Right?"

"Hell, yeah. She's scary when she's mad." Aiden grimaced.

Finn moaned and sat up. He blinked through the lenses of his glasses and pushed forward, his small hands gripping the console in front. "Aunt Jo's here." He pointed at the dark SUV Rafe had parked next to and turned to Rafe and squinched his nose at him. "You think they're having a sleepover?"

Whether they were or weren't was of little concern, except his plans for sneaking up into Bren's bedroom, after judiciously sending his nephews to bed, just got a little bothersome.

Rafe shut off the truck. "Remember, stealth. To your beds and lights out." He peered back at Roscoe, still resting his heavy, slack jowls on a rolled-up sleeping bag, and turned hard eyes toward the boys. "I'm not looking to get my butt chewed by your mother. Keep the hound outside. I'll deal with him."

They both nodded. He unlocked the doors, and they piled out. The rain began to pick up. Rafe drew up his hood and opened the back door. Roscoe jumped out, all four paws splashing in the muck, and Rafe grimaced. Looked like the hound would be coming with him and the gear. He'd sort it out tomorrow, along with his life.

The boys ran ahead of him, the hound bounding behind them. Rafe kept his head down, avoiding the fat raindrops spotting his jeans and boots. The steps came up fast, and he climbed them two at a time. Once he reached the landing, he flipped his hood off and stopped and winced.

"What the—"

The boys stood on either side of the door, their eyes wide, their only responsibility halfway through the door. Roscoe's paws, mud slicked, slapped the wooded foyer, the thrash of his wet tail smacking against one side of the wall. "*Shit*. I thought I said to keep him on the porch." Texas was looking a might safer.

"But we didn't—"

Rafe put up his hand. He didn't want to hear their excuses. He was wet, bone-tired, and the hound had just put Rafe alongside him in the doghouse.

Finn yanked on Rafe's jacket. The soft underside of his neck craned up, and his brown eyes, resembling black marbles in the dark, widened with worry. "But, Rafe, we didn't open the door."

"What?"

"It was already open." Aiden's wary voice sent a chill racing down Rafe's spine.

"Maybe the wind blew it open," Finn said.

Rafe ruffled his soft blond head. "It's a starting point." Although his gut told him otherwise, he didn't want to frighten him. He glanced at Aiden. "Stay with your brother. I'll get the dog, check things out, and be right back."

Aiden's lips thinned, and his face took on a more serious expression. "You don't think—"

Rafe frowned, hooked his chin toward Finn, and shook his head a definite no. Aiden nodded his point and pulled his brother next to him. "Come on, squirt. Let's see how many puddles we can find."

Rafe stepped over the threshold and reached in to hit the light switch. It clicked, but still he remained standing in the pitch black. He cursed under his breath and turned back toward the boys. "Aiden, go to my truck and get me the flashlight. It's in the glove compartment. The lights are out."

Aiden grabbed Finn's hand and headed for the truck. While he waited, Rafe peered into the front rooms. The living room, off to the left, which he'd rarely been in, looked untouched. The dining room on the other side the same, from his vantage point.

"Here." Aiden shoved the flashlight at him.

Rafe took it, the metal cold against his palm. He moved forward. They should be in bed. The first logical place to look for them would be upstairs. Rafe turned on the flashlight. The bright beam angled up the stairs, and he climbed to the second level, Bren's bedroom two doors down. He moved in that direction and placed the light directly on the four-poster bed and a bundle of covers on top. Edging toward the bed, he pulled them back. She wasn't there.

Rafe's pulse sped up. He checked the master bathroom. It was empty. Heading down the hall, his eyes hunted each room, hoping to find either woman. The boys' beds were made. He swung into and flashed the light into the last bedroom. The bed was unmade and also empty.

Son of a bitch.

Something was wrong. He flew down the steps and rounded the banister. Roscoe came around the corner, and they collided, Rafe stepping on his paw. Roscoe yelped. Rafe cursed, pushing him out of the way with his foot.

"Bren!" If she was trying to teach him a lesson for lying, he wasn't the least bit amused. His heart thumped like a jackhammer. "Answer me, damn it!" He swung into the kitchen and stopped dead—broken glass, a milk jug lying on its side, a puddle seeping under the refrigerator. He took measured steps.

"Jesus."

Jo lay silently on her side, her long black ponytail draped across her face.

Rafe rushed to her and kneeled, ignoring the milk soaking through his jeans. The wound to her head and the blood saturating that side of Jo's pretty face made his jaw clench. What kind of a son of a bitch attacks a woman? He placed his fingers along her neck, her pulse faint but there. He fumbled for his phone on his belt to call 9-1-1, but wet sneakers squeaking behind him brought him around.

"Damn it, Aiden, I told you to stay outside."

"Is . . . is that my mom?" Aiden's voice cracked. He stood with Finn, looked down at his brother and yanked him next to him, wrapping his arm around him. He pulled Finn even tighter. Aiden's eyes and now those of Finn's gleamed in the dark, staring at Jo's body.

"No. It's Jo."

They took a step closer.

Rafe put out his hand. "Stay put. I'll take care of Jo. She's going to be fine." He held up his phone. "I need you to call 9-1-1 for me while I see what I can do for her."

Aiden made a tentative move toward him.

"It's okay. Come take my phone."

Aiden moved closer, craning his neck. "Man, she's covered in blood." He reached for the phone.

Rafe handed it to him. "Call 9-1-1. Ask for an ambulance and the sheriff to be sent to Grace."

Aiden nodded and took the phone.

Rafe eyed Finn. "Hey, buddy. I need you to find some towels. Can you do that for me?"

Finn nodded and made an about-face, his tennis shoes giving a loud squeak, and headed down the hall.

Rafe concentrated on Jo. What the hell had happened? Wes was in jail. Was it a home invasion? What? As much as he wanted to rip through the house for Bren, he couldn't leave Jo. Her breathing was shallow, her pulse weak. His gut told him Jo's unexpected presence had made her expendable.

Whoever did this to her had Bren.

❦

Where was Bendix? Last he'd seen, the sheriff was nursing his conscience, barking out orders in an attempt at command and control. He'd been too close to this one, to her, believing it was just Bren being Bren.

It cost Rafe his pride, but if he wanted her back, it was up to him to swallow it and call the old man. So he made the call. Hell, he didn't even know what to call him, what to say, except *I need your help.* To the old man's credit, he didn't pepper him with questions. Only said, *I'm on my way.*

Rafe paced the front porch, the damp air cool against his face and hands. Like the total pain in the ass the woman had proven to be, she couldn't have been dressed for the weather when she'd been abducted. If she looked anything like Jo, she was prepared for a pajama party, not the elements.

Damn it, but he'd miscalculated this one. He'd just assumed the danger had passed. Wes was in jail, for crissake. If he was that bent on revenge and had hired a hit, it would have been clean. Kidnapping didn't seem logical. If that's even what this was. Hell, he didn't know what to think. But she was gone and not by choice.

His gut told him this wasn't about revenge or Wes.

He took a deep breath.

No, this guy had plans for Bren. And it wasn't vengeance. Rafe sensed it with every tightening muscle. He'd been watching her, waiting for an opportunity. Rafe's newly acquired title as uncle and his need to make his point and enjoy Bren's aggravation gave the bastard his edge.

Fat raindrops landed on the wooden steps and Rafe's jaw tightened. *Relax.* It had been doing this all night. It wasn't enough to kill a scent. That was his worry—a downpour. He only hoped that damn hound lived up to his breed.

Paddy's black Suburban pulled in and maneuvered around sheriff cruisers parked in and around the driveway and parking area. Their lights a constant flash of red and blue made everything blend into a purple haze of confusion. Bendix, for all the eye-rolling he'd done around Bren with her crazy theories of murder, looked like a guy solidly punched in the solar plexus. He'd been wrong, they'd all been wrong, including Rafe, and it could very well cost Bren her life.

Rafe rubbed the back of his neck. How long did it take to set up a damn perimeter? Rafe stepped off the porch and came around to the driver's side of the Suburban. Taking a solid breath, he promised himself he'd keep it together for Bren's sake. Patrick Ryan had something he didn't have—a knowledge of Clear Spring and all its hidey-holes. Something told him she was within a whoop and a holler. He needed only a guide and a sharp nose.

Rafe gripped the door handle and opened it, swallowing his anger. "I didn't know who else to turn to."

"I'm glad you called." Patrick Ryan swung his jean-clad legs out and rested his work boots on the running board, the spat of rain hitting his rain slicker. His expression, left to Rafe's imagination, was hidden in shadow beneath the bill of a John Deere baseball cap. "How are the boys?"

Rafe nodded toward the house. "Inside. Worried about their mother. A deputy is with them now."

Paddy got out and shut the door. "How about Jo?"

Jo's sweet face invaded Rafe's thoughts, and his hands became iron fists. "She's conscious, but barely."

"She give a description? Know which way he took off?"

"No. Nothing." He met his gaze. "She can't even form words. The bastard beat her senseless. Bendix sent a deputy with her. If she becomes coherent, he'll get a statement."

Rafe handed the old man the semiautomatic he'd picked up the other day in town, grateful he'd started the paperwork on getting a permit early. The laws definitely differed from Texas.

Paddy took the gun, hiked up his slicker, and stuck the gun in the back of his jeans. "What about you?"

"I've got Tom's shotgun."

Paddy nodded. "Where's Jeremy?"

"Kentucky." Rafe shook his head. "I left a message at his hotel to call. Didn't want to drop that kind of news in a voicemail." Rafe scratched his head. "You think Wes is behind this?"

"He's in jail, isn't he?"

"Yeah."

Paddy squeezed his shoulder. "What do you make of it?"

Rafe eyed the old man. "Whoever he is, when he's done with her, he's going to kill her."

Chapter Thirty-Five

B REN'S HEAD COLLIDED WITH THE METAL EDGE OF THE BED FRAME.
She cursed and ducked underneath. Lying on her side, she wanted to
dissolve into the cold stone against her back. She reached up and felt around,
her fingers latching onto springs. With all her strength, she pried one off,
either end a curved hook she'd jam in his eye if he got close.

The scrape of a door, the clip of a hard-soled shoe on wood, the pop of a
light, and the room, which had frightened her in all its darkness, terrorized her
with its brilliance. Sweat beaded her brow and the indentation above her lip.

Footsteps deadened by the compact soil floor only made a thunk as they
neared closer. A pair of black dress shoes, the light reflecting off their polish,
stood directly in front of her, a pair of charcoal dress pants, their cuffs resting
perfectly even against the black tips of his shoes.

The spring she held in a death grip bit into her palm, the sharp coil at
the top digging into the back of her hand. What the hell was he waiting for?
From where she lay curled under the bed against the back wall, she could
make out four metal table legs a few feet past where he stood. Down by her
feet and a little ways beyond the end of the bed were two wooden steps, she
guessed leading to the door. The room was no bigger than a small shed, its
damp stone walls and dirt floor making her shiver.

He had to know she hadn't escaped. The only place left for him to look
was under the bed.

"Bren?"

The voice gave her a jolt, and her head hit the metal crisscross of springs.
She bit down on her lip, but not before a whimper escaped. *Shit.*

The charcoal pants started to move, a knee hitting the floor, a blond head and serious blue eyes beaded in on her. "God, you okay?" Familiar hands reached under, and Bren dropped the spring and clasped onto him.

Her heart, beating a frantic pace, slowed, and she held tight, letting him pull her to her feet. Bren's toes curled inward against the chill of the floor, her legs wobbling fiercely. She struggled to remain standing. Strong arms encircled her waist, and she clung to him. "Oh, my God, Robert. We need to get out of here."

His hand moved to the back of her head. "Shhh. I've got you." His fingers cradled and slipped under her hair. "You're awake. I'm glad."

Bren stiffened. *Awake.* Like he knew she'd been asleep. Bren's eyes widened, and it was only then she took in her surroundings. The steel table she'd found in the dark was in front of her. On it lay what was left of the sticky paper that had clung to her palms, she now knew to be photographs of her. The rest littered the floor.

In the corner sat a thick roll of duct tape and scissors glinting menacingly. The fear of bondage rose bitter and all too real in her throat. But it was the photos she'd seen in an instant by match light she concentrated on now. They grew sharper in detail.

And the hideous possibility that the man who'd showed her such compassion following Tom's death, the man who ran interference between her and his father, and the man she neither hesitated to accept when he'd reached for her nor questioned coming to her rescue, now holding her offering his strength, could be the one she should fear most.

Rafe dodged patrol cars and hit the steps of Bren's farmhouse at a dead run, swinging open the door. Ahead of him in the kitchen, uniformed sheriff's deputies and plainclothes detectives from the state police were working the crime scene. The living room and dining room were empty.

"Aiden!" He cleared the hall and almost collided with the boy. Rafe grasped his shoulders, their gazes met, and it was the first time he'd seen any real emotion in Aiden's eyes. They were strained and glassy with unshed tears. "What were you doing in the kitchen?" Rafe's voice was sharp. What the hell was Bendix thinking, letting her teenage son anywhere near that area of the house?

"Sheriff in there?" Rafe hooked his chin toward the kitchen.

"I thought he was her friend. She tried to tell him about my dad. But he wouldn't—"

He gave him a hard shake. "Doesn't matter, son. We just have to work to get her back."

"We going after her?" Aiden's shoulders rose, and his voice perked up.

"No we, Aiden. I called your grandfather. Paddy's in the barn saddling up two horses. I need a long lead and Roscoe. Can you handle that for me?"

Aiden tore himself away from him. "You're just like everybody else."

Rafe grabbed for his arm, holding him in place. "Hey. What's that supposed to mean?"

His lips trembled. "I'm no tool."

"A what?"

"Means I'm not stupid. I'm old enough to drive."

He'd have argued that point if it weren't for the urgency at hand. He understood where Aiden was coming from, and Rafe needed to respect that. Or, at the very least, honor his own words to Bren. Aiden wasn't a boy. He was becoming a man.

"You think you can control Roscoe? Get him to track your mother's scent?"

"Yeah. I know how."

Rafe clamped down on his shoulder. "Where's your brother?"

"One of the deputies took him upstairs to bed."

"I'll meet you in the barn with Paddy. Tell him to saddle another horse. I want you riding with a long lead and Roscoe out front. We don't have time to go on foot."

Aiden's lips parted.

"No more questions. Get your dog. You see Kevin, tell him I want to talk to him. I need to go up to your mom's bedroom and find some of her clothing. I'll meet you in the barn. Get yourself a raincoat. We're expecting heavy rain."

"What about her scent?"

"It makes it more difficult. The sooner we get a move on, the better."

"Let me see your head." Before Bren could utter a protest, Robert turned her around and moved his fingers under her hair, probing her scalp.

"Ow." Bren jerked her head away.

"Hurts?" He frowned at her. "You always were a fighter. Even when we were kids." His eyes lingered on her face, his one hand reaching up to caress her cheek.

Bren backed up, her knees hitting the edge of the bed.

"You don't want me to touch you?" His lips thinned.

Touch her? When had she ever given Robert Connelly the impression she was attracted to him?

"I think you've done enough touching." Keeping him accounted for, she locked onto a black-and-white newspaper photo taped to the wall with duct tape. It had begun to yellow at the edges. But even with the affects of time and the distance from where she stood, she recognized it immediately. Her heart clenched, and her brain spun with understanding. Tom had been marked for murder the moment the small article hit the *Hagerstown Herald*. The neat, black X drawn over Tom's face, her first indication she'd really screwed up.

It wasn't the father she should have feared, but the son.

In this insidious room, the photos of her plastered over the wall in the eye of the gathering storm—the photo with its caption she could recite by memory, *Brenna Maeve Fallon and Thomas Patrick Ryan, both from Clear Spring, Maryland, announce their wedding engagement and their plans to marry, June 9, 1996*—she realized Robert Connelly was the enemy she never saw coming.

"He didn't deserve you."

Bren jumped. His voice was edged with a hint of suppressed anger and jealousy she never knew existed. Her mind struggled to connect the Robert Connelly she thought she knew with the man standing beside her. "He was your friend," she said. "We were all friends."

Robert gave a short laugh, his usual caring eyes hardened. "What were we . . . nine, ten? We." He cleared his throat and nodded to the newspaper clipping. "*He* stopped being my friend a long time ago." The edge to his voice returned, and he took a step toward her. "The only one I wanted to be close to was you. I never stopped wanting you . . . loving you . . . looking at you."

No doubt. His photos proved his eye had been zooming in on her for years.

"We were just kids, Robert." Bren inched sideways, heading toward the end of the bed, her destination the steps, then she'd have her hand on the door.

"It's locked."

Her head swung back. The smirk, so unlike any expression she'd ever seen on Robert's face, chilled her blood.

He dangled a small key in front of her. "This is going to be our special place."

Like she'd ever come back to visit? But the irrational gleam in his eyes had her seriously thinking her next move. She wanted to wrap her hands around his neck and squeeze until the murdering bastard turned a nice shade of purple like Tom.

But reality shook her hard, and she gritted her teeth and smiled. "It's nice, Robert. But I really need to get home. I don't want my boys to worry."

He shoved the key in his pocket. "Are you hungry, sweetheart?" He moved closer.

"Robert, please take me home. We can come back another time." She shivered and wrapped her arms around her.

"You're cold." He took two long strides and pressed her against the stone wall and his body. He rubbed her arms. "Let me make you warm."

Bren's heart thumped with warning. "I don't want to be warm. I want to go home." She pushed on his chest.

"I can't do that. This is your home now." He pressed a shaft of her hair back behind her ear.

She remained painfully in place, her insides trembling. Her new home was a cold, damp place, dark and frightening, and the thought of remaining in this closed-off hole, underground, made her chest constrict and breathing more difficult.

Bren flashed him an ireful gaze. "I see. I'm not good enough to move into the big house." She raised her chin. "What would your father say if he knew you'd fallen for the 'girl?'" Bren hoped that was enough to cause his demented head to spin.

He cupped her chin. "God, I've hurt your feelings." His voice gentled. "It's not like that, sweetheart." He crowded her once more, the uneven stone wall poking her back. "We need time to get reacquainted." He pressed his body to hers, the proof of his arousal riding hard along her stomach.

She suppressed every urge to push him away. Her mind raced. "What about Susan?"

"I'll tell Susan." He made a move to kiss her.

Bren turned her face, his lips grazing her cheek. She refused the grimace threatening the corners of her mouth and concentrated on the door and her response.

Keep him off balance.

"You've been two-timing me, Robert." She met his gaze. "You can't expect me to kiss you."

He laughed and backed away slightly. "You should talk. If it weren't for that cowboy's interference, I would have been able to court you the way I wanted. He forced me to take you tonight." He touched her throat. His finger traced lazily down to the open collar of Rafe's shirt to rest above her breasts. "I hope you didn't do anything with him when you were in Mexico. I wouldn't like that, Bren."

It was on the edge of her tongue to give him an earful. Maybe if he knew she'd made love to Rafe, and he'd jolted her world, Robert would consider her damaged goods and return her. But the all-or-nothing look in his eyes told her that would be a serious infraction.

She stood in his menacing shadow, his head blocking the only light. She suddenly realized she recognized this place. They had played here as kids. There hadn't been electricity in the root cellar then, abandoned years ago. Straddling Connelly and Fallon land, they called it their fort. Since then, the woods had taken claim to it. Two-thirds buried underground, only the roof, which blended into the landscape, remained visible. Other than her father and Kate, only Kevin knew it existed. Would he remember it?

Keep him off balance.

"You've done a lot with the place. How'd you wire it for electricity?"

"Did he touch you?" He gripped her chin, forcing it up, his fingers tightening incrementally.

His face, which she'd come to rely on as so familiar and welcome, was strained and angry, waiting on her response. "No. There's nothing between Rafe and me."

"That's wonderful news." His fingers relaxed. "Except he believes there's more. In order for us to be together—sharing my name, the house . . ."

Bren stiffened.

"Relax, sweetheart." He ran his fingers down her arm and held her hand. His palm was clammy and cold, and she swallowed the unease of his touch like medicine. "I plan to make an honest woman of you."

Oh God, he is going to take me against my will!

"Bren?" He shook her hand lightly.

She couldn't speak. Her voice was lost, drowning in the hidden undertow of his deceptive, placid blue eyes.

"You need to remain here until he moves on. He won't until he believes you're not coming back."

She wanted to laugh at the absurdity. Wes Connelly would never allow his son anywhere near a Fallon. Rafe would never leave her. Even if he believed she'd met a tragic end, he wouldn't leave her boys. He loved them. She'd be left to rot in this grave alive because she wouldn't starve to death. Robert would see to her every need, or rather his needs, and that made her skin creep.

"I'll tell him I care for you."

He cocked his head. "He does seem too proud to grovel." He pulled her hands up and placed them on his shoulders. His arms sliding around her waist, he held her tight to him. "Prove it to me, Bren." His thoughtful tone hardened, demanding her compliance.

Hell, no! Bren's fingers curled inward along the fine linen of his dress shirt. She wasn't touching him. There was only so much negotiating she was willing to do. What she needed was a weapon. She searched frantically and stopped. Beyond his shoulders, the scissors sitting on the metal table flashed—sharp, deadly. But if he knew her intentions, the blades could end up buried to the hilt in *her* chest. She didn't need to worry herself. In order for the weapon to be used against her, she'd have to get to it first.

Damn it. She was going to have to initiate touching him.

Chapter Thirty-Six

Rafe pulled the brim of his Stetson down to avoid the swirl of mist in his eyes. He clamped down on Ryan's shotgun across his lap and urged his horse forward with the old man at his side. Aiden was riding ahead with Roscoe out in front, tracking the scent from Bren's pajamas. They drove further. The cornstalks cracked beneath the hooves of their mounts, hollow and empty, like his life before he'd met Bren.

The squawk and static of the police radio on his hip kept him alert. Kevin's search team was working out on Route 68. A team of neighbors worked Bren's hundred or so acres, while Rafe's team searched the property along the back forty that bordered Connelly land.

Aiden remained only a dark silhouette against the curtain of night and mist, his face hidden beneath the hood of his rain poncho. He hadn't said much before they headed out. Only took Rafe's orders like a soldier would from a drill sergeant—a lot of yes sirs, showing a determination Rafe always knew the boy possessed. Even if it was hidden under that obstinate teenage persona he worked like hell to aggravate his mother with and had perfected over time.

They'd decided to let the dog do the work. If they called out, it could very well tip her captor off. The element of surprise was their best hope. Roscoe's lead remained taut, the hound's legs working the field behind his property, his nose pressed toward the ground, giving every indication he had Bren's scent and was moving in the right direction.

But that didn't lift the sick uneasiness tight across Rafe's chest—Bren was slipping farther away from him, and it clung heavy and inescapable like the bleak, gray night surrounding him.

"She's a fighter, son." Paddy's bay moved alongside him and reminded Rafe he'd asked for the old man's presence.

Was the old man's comment supposed to console him? It only made him acutely aware Patrick Ryan had years of knowing Bren. Years Rafe was never afforded, and that burned low in his gut.

"It'll also get her killed."

"She's smart."

Rafe's gaze cut to Patrick Ryan, his features hidden under a moonless sky. He could only make out the old man's silver crew cut around his ears, the brim of his cap turned down, his expression left to Rafe's imagination, except he recognized the jut of his chin—stubborn like Rafe's. He grunted in amusement, but sobered quickly. He wanted nothing to do with Patrick Ryan after tonight, and being reminded that he was related to him pissed him off.

"I brought you for guidance, not your insight." It also riled Rafe the old man hadn't given him enough credit to figure Bren out. "I know her, too. No thanks to you."

"You look like her." Paddy's head dipped as though it made him nervous to talk to Rafe, and he stroked his horse. "I recognize that now."

Her? He must mean Pamela Ryan, Rafe's biological mother. Rafe guessed resembling a person who had been dead for almost forty years, her photo forgotten in the corner of a room, had helped keep his identity a secret.

"You have her eyes."

"Stick to tracking." He clenched the reins. He could care less about the past now.

"Rafe!" Aiden peered over his shoulder. "I think he's got something."

Rafe kicked his horse in the flank and moved to Aiden's side. "Ease up on his lead."

Roscoe pulled to the right. He came upon the charred earth, what was left of Aiden's bonfire from several weeks ago. Rafe smiled inwardly. His feelings toward that defiant, moody teenage delinquent had changed considerably, and Rafe concentrated on the responsible man Aiden was growing into.

The hound continued toward the woods.

"What's beyond the trees?" Rafe called back to Paddy.

"Connelly land."

"How far back?"

"Not far. There's an old root cellar that straddles Fallon and—" The old man stiffened in his saddle. "They were a group, those kids." The comment sounded more like a walk down memory lane. "You don't suppose . . ." His voice lowered when he came up alongside Rafe and Aiden.

"This have something to do with Bren?" Rafe gave him an irritated look.

"Not sure. I never let on to Tom I knew about their fort. Daniel told me."

A childhood fort? "Where is it?"

The old man motioned at the hound heading toward the woods. "It's maybe a hundred yards past the wood line. You'd trip over it. It's buried so—"

"I know what a root cellar is," Rafe snapped. *God, I'm a bastard.* The old man was only trying to help. He loved Bren like a daughter. This had to be tearing him up as well. But Rafe's nerves were taut as a lasso with a longhorn steer at the end of it, its horns sharp and ready to jab him in the belly if he didn't come up with a plan of attack.

"Who knows about it?"

"The kids—Tom, Bren and Kate, Kevin." He rubbed his chin. "As I recall, even Connelly's son was part of that group."

He leaned over the saddle. "She never mentioned they had a long-standing friendship."

"They don't. At least not that I ever knew. Wes ordered that boy around. Wouldn't permit him to associate with farmers. It's just been recent . . . since Tom's death, he's been around more frequent."

There it was. What he'd been missing. His body went cold, and it scared the shit out of him. He turned abruptly in the saddle, giving the old man an incredulous look. "You don't think that's odd? The guy has a habit of showing up whenever she's around."

"I can't believe Robert Connelly would want to hurt Bren."

"Not hurt. Have."

Rafe pulled back on the reins and brought his horse to a stop. "Aiden, hang on to Roscoe and dismount. We need to go in on foot." He motioned to a stand of trees at the wood line. "Tie your horse off."

Rafe made a move to do the same when the old man gripped his arm. "You really think *he* killed Tom?"

Rafe considered it. If he was right, Connelly had been coveting Tom's wife for a long time. "I'm not sure. But it makes good damn sense."

Paddy released Rafe's arm and slumped in the saddle. "I never saw it coming."

"And neither will he." Rafe stepped down with the shotgun and tied off his horse. He was prepared to end the sick son of a bitch's life if it came to it.

The old man came up next to him and tied off his horse.

Rafe hooked his chin toward Aiden. He and the hound were several feet in front with little more than a few yards before the hound entered the woods. Aiden worked the dog well, giving Roscoe words of encouragement. The hound kept a steady pace, his gangly legs and clumsy paws plodding through what remained of the cornfield.

"He's a great kid." Rafe glanced over. "A bit hardheaded." The old man stood next to him, close enough that their breathing was one. The inner strength and warmth of Paddy Ryan's body was suddenly comforting. Whatever the man had done, he was here now, and that counted for something. That day in his house, Rafe had connected with Paddy's eyes. Brown and murky from age, they'd revealed to Rafe the loss and regret of a decision made under duress. Rafe hadn't wanted to admit it then, but his stance was softening now. "But if his father was anything like me growing up, his hard head will make him fight for what he wants in life."

The old man gripped his shoulder and tipped his head toward Aiden. "Right now he's got the fight, but if things don't go our way . . . He can't afford to lose his mother."

"I can't afford to lose either one of them." He meant it. He loved Bren with an ache. But her boys had carved out a place in his heart, too. "Let's hope it's the fort. Once we find them, call Bendix. Then take Aiden and the dog and find cover." He handed him the radio but hesitated. He wanted to say, "I'll work on this thing"—forgiveness. Instead, he let go of the radio and shrugged. "Your son raised a great kid. Keep him safe."

Family's not something I'm looking for. What a total ass he'd been.

Now he wanted it all, and he meant to protect all of them, including the old man, until he could make that happen.

Chapter Thirty-Seven

ROBERT STOOD BEHIND BREN, HIS ARM AROUND HER WAIST, HOLD-ing her against him. He caressed her neck, the touch of his fingertips like nails to a chalkboard. She wanted to cringe. But she endured because if he believed she belonged to him, had belonged to him since they were kids, then perhaps he'd be blinded to what she was really up to.

"The lens loves you, sweetheart." His mouth and hot breath, unbearably close to her ear, made her lips tremble.

She'd maneuvered him to the table. Pretending to be attracted to him had made her nauseous—touching him, equivalent to charming a snake. But the result put her within an arm's reach of the scissors. The sharp point with its nearness taunted her. No way could she grab it in front of him. Robert wasn't ripped with muscles, but he was tall, agile, and a man—three strikes.

She needed to turn him around. Put his back to the table. In order to do that, Bren needed to block out her derision for him and focus on the result—escape.

Bren closed her eyes tight. *Turn around and touch him.*

"Robert." She ran her hand along his forearm that held her to him. "Loosen up. I want to see you." His hold gave slightly, and Bren turned in his arm.

"Better?" The tenor of his voice, edged with his usual concern for her, took on a frightening parallel. This Robert lived within the same body as the other one. She couldn't tell them apart at the moment. His easy smile brightened the strong lines of his fine-boned face. Blue, peaceful eyes watched her with interest.

She wouldn't be lulled into thinking she could reason with him. This

Robert would surely disappear, and she'd be left to deal with the bastard that lurked below the surface.

"The table's poking my back. How about we switch." She cupped his cheek. Unlike Rafe's, it was too smooth. He was smooth, too put-together. How could he have ever believed she would want him with his perfectly pressed pants, starched shirt, and glaringly polished shoes?

We're complete opposites.

"The bed's more comfortable, Bren. I can lie next to you." He said it with such seriousness that every nerve ending she possessed went on alert, and the bed loomed with what he had in mind.

"We'll get to the bed, baby." Her hand slid down his shirt and rested on his tie. She tugged it. "I thought I'd undress you first."

He smiled wickedly, hopped up on the table, and pulled her to him, placing her between his thighs. "I'm all yours."

Oh, yes. He was definitely hers. Only with the height of the table, he'd grown by several inches, and his body blocked the scissors. She could reach them. But she still needed to do it without calling attention.

Touch him.

Bren took a breath and continued to work on his tie until she pulled it free. The buttons came next, and she pulled his shirttails from his trousers.

He unbuttoned his cuffs and pulled off his linen shirt, leaving him bare chested.

Okay, more skin in which to plunge the scissors. This was a good thing. Except the thought of how she would accomplish it made her queasy. But as accommodating as he was at that moment, seeing he was going to rape her with her consent, the queasiness settled into hardcore survival mode, and she moved to his belt.

He grabbed her hand. "My turn."

Shit!

"No fair," she teased. "You've got far more clothes on than I do."

He'd put her at a disadvantage when he'd stolen her from her home in the middle of the night. Bren aimed to equalize the situation.

"How about you give up your shoes and socks?" She touched his arm lightly. "You don't make love with your shoes on, do you?"

He laughed and kissed her forehead. "Then we move to the bed."

She smiled back, tried like hell to ignore the wet outline of his lips on her skin, said nothing, and bent down to untie his shoes to remove them. When she'd gone to bed last night, she hadn't dressed for the fight of her life. But she could outrun him if they were evenly matched, and something told her Mr. Perfect had tender feet. She did not. If her aim missed a vital organ or only grazed him, he would come after her. With that in mind, she removed his socks.

Crap—except for the damn key. She'd work on that. It was in his back pocket.

He slid off the table and pulled her to him. His head bent slightly; he had every intention of kissing her. It was the only chance she had at retrieving the key.

His lips came down tentatively. Bren held still. He could search for her tonsils before she'd respond. She closed her eyes and tried to ignore his soft lips, wide and clumsy, tasting her mouth. She wrapped her arms around his waist and touched his butt cheeks, rubbing for the key. The hard shape of it rested in the right rear pocket of his pants, and she began to work it out under the pretense of groping his ass.

He moaned into her mouth, his tongue pushing its way inside. It took every ounce of resolve not to bite him. She continued her manipulation of the key until she pushed it out and into her hand.

Bren pulled away. "You kiss like you mean it." She rolled her lips in. They were swollen and wet.

"I want you. Enough petting, Bren." He grabbed her arm and tugged her toward the bed.

She ran her hand along the table and snagged the scissors. Raising it, she jabbed it hard into him aiming for his heart, but he dodged to the right.

It was like cutting into a tender chicken breast, the give of flesh, and Bren let go, the scissors falling. It hit the table with a resounding clatter, then a light thud onto the floor.

Robert groaned in pain, his grip falling away. "What the hell?" He gave her a confused look and grabbed his arm. "Bren?"

Not good. He shouldn't still be standing . . . or talking. She glanced up. His eyes were wide with shock, and then they pierced her with understanding. "You bitch."

Shit. No one died from an injury to the shoulder unless a major artery was hit. There was blood, but not enough to suggest he was going to bleed out. God, she sucked with her aim, but he was off balance and she had the key. She ran to the door. He stumbled behind her. Things fell to the floor, and she didn't look back. She concentrated on the lock and the key. Her fingers shook with fear, and she cursed.

Dear God, help me find the hole, or he's going to kill me.

As though God had heard her prayer, the key slipped in the lock and clicked. She yanked opened the door. The scent of pine greeted her, a chorus of spring peepers beckoned, and she took her first step toward freedom—when an arm reached out and hauled her back. She screamed. The sharp point of the scissors, coated in Robert's blood, pressed into her stomach, and she clamped her lips shut and swallowed a whimper.

He grabbed her by the hair and pulled her face against his smooth cheek. "I'm going to take you now as your punishment." The engaging voice of a new lover disappeared, replaced with the edge of reprisal. He yanked her off her feet and dragged her to the bed and pushed her down.

Sitting on top of her, pinning her arms under his thighs, he pressed the scissors to her throat with one hand and with the other unbuckled his belt and worked the button and zipper of his pants.

Bren squirmed beneath him, screaming her head off. If someone was out there, she prayed they'd hear her.

"Don't fight me." He pressed the scissors into the soft hollow of her throat. "It can go the hard way or the easy way."

Oh God, he was going to rape her! He was going to keep her captive. And he was going to punish her again and again for deceiving him.

He moved down to her thighs, and grabbed for her hands at the same time, still keeping her pinned beneath him. His lips came down hard, his tongue relentless. He tore at her mouth until she unclenched her teeth. Bren choked out a cry when his tongue darted into her mouth. Tears, hot and wet, ran down her cheeks. Consumed with taking what was not his, he had left the scissors on her chest, leaving its sharp point between their bodies to graze her neck and throat repeatedly with their movements.

Bren moaned into his mouth to stop. The point pierced her skin, and she gulped down a cry. Her eyes flew open and locked into his. They were wild and intent on conquering.

"Please, Robert, stop!"

He pulled away suddenly, the scissors falling into the crack between the wall and the mattress. Robert studied her intently. His brows furrowed, and he touched the hollow of her neck. "Sweetheart, you're bleeding."

No shit.

He brought his finger up. Bren's dark, red blood covered his fingertip, and he tasted it, smiling pleasantly like a vampire after a meal.

Bren wanted to gag. All that she knew of Robert Connelly became distorted. His attractive patrician features twisted with anger, and she didn't recognize the childhood friend or the man who had been so compassionate toward her.

His hand came down on her breast. Roughly, he pinched her nipple through her shirt.

Bren gasped in pain. "Don't, Robert. You're hurting me."

"Like you hurt me." He glanced at his shoulder. His pale skin oozed with blood. Robert's lips thinned. "Our first time could have been sweet . . . sensual." His eyes hardened, and he reached under her shirt and tugged on her panties.

"God no. Please don't." She'd die before she'd let him invade her. She reared up and screamed.

"You son of a bitch." The deep drawl filled the room accompanied by the racking of a shotgun.

Robert's eyes grew large and his hand stilled, clenched around the satin of her panties.

Bren couldn't see him, but she recognized the slow, pissed-off tone of Rafe's voice with utter relief.

His powerful hand gripped Robert's arm—the difference in strength between the two men evident when Rafe's fingers wrapped around Robert's bicep and plucked him off her. He flew back into the metal table and fell to the ground.

Tall and angry, Rafe loomed over him, a shotgun shoved against Robert's skull. "I should kill your miserable ass."

Robert remained still, his eyes closed.

The tightness in Bren's chest eased.

Rafe glanced at Bren. "He hurt you?"

She shook her head, her hand instinctively going up to her throat.

"Jesus. You're bleeding!" He lowered the shotgun to his side and moved toward her.

Bren scrambled to the far corner of the bed and tucked herself into a small ball.

Rafe's face tensed. "What'd he do to you?"

Bren's heart sped up. She couldn't speak. She felt dirty. She wanted to go home. Bren shook her head. "Not now," she whispered and bit down on her lip, helpless to stop the tears welling in her eyes.

A hand grabbed for the table, and Bren gasped. Robert hoisted himself up. "Rafe!"

Rafe flinched and raised the shotgun.

Robert grabbed for the barrel. "I'm going to fuck you up, Langston." His language, sharp and vulgar, made Bren recoil deeper into the corner. Sweat beaded Robert's forehead, his usual pale complexion now a flush of repressed rage as he wrestled Rafe for the shotgun.

Rafe's dark brows knit, and he beaded in on Robert. "It's over, Connelly. Sheriff's right outside the door."

"You're lying."

Rafe forced Robert back against the table. He motioned with his head to Bren. "Get out of here."

She wanted to. But she wouldn't leave him. If Kevin were right outside, why wasn't he drawing down on Robert? No. She wasn't leaving Rafe.

"Move it, Red," Rafe growled, the gun slipping from his hands.

"Rafe!" Bren screamed.

"Connelly." The gruff voice seemed to stop time—and Robert.

Paddy stood in the small doorway, hunched over, holding a pistol at the ready.

Cursing, Rafe shot Paddy an irritated gaze. "Old man, I got this."

Bren moved to the bed and struggled to get to her feet. Rafe glanced over his shoulder. "God, Bren. Stay—" Rafe swung his head back toward Robert. "*Shit.*"

Robert twisted the gun away from Rafe and pointed it at him.

"Rafe!" Bren held her breath.

Paddy's heavy boots clomped down the wooden steps. "God damn it!" He kept his gun trained on Robert. "I'm not losing another son."

Robert sneered and took aim at Rafe's chest. Rafe backed up and struggled for balance when his leg hit the end of the bed. A single gunshot exploded, echoing inside the stone walls of the cellar.

Bren glanced at Robert still holding the shotgun now aimed at her. Glued to Robert's menacing eyes, she prepared to die. But his look changed slowly to one of terror, and the shotgun slipped from his hand and hit the floor as he clutched the grisly hole in his chest.

Blood trickled through his fingers, and he collapsed.

Bren's body trembled, and her hand flew to her mouth. "Oh my God."

Rafe grabbed the shotgun from the floor and knelt down to check Robert's pulse. "He's dead." He stood and came to her, pulling her quivering body to him.

"He killed Tom," she managed to whisper.

"I know, honey." He held her at arm's length, doing an inventory of her when his eyes landed on her throat. "He cut you."

She didn't miss the edge to his words. "It doesn't hurt."

He probed her throat gingerly with his finger. "It's a flesh wound," he said, relief in his voice. Their gazes met. His eyes swept her as though he was unsure she was real. "You're wearing my shirt."

His matter-of-fact tone made her laugh. "I couldn't fall asleep."

Rafe's lips quirked. "I love you." His voice was hoarse.

Bren caressed his dark, bristly cheek. "I love you, too."

His warm, firm lips kissed her mouth. She kissed him back.

He set her away from him and dug into the front of his rain jacket, pulling out something soft and familiar. "You're near to naked, darlin'. This should warm you up."

"My pajamas?"

"Thought we'd give that hound a test run."

"We?"

She remembered Paddy then. He remained in the doorway, his face ashen under the glow of the glaring single bulb. His eyes were lost. He still held the pistol, shaking in his trembling hand.

She squeezed Rafe's hand, nodding behind him. "He needs you."

Rafe glanced over his shoulder. "I got him." He stepped over Robert's body and Bren wanted to gag. The sooner they got out of here the better.

Rafe moved to Paddy's side and pried the gun from his arthritic fingers then shoved it in his waistband.

Paddy grabbed Rafe's shoulder. "I had to, son."

He was his son. If or when Rafe chose to recognize it, the man she'd known most of her life would be waiting to receive him.

Rafe moved him to the bed and sat him down. "Don't keel over on me now, old man." Rafe crouched down in front of him, then grinned at Bren.

"We've been at each other since we left Grace." He squeezed Paddy's jean-clad leg, feeling forgiveness creep in whether he wanted it to or not. "It's just going to take some getting used to. I don't even know what to call you."

Paddy placed his hand over Rafe's. "Anything but old man."

Rafe laughed. "You don't like it?"

"Hell, no," Paddy grumped. "When you say it, you're always scowling at me."

Rafe gave a deep-throated chuckle. "Then I'll try not to scowl."

They were like two thunderheads clashing. If it wasn't for the smell of blood and death around her, Bren might have laughed. But her humor faded with the commotion coming from the doorway.

Kevin with his Stetson poked his head through the door. "Ryan, you're the biggest pain in the ass." She recognized his mock anger and crooked smile.

"Mom!" Aiden's head, slicked back and wet from rain, emerged from under the hood of a rain poncho.

Rafe nodded to Bren, and then grabbed Paddy's arm, pulling him up. He hooked his chin toward the door. "Let's take this outside."

Fat ran drops hit Bren's face the moment she emerged from underground. Aiden had been pulled back, a sheriff's deputy standing next to him. Rafe came up behind her and reached for Aiden's arm. "I'm proud of you."

Aiden smiled.

One of the deputies threw a yellow raincoat over Bren's shoulders. Barefoot but safe, she headed toward her son.

Aiden swooped in on Bren, his poncho reminding her of a bat's wingspan. He wrapped his arms around her waist.

Ignoring the water seeping through her shirt from his poncho, Bren hugged him back and gave Rafe a quizzical look over Aiden's cold, wet hair.

"Your boy found you."

Aiden squirmed, and she let him go.

So much for their loving embrace.

He angled his head toward Rafe and Paddy, but in particular his grand-father. "I heard Kevin talking. He said when Aunt Jo was able to talk, she told him Rafe was your son. Is he?"

Paddy looked to Rafe, his expression more of a question.

"It's a long story, Aiden." Rafe grimaced. "It's confusing."

"Holy shit!" He looked from Bren to Rafe to Paddy. "Rafe's my uncle." The awe in which he said it left Bren in a quandary as to how he truly felt about it. Almost like he was trying the title on for size to see how it fit or sounded coming off his lips.

"That's cool." Aiden shook his head in an I'm-down-with-that kind of motion, which Bren was fairly sure was a good thing.

She'd leave it to father and son to explain details because she was done with convoluted issues. Cold but relieved, tired although she wouldn't be able to sleep, Bren Ryan was officially off the clock trying to save the world.

She smiled to herself. *Well . . . at least my world.*

Chapter Thirty-Eight

BREN STEPPED INTO JO'S BEDROOM. THE SHADES WERE OPEN, ALLOW-ing a gray afternoon light to spill in across the king-sized bed where Jo sat propped up by pillows. Swallowed up by a bulky floral comforter, she seemed small and vulnerable.

Bren moved closer and frowned at the dark circles ringing Jo's eyes.

She should have been recuperating in the hospital. But she had checked herself out within twenty-four hours saying all she had was a killer headache.

"Who was that at the door?" A shapely dark brow rose over Jo's eye. As a pair her eyes were tired and fluttering toward sleep. Only Jo was obstinately holding them open.

"Why aren't you asleep?" Bren narrowed in on her. "You did take those pills I gave you?"

"Answer the question, Ryan."

"Kevin." Bren sat down on the bed next to her. The big, pillow-topped mattress hugged her bottom.

"What did he want?"

She slumped against Jo's legs under the plaid comforter and toyed with the stitching. "You know Wes is friends with the judge."

"Yeah."

"Being friends with the judge gets you privileges most prisoners don't get."

"So?"

"When they told Wes the news about Robert, he fell apart. Cried like a baby. When they came back to check on him an hour later, he'd hung himself."

"Bren!" Jo's hand flew to her mouth. She slid it down. "I don't understand.

What could he possibly use? He should have been wearing a jumpsuit and slip-on tennis shoes."

"Seems Wes is used to sleeping in satin sheets."

"That's awful."

"Unfair is more like it. Wes gets his sheets, and I get screwed. I wanted that bastard to suffer."

"He's dead, Bren. I wouldn't take death lightly."

Bren could attest to that. Jo had been lucky she'd gone down with one blow. Had she struggled with Robert or been able to unmask him, he would have killed her. As it was, she looked exhausted, her head taped up like a busted piñata.

Bren squeezed her hand. "I don't care about Wes. He got what he deserved. I'm worried about you. I can't believe you signed yourself out."

"I hate hospitals. Plus I have work."

"You can't be serious." Bren eyed her and then the lump next to her under the comforter. "Is that what I think it is?" She grabbed the covers and pulled it back. "What the hell do you need a briefcase for?" Bren went to grab for it.

Jo slammed her hand on the black leather case. "Leave it. It's important."

"The PI business picking up?"

"You know I can't discuss it." She frowned at Bren.

Since when? Maybe she shouldn't have, but she had, on numerous occasions. Why the secrecy now?

Jo's hand remained glued to the case, her expression tense.

"Okay." Bren moved off the bed. "Keep your briefcase." She walked to the window and peered out. It was cloudy and chilly—the norm for an afternoon day in March. "You know he doesn't like being away from you."

"Jeremy." She spoke his name with little feeling.

"What's wrong?"

"All he does is travel lately."

"For his job, Jo."

"Nice he could find the time to fly back and check on me."

"Be fair. He'd been out all night on an emergency call."

"He called *you* this morning—not me."

Where was all the hostility coming from? He'd called just as soon as he got word. He'd tried her hospital bed, but she'd already checked herself out. She had no cell phone—only her stupid penguin pajamas when the cab dropped her off.

"You know why."

Jo shrugged. "I'm tired, Bren."

Bren shut the shade. "I didn't mean to upset you, honey. Take a nap. I'll be downstairs." Bren started to walk away.

"Bren." Jo grabbed her wrist. "I'm sorry. We've both been through a lot. You don't have to stay with me. Jeremy will be home soon."

"I'm not leaving you alone."

"What about Rafe and the boys?"

Bren smiled. "You mean Uncle Rafe. He's over at Paddy's replacing a belt on his tractor. And the boys are with him."

"So he's forgiven Paddy?"

"He's trying."

"And the boys . . . they've taken to their Uncle Rafe?" Jo gave her a tired smile.

"They've been inseparable. I don't think the three of them have stopped smiling."

"And you?"

"I love him, Jo."

"You deserve to be happy, honey."

"I am." Bren turned off the light on the nightstand. "Get some rest."

Bren grabbed the phone on the first ring. "Breakstone residence."

"Please tell me you take out the trash and cut the grass, too."

"Funny. Why are you calling? You should be getting ready to land."

"Early flight."

"Then you're on your way."

"Not quite. My battery's dead. I need a ride."

Bren glanced up toward the stairs of the Breakstone home. "Let me check on Jo. If she's still asleep, I'll come get you."

"I'm not around the corner, you know. I'd rather you stay with her."

"Okay. Let me see what I can do. Someone will be there by five."

CHAPTER THIRTY-NINE

BREN PUSHED THROUGH THE CROWD SURROUNDING THE BAGGAGE carousel on the bottom level of Baltimore's Thurgood Marshall Airport and searched the faces of those coming down the escalator. She caught Jeremy stepping off.

"Hey." Bren gave Jeremy a quick hug. "I'm your ride."

"Jo okay?" He frowned. "You could have sent Rafe."

"I tried. I think he and the boys are up to something. I have the sneaking suspicion they were not where they said they were. Jo was still sleeping when I left, but Rafe's on his way over to stay with her." She picked up his wrist and turned it to check his watch. "He should be there now."

Jeremy grabbed his suitcase off the luggage carousel. "Looks like I missed a lot of excitement."

"You should stay home more often." She jabbed him playfully in the side. "Maybe you need to be grounded, mister."

"What?" He looked confused.

"Jo. I think she's worried you're two-timing her."

His pale cheeks took on an irritated pink glow. "That's ridiculous. I've missed her like hell." His expression softened. "How's she doing?"

"She has a nice-sized knot on her forehead, but she's going to be fine."

"Rafe's phone call scared the hell out of me."

"I think he scared the hell out of himself."

"Can you blame him?"

She didn't want to talk about it. It only reminded her that instead of being here with him at the airport, she could very well still be underground, broken and lost.

"I'll take your bag." Bren grabbed the smaller medical bag in his hand, but came up short when he held it tight. She gave him a quizzical look.

"I've got it. Just get me home."

"Sure, you've got to be beat." She led him through the baggage claim area and out to satellite parking. "The truck's this way."

He followed, and within a few minutes she was unlocking the truck doors. "The back seat's kind of full. How about we put your stuff in the bed?"

They stowed his bags and got on their way. She filled him in on the ride home, starting with Mexico.

"Bren, that's barbaric."

The Mexican's head swirled before her, and she swallowed. "Tell me about it."

"What about Robert? You need to fill me in. I never would have guessed he had a thing for you."

She gripped the steering wheel. Just his name made her tremble. Jeremy didn't know yet that Robert had killed Tom. "He—"

Her cell phone went off. With one hand on the steering wheel, she popped it off her belt holder and checked the number. "Hang on. I should take this, but I still need to tell you the rest." She took the call. "Clinic. How's she doing? That's good. No, we're in Baltimore. Probably an hour and fifteen minutes. I'll get someone out there." She snapped her phone shut and frowned

Jeremy grabbed her arm. "Is it Jo?"

Bren glanced over. "No." She then transferred her eyes back to the road. Keeping her eye on traffic, she pulled the phone away from her mouth, pressing it to her cheek. "It was Joan Bartlett. It's Tiger Lily—they think she's breech."

Jeremy moaned, his head hit the back of the seat, and he closed his eyes. "God. Doesn't this job ever end?"

Bren glanced over frowning. "I'll see if one of the vets on call can swing by."

His eyes opened and he sat up. "Tractor trailer," he warned, and the heavy rig thundered by on her left. "Keep your eyes on the road. Tell them we'll swing by."

"But—"

"You said Jo's fine. She knows the responsibilities I have." He motioned with his hand. "Give me your phone. I'll call them back." His tone left no room for argument.

Bren handed it to him. "I should be taking you home."

"Trust me, she'll understand."

After all these years she must. But these weren't normal circumstances. Something was definitely off with these two. The last time she'd seen them together, she was dealing with an extremely intoxicated Rafe Langston doing his best to irritate her. Jeremy and Jo were as close as they could be for a married couple working toward their seventh anniversary—not the seven-year itch.

He seemed relieved she was fine, but didn't seem too eager to get home.

Jeremy finished the call and shoved her phone in Bren's front coat pocket. "I'll check on Jo later. If she's asleep, I don't want to wake her."

Rafe sat back on the navy-leather couch with the TV clicker and flicked through the stations in Jo and Jeremy's family room. He'd showered real quick and left Aiden and Finn at Paddy's.

Rafe grunted to himself—*no, my father's house.*

How in the hell was he going to get used to that? Truth, he had a daddy back in Texas. One he loved and respected. Not that he didn't respect Patrick Ryan in some ways. He'd been good to Bren and his grandsons. Good to his son Tom. He would have been good to him, too, had he kept him.

But he hadn't, and it still bothered him.

Course, he'd almost looked that devil in the eye himself. He now knew what it was to love a woman so completely and without end. If Connelly had killed Bren, he'd have been inconsolable. The equivalent of Patrick Ryan when he'd lost his wife.

Could he have made the right decision and stayed to see to his nephews' upbringing? Looked into their eyes every day and caught glimpses of their mother in their smiles and mannerisms?

He hoped he would have. But, realistically, he may have turned tail and gone back to Texas and tried to forget everything about this place called Clear Spring. Almost losing Bren had gotten him an up close and personal glimpse into Patrick Ryan's private hell. Only he wasn't married to Bren. But he was working real hard at rectifying that.

Rafe dug into the pocket of his black suede jacket resting over the arm of the couch and pulled out the small velvet box and flipped the top open.

He'd have bought the biggest diamond out there. But Bren was a practical woman—a farm girl. She wasn't prissy or pretentious. So he went with the three C's—cut, clarity, and color.

He wanted to take full credit for the purchase he made today, but in all fairness it had been a joint effort of four: himself, Aiden, Finn, and the old man. He'd wanted to feel the boys out. They had only one daddy. He knew he could never replace Tom—not his intention. He shouldn't have worried. They'd taken his hints and ran with it right to their grandfather. Before long, they were standing in Hagerstown Jewelry off of Clear Spring's Main Street, picking out Bren's engagement ring when she called with a favor.

The thump of Jo's cane brought Rafe around, and he snapped the box shut and shoved it back in his coat pocket. He leaned over the couch and toward the steps.

"Whoa." He hopped up and came around the couch and into the hall. "You're retired, right?" He took stock of her black running shoes, jeans, and white T-shirt, his eyes coming to rest on the black shoulder holster and semiautomatic handgun with her hand curled around her cane.

"Where's Bren?" She placed her cane against the wall and snagged a black windbreaker from the hall closet and slipped it on.

"Jeremy called. His car wouldn't start. She went to get him."

"Why didn't she tell me?" she snapped.

"She didn't want to wake you."

"How long ago?" Her words were impatient.

"She's been gone about two hours. Why?" And he was quickly losing *his* patience.

"You didn't block me in?" She grabbed her cane.

Actually he had. Damn good thing.

"Didn't think you needed to go anywhere, Jo." His voice grew irritated.

"I do." She moved toward the door. "Can you move your truck?"

Rafe leaned up against the wall and folded his arms. "Depends. You didn't answer my questions."

"Rafe, I don't have time for this. I need to go. Can you move your truck?"

He didn't know what to make of her behavior. This wasn't the Jo Breakstone he knew.

"Jo, tell me what's going on. I know you're retired, so why the gun? More to the point, why the hell are you dressed? You have a concussion—you should be resting."

"I work for the FBI on a contractual basis. I'm authorized to carry a firearm."

Maybe. But did they know their subcontractor was not fit for duty? Deep shadows ringed her eyes. She had a bump the size of a goose egg, and he wasn't exaggerating—he'd seen it. From the looks of that bump, if it had gone down, it wasn't apparent.

"I can't let you leave."

"This is ridiculous. I'm going. I *have* to go." She flung the door open and grappled with her cane, placing it out in front.

Before Rafe could stop her, she began her descent down the front steps, the rubber of her cane making a thump, thump, thump.

"What the hell?" He made his way back to the couch and slipped on his jacket and bolted out the front door.

Jo worked to seesaw her Tahoe between the house and Rafe's truck. It was like the woman was trying to head off a disaster. Her steadfast determination concerned him. Rafe took the steps two at a time and came around to her passenger side and swung the door open.

"What in hell are you doing, Jo?" He peered into the truck, the glow of the interior light leaving nothing to his imagination. Tears streaked her face. Her hands were glued to the steering wheel, and her body shook with sobs. "Shit. You're in no condition to drive." Rafe reached over and put the truck in Park and took the keys from the ignition. Only Jo's gentle weeping filled the cab.

Rafe hopped in and shut the door, the interior light popping off. Weepy women and their unpredictable emotions—he'd tried to stay clear of them most his life. His mother was an enterprising woman full of vigor and rarely wept—probably too busy chasing two hellions to succumb to such frivolity. That was probably what attracted him to Bren. But this was Jo and damned if he knew how to console her.

He touched her shoulder and leaned in. "I'm thinking this is more than work related. I can't let you drive. You know that." He bent in to get a better look at her.

She sniffed and shook her head in the affirmative.

He squeezed her shoulder. "I'm real good at listening."

She sat back in her seat and placed her hands in her lap and closed her eyes. Silent and relentless, the tears continued to escape down her cheeks. "It's J-Jeremy."

"Bren's bringing him home, honey." He patted her arm.

She angled herself in the seat so she faced him. "N-no. They won't m-make it home."

He couldn't see her face—too dark. But the words she'd strung together and her despondent tone had him searching for the interior light. The overhead popped on and lit her face. Tear-stained he expected, but the look of complete despair in her eyes sent his pulse into overdrive.

"Tell me what I need to know, Jo. Bren's with him."

She nodded. "J-Jeremy's b-being investigated by the FBI," she said, gasping through sobs.

"For what?"

"Gambling."

"Jesus." Stunned, Rafe dropped back into his seat and rubbed his jaw, trying to sort out what that all meant. "Where were you going?"

"The clinic. They . . . want his hard drive."

"You're working for them." If it sounded like an accusation, it was. Since when did the FBI send an agent—subcontractor, whatever—to seize her own husband's computer? He was missing a chunk of information here. "Tell me what's going on."

She shook her head. "I will. But we need to get on the road."

"We're taking my truck. I'm driving." Rafe opened his door and grabbed her cane in the footwell on his side of the truck. "Let's go." He came around and helped her out.

He pulled out, heading east on 68. "Help me out, darlin'. What the hell are we doing here?"

"Take 70 toward Baltimore."

He took the exit onto 70. But, honestly, he had no idea where the hell they were going. His hands gripped the steering wheel. "We headed to the airport?"

"We need to find them."

"Am I looking for Bren's truck? What?"

"Yes."

"Someone call you? Tip you off?"

This was a real bitch. Clearly she was trying to hold it together. But every one of his questions, although necessary, brought panic to her voice.

"An agent friend called me this morning at the hospital. Told me they were going to intercept Jeremy at the airport in Louisville before his flight left at seven tonight. The agent called back this evening. They found out too late he'd grabbed an earlier flight."

"He called Bren when his car wouldn't start." Then something occurred to him. His shoulders tensed, and he glanced at Jo. "Were you planning on making a break for it?" Which was stupid as hell. And not something he thought Jo would consider with her law enforcement background.

"No! I couldn't let them take him without explaining why I turned him in."

Rafe fell back in his seat. "You turned him in?"

"I had to. These people he's dealing with will slit his throat. Eventually, they were going to kill him." Her voice cracked.

"How much is he into them for?"

"Close to half a million."

"Christ." He glanced at her. "That's heavy."

She wiped her face. "Tell me about it. When you wake up to find you can't buy groceries it kind of pisses you off."

"He clear out your savings?"

"Every penny."

"That's rough."

She started to cry again. "He needs help, Rafe. I tried. Trust me, it's a disease. I love him, but spending a few years behind bars seemed like the only answer. He would have gotten the help he needs. I would have seen to it."

"You're worrying me. You sound like it's not an option."

"It gets much worse. I can't save Jeremy now."

Not what Rafe wanted to hear, and his girl was with him. With only one number on his mind, Rafe grabbed for his cell phone.

CHAPTER FORTY

Bren carried Jeremy's medical bag out to the truck and pulled down the tailgate. By the time they pulled in, the foal had righted itself. But at the urging of Joan Bartlett, the stable owner, they had remained until the birth. When the colt arrived, he was perfect, wobbly to start and nursing contentedly when they'd packed up.

While Jeremy was busy chatting to the Bartletts about the colt, Bren grabbed his bag from the stall and stepped out to check her messages. She dug out her phone and fumbled it. The bag that she intended to sit on the tailgate fell to the ground, the contents spilling out.

"Crap."

She glanced at the phone—two messages. *Shit.* She'd forgotten to call Rafe. He'd have to wait. She put her phone back into the pocket of her coat. Dropping down on her haunches, she gathered up pill bottles, and cellophane-packaged syringes and stuffed them back into his bag.

Jeremy was a freak about the bag to begin with. He'd be pissed to know she'd dropped it.

She righted the bag, and anything near to falling out fell back into place, except for a dark cord that had looped its way out. She shoved it back in, but the obstinate thing kept popping out.

"Err." She stood and set it on the tailgate and pulled the wire, prepared to wrap it nice and neat and put it back. But the ends got hooked up on something in the bag. She managed to pull the entire wire out, stretching it the full length of the tailgate, and found the culprit. At one end hung two metal clips.

"What the hell would he use this for?" On the other end was an electric plug. But extension cords didn't look like this one. Yet it looked oddly familiar.

Where had she seen it before?

"Bren? You seen my bag?" Jeremy cleared the barn and slipped on his suit jacket. Pulling up his collar, he shoved his hands in his pockets and walked toward her.

She shivered, too. But it wasn't from the night air. She turned and placed her hand that held the wire behind her back.

"I couldn't find it in the stall." His pace slowed when he got closer. He stood next to her now. "It's freaking freezing out here. It was warmer down south."

"I brought it out. I didn't think you needed it."

He glanced at the bag sitting on the tailgate. It was a black leather bag, large with stiff leather handles. She could fit a large cat inside and still have room. She'd shut it but hadn't yet snapped the small leather strap with the lock closed.

Her adrenaline spiked. *What had he been doing in Kentucky?*

Jo had said getting ready for the Derby. Where had he been all the other times on his business trips?

She kept going back to the wire hidden behind her back. She'd seen this type of device before. Sketched it out and tossed the paper when she realized it was an effort in futility. Tommy "The Sandman" Burns, a.k.a. horse executioner, existed, but only in the past.

Then why did Jeremy have the identical device in his bag—handmade and designed to kill, not support, life?

Horses had perished in Maryland and other nearby states. It had happened a handful of times—West Virginia the most recent.

Jeez, I'm reaching. This is Jeremy, for God's sake!

"You okay?" He moved closer.

"Fine." She shrugged. "Tired is all."

"You've been through a lot." He moved still closer and tilted his head. "You sure you're okay?"

Bren pressed back against the tailgate. The clips hit the truck and clanged. She stiffened.

"What's that?"

"What?"

He pointed. "You look like some damn stuffy waiter taking an order at Clear Spring Horsemen's Club, ramrod straight with your hands behind your back."

Before Bren could respond, her cell phone went off. She could ignore it, but she'd already called attention to her odd behavior. It pealed again.

"You going to get that? It could be Rafe or Jo." Concern and irritation edged his voice.

"Yeah, sure." She transferred the device.

Jeremy reached in her pocket before she could get her hand around and pulled out her phone. He flipped it open and placed it to his ear. He pulled it away, looked at the screen, and frowned. "Sorry. It was Rafe. He must have gone to voicemail."

He leaned against the tailgate and looked at her, his hand resting on the bag. "What's going on, Bren? Something happen to Jo you're not telling me?"

"She's fine."

"Then what gives?" His hand moved against the leather strap. Her attempts to concentrate on his face proved difficult with his insistent fingers manipulating the lock. "You opened my bag."

"It fell, and the lock broke open."

"Uh-huh." His tongue pressed against the inside of his cheek, and he hooked his chin toward her. "What's behind your back?"

Something told her to fear him. The instinct, foreign where Jeremy was concerned, made her stomach flip with confusion. They were friends—she loved him. He'd helped her through the rough patches. He and Tom had been best friends. She was best friends with his wife. Her suspicions had to be unfounded.

Show him, and he'll explain.

That was what she was afraid of. Bren pulled it out from behind her back and laid it on the truck. "It fell out of your bag."

His face stiffened, and he grabbed it off the tailgate. "You know how I feel about my medical bag."

"I'm Bren, Jeremy. Your friend. Your assistant, remember? Don't treat me like a child." She grabbed it out of his hand. "And I'm not stupid. I know what this is."

"It's not what you think."

She'd read it. It had been done before and successfully until Burns had gotten caught. "No? Mr. Tommy 'The Sandman' Burns. Or is it Breakstone now?"

"What?"

"I know you know what I'm talking about." She took a step toward him and let the plug dangle but held the thick alligator clips in each hand. "How about I attach this to your ear and rectum and plug it in?"

He moved away. "They don't feel a thing. It's humane."

"You are so full of shit, Jeremy." She wanted to slap him. She'd dedicated her life to saving them and he had . . . what? Built a business? Bought a vacation home? Hell, she didn't know. Burns got paid, so she assumed he was, too. "Humane, my ass." She bore into him. She wanted answers. "For who? You? Why, for God's sake? You're a vet. You save lives, not end them."

She'd seen him work on horses. He had compassion. When he'd lost one, he felt it. Just like the one they'd put down in the cattle trailer. He'd agonized over shooting her.

He stepped forward. "Give it to me."

She moved away. "Not till you tell me what's going on."

He stopped and took a belabored breath. "All right. I'm owned."

"Owned? What does that mean?"

"Means I owe a lot of money. Money I can't make doctoring horses."

"For what? You mortgaged to the hilt? Gambling? What?"

His shoulders sagged.

She took a step back and looked him in the eye. "You're serious?"

He nodded. "I'm in for about half a mil."

"Good God!" Her hand flew to her mouth. He *was* serious. She could tell, and embarrassed, too. "Jo know?"

"Only about the gambling."

No wonder she'd been grumpy. She'd probably ripped him a new one. Plus, these were her finances, too. Poor Jo.

"You have to stop."

"I can't."

"Come again?"

"You heard me."

"Which we talking about?" Because if he wanted to fritter his life savings away, she couldn't help him. He needed serious therapy for that. But the horse thing was non-negotiable.

"Do you know what they do to those who can't pay up?"

"You should have thought about that before you did whatever you do when you gamble."

"God, you're so self-righteous. I can't. They won't just kill me. They'll kill Jo first, then me."

"You're an idiot, Jeremy." She fell back a step and dropped the wire on the tailgate and placed her hands on her hips. "We're going back to your house. You're telling Jo. Then you're telling Kevin." Bren grabbed his case and the wire and slammed the tailgate. "I can't even stand to look at you." She turned to get in the truck when he grabbed her arm, pulling her toward him hard.

"I'm not turning myself in, Bren. I'm not going to prison. I'm asking you to let me finish this thing. I only need a couple more, and I'll be paid up."

"You bastard." She yanked on her arm. "You're asking a hell of a lot from me. You killed that Thoroughbred at Charles Town." She shook her head. "You were just at Churchill Downs. You son of a bitch. You killed that one in Louisville, too. You're my friend—Tom's friend. How could you do this?"

His eyes pierced hers, and his grip tightened. "You're just like him. High and mighty. Never made a mistake. Never needing to ask for forgiveness. It's not always black and white. He didn't understand that, either. I asked him to look away. He couldn't or wouldn't."

"Tom knew about your electrocution scheme?"

"Someone told him. I've never figured out who. He wouldn't say. He was going to turn me in."

"What are you saying?" Her legs began to tremble.

"It was an accident, Bren, I swear. I agreed to meet him up in the barn. Said he had a proposition for me. Then he laid the guilt trip on me. Told me he knew about the insurance fraud. About the horses."

He tightened his grip. His eyes, now only inches from her face, were desperate. She didn't recognize him so angry and frightened.

"H-he never told me." He'd never had a chance.

His face softened, his fingers lightening up a fraction on her arm. "I didn't plan it, Bren. I swear. It just happened. He was wrapping up that damn rope as he laid down his demands. I was so pissed off. Who was he to tell me what to do? I told him to go to hell and walked away. But he grabbed me. I pushed him." He ran his fingers through his strawberry-blond hair roughly, as though he wanted to pull it out by its roots. "*God, Bren.* It happened so fast. He stumbled. His legs got twisted up in the rope, and he cussed up a storm. I tried to help, but he pushed me away and fell back into the hay door. I tried to grab him, but I couldn't."

What was he saying? It had been him up in the loft with Tom?

Bren grabbed her mouth in disbelief. Tom *had* gotten tangled up in the rope—but not all by himself. The back of her eyes burned with understanding. "You let him die, you bastard. You could have saved him." She clenched her hands to her side, her nails digging into her palms. "Why didn't you help him? You watched him die. You bastard!" She came at him, swinging.

He dodged her hands and managed to grab one arm and spun her around. He held her hard against him, pinning her arms down to her side. "I panicked." His voice was rough against her ear.

Panicked? That was his excuse?

"You murdered him!" It came out a wail, low in her gut. She went limp in his arms, and he allowed her to fall gently to the ground.

He came down on his haunches and smoothed back her hair. "Please forgive me." He began to cry. "I lost it, Bren. It wasn't me. I was sick and confused. Desperate." He pulled her up to him and hugged her. His chest rocked with his own sobs, shook her.

A freefall of emotion came over Bren. Tears flowed down her cheeks, and she couldn't even blink them away, her eyes open but not seeing. He wasn't Jeremy. He was a murderer. How could he ask her to forgive him? Bren yanked away from him. "*You* have Tom's phone. Why did you take it?"

He wiped his face. "All the cops had to do was listen to his voicemails. They would have known I was the last one to see him alive."

"You sick son of a bitch. You were the one calling me. Why?"

"I don't know. I should have known trying to frighten you would have the opposite effect." He took a step forward. "I couldn't let you find out it was me."

Her throat went dry.

My God. What would he do to her?

He pressed his hands to his face and wiped hard. Although his eyes glistened with emotion, there was a hardness of resignation and understanding.

Run, Bren, before he kills you.

She stepped away from him. Eyed the wired device and grabbed it.

He reached for her. She ducked and took off toward the barn. The Bartletts still had to be in the barn.

"Bren!" he yelled.

She glanced back. He wasn't going after her. He remained at the back of the truck. He'd opened the tailgate and was reaching into his bag while he kept a visual on her. What was he looking for? She made it to the barn. It looked dark. She called out and slid the heavy barn door open, the stubborn track screeching in protest.

Quiet, except for the gentle stirrings of the horses; there was no one inside. They must have gone up to the house. Too far for anyone to hear her if she screamed. Jeremy would hear her, though.

He yelled her name, his voice low and desperate. The distinct heel of his dress shoes connected with the gravel until she could no longer hear it. He was in the barn now. The dirt floor deadened his footfalls.

Bren hid next to one of the stalls. He was checking them, opening the doors, his breathing heavy and more irritated with each slamming stall door.

"Bren, let's talk about this."

They were done talking. She'd been talking to the enemy all this time—filled him in—told him her plans to catch Tom's killer.

He liked to listen.

"I helped you, didn't I? Gave you a job."

Damn right he'd offered her one. He felt guilty, the son of a bitch. She'd lost half her farm because of him. He'd ruined her life, and now that she had a new one, he was going to take that away from her, too.

"Bren. Come on. This is childish. Stop hiding. I wouldn't hurt you."

Liar. He killed Tom to save his miserable ass. He'd kill her, too.

She ached with sadness and trembled in fear. Everything she'd believed Jeremy Breakstone to be—trusting friend, compassionate healer, loving husband—had melted together and hardened into something ugly and perverse.

Bren grabbed for her phone. The irritated snorts and whinnies of the horses in front of her put her on alert. She peered through the wooden slats of the stall she was leaning on. He was in the next aisle. Her hands tightened on the electrical cord, and she tried to flip through her contacts for Rafe's cell phone. She waited. The phone clicked, then went to dead air before it began to dial the number.

"Bren?" Rafe's voice sounded in her ear.

She dropped the wire. "Rafe. God—help me. I'm at the—"

"Got you." Jeremy yanked her arm up.

She dropped the phone and tried to grab it off the ground. But Jeremy kicked it from her. Bren glanced over her shoulder. Moonlight filtered through the barn. Jeremy loomed over her. His arm rose, and the glint of something came down toward her and pierced her skin.

"Ow!" She pulled her arm from him, and he let go. She stumbled and tried to run, but her legs were clumsy. She teetered. "Damn it!" She rubbed her arm and zeroed in on him. "What did you poke me with?"

He was close. His face, level with hers, looked distorted, a reflection of a man she once trusted. Her vision blurred, but she could still make out his face. He was frowning at her. His arm shot out and helped her to the ground.

"It's a sedative. You need to calm down, Bren."

A low, garbled voice came from the right—her phone. *Where did he kick it?* It was Rafe. He was talking to her. Drowsy, unable to move, she recognized his demanding yet anxious voice drifting off with her as she slipped deeper into nothingness.

Rafe swung on Jo. "She drew it out on a piece of paper."

He'd picked up the crumpled paper under her bed after he'd tucked her in and gone downstairs with the laptop. While he waited for Bendix, he went on the Internet and checked it out for himself, which was easy. She'd saved it to her favorites.

Of course he'd showed it to Kevin, who had dismissed it, saying the FBI knew all about what happened in the past.

Only thing was, it was also happening in the present.

"If it's in his bag, she'll recognize it." He couldn't believe this shit. The vet. He'd never have guessed it.

Guess ol' Tom and he had something in common after all. Only Rafe wouldn't have found himself at the end of a—

Rafe's phone rang next to him on the seat. He grabbed it. Bren's name glowed on the blue screen and he flipped it open. "Bren?"

"Rafe. God—help me. I'm at the—"

"Bren!" Rafe kept his ear glued to his cell phone. The voices were distant now. His body tensed, and cold panic surged up his chest.

"Bren, honey, talk to me. Where are you?" The voices gave him hope. Then someone fumbled the phone, and the only connection he had to Bren was severed. It was the sound of silence that brought true fear.

Jo tugged on his arm. "What's happening?"

He shut his phone and tossed it to the seat. "She knows. Damn it." Rafe cut across all four lanes of traffic and slammed the car into Park. "Where would he take her?"

Jo shook and brought her hands to her face. "I-I don't know. They could be anywhere."

It had been several hours since Jeremy's flight had landed. They were obviously on their way home. They'd have to be somewhere close by.

Rafe pulled onto the interstate. "We're going back." He nodded to his phone on the seat. "Call Paddy. Tell him to go to Bren's and wait there for us. Then get a hold of Bendix and tell him what's going on. He can alert the FBI and put a lookout for Bren's truck. Someone might spot it."

"Where are we going?"

It was all that was left. "The clinic." Rafe caught the ramp at Frederick and flipped around to go west. They were about an hour away. He could get there in forty if he hauled ass. He'd find her. And when he did, he'd protect her with his life because, the simple truth was, without her he had none.

CHAPTER FORTY-ONE

B REN AWOKE SLOWLY TO DEEP SOBS. ABOVE HER, A GLARING FLUO-
rescent light made it difficult to open her eyes fully. But the movement to the right of her, the shutting of drawers and the echo of clinking
metal, brought her around.

Jeremy's back was toward her, in a dress shirt with the sleeves rolled up to
his forearms. His pale but capable hand reached into a jar with fluffy white
clouds—cotton balls. His other hand held something crinkling between his
fingers while she seemed to float on her back several feet away.

Oh God, am I dead?

Terror washed over her, and she jerked up. She couldn't. Glancing down,
gray, thick straps restrained her chest, hips, and legs. She tried to move her
arms, but they were pinned, too. The room with its yellow walls closed in,
and she knew she was in one of the examining rooms at the clinic.

How had she gotten there? Last she remembered, they were in the
Bartletts' barn, and Jeremy had poked her hard in the arm. It had been a
needle. He'd told her it was a sedative. So she'd been out for a while.

"Jeremy." The word tore from her throat. It startled her—the roughness.
It was edged in concern, and her brain couldn't understand why she should
fear him. She tried to remember, but her mind stumbled on the periphery
of a dark truth that lay bare if only her memory could grasp it.

He turned to her. "Bren?" He was startled, too. Startled she was awake.

"You look like hell." She'd meant to say it to herself. But he did. Deep
lines bracketed his usual smiling mouth. His blond hair stuck up in places.
His eyes were rough and red. He'd been crying—sobbing when she awoke.
Bren pulled at the straps with her wrists. "I want to get up."

He rolled a stool next to her and sat down. "How do you feel?" He patted her arm, and his cold, clammy palm made her shiver.

"Like I've been kicked in the head by a horse." The hum of the overhead light and its brightness made her head ache. His intense gaze made her uneasy. "What's wrong with you?"

"You were upset. How do you feel now?"

"I don't like these straps, for one thing." She tugged on them.

He glanced down at her body and frowned at her. "I didn't want you to roll off."

"That's nice. Now can I get up?" She smiled sweetly because when he let her up, she was going to brain him for treating her like some patient in a psych ward.

"Where do you want to go, Bren?" He talked to her in slow, deliberate syllables.

Home. What a ridiculous question. "I'm not stupid."

He studied her with avid curiosity but said nothing.

"You're acting weird."

He stood up and walked away.

"Hey, Doc, I mean it. Let me up." She tugged on the straps again with her wrists. She wriggled to free herself but couldn't. *Why so damn tight?* "Jeremy." His name came on an irritated burst. She lifted her head. "I'm freaking out here."

"You were upset with me. Do you remember?" He kept his back to her.

"You poked me in the arm. It hurt."

"Before that." He reached for something in the cabinet above.

Irritated he wanted to play Freud, she let her head drop against something lumpy, yet soft and dark, and she remembered something. "I picked you up at the airport." He'd been wearing a navy-blue suit jacket, the one her head probably rested on. Where had he been coming from?

"After that."

"Damn it, Jeremy, this is crap. I want to go home!"

Wait. She was supposed to take *him* home. Where was Jo? The metal table radiated cold through her palms, and she remembered the cellar—Robert. She stiffened. He'd hit Jo, given her a concussion. He'd killed Tom, tried to rape her.

But he was dead. Paddy had killed him before he could . . .

Relax. Rafe was alive and with Jo. The only one who didn't know the full story was Jeremy. "Wait. I know. Robert killed Tom. I forgot to tell you." More like, she didn't get a chance. But why?

"You sure about that?" He raised a needle in the air.

Yes. He'd killed Tom to get to her. Jeremy was confusing her. "I told you he did," she snapped.

She concentrated on the needle still held in the air. He clicked it with his finger to get the air bubbles out, shooting liquid out the end. She'd seen him do it numerous times before he gave an injection.

Bren's heart raced. Was he planning to sedate her again?

"Hey, stop ignoring me and turn around."

He did and leaned back on the edge of the counter.

"You're pissing me off. I know that." She clenched her teeth and tried to calm down.

He grabbed his medical bag and placed it on the counter, his expression grim.

It was open at the top with a brown wire hanging out. He snagged the wire and came toward her, holding it out, a plug dangling from one end.

"Shouldn't that be attached to a lamp?" She smiled at her humor, but he didn't.

"How about this end?" He held it out. Two metal clips swung with angry teeth, and her brain scattered. But fragments, sharp and uncomfortable, thrust themselves into her memory. The ugly truth of who Jeremy was and what he had done took hold of her sanity and shook her without mercy.

Bren's hands fisted. *Don't let him know you know.* She let her fingers unfurl slowly.

"You use those to hold up your pants?"

This time his mouth quirked. "Pants?"

"They're suspenders, right?"

He laughed and did his best to hug her, catching her by surprise.

His chest rumbled against hers. "I love you so damn much." But his laughter changed to drawn-out breaths, and she realized he was crying, again. Wet, warm tears rolled onto her neck. "It's fast. You won't feel a thing. I promise. You'll go off to sleep."

Fear, sudden and suffocating, like the weight of his body, stole her breath. "Get off me." She squirmed beneath him. "You bastard. Stop crying."

He moved off her, his face rosy with emotion and wet with tears. "Bren, I'm sorry." He placed a small silver tray on her stomach. He grabbed the needle from the tray.

"No!" She struggled, the straps only giving incrementally. Tears pinched her eyes and ran down her cheeks. The needle glittered above.

You'll go off to sleep.

"Jeremy!" she cried out. "I don't want to die." Her heartbeat gave witness—quick and clipped, it beat faster.

"I never meant to hurt you. I didn't." He wiped his face with his arm and bent over her.

"You have, Jeremy." She needed to keep him talking. Jeremy still existed. She needed to reach him. "Look at me."

"I can't." His body shook, and he sobbed.

"You will, damn it. Look at my face. If you're going to do this, then I want you to watch the light go out of my eyes. Remember it when you're lying to my boys." Her nose ran, and her face warmed like a fresh sunburn on her cheeks.

His eyes connected with hers, and for a brief moment she saw surrender, but then he looked away.

Her temples thumped. She would be dead soon. She couldn't stop him. There was no one to stop him. He'd dispose of her body, lie like nobody's business, and everyone would continue to believe Robert Connelly had killed Tom.

They'd search for her body, but they'd never find it. Jeremy had connections to crematories with incinerators. He'd find a way to turn her to ash, once he pulled himself from his self-indulgent tears.

All this time, Tom's killer had moved within a circle of those she trusted and loved. He wasn't an enemy, as she'd originally thought. She knew him—loved him. She'd never suspected he had the capacity to deceive or to murder without conscience. He said he had one. But the bastard had walked away from Tom, leaving him to struggle to remain of this earth.

Tom hadn't, and that made Jeremy a murderer.

Jeremy held her arm down.

She drew in a sharp breath.

His fingers were strong and pressed hard into her flesh. "Relax, Bren. I want you to go easy."

"Then you should have put a bullet in my head."

"I'm not laughing."

"I'm not joking."

He put the syringe between his teeth and took a piece of cotton from the tray. He swabbed her arm. Heart pounding, chest heaving, the simple prep brought death closer—colder.

It's fast.

She didn't want fast. She wanted to grow old with Rafe, see her boys grow up.

Jeremy frowned down at her. "I'm so sorry," he cried, his lips wet with tears.

Yet, if he truly felt remorse, loved her like he claimed, it didn't deter him. He raised the needle. The tip glinted sharp and deadly. He touched the slender metal needle against her forearm, and she gasped with the impending sting. "Ah, Bren. I never meant to torture you this way." He sighed. "It'll be over soon. I promise."

CHAPTER FORTY-TWO

INACTION TWISTED RAFE'S GUT. BENDIX HAD SENT A PATROL CAR TO meet them, but the only vehicle in the clinic parking lot was Bren's truck parked in front. Rafe cut his lights and parked at the far end of the parking lot. She was in there, and every second of indecision on his part could mean a bad return on his life investment—one five-foot-six Irish redhead he couldn't live without.

"The hell with it." Rafe opened the door and glanced back at Jo. "Tell them I went ahead."

"Wait." Jo grabbed his arm. Her eyes, distressed and a little uncertain, locked into his. "I don't know what he's capable of." She grabbed her gun from its holster. "Take it. From what Bren told me, you know how to use it."

Rafe hesitated. Jeremy was Jo's husband. She loved him. But a gun was a great equalizer. Whatever he was about to walk into, it could make the difference between walking away with his girl or not.

He took it and squeezed her shoulder. "I don't plan on letting it get that far."

Tears in her eyes, she nodded, and Rafe stepped from the truck, sprinting toward the clinic. He shoved the gun into the waistband of his jeans. He didn't want to have to use it, but it was insurance.

He tried the door first—locked—then he kicked it in with his boot. The wooden door thumped and splintered from the doorframe. He muscled it the rest of the way with his shoulder. "Bren!"

"Rafe!" she called to him, her voice strained and coming down the hall.

He headed that way. Light flooded the dark hallway, and he swung into the doorway and froze. *Son of a bitch.*

Jeremy stood over Bren. She was strapped to an examining table, the vet holding something above her.

Bren's eyes met Rafe's, hers were rough and tormented.

Every muscle in Rafe's body tensed. "God, Bren." He exhaled her name. His hands, usually steady and sure, trembled slightly, and his fingers tightened on the doorframe. "Let her up." His voice snapped like a whip. He pushed off the frame, his target Jeremy.

"Rafe, stop! God, stop!" she shrieked. "He's got a needle." Tears rolled down her pale cheeks.

Cold fear wound itself tight as a coil inside his brain.

Jeremy straightened. "I'll kill her if you come any closer, Rafe." With an unstable voice, eyes glassy with tears, he held up the needle.

Rafe slowed. Jo's gun pressed into his back, and he stopped. Mindful of the needle and the distance, he didn't go for the gun.

Shit! He caught the gentle thump, thump, thump of Jo's cane. He should have known she'd come behind him. It grew louder—the effect, more a culmination of an end. Rafe wondered whose end it would be.

"Jo's behind me. *Damn it*." He scowled at Jeremy. "She's been with me all night trying to save your ass. She knows. I know. Killing Bren isn't going to make this go away. The FBI's been working this case for months. They're on to you."

A siren wailed, red and blue lights bounced off the clinic walls, backing up his words, and Rafe relaxed a fraction.

Bren managed to touch Jeremy's leg with her fingers. "Don't let her see you like this."

Fear and uncertainty lined Jeremy's face. The usual smiling eyes Rafe associated with the vet looked desperate. Jeremy glanced down at Bren and then the door, but kept the needle aimed at Bren's arm.

"Jeremy." Bren snagged his pant leg and tugged.

His head jerked down toward her. He was breathing heavy. "I don't deserve her." Silent tears rolled down his cheeks.

The thumping stopped.

Bren drew in a sharp breath. "Jo."

"I'm okay, Bren." Jo leaned heavily on her cane in the doorway.

If hearts could break, Rafe's broke for Jo. Busted up with a bandage on her head, dark circles ringing her eyes, she took a step forward and concentrated on her husband.

"I love you."

"Jo, don't." Jeremy's voice faltered.

"You trust me?" She took another step and leaned on her cane for support.

"I've hurt you."

"You're hurting, too, baby. Just put the needle down."

Jeremy stepped back. "I don't want to go to prison, Jo."

Heavy footsteps came from the hall. Jeremy's eyes darted to the doorway. "It's okay, baby." She moved closer. "You don't want to hurt anyone."

He dropped onto the stool. His hand, holding the needle, fell to his lap. "I need help, Jo."

"I know, baby."

Jo stood in front of Bren, her body using the table for support. She touched Bren's shoulder and began to work the straps free, never taking her eyes from Jeremy. "Put the needle down on the counter."

He gnawed on his lower lip, idly spinning the seat back and forth.

The last of the straps lay loose about Bren's body. Bren gave Rafe a measured look. He shook his head a definite no. The fragility of Jeremy's mind warned that any sudden movements could counter Jo's negotiations, and Bren could pay with her life.

"Jesus." Kevin and several men wearing suits spilled into the room.

Jeremy's head shot up. His stricken expression made the hairs on Rafe's neck spike with warning.

Jeremy's armed jerked suddenly.

"No!" Jo screamed and reached across the table.

Rafe's eyes went right to Bren.

Bren glanced sideways at Jeremy, right as he jammed the needle into his arm and pushed the syringe. She hopped off the table and came around. "Damn it, Jeremy. What did you do?"

He slumped against Bren and slid off the stool, his weight taking her with him. Kevin and his men rushed forward, and Jo struggled to get around the table, collapsing next to them.

"What was in it?" Jo shook him. "Jeremy, answer me." Then she grabbed his arm. "*God*. He hit an artery."

Jeremy reached for her hand, his grip weakening as his body relaxed.

Rafe came up behind Bren and crouched down beside her. He stroked her back. Damn but he wanted to burn with vengeance. Jeremy had killed

Tom. He wanted to kill Bren. Jeremy was getting what he deserved—but it wasn't as neat as all that. And the irony was, he'd liked the guy.

Jeremy's breathing became shallow, and Bren concentrated on his eyes. Conscious, his blue eyes seemed to be taking in Bren and his wife, but then they stilled.

"He's dead," Bren cried softly, trembling. "He said it would be fast." She glanced back at Rafe, and her eyes flashed with understanding. "My God."

Rafe's blood slugged through his veins. He couldn't move—it could have been Bren.

Bren pushed up against Rafe frantically, trying to stand.

He pulled her out from under Jeremy's body and turned her into him. She glanced back to Jo weeping on the floor, holding Jeremy to her. Bren reached for Jo, her hand only brushing the air when Rafe scooped her up in his arms.

"Jo-o," was all she could manage, her chest battered by short, labored breaths.

"I got her," Kevin said, and he motioned for Rafe to go.

Bren buried her face into his chest and clung to him.

"It's over, darlin'," Rafe soothed and angled his body through the doorway when a hand shot out.

"We need her statement." The hand was connected to a man—dark suit, penetrating eyes, and a crew cut. FBI.

And Rafe didn't give a damn. "Get it tomorrow." Rafe's eyes flashed, and his chest constricted. "I'm taking her home."

Kevin stood up and moved toward them. "He's right. I'll make sure you get it in the morning."

The agent nodded and let go. Stepping back, he allowed Rafe to continue down the hall.

Rafe carried her out the door. The night air, crisp and alive, ran over his skin. It caught a dark, red wisp of Bren's hair and brushed his cheek.

He cleared the police tape the deputies had strung around the entrance. The squawk of police radios faded the farther he walked toward his truck. He opened the driver's side door and sat her down on the seat. Crouching in front of her, his arms slid to her waist. "Is that you shaking or me?" His fingers slipped under her sweater and pressed lightly into her warm skin.

"It's you." Her eyes were moist under the interior light, but her tears had stopped. She smoothed her hands along his shoulders and down the length of his arms. "You're trembling."

"Hell, I'm not surprised." His hand came up and tilted her head back, probing her face. "He hurt you?"

She bit down on her lip. "He would have, if you didn't come for me."

"Was there any doubt that I would, darlin'?" He searched her eyes. Familiar and lovely, and staring back at him, they were the only pair he wanted to wake up to—and to think he'd almost lost that chance, again.

He cupped her chin and ran his thumb over her quivering lips. "Is there anything else I should know, Red? Any more adventures you want to take me on? Because my heart is just about wore out."

Her lips quirked.

Color began to creep into her cheeks. "Not up for the challenge, cowboy?"

"Nope. The way I see it, that makes it impossible for me to leave you to your own devices." He wasn't waiting another minute. It wasn't how he'd pictured it—lights and sirens, loss and heartache, and yellow crime scene tape—the two of them smarting with grief.

But that damn black velvet box kept nudging his side. It remained in the pocket of his jacket. She'd probably knock him in the head for being insensitive. He'd had it all planned out—flowers, the works. She was his girl, and he wanted it to be special. But he couldn't take another minute without some assurances she'd be his.

He'd never been so nervous in his life. He was back to shaking with it—nerves.

"I'm not one for convention, Bren. I love you with all I have in me." He dropped to one knee and edged her forward. "I told you when I met you, family wasn't something I was looking for. That couldn't be further from the truth now. That's all I've been thinking about tonight. Not knowing where you were, what he was doing to you."

"Rafe." She glanced around. "Baby, get up off the ground."

"Bren, honey, let me do this proper. We had this thing all planned out."

"We?" She gave him a curious look.

"The old man—"

She arched a well-shaped brow.

"Sorry." He grimaced. "I mean my father and the boys."

"Aiden and Finn?"

"Since your father's not here, it seemed fitting I should ask their permission."

"For?"

"I'm getting to that." He took a breath and steadied himself. "The hell of it is, Bren, I want that family. I want you. I'll help you raise Aiden and Finn. I know I could never replace their daddy. I don't expect you to move to Texas. There's no reason we can't have two homes." He took a breath. Damn, but he was rambling. "Now I'm getting ahead of myself."

Her lips trembled, and her eyes filled with tears.

Shit.

"Hey, don't cry on me, Red." A tear got away, and he brushed it with his thumb.

What the hell was I thinking?

"You've been through hell. This can wait." He made a move to stand up.

She caught his arm. "I want to hear what you have to say."

He took her hands in his and experimented with the weight and size. It was right. He lifted his face to hers. It was the face in his dreams—soft angles, pink, pliable lips that fit perfectly with his, eyes that corralled his heart.

Ah, but he was suffering—trembling, too. He'd never proposed—never found a woman he'd willingly give his heart to. He dug into his coat pocket and pulled out the box.

Her lashes lowered, and her fingers, still wrapped in his one hand, tightened. Her gaze shifted up again. Those brown eyes were aware, and a little guarded.

Rafe popped the box open with his thumb and loosened one hand from her grip. Taking the ring from the box, he held it between work-roughened fingers. The diamond, catching the interior light, sparkled with promises of the future—a future with Bren.

He picked up her hand, his finger running nervously over her knuckles. Intent on her face, he took a deep breath. "I know you're a package deal, Bren. And I wouldn't have it any other way. If you'll have me, I want you to be my wife. Will you marry me, darlin'?"

Her eyes watered, but a faint smile crossed her lips. Sniffing again, she stroked his face. "I thought you said you weren't good with words."

Rafe's cheeks warmed. "Don't make fun. I'm sweatin' like a plow horse here. Is that a yes?" He waited, his stomach tightening like a clenched fist.

"Yes." Her voice was soft, quiet. "You're my best friend." She smiled up at him. "I love you."

He slipped the ring on her finger and pulled her from the truck, giving her a quick, hard kiss. "What am I going to do with you, Red?"

Their eyes connected and held.

"Never leave me."

He slipped his arms around her waist. She was warm and soft, and he held her to him. Her heart pounded. Or maybe it was his heart. He'd found what he'd been looking for—the love of a good woman . . . a family.

"No way in hell, darlin'." He kissed her hair, forehead, and then her mouth, his lips moving against hers. "But I'm not one for long engagements."

Hell, his timing couldn't have been worse. He didn't need a fancy wedding. He only needed her. As far as he was concerned, the only thing standing in his way was a piece of paper. He'd work on the technicalities. But for now, he'd concentrate on the moment, and he kissed her long and deep.

EPILOGUE

B REN STEPPED FROM THE MASTER BATHROOM.

Rafe stood in the doorway to their bedroom. Wearing a pair of blue-plaid pajama bottoms and a white T-shirt, he grinned at her. "Sexy." He crossed the hardwood and pulled her to him. "No horses?" He brushed her bare shoulder with his knuckles before slipping an inquisitive finger under the thin strap of her silk nightgown.

"It's our wedding night."

She'd let Rafe have his way—quick, quiet wedding with no fuss, out in the back garden. With God and, she hoped, Tom's blessing, Father Noonan from St. Michael's performed the ceremony, with their fathers—that would be Paddy on Rafe's side—the boys, and Jo.

Jo . . . She loved her, wept with her, and would always be there for her like she had during Bren's darkest moments.

As far as Jeremy was concerned, she'd remember the heart of the man— not his weakness or wicked actions that had altered her life forever.

"I like it." Rafe's hand reached under the hem to caress her thigh.

Bren connected with her husband and smiled into his rugged, loving face. "I'm glad you approve." Her hands rode over his muscled chest and broad shoulders. She lifted her chin to accommodate his height. "Where were you earlier?"

"Tucking the boys in." He scooped her up in his arms.

"Oh." Her arms slid around his neck for support while his arms flexed with strength, holding her to him with little effort.

"Now I intend to tuck their mother in." His eyes glittered with mischief, and he strolled to their bed that she had turned down, placing her in the center. He kissed her quick and hard and turned away.

"Where are you going?"

He opened the top drawer to the tall dresser and pulled out a file. "I haven't given you your wedding present yet, Mrs. Langston."

She frowned. "But I haven't gotten you anything."

"I think you have. The sign company called today." He laughed. It was deep and genuine, and it warmed her heart.

"You weren't supposed to know about that. I wanted to surprise you."

He snuggled down next to her and drew her close to him. He kissed her nose. "And you did, darlin'. But there's no other gift I'd want, except you and the boys. But I will need to eke out a living. I guess you figured me out."

She smiled at that. He'd given her cause to question his motives that night in the barn. "I never did take you for a dairy farmer."

"And you'd be right." He twined his fingers through her hand. "But I like the sound of it. It's enterprising, don't you think? 'Grace Equine Sanctuary and Cattle Ranch.'" He said it as if deciding how it fit together.

"It's perfect."

He handed the folder to her.

She gave him a curious lift of her brow.

"Open it."

She sat up, his arm coming around her. She sifted through the papers. It was the deed to Grace—all of it. She looked up. "I don't understand."

"It's yours, sweetheart. I paid it off and put it back in yours and your father's name." He settled against the pillows and brought her hand up and kissed her palm. "It was never my intention to take it from you."

She cupped that stubborn chin of his, tantalizingly smooth. He'd surprised her by shaving for the ceremony. Handsome with or without whiskers, she loved him. "Why would you help me in the first place? You didn't even know me."

"I think when I hopped the rail at the sale barn, I knew you were going to steal my heart."

Her throat went dry, and tears pinched her eyes.

His head dipped. "Bren, honey, you're not crying?"

"I'm not." She sniffed. "You're a good man, Rafe Langston."

"And, *you*, Mrs. Langston need to stop talking."

He kissed her, his lips slow and deliberate, and she moaned with pleasure. Her hands let go of the folder, and she slipped them around his neck, her fingers inching toward the crisp, dark locks curling at the nape of his neck.

Tom would always hold his place in her heart. He was her first love, the father of her children. But she was Rafe's now. Perhaps she had always been.

Bren Langston.

She liked the sound of it, although, she'd been tempted to ask Rafe to change *his* name. He was a Ryan, after all. But Langston suited him. It was a Texas name, and he was a Texan. The child born to a farmer in a small town back east, but raised out west by a rancher, had become and remained every bit the cowboy.

She loved him completely, and it was almost more than she could bear. But she promised herself one thing.

I will grow old with this one.

Keep reading for an excerpt from P. J. O'Dwyer's next novel

DEFIANT

The second book in the

FALLON SISTERS TRILOGY

Available from Black Siren Books in September 2012

DEFIANT

CHAPTER ONE

THREE YEARS LATER . . .

Kate Reynolds kept her foot on the accelerator. A cold, uneasy feeling settled in. The heated seats of her BMW offered little in the way of warmth to alleviate the chill riding along her spine. Glancing down into the darkened interior of her car, she frowned at the green glow of the clock. Too early to call her sister Bren. She'd only worry, and fumbling for her cell phone would only slow her down. If she cleared this side of the Chesapeake Bay Bridge, he'd be less likely to catch up to her. She'd fill Bren in once she made it to the family farm.

The island of Tilghman a memory, she concentrated on the double-yellow center line and putting miles behind her. The side street came up fast. She swiveled her head to check for oncoming traffic and caught her reflection in the rearview mirror. She groaned and grudgingly transferred her eyes back to the road. Unable to ignore the sensation, she ran her tongue along her swollen bottom lip; the bitter taste of blood filled her mouth.

Damn him.

The light changed from yellow to red when she approached the intersection of Routes 33 and 322. The brief stop allowed her another look at her face. She raised a finger toward the haze of purple, and then pressed the pad of her finger against her lid. The skin, plump like a marshmallow, made her grit her teeth. She grabbed for the steering wheel and held it tight. Eyes forward, she let off the brake, easing back up to forty.

Her muscles bunched. The unexpected bright lights filled her rearview mirror, and she sucked air through her teeth. Kate reached to adjust her mirror and flew forward with the sudden impact. Her seat belt pressed against her chest and hips like a vise.

Shit! He found me!

She punched the accelerator and kept up the pressure. But the lights in her rearview mirror never wavered. The force of the second collision sent her vehicle into a spin. The car slid off the road and struck the guardrail.

Everything stopped.

Kate's forehead rested against the cushion of the airbag. The powder that had exploded upon impact filled the air, making everything seem muzzy, her head a boulder too heavy to move. A stab of pain radiated down her back when she tried to turn her neck. She reached for the door handle, but before she could grasp it, a rush of cold air hit her body. Strong fingers dug into her shoulders. She moaned, and her eyes fluttered open. The interior light, a halo of brightness, illuminated steel-blue eyes, glassed over and bloodshot, spearing into her.

"Where the fuck were you going, Kate?"

A blast of bourbon singed her face, and she recoiled into the opening of her sweatshirt—not good. Making her mind up tonight had weighed heavily. She and Jack had a love-hate relationship. But tonight, she hated him, and the decision was easy.

Jack dragged her from the driver's seat, slammed the door, and sprawled her across the side of the car. Her breath caught, and her heart dove straight for her stomach.

"Look at me." He grabbed her face. "You're the most ungrateful bitch. I've given you everything."

The pressure of his fingers bit into her flesh, and she shook. The darkness frightened her, but his expression frightened her more. Kate pulled wildly at his hands. She brought her knee up in between his legs. He groaned. The pain along her jaw line disappeared. The quick release had her staggering, desperate to find her equilibrium. Her eyes shifted. Her trembling fingers reached for the car, only to find he'd locked it. Cursing under her breath, she ran up the embankment into the woods.

Darkness enveloped her. She dodged tree stumps and vines, but kept moving. Branches slapped her face, and her lungs burned as she gulped for air. She stopped to catch her breath, placed her hands on her knees, and hung there a moment. Her eyes scanned the area—nothing.

But her heart quickened. In the distance, leaves and underbrush crunched and snapped, so she ran even harder, her tennis shoes sinking into the soft earth until she came upon a ravine. She slid down a small slope, the ride like a pothole-laden street; her butt took most of the shock. A thin sapling whipped across her cheek. She placed her hands out front to shield her face and pushed away spindly, outstretched limbs until she hit bottom. She spied a tangle of underbrush several yards away and started toward it. Kate shoved her body deep into the entanglement of vines, ignoring their sharp points as she nestled down among the decaying leaves. Her breath mingled with the autumn air, causing bursts of white steam. Afraid he'd see it, she cupped her mouth with her hands and breathed into her palms, the warmth damp against her skin.

The single beam of light shimmered in the distance. It moved closer and then veered off in a different direction.

"Kate, I know you're here," he called out.

She squatted lower to the ground and pressed her head to her knees.

"I'm not leaving until I find you."

His voice grew closer; the white haze from his flashlight became brighter. She had to move. But her hands stung. Pushing through vines and thorns had her weighing her options. They weren't good. She yanked her sweatshirt sleeves over her hands, placed her arm in front of her face, and propelled forward.

She ran from the light, refusing to glance backward, hoping she could outrun him. Those thoughts slipped away when the woodland floor crunched behind her. A blinding force collided with her back, sending her sprawling onto the unforgiving earth. Her eyes popped wide, her mouth agape with her desperate attempt to take a breath—no air. She struggled for oxygen while clawing, trying to wriggle free, but his strong hands rolled her on her back. He straddled her torso, clenched her arms above her head, and pinned them to the ground. The flashlight he kept raised, the bright glare glancing off her face.

He leaned into her, his chest expanded with every breath. For a moment, he only stared at her, his dark brows furrowed together. "Don't look at me with those damn brown eyes."

His hand flinched, and she jerked her head to the side, the sudden movement a reminder of earlier. "Relax. I'm not going to hurt you." Gentle outstretched fingers examined her eyelid, and he winced. "I'm sorry. I never meant to hit you. It won't happen again. I promise. But you make me so damn angry sometimes."

Same old Jack—blameless.

Rotting branches and twigs pressed into her back. She struggled against his weight and began to hyperventilate. He readjusted his weight, and his expression softened. He moved his hand toward her cheek and gently caressed her skin. "Kate," he whispered. "Stop fighting me. You're going to make this worse."

"Let go of me." She tried to rise up against him, but her body only made an upper thrust before coming back to rest on the hard ground.

"Not on your life, sweetheart."

"You tried to kill me."

"I tapped your car."

"You sent me into a ravine."

"You lost control."

His steel-blue eyes hardened—her cue to tone it down. Or he'd make her regret her show of bravado.

"You hit me, Jack." Her voice cracked. The tears burned the backs of her eyes. She had loved him once—forgave him when he hurt her feelings with his cutting words. But forgiveness she was all out of, even if this was the first time he'd actually struck her.

But he'd caught her, and the only thing left was to play by his rules—for now. Because her husband, the U.S. District Attorney of Maryland, would be revealed for the abusive bastard he was in time. What she needed was a plan. She might not escape him tonight, but patience and placating Jack she'd mastered long ago.

"Because you pushed me to the limit tonight, to the point I thought I'd explode." He took a deep breath and continued, "When I said I didn't want to talk about it, I meant it."

"So to shut me up you took a swing at me. Twice."

"You left me no choice."

She refused to answer. Like this was somehow her fault.

He eyed her suspiciously. "Why were you rifling through my desk?"

Snooping. But she wouldn't admit to it. "I thought I left one of my case files in your office." His weight unbearable, she shifted. "You need to get up."

He slid down onto her thighs. "The drawer was locked."

"Okay, it was locked. I'm sorry." She needed to change the subject—namely, her. "Have you always known?"

"If I did, how would that change anything?" he snapped and lowered his head so she could see him better, his eyes pinning her. "It doesn't concern you." He relaxed his hold on her wrists.

Not directly, but anything he'd go to such lengths to hide from her had to be something she could use against him. Too bad for her she'd only had time to glance at the document, and what she could gather in that split second wouldn't raise suspicion or tarnish a reputation . . . unless there was more to it.

"No . . . but I know how much the Reynolds name means to you. How long have you known you're—"

The corners of his mouth tipped into a smile, and he chuckled. "I see." He tilted her chin up slightly. "Kate, how much did you read before I walked in?"

"The header . . . your father's name." She took a huge breath through her nose. "You have to get up. You're squishing me. I'm going to freak out."

He hoisted her up to a sitting position and leaned her back against the wide trunk of a nearby poplar. He squatted next to her, studying her briefly. "Where were you going, hmm?"

The truth would only earn her his anger. He knew, and he was baiting her. "Away . . . away from you." Kate's hands sat restless in her lap, her fingers picking at her nails. She hated when she did that. He could read her every movement. She stopped, quelled her hands, and placed them on the ground on either side of her. "You get angry. You yell, throw things. I deal with it because I know the stress you're under."

The corners of his mouth lessened.

Pity was good—surprisingly easy to accomplish. But she'd take it and go for a few bonus points because she wanted him to know what he had done to her. How he had taken something so precious. Something she feared she'd never regain. "I'm a grown woman." She laughed, the sound mocking. "I sit next to and defend criminals every day. But I fear you more." She reached out tentatively and touched a lock of his dark hair that fell across his forehead, hoping to connect with him. "I want to love you—I do love you—I'm your wife." Her hand slid down against his face, his chest, and then the ground, resigned to rest against the cool, damp leaves.

How had she allowed a man to control her? To her credit, outwardly she appeared functional. Her colleagues would never guess that the Kate Reynolds they knew and respected was a complete and utter mess who could not rid herself of one psychopathic husband. But why would they? No one else knew *this* Jack.

He looked deep into her eyes. "Yes, you are."

A knot formed in her throat, and she was unable to read him. He raised his hand to her face, and she remained stoic, refusing to flinch a second time. He touched her temple, his fingers gentle, and then slid his hand down her cheek, the palm of his hand resting against her beating pulse. Gliding fingers tightened slightly around the back of her neck, and his thumb pressed into the hollow of her throat. "No one leaves me, Kate." He paused. "Unless I say so."

He said nothing for the longest time, but his thumb remained. She swallowed hard, her throat bobbing against his thumb.

"Do you understand?" he asked.

Completely. The only way to escape Jack was to bring him down. And abuse was a good start. Only if she went to the police, put a restraining order out on him, he'd find a way to make her regret adding a blemish to his fine reputation. Based on his reaction tonight after finding that she'd jimmied the lock on his desk, he *was* hiding something, and she would find it. Before long, he wouldn't be so hung up on divorce. He'd be too busy salvaging more than just his marriage.

She nodded. He leaned in, his broad shoulders casting her in shadow against splinters of moonlight. He kissed her forehead, and she shivered.

A Message from the Author

Relentless, the first book in the Fallon Sisters Trilogy, tackles the controversial and often heated debate about horse slaughter. Writing a story that is relevant to our time is a precious opportunity.

This story, Bren's story, although fiction, represents the struggles that horse rescues and animal activists face each day in advocating for the protection and humane treatment of horses and other equines that suffer from ignorance, neglect, and—most dreaded of all—kill buyers and the horse slaughter industry.

It has become more than a story line for me. Having a love and respect for animals, I felt compelled to assist this noble cause.

In an effort to support horse rescue organizations and their mission of rescue, rehabilitation, and education, I am donating a portion of all Fallon Sister Trilogy book sales and all future literary works, purchased through www.pjodwyer.com or the publishing house of Black Siren Books www.blacksirenbooks.com, to horse rescue.

As a consumer, you may choose the horse rescue where you want your donation to go. A list of participating horse rescue affiliates can be found in the Horse Rescue Affiliate Directory on the following pages or either website where *Relentless* is sold.

The ability to assist with the protection and humane treatment of these graceful creatures is only available through the author and publishing house websites.

If you are a horse rescue organization interested in becoming an affiliate with P. J. O'Dwyer and Black Siren Books, you can visit our websites to complete an online affiliate application.

By working together to bring awareness to the plight of all equines, I truly believe we can make a difference, and, hopefully, end overbreeding, abuse, and neglect, and the most horrific means of dealing with these overwhelming problems—horse slaughter.

~ P. J. O'Dwyer

HORSE RESCUES AND ADVOCATE DIRECTORY

UNITED STATES HORSE RESCUES

ALABAMA

Dusty Trails Horse Rescue
P.O. Box 250191
Montgomery, AL 36125-0191
info@dthr.org
www.dustytrailshorserescue.org

ALASKA

Alaska Equine Rescue
P.O. Box 771174
Eagle River, AK 99577
aer@alaskaequinerescue.com
www.alaskaequinerescue.com

ARIZONA

Dreamchaser Horse Rescue and
Rehabilitation
48019 North 7th Avenue
New River, AZ 85087
susan@dreamchaserhorserescue.org
www.dreamchaserpmu.org

Reigning Grace Ranch
30514 North 162nd Street
Scottsdale, AZ 85262
joey@azrgr.org
www.reigninggraceranch.org

ARKANSAS

Proud Spirit Horse Sanctuary
1210 Polk 48
Mena, AR 71953
proudspirit@juno.com
www.horseofproudspirit.com

CALIFORNIA

Lifetime Equine Refuge
WFLF Garden of Equine Sanctuary
Riverside, CA
www.LifetimeEquineRefuge.org
info@lifetimeequinerefuge.org

Saving America's Horses
WFLF Humanion Films
Studio City, CA
www.SavingAmericasHorses.org
info@savingamericashorses.org

Wild for Life Foundation
One Vision Equis
Studio City, CA
www.WildforLifeFoundation.org
info@wildforlifefoundation.org

After the Finish Line
10153 Riverside Drive
Suite 397
Toluca Lake, CA 91602
dawn@afterthefinishline.org
www.afterthefinishline.org

Safe Haven Horse Rescue and
Sanctuary
3950 W. Anderson Drive
Cottonwood, CA 96022
safehavenhorse@gmail.com
www.safehavenhorserescue.org

Return to Freedom
P.O. Box 926
Lompoc, CA 93438
www.returntofreedom.org

Honest Horses Magazine
Ms. Cheryl Caldwell
172 Horse Run Lane
Chico, CA 95928
Cheryl@honesthorsesmagazine.com
www.honesthorsesmagazine.com

COLORADO

Colorado Horse Rescue
10386 N 65th Street
Longmont, CO 80503
info@chr.org
www.chr.org

CONNECTICUT

Horse of Connecticut
43 Wilbur Road
Washington, CT 06777
horsectinfo@gmail.com
www.horseofct.org

DELAWARE

Changing Fates Equine Rescue
29573 West Elliotts Dam Road
Laurel, DE 19956
cferdelaware@aol.com
www.changingfates.rescuegroups.org

GEORGIA

Dancing Cloud Farm Horse Rescue
P.O. Box 6
Ochlocknee, GA 31773
dancingcloudfarm@gmail.com
www.dcfhr.com

HAWAII

Equine 808 Horse Rescue
Ranch Location
Kunia Loa Ridge Farm Lands Lot 21
Kunia, HI
Mailing address:
P.O. Box 2817
Ewa Beach, HI 96706
director@equine808.com
www.equine808.com

IDAHO

Panhandle Horse Rescue
P.O. Box 2832
Hayden Lake, Idaho 83835
1panhandlerescue@gmail.com
www.northidahohorserescue.com

ILLINOIS

Crosswinds Equine Rescue, Inc.
8182 E. 200 North Road
Sidell, IL 61876
info@cwer.org
www.cwer.org

INDIANA

Friends of Ferdinand
P.O. Box 1784
Indianapolis, IN 46206
contact@friendsofferdinand.org
www.friendsofferdinand.com

344

IOWA

Hooves and Paws Rescue
27821 US Hwy 34
Glenwood, Iowa 51534
legs1212@aol.com
www.hoovespaws.org

KANSAS

Rainbow Meadows Equine Rescue
and Retirement
1949 Dalton Road
Sedan, KS 67361
Karen.everhart@
rainbowmeadowsranch.com
www.rainbowmeadowsranch.com

KENTUCKY

Old Friends
1841 Paynes Depot Road
Georgetown, KY 40324
www.oldfriendsequine.org

LOUISIANA

Louisiana Horse Rescue Association
P.O. Box 24650
New Orleans, LA 70184
admin@lahorserescue.com
www.lahorserescue.com

MAINE

Ever After Mustang Rescue
463 West Street
Biddeford, ME 04005
mustangs1@maine.rr.com
www.mustangrescue.org

MARYLAND

Alex Brown Racing
Fair Hill Training Center
719 Training Center Drive
Elkton, MD 21921
alexbr.brown@gmail.com
www.alexbrownracing.com

Days End Farm Horse Rescue
1372 Woodbine Road
Woodbine, MD 21797
info@defhr.org
www.defhr.org

Gentle Giants Draft Horse Rescue
925 Lady Anne Court
Mount Airy, MD 21771
gentlegiantsdhr@aol.com
www.gentlegiantsdrafthorserescue.com

Tranquility Farm Equestrian
Education and Renewal Center, Inc.
16371 Glen Ella Road
Culpeper, Virginia 22701
tqfarm@aol.com
www.tranquilityfarmequestrian.com

Horse Lovers United, Inc.
P.O. Box 2744
Salisbury, MD 21802
boxwood3684@comcast.net
www.horseloversunited.com

Chesapeake Sporthorse
10716 Todd's Corner Road
Easton, MD 21601
speedjumpr@aol.com
www.chesapeakesporthorse.com

Windy Rock Equine Rescue
12324 St. Paul Road
Clear Spring, MD 21722
windy-rock@hotmail.com
www.windyrock.org

MICHIGAN

Horses Haven
P.O. Box 166
Howell, MI 48844
horseshavenmi@gmail.com
www.horseshaven.org

MINNESOTA

RIDE-Minnesota
4505 Viola Road NE
Rochester, MN 55906
info@ridemn.org
www.ridemn.org

MISSISSIPPI

Dark Horse Rescue
P.O. Box 781
Hernando, MS 38632
info@darkhorserescue.org
www.darkhorserescue.org

MISSOURI

The Shannon Foundation
744 Cross Creek Valley Lane
St Clair, MO 63077-3462
Rhonda@theshannonfoundation.org
www.theshannonfoundation.org

MONTANA

Western Montana Equine Rescue and
Rehabilitation
P.O. Box 1168
Corvallis, MT 59828
info@westernmontanaequinerescue.org
www.westernmontanaequinerescue.org

United In Light
Home to the Draft Horse Sanctuary
101 Billman Lane
Livingston, MT 59047
unitedinlight@mac.com
www.draftrescue.com

NEVADA

Miracle Horse Rescue and Sanctuary
2091 W. Quail Run Road
Pahrump, NV 89060
Miraclehorserescue01@gmail.com
www.miraclehorse.com

NEW JERSEY

Helping Hearts Equine Rescue
P.O. Box 342
Perrineville, NJ 08535
hheartsequine@optonline.net
www.hher.webs.com

NEW MEXICO

Four Corners Equine Rescue
22 CR 3334
Aztec, NM 87410
contact@fourcornersequinerescue.org
www.fourcornersequinerescue.org

NEW YORK

Akindale Thoroughbred Rescue
323 Quaker Hill Road
Pawling, NY 12654
akindalefarm@comcast.net
www.akindalehorserescue.org

Equine Rescue League of
Cooperstown
3018 County Highway 35
Schenevus, NY 12155
equinerescueleague@hotmail.com
www.equinerescueleague.weebly.com

NORTH DAKOTA

Triple H Miniature Horse Rescue
P.O. Box 4125
Bismarck, ND 58501
hhhmhr@mac.com
www.hhhmhr.org

OHIO

W.H.I.N.N.Y. Horse Rescue
(W.H.I.N.N.Y. is an acronym for
"why horses in need, need you")
14076 Township Road 203 N.E.
Crooksville, OH 43731
mary@whinnyhorserescue.org
www.whinnyhorserescue.org

OKLAHOMA

Horse Feathers Equine Rescue
P.O. Box 1372
Guthrie, OK 73044
plainswindrdr@gmail.com
www.horsefeathersequinerescue.org

OREGON

Equine Outreach Inc.
63220 Silvis Road
Bend, OR 97701
joan@equineoutreach.com
www.equineoutreach.com

PENNSYLVANIA

Angel Acres Horse Haven Rescue, Inc.
P.O. Box 62
Glenville, PA 17329
angelacreshorsehaven@yahoo.com
www.angelacres.net

R.A.C.E. Fund, Inc.
Retirement Assistance and Care for
Equines
8031 Rabbit Lane
Harrisburg, PA 17112
info@racefund.org
www.racefund.org

SOUTH CAROLINA

South Carolina Awareness and Rescue
for Equines
312 Shetland Lane
Lexington, SC 29078
elizabethwood1@cs.com
www.scequinerescue.org

SOUTH DAKOTA

Black Hills Wild Horse Sanctuary
Program Development
Institute of Range and
American Mustang
Box 998
Hot Springs, SD 57747
iram@gwtc.net
www.wildmustangs.com

TENNESSEE

Mustang Alley Horse Rescue and
Riding Stable
1020 Walters Road
Greeneville, TN 37743
mahr@mustangalley.org
www.mustangalley.org

UTAH

Madaresgold Horse Rescue
13496 S. 7300 W.
Herriman, UT 84096
madaresgold@yahoo.com
www.mghr.com

VERMONT

Spring Hill Horse Rescue
175 Middle Road
North Clarendon, VT 05759
springhillrescue@aol.com
www.springhillrescue.com

VIRGINIA

Central Virginia Horse Rescue
389 Boydton Plank Road
Brodnax, VA 23920
rescue@centralvahorserescue.com
www.centralvahorserescue.com

WASHINGTON

Hope for Horses
P.O. Box 1790
Woodinville, WA 98072
info@hopeforhorses.net
www.hopeforhorses.net

People Helping Horses
24717 43rd Avenue, NE
Arlington, WA 98223
info@peoplehelpinghorses.org
www.peoplehelpinghorses.org

Seattle Times
NW Horse Forum
Seattle, WA
www.seattletimes.com

WASHINGTON D.C.

American Horse Defense Fund
P.O. Box 96503 #66433
Washington, DC 20090-6503
president@ahdf.org
www.ahdf.org

WEST VIRGINIA

Horse Haven Hollow
988 May Ridge Road
Ellenboro, WV 26346
adopt@horsehavenhollow.org
www.horsehavenhollow.org

WISCONSIN

Midwest Horse Welfare Foundation,
Inc.
10990 State Highway 73
Pittsville, WI 54466
scott@equineadoption.com
www.equineadoption.com

WYOMING

Reaching Hands Rescue
P.O. Box 656
645 RD9
Powell, WY 82435
info@reachinghandsranch.org
www.reachinghandsranch.org

CANADA HORSE RESCUES

ALBERTA

Dare to Dream Horse Rescue
Box 335
Dalemead, Alberta
CANADA T0J 0V0
Brenda@dare2dreamhorserescue.ca
www.dare2dreamhorserescue.ca

BRITISH COLUMBIA

The Voice of the Horse Foundation
P.O. Box 12072
Langley, British Columbia
CANADA V3A 9J5
www.voiceforthehorse.com

New Stride Thoroughbred Adoption
Society
17687 56A Avenue
Surrey, British Columbia
CANADA V3S 1G4
memery@newstride.com
www.newstride.com

Dreams Aloud Promotions and
Co-founder
Sunshine CoastSchool of Writing
Ms. Carol Upton
Gibsons, British Columbia
CANADA
Carolup@telus.net
www.dreamsaloud.ca

MANITOBA

Papas Ranch Horse Rescue
Box 291
Selkirk, Manitoba
CANADA R1A 2B2
info@papasranch.ca
www.papasranch.ca

NEW BRUNSWICK

Earth Spirit Horse Rescue
1 Spruce Street
Rothesay, New Brunswick
CANADA E2E 2H3
Marilyn@earthspirithorserescue.com
www.earthspirithorserescue.com

NOVA SCOTIA

Earth Arc
644 Heron Road
RR#3 Scotsburn
Pictou County, Nova Scotia
CANADA B0K 1R0
raveneartharc@gmail.com
www.piczo.com/eartharc

Maritime Horse Protection Society
1283 Northfield Road
RR#1 Blockhouse, Nova Scotia
CANADA B0J 1E0
maritimehorseprotection@gmail.com
www.maritimehorseprotection.ca

ONTARIO

Canadian Horse Defence Coalition
150 First Street
P.O. Box 21079
Orangeville, Ontario
CANADA L9W 4S7
info@defendhorsescanada.org
www.defendhorsescanada.org

Refuge RR
21305 Concession 10 RR 2
Alexandria, Ontario
CANADA K0C 1A0
refugerr@xplornet.ca
www.refugerr.org

PRINCE EDWARD ISLAND

Sadie's Place Equine Rescue
18457 Rte 2
Brookfield, Prince Edward Isalnd
CANADA C0A 1Y0
sadie@sadiesplace.ca
www.sadiesplace.ca

SASKATCHEWAN

Paradise Stable Horse Rescue
RR4 GB603
Saskatoon, Saskatchewan
CANADA S7K 3J7
blharasym@sasktel.net
www.paradisestablehorserescue.weebly.
com

AUSTRALIA HORSE RESCUES

MELBOURNE

Project Hope Horse Welfare Victoria,
Inc.
GPO Box 1991
Melbourne 3001
Australia
info@phhwv.org.au
www.phhwv.org.au

NEW SOUTH WALES

Quest Equine Welfare, Inc.
P.O. Box 604
Lithgow, NSW 2790
Australia
enquiries@questequinewelfare.org
www.questequinewelfare.org

QUEENSLAND

Save a Horse Australia Horse Rescue
and Sanctuary
Ms. Amanda Vella
P.O. Box 451
Henensvale, QLD 4212
Australia
saveahorseaustralia@yahoo.com.au
www.saveahorseaustralia.blogspot.com

NEW ZEALAND HORSE RESCUES

Last Chance Equine
288 State Hwy 30
Tikitere
Rotorua 3074
New Zealand
lastchance.equine@yahoo.co.nz
www.lastchanceequine.webs.com

Horsetalk Ltd
Equestrian News and Information
North Canterbury
New Zealand
info@horsetalk.co.nz
www.horsetalk.co.nz

UNITED KINGDOM

Redwings Horse Sanctuary
the Largest Horse Sanctuary in the
UK
info@redwings.co.uk
www.redwings.org.uk

Follyfoot Horse and Pony Sanctuary
23 Saffron Close
Meir Park
Stoke-on-Trent
Staffordshire
ST3 7FB
jaynebowles@hotmail.com
www.follyfoothorseandponysanctuary.
weebly.com

Shy Lowen Horse and Pony Sanctuary
Buckley Hill Lane
Sefton
Merseyside
L29 1YB
Shylowen@aol.com
www.shylowen.com

IRELAND

Sathya Sai Sanctuary Trust for Nature
Castlebaldwin
County Sligo
Ireland
sai.donkeys@gmail.com
www.donkeys.ie

HELP GAIN AWARENESS
FOR THE PLIGHT OF OUR
WILD AND DOMESTIC HORSES

SUPPORT THE FILM

SAVING AMERICA'S HORSES:
A NATION BETRAYED

SAVING AMERICA'S HORSES

Filmmaker Katia Louise masterfully presents a passionate reverence for all animals in her international award winning film, SAVING AMERICA'S HORSES—A NATION BETRAYED. This landmark feature documentary film explores the human-animal bond of horse and man through an illuminating humanitarian lens. It's an intelligent and inspiring exposé about today's horses and the need to protect and preserve them. Viewers venture across the nation's sweeping landscapes to witness the magnificence, power and free spirit of one of America's most treasured icons, the horse. Audiences rediscover the relationship we share with these animals through following the life of a champion racehorse. With an up close look at the America's wild horses, we get a glimpse of the controversial world of wild equines in captivity and the government elimination process that threatens their very survival in the wild. SAVING AMERICA'S HORSES also explores the routine practice of sending equines treated with banned lethal substances to slaughter for human consumption. This compelling and passion driven film concludes with an awe inspiring presentation of empowering alternatives and solutions for change.

Celebrity appearances include Paul Sorvino, Michael Blake, Tippi Hedren, Linda Gray, Willie Nelson, Chief Arvol Looking Horse, the Barbi Twins, Ken Wahl and more! Geared for the conscience consumer and suitable for all audiences; SAVING AMERICA'S HORSES—A NATION BETRAYED is a feature length educational documentary film project under Wild for Life Foundation, a 501 (c)(3) nonprofit.

SavingAmericasHorses.org

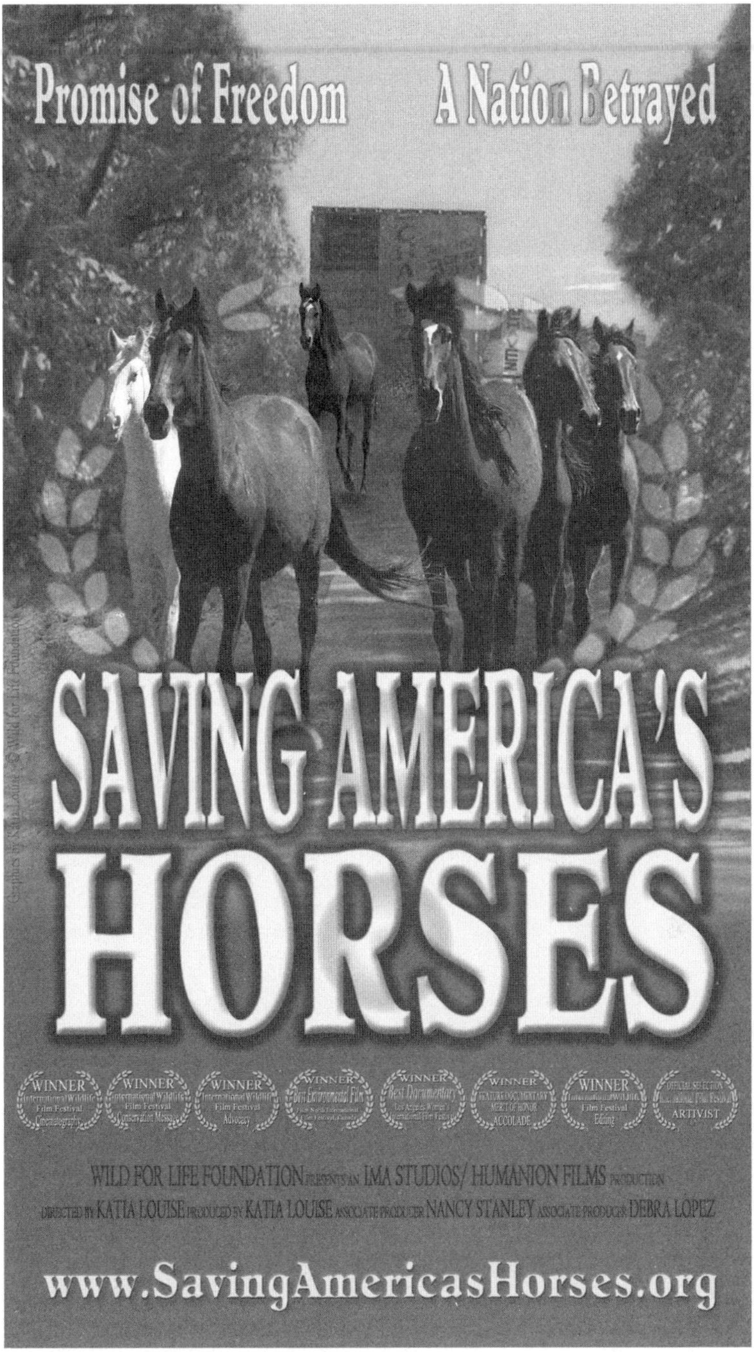
Promise of Freedom
A Nation Betrayed
Graphics by Katia Louise © Wild for Life Foundation
SAVING AMERICA'S
HORSES
WINNER International Wildlife Film Festival Cinematography
WINNER International Wildlife Film Festival Conservation Message
WINNER International Wildlife Film Festival Advocacy
WINNER Best Environmental Film
WINNER Best Documentary Los Angeles Women's International Film Festival
WINNER FEATURE DOCUMENTARY MERIT OF HONOR ACCOLADE
WINNER Film Festival Editing
OFFICIAL SELECTION ARTIVIST
WILD FOR LIFE FOUNDATION PRESENTS AN IMA STUDIOS/ HUMANION FILMS PRODUCTION
DIRECTED BY KATIA LOUISE PRODUCED BY KATIA LOUISE ASSOCIATE PRODUCER NANCY STANLEY ASSOCIATE PRODUCER DEBRA LOPEZ
www.SavingAmericasHorses.org

About the Author

Born in Washington, D.C., and the oldest of five children, P. J. O'Dwyer was labeled the storyteller of the family and often accused of embellishing the truth. Her excuse? It made for a more interesting story. The proof was the laughter she received following her version of events.

After graduating from high school in the suburbs of Maryland, the faint urgings of her imaginative voice that said "you should write" were ignored. She opted to travel the world instead. Landing a job in the affluent business district of Bethesda, Maryland, as a travel counselor, she traveled frequently to such places as Hawaii, the Bahamas, Paris, New Orleans, the Alaskan Inland Passage, and the Caribbean Islands.

Today, P. J. lives in western Howard County, Maryland, with her husband Mark, teenage daughter Katie, and their cat Scoot and German Shepherd FeFe in a farmhouse they built in 1998.

P. J. is learning that it takes a village to create a writer and relieved to know she's not in this alone. She's an active member of Romance Writers of America. She also participates in a critique group, which has been an invaluable experience with many friendships made and an abundance of helpful praise, and, yes, criticism. But it's all good. Improving her craft is an ongoing process.

Writing is a passion that runs a close second to her family. When she's not writing, she enjoys spending time with family and friends, fits in her daily run with her husband, and tries heroically to keep up with her daughter Katie's social life. Who knew how demanding the life of a teenager could be, especially for Mom?

When asked where she gets her ideas for her stories, she laughs ruefully and says, "It helps being married to a cop." Actually, she admits, "Every day I find a wealth of possible stories and plots in the most unsuspecting place—my daily life."